BOOKS BY J.D. KIRK

A Litter of Bones

Thicker Than Water

The Killing Code

Blood & Treachery

The Last Bloody Straw

A Whisper of Sorrows

The Big Man Upstairs

A Death Most Monumental

A Snowball's Chance in Hell

Ahead of the Game

An Isolated Incident

Colder Than the Grave

Come Hell or High Water

City of Scars

Here Lie the Dead

Northwind: A Robert Hoon Thriller

Southpaw: A Robert Hoon Thriller

CHAPTER ONE

HE SMELLED THE SMOKE FIRST. Thick. Acrid. Jarringly out of place in the otherwise crisp night air. It snagged in his throat as he opened the door of the cab, throwing the shell-shocked driver a couple of bloodied, scrunched-up tenners before falling out of the car onto the towpath.

The pain skelped his arse. Stole the breath from him. Made the world spin. They had done a number on him, no doubt about it. The fact that he was alive was something of a miracle. Even more so if he remained that way until morning.

That he could smell anything at all was also miraculous. His nose was blocked by two fat corks of blood, but there was something about smoke—about this particular sort of smoke—that seemed to bypass the senses completely, targeting instead some ancient and primal part of the brain.

DANGER, it screamed. *BEWARE.*

The boat was a hundred yards up the towpath, around a bend, overlooked by two tall towers of flats, whose lights guided him to the place he had temporarily called home.

The place that he already knew no longer existed.

Still, he had to see. Had to be sure. And so, with a crescendo of pain building in his legs, and his back, and most of the rest of him, too, he set off along the path.

He was barely halfway to the bend when he saw them through the trees—the oranges and reds dancing in the darkness, a mad and frenzied celebration of chaos and destruction. The smoke lined his throat, and he imagined his tongue and gums turning black as he pressed on through it, eyes streaming in the charring heat.

Sirens rang out in the distance. But then, they always did. Since coming to London, he couldn't remember a time when he hadn't been made aware of some distant emergency or other by the panicky squeals of the emergency services.

He limped on, ignoring the protests from his body, the lightness in his head, and the tickle of the blood as it trickled down his arm and along his fingertips. He had to see it. He had to see what they had done.

The boat wasn't his. Not technically. He had... inherited it from a friend, though not through any official channels.

Well, a *former* friend.

In every sense.

It had proven itself useful during his time here, though. It had been one of a very small number of things he'd known he could count on.

Had been. Emphasis on the past tense.

The smoke had already done a number on his breathing on the way up the towpath. The sight that presented itself as he rounded the bend stole the rest of it away and finished the job.

The glimpse he'd had of them through the trees didn't do the flames justice. They sprouted from the skeleton of the old yacht like flowers blooming to the sky, hissing, and crackling, and spitting their sparks into the surrounding darkness.

"The cockrags," he said, coughing the words through his tightening throat. "The weasel-eyed fucking cockrags."

He let out a pained groan as a thought struck him.

"My fucking sparkly notebook was in there!" he announced, then he hung his head for a moment, mourning its passing.

There were a few randomers standing around, watching the boat burn. The owners of the boats moored on either side of his were working quickly to move them, lest a stray spark should light those up, too.

At the sound of his voice, the inky black silhouette of a woman turned. Short. Stout. He dimly recognised her as one of his fellow water-dwellers. She nudged her husband, and they both started walking over.

Even cast in shadow, he could see the horror registering on their faces when they noticed the state of him. It didn't deter them, though. If anything, it just made them pick up the pace.

No surprise. From what he could gather, they were a right pair of nosy bastards. After the day he'd had, a conversation with these two arseholes would be the icing on the cake.

And to think, it had started as a day like any other...

CHAPTER TWO

SEVERAL HOURS before the boat was set on fire, Bob Hoon came to the conclusion that he had no idea what he was doing here. He didn't like London. He'd *never* liked London. He hadn't wanted to come here, and had actively fought against it, in fact. But, in the end, he'd had no choice.

He had a choice now, though. His reason for being in the capital no longer applied. His mission was over. He could leave anytime he wanted. Head north. Go home. Step back into the life he'd been forced to abandon.

"What fucking life is that, exactly?" he muttered, and the dishevelled reflection in the bathroom mirror mocked him with its hollow-eyed sneer.

He looked, not to put too fine a point on it, like a sack of shite. His skin was pale and sallow, his bloodshot eyes surrounded by big black circles. He looked like a panda with a smack habit, though with none of the cuddly charm.

The boat rolled beneath his feet as he reached for his razor. Dried shaving foam and short pieces of lightly greying hair still clung to it from when he'd last used it. How long ago had that been? Two weeks? Three? His beard was a ramshackle, scattergun thing, like the lower half of his face had been dipped in treacle and dragged across a barber's floor. It wasn't a good look, not by any stretch of the imagination.

And yet, he just couldn't bring himself to care.

He returned the razor to the edge of the sink, next to his equally neglected toothbrush, and resorted to the same self-care techniques he'd fallen into in recent weeks—a splash of cold water to the face, and a withering look at the man in the mirror.

The sun was streaming through the boat's porthole windows when he returned to the main living area, and while most people would see this as a good thing, it did his mood no favours whatsoever. Those beams of sunshine were brimming with the promise of a brand new day, and it was the level of expectation that came with them that he couldn't abide. You were supposed to be happy when the sun was shining. You were supposed to be —he physically winced as the word entered his head—*positive*.

Well, the promise of a brand new day could, quite frankly, go fuck itself.

He stumbled, eyes screwed half-shut, into the kitchen and opened the closest drinks cabinet. Technically, it was just a regular kitchen cupboard, but as it—and all four of the others— held almost exclusively alcoholic beverages, they had defaulted to being drinks cabinets.

He removed a half-bottle of *Famous Grouse*, unscrewed the lid, and took a swig. He considered *Grouse* to be the ideal break- fast whisky. It wasn't as rough as some of the supermarket own- brand stuff he might knock back around lunchtime, but equally not as smooth as the malts he'd almost certainly enjoy as the day wore on.

It had enough of a kick to get you going, but not so much that you'd have to write off half the morning. It was the alco- holic's equivalent of a hearty bowl of *Weetabix*, and an effective middle finger to the promise of a brand new day.

Still, food would be a good idea. Man could not live on the

bevvy alone, much as he might like to. At some point, you had to succumb to solids.

He opened the fridge and considered its contents. As these amounted to a single block of cheese, this did not take him long.

Removing the pack, he peeled back the plastic and gave the block an experimental sniff. It was an artificial orange in colour, and he'd picked it up late one night at a corner shop that was staggering distance from the nearest pub. The description on the front label read simply, 'Cheese,' with only the bare minimum legally required additional information available on the back.

It smelled alright, though. Not great. Not even good. But alright. He took a bite from one corner, clumsily rewrapped the plastic, then returned it to the dookit in the door where he'd found it.

Breakfast done, he headed for the living area, flopped down onto a seat, and turned on the TV. The television set was knocking on in years, and the sound always came blaring out a few seconds before the picture arrived.

A braying, nasal sort of laughter assaulted him from the speakers, and he hastily thumbed the power button, shutting the TV off before the images had a chance to arrive.

Christ, that had been close.

"*Loose* fucking *Women*," he grunted. He ran a hand down his face, asked out loud what time it was, then checked his watch.

Afternoon, then, although only just. He'd overslept.

Well, no. Not exactly. 'Overslept' suggested there was something to get up for—a deadline for waking, a reason to rouse. He had none of those, so had simply *slept longer than expected*. Not a problem when your time was your own.

Every damn minute of it.

Still, on the plus side, that meant it was almost time for the lunchtime whiskies. The days tended to fly by after those. If he knocked a few back and kept his head down, it'd be night before he knew it, and another day could be torn from the calendar forever.

He was considering his options—the *Spar* stuff was particularly bracing, but the *Tesco* bottle was closer—when he heard the unmistakable creaking of the deck above him.

The boat was a noisy bastard of a thing at the best of times, always groaning and squeaking as it shifted on the tide, but he'd come to know all those sounds like he knew the clicks and wheezes of his own body, and he'd long-since stopped noticing them.

This one was different, though. This one was new.

He reached under the table, to where he'd taped one of the many handguns he had stowed around the boat.

There was someone up there. Someone was sneaking around on the boat. Someone who didn't want him knowing they were—

"Coo-ee! Hello? Anyone home?"

It was a woman's voice. Young. He'd just processed this information when footsteps descended the stairs and knuckles rapped on the door.

"Um, Mr Hoon? Robert? Are you in there?"

Not one of the neighbours, then. He'd made a point of never identifying himself to any of those stuck-up snooty bastards. But she knew it. She knew his name.

How the fuck did she know his name?

He gave the gun a moment's consideration, then elected to leave it where it was. He reached the door just as she started to knock again, and she jumped back in fright when he tore it open, presenting himself in all his full, smack-panda horror.

"Keep your fucking voice down," he spat, and she danced skittishly back up the steps, stopping halfway but ready to flee farther at a moment's notice. "What do you want?"

She was a little older than her voice had suggested, but not much. Thirty, maybe. Thirty-five. Despite the light-footed elegance of her retreat, she looked sturdy, like she was no stranger to physical labour.

Her hair and fingernails were both kept to practical lengths, and her clothes were dark denim, like a cowboy in mourning.

It was her eyes that Hoon noticed most of all, though. They had a troubled, haunted look to them that he didn't think even his startlingly awful appearance could fully explain away.

They reminded him, in many ways, of his own. Not the bags —she didn't have those—but the trauma.

"Are, um, are you Robert?" she asked, and he realised the levity of her original *coo-ee* had been forced. Now, up close, her voice was flattened by worry and fear. "Are you Robert Hoon?"

Hoon looked past her to the top of the stairs, and the rectangle of blue sky he could see overhead.

"Who's asking?" he demanded.

"I'm... My name's Suranne. I need your help."

"Aye, well, tough luck, sweetheart," Hoon said. He closed the door with an emphatic slam, slid the locking bolt across, and his thoughts returned to his lunchtime tipple.

"Gabriella!"

Mention of that name stopped him, mid-step. He turned, unfastened the lock, and pulled the door open even more sharply and suddenly than before.

Suranne was still standing there, halfway up the stairs, ready to run.

"The fuck did you say?"

"She, uh... I'm a friend of..." Suranne descended a couple of steps, her voice lowering into a whisper. "Gabriella. She told me about you. She told me where to find you." Her hands clasped together, the fingers entwining. "She said... She said you might be able to help."

"Gabriella?" Hoon replied, unable to hide his surprise. He

looked Suranne up and down, as if only now seeing her. "What, you've spoken to her? You've spoken to Gabriella?"

"Yes."

"How the fuck can you have spoken to Gabriella?"

"I... Sort of spoke to her. Not exactly. I can explain," said the woman at the bottom of the stairs. "I just... I've got no one else to turn to. She told me you could help. She said that's what you do."

Hoon let out a snort at that. "Aye, well, she's stitched you up a fucking blinder there, sweetheart. Look at me." He pointed to his face. "You think that's helping anyone?"

Suranne looked like she wanted to agree. Like she wanted to take back everything she'd said, turn around, and get the hell out of there.

But she didn't. She couldn't.

"Please," she said, and her voice broke on the word. "Someone's taken my Ollie. I don't know what to do. I don't know where else to go."

Hoon tutted. Sighed. Groaned. All for her benefit. This was an unwelcome interruption to his day. This was a fucking liberty. And he was damn well going to make sure she was aware of that fact.

"Right, well," he grunted, stepping aside and opening the door. "I suppose you'd better come in."

———

He made them coffee. Black by necessity, as the last of the milk had crawled away days ago. She accepted it gratefully, though had declined his offer of cheese with an almost superhuman level of politeness.

They sat at opposite ends of the small dining table. She didn't seem like a threat, but Hoon had positioned himself at the end with the gun taped to the underside, because he'd had it repeatedly hammered into him over the years that you couldn't trust anyone.

He gave her a chance to take a sip before asking the question that had been burning a hole in his head since she'd called to him through the door. It wasn't actually a question at all. At least, not a fully formed one.

"So. Gabriella?" he said, then he sat back and observed her reactions.

"She's um, I used to help her sometimes. With Welshy," she offered, hesitating over the words like she was sharing a secret she'd sworn to protect. "It was difficult for her sometimes. On her own. So I'd give her a hand. With his care. Or, you know, if she needed a break, we'd do a sort of... a swap."

"A swap?" Hoon asked. "What do you mean?"

"She'd look after my girls on the farm for a couple of days, and I'd move into hers and look after Welshy."

"She never mentioned you," Hoon said. It came out like an accusation. Which was precisely what it was.

"Well, snap. She never mentioned you to me, either," Suranne replied.

"And yet here you fucking are," Hoon countered.

"Until yesterday, I mean."

Hoon sat forward, resting his elbows on the table. "See, that's where I'm confused. Gabriella's not around at the minute. She and Welshy are... elsewhere."

Exactly where they were, he didn't know. Almost nobody in the world did. But they were safe. He'd been promised that much.

"I know. I've been messaging her. For weeks. On the phone. Email. On *Facebook*. I went to the house, but it's empty. There's a sign out front saying it's for sale. I just..." She looked down into the murky black depths of her coffee. "I thought something must have happened. And then, I sent out a message yesterday about Ollie being taken—sent it to everyone I know—and a couple of hours later I got a message back."

"From Gabriella?"

Suranne nodded.

"Saying what?"

"Saying she and Welshy had to go away. She didn't say why. Just gave me your name and where to find you. Told me you might be able to help get Ollie back. Said you'd helped someone else."

"Did she say anything else?" Hoon pressed. "How they were?"

"No. No, nothing. Just that."

"Show me," Hoon said, holding out a hand.

Suranne didn't hesitate. She took out her phone, tapped the screen a few times, then presented the message exchange to Hoon. There was just the one from Gabriella, pretty much word-for-word as Suranne had said.

She'd followed up with four further messages, but without any further response from Gabriella's account.

He placed the phone on the table and slid it back across the smooth Formica.

"Sorry. I can't help you."

Panic contorted Suranne's face until it looked like she might burst into tears. "What? But she said that this is what you did. That you helped people."

Hoon laughed. It would've been impossible not to. "Aye, well, she doesn't know me as well as she might think."

"Or maybe she knows you better than you know yourself," Suranne said. "Please, Mr Hoon. I have money. I can pay. I just... Someone took him. Ollie. Someone's taken him, I know they have, and I don't know what else to do."

"Call the police. This sort of thing's right up their street."

"I've tried. I called them right away, of course, but they're not interested. Ollie's 'not a priority at this time.'"

Hoon frowned. "How old is he?"

"What? What does that have to do with anything?"

"How old?"

"He's nineteen."

Hoon sat back. "There you go, then. Probably just gone clubbing."

Suranne's face became a mask of confusion. "*Clubbing*?! What are you...? Is that a joke? Someone took him, Mr Hoon. I know they did. It's the only explanation."

She slipped a hand into her bag and produced a thick white envelope that was splitting at the seams. It landed on the table with a satisfyingly heavy *thunk*.

"That's two thousand pounds," Suranne said. When Hoon didn't offer any response, her eyes flitted briefly to the offering. "For starters. You'll get twice that if you find him."

Hoon didn't look at the money. He daren't. He'd been surviving on savings for a while now, and neither cheese nor booze were getting any cheaper. Six grand would make a difference, no denying that.

He looked at her, instead. Into those haunted eyes. She held his gaze, pleading with him, her whole body wound tight by anxiety and stress.

Hoon knew he should keep his mouth shut. Knew that he should turn her away, tell her to find someone else. Someone better.

But, as with most things, he fucked that up, too.

"How long's he been missing?" he asked.

"Since the night before last," Suranne replied, grasping at the question like it was a handhold that might keep her from drowning. "I woke up early to get breakfast for him and the girls, and he was gone. He was just... He was gone."

"And you'd last seen him when?"

"Night before. About half-ten."

Hoon finally looked at the money on the table. He clicked

his tongue against the back of his teeth, then reached for the envelope. "If he wanders back by himself, I keep this."

"Of course! Of course, yes, no problem. Of course!" She swallowed, tears pooling at the corners of her eyes. "So... you'll help? You'll find him?"

"No promises," Hoon told her. "You got a photo?"

She picked up her phone.

"Hard copy, preferably."

Suranne's finger hesitated over the screen. "Uh, not with me, no. But I can show you one on here."

Hoon waited as she swiped frantically through her photos.

"I'll need a description, too. Height. Build. Distinguishing features..."

Suranne didn't look up from her screen as her finger flicked through the pictures.

"Yes. Yes, of course," she said. "He's about seven-foot-nine..."

"Jesus fuck! Seven-*nine*? Who's his dad, the fucking *BFG*?" Hoon shot back.

"I'm sorry?"

"Seven-foot-fucking-nine!" Hoon continued. "What've you been feeding him? And how the fuck did you manage to lose him? He's a giant!"

Suranne's eyebrows were united in their confusion. "Wait. Didn't I say? Oh, God! I thought I said."

"Say what?" Hoon asked. "What didn't you say?"

"Ollie. He's not a giant," she said.

She turned the phone towards him, and the face that looked back at Hoon was some way removed from anything he'd been expecting.

It had a beak, for one thing.

"He's an ostrich."

Some time passed while Hoon regarded the photograph.

Some more time passed while he studied the woman sitting across from him, trying to decide if she was winding him up.

"An ostrich?" he said, after both these periods had passed. "Are you taking the piss?"

"No. No, I'm not," she insisted. "I run an ostrich farm. Ollie's our stud."

"Why the fuck would anyone steal an ostrich?" Hoon asked.

"For his semen."

"Course. Aye. Yep." Hoon nodded. "Should've seen that coming. Walked straight into that one." He stabbed a finger against the tabletop. "You sure this isn't a fucking wind-up?"

"No. I promise," Suranne said. "Do you have any idea what Ollie's semen would sell for?"

"Why the fuck...? No. Why would I know that?" Hoon fired back. "Under what fucking set of circumstances would that information have come into my possession?"

"It's a lot. Up to five hundred quid per load."

Hoon raised an eyebrow. "Per load? As in...?"

"Per ejaculation."

"Right. Aye. Thought that's what you meant," Hoon muttered. He sighed, massaged his eyes with a thumb and finger, and muttered below his breath.

"I really don't have anyone else to turn to," Suranne reiterated.

"Aye. You said that." He sighed again, louder this time, then shook his head. "Look, sweetheart, missing people is one thing. I wouldn't have the first fucking clue how to even start looking for an ostrich. I can't help."

"You don't have to look for him."

"How do you mean? I thought that was the whole fucking point of you coming here?"

"No. I'm pretty sure I already know where he is. I know who took him. I just need you to go and get him back."

"Oh. Right. So we're talking ostrich retrieval?" Hoon said.

He picked up the envelope of cash and hefted it from hand to hand like he was checking the weight. "And I get six grand just for that?"

"It's, um... the men who took him. They're not really people you want to mess with. They're dangerous. You'd have to tread lightly."

A smile crept across Hoon's face, showing an alarming number of teeth. "Don't you worry about that, sweetheart," he told her. "Treading lightly is what I do best."

CHAPTER THREE

"RIGHT, YOU BIRD-COCK-TUGGING NO-MARKS,"
Hoon boomed. "Which one of you jizzy-fingered fat fucks is in
charge?"

There were four of them, sitting around a cluttered table in
the manky, run-down kitchen of a farmhouse whose rightful
owners had given up on long, long ago. The wallpaper looked
like it had been applied in the forties, started peeling in the
seventies, and been gradually flaking its way out of existence
ever since.

Mice had been chewing at the dirty linoleum for decades.
Judging by the smell in the place, many of their remains were
still lingering behind the skirting boards.

The men around the table were big lads, but judging by the
time it took them to register Hoon's presence in the kitchen,
they weren't the brightest.

They ranged in age from mid-twenties to late-fifties, and all
dressed like they spent most of their day rotating crops, or
combine harvesting, or whatever the fuck it was farmers got up
to when left to their own devices.

He silently counted all the way to six before any of them so much as moved. The two youngest lads scraped their chairs back and heaved themselves upright. There was no show of urgency to it—that ship had sailed—with their focus instead being on a sort of slow, calculated menace that had presumably proven to be an effective way of scaring people away in the past.

Not today, though.

"Defuck're ye?" one of them demanded, and his accent was so densely Irish as to be almost incomprehensible. If it wasn't for Hoon having spent most of his life surrounded by a variety of Celtic accents, he'd have been completely lost.

"You fucking deaf, son?" Hoon demanded. "I asked which one of you ostrich-blowing pricks is in charge."

The other lad—the one who'd risen to his feet but hadn't yet said a word—came lumbering at Hoon with his arms raised. It was a real Frankenstein's monster move, and one that ended with him face down on the floor with a boot on the back of his head.

"Let's fucking try that again, shall we?" Hoon suggested, pressing his attacker's face more firmly against the lino for emphasis. "Which one of you avian cum harvesters is the boss here?"

"I'm the boss. What do ye want?"

Hoon turned his attention to the man who had spoken. He wasn't the oldest of the group, which was a surprise. He was in his forties, and sat with his back to the door and, by extension, to Hoon. He'd eventually turned at Hoon's arrival, but was now back facing the table, fingers pincering around a glass of something the colour of old piss.

Releasing the pressure on the back of the fallen man's head, Hoon crossed to the table, took the empty seat, and sat back with his arms folded.

"I'm a pal of Ollie's," he said.

"Are ye now?" the Irishman replied. He was the largest of the four men, with most of his bulk contained within a dirty donkey jacket that probably had a few stories to tell. He wore a flat tweed cap that wasn't quite big enough for his head, and his general appearance—from his wild red beard to his puffy grey skin—made Hoon look like he'd stepped off a cover shoot for *GQ* magazine.

Hoon had seen plenty of bloodshot eyes in his time—his own, mostly. This was the first time he'd ever seen a bloodshot face.

The boss waved a hand, and four sovereign rings flashed in the sunlight. On his left, the younger man lowered himself back onto his seat, directly across the table from Hoon.

"I don't know no Ollie," the group's leader declared.

"Aye, you do. Big lad. Long legs," Hoon said. He looked around the table. The oldest man on his right was the only one not making eye contact. Well, him and the oaf on the floor. "No? Not ringing any bells? He's got feathers and a beak, if that helps, any? You'd know him if you'd seen him."

"Suppose that tells ye we haven't seen him, then, don't it?" garbled the younger of the three men. He leaned closer, face twisting up in rage. "So, why don't ye fuck back off the way ye fucking—"

His head hit the table with enough force to swirl the liquid in the glasses, and elicit a high-pitched yelp of shock from the man now face-down between them. The lad's hair was too short for Hoon to grip, so he splayed his fingers wide like a claw, and dug them into the back of his skull to pin him in place.

"Grown-ups talking, son. Do us all a favour and shut the fuck..."

The command fell away into silence as cool metal was pressed against his jaw. He tried to turn to look at the oldest of the men, but the pressure of the sawn-off shotgun barrels held his head in place, so all he could move were his eyes.

The older man said something, but the accent was so incomprehensible that it might as well have been Martian.

"Aye, whatever you say, pal," Hoon told him. "Just you go fucking steady there."

The man with the shotgun ejected another slur of syllables. These sounded angrier and more aggressive than the last lot, and were further hammered home when the gun was pressed harder against his jaw, turning him to face the man who had introduced himself as the boss.

"I think you'd better do what he says there, now," the leader urged.

"Aye, easy for you to fucking say," Hoon retorted.

This earned him a furious—but still completely indecipherable—outburst from the older man, and the *cli-click* of two hammers drawing back forced Hoon to take a leap of faith. He removed his hand from the back of the younger man's head, and raised both arms in a gesture of surrender.

"Right, cool the fucking beans, you mad old bastard," he said. "In hindsight, I may have come in a wee bit on the heavy-handed side. I'm sure we can discuss this like fucking adults, can't we?"

The pressure of the gun eased off, but while it was no longer jammed against his jaw, it was still pointing directly at his face. The old man's reactions may not have been world-class, but they didn't need to be with that weapon at this range.

"I don't reckon so now, Robert," the boss-man said. "I reckon that time's passed, sure, don't you?"

Hoon picked up on it immediately. His mind raced ahead, second-guessing the possible answers before he'd even asked the question.

"How the fuck do you know my name?"

Across the table, the lad whose face had moments before been mashed into the table now laughed until his shoulders shook. "Ollie the fucking ostrich? Are ye wise?"

Shit.

Fuck.

Bollocks!

Hoon threw himself backwards, away from the table, rolling the chair onto its back legs. The shotgun thundered. The boss, sitting directly across the table, emitted an animal squeal of pain, and blood misted the air.

The old man shouted something—Christ alone knew what —and then Hoon was on his feet, grabbing for the gun, the metal hot against his hand.

He powered his fist at a spot two inches behind the old man's nose, wasted half a second celebrating the sound of the impact, then wrenched the shotgun from his grip. Spinning with it, he took aim at the younger man across the table, who sat motionless, his eyes wide and staring, his jaw hanging open like a broken hinge.

On his right, the old geezer was coughing up what was left of his nose. On his left, the boss was half-blinded, and trying desperately to slide his scalp back on.

That made three.

He stole a sideways glance at the floor where the fourth man should've been.

Empty.

The old floorboards squeaked behind him. Too close. Way too close.

A bomb-blast of pain exploded against the top of his head. For a brief, fleeting moment he imagined his whole body being compressed, concertina-like, and then his legs became liquid.

He heard the clatter of something hitting the lino, then tried to squeeze the trigger of a weapon he was no longer holding. The room turned ninety degrees. He smashed against the floor by way of the table, but by the time he'd connected with either of those things, he was too far gone to notice.

CHAPTER FOUR

HOON WOKE TO DARKNESS, cold, and the pungent stench of shit. Probably not his own, though it was still too soon to write off the possibility.

His face was pressed against something rough that shifted around beneath him, rubbing across his cheek and wearing it down like sandpaper. It hurt. At least, he assumed it did.

Again, it was still too early to be sure.

He didn't move. Not yet. Moving would give away the fact that he was awake to anyone nearby. And, more importantly, he suspected any movement on his part was going to lead to some immediate and not insignificant discomfort.

There was already a pain burrowing into his skull like a one-inch drill bit. He could account for that one, at least. Something hard and heavy had struck him like a hammer blow, immediately dropping him to the floor.

After that...?

What had happened then?

There were flashes, he thought. Glimpses of half-conscious memories that swam in the darkness, just out of reach.

Flashes of fists. Of boots. Of a bat or club of some kind,

maybe. He couldn't remember the impacts themselves, just a hazy impression of the brutality with which they had been inflicted.

Probably for the best.

A sound thrummed inside his head, vibrating his skull until he felt like his eyes might come rolling out of their sockets. Assuming they hadn't already. Which, given that he couldn't currently see a bloody thing, was not necessarily a safe assumption to make. The sound was a low, persistent rumbling, like a clap of thunder that had long overstayed its welcome.

Was this it, he wondered? Was this what a blunt force trauma-induced aneurysm sounded like? Was that what was happening now?

From somewhere below the floor, he heard the *hiss* of hydraulics.

An engine. That was what the sound was. The revving of an engine, and the rumbling of wheels on tarmac.

Thank fuck for that.

So, probably not a brain bleed, then. That was something. And being in a moving vehicle also explained the way the floor was shifting around beneath him. Much better that, than the permanent inner ear injury he'd started to suspect he might be suffering from.

He lay there, silent and mostly motionless, as he rattled through some quick diagnostic checks.

He was alive. That was both the headline news and, frankly, a welcome surprise. He had been shocked to avoid the blast from the shotgun, and when the blow to the back of the head had come, he'd assumed his time was up.

His life hadn't flashed before his eyes, although given that he'd forgotten most of the good bits, and would desperately like to forget the rest, he hadn't been too disappointed.

So, alive. Tick. What next?

He was conscious. Maybe not fully—maybe not all the way —but more or less.

Not only that, but he was reasonably confident that he knew his name, date of birth, and full home address. He didn't know what day it was, but then, that was pretty much par for the course, and completely unrelated to the head injury.

So, little to no lasting brain damage sustained, then. That was another cracking result, all things considered.

He still had no idea if he was alone in what he now reckoned to be the back of a lorry, so he didn't dare make any big sudden movements yet. Instead, he tried wiggling his toes. They responded, though he paid the price with some shooting pains up the backs of his thighs.

Alive, no brain damage, and he wasn't paralysed, either. Christ. This was shaping up to be his lucky day.

He tried moving his fingers next. They were present, but painful. Very fucking painful, in fact, and he dimly recalled some big Irish bastard stamping down on them. Still, pain was good. Pain meant his hands were still attached to his wrists.

Even with that established, it took him a few moments to figure out where his hands were positioned. They weren't under him, he could tell that much. Not at his sides, either. He eventually concluded, to his dismay, that they were resting at the top of his arse, tightly bound together with something that was currently cutting grooves in his flesh.

Just fucking marvellous.

He thought about wrenching them apart, struggling against the bonds either until they snapped, or he could work his hands free. The rest of his body had a quiet word with him, though, and he eventually concluded that this probably wasn't in his best interests. Also, it felt like it would be quite a lot of hard work, and he still hadn't woken up to the point where he could be arsed even giving it a go.

No point exerting all that energy for no reason, he thought.

Besides, unlikely as it sounded, he was actually quite comfortable where he was. Or at least more comfortable than he'd be if he stood up, say, or otherwise attempted to move a muscle. Moving, he thought, was a mug's game. Lying motionless, that was where it was at.

And so, he just lay there for a while, listening to the rumbling of the engine, letting the floor wear away at his cheek, and the malodorous stench set up camp in his nostrils.

Sheep shit. That was what it was, he was sure of it. He was amazed he hadn't recognised it earlier. You didn't spend half your life in the Highlands of Scotland without being able to identify the smell of sheep shit, especially when your nose was partially buried in it.

It could be ostrich shit, he supposed. Never having come across that particular substance before, though, he had no basis for comparison. His money was still on sheep.

There was another hiss of brakes from below him, and the truck slowed suddenly to a stop. He felt the laws of physics pushing and pulling at him, then his momentum slid him across the floor until he hit the front wall of the big box trailer with a *thump* and an involuntary, "Fuck!"

Nobody reacted in the darkness behind him. Nobody moved. Nobody uttered a sound.

He was alone, then. He had to be. If anyone had witnessed the previous few seconds, they'd be laughing their arse off right now. He knew he would be, if the shoe was on the other foot.

Alone, then. Alone, tied up, and being transported somewhere in a big smelly lorry.

"All this over a fucking ostrich," he muttered.

Worse—all this over a fucking ostrich he was now reasonably confident didn't even exist.

The engine rumbled beneath him again. The truck pulled away, headed uphill, and he slid several feet backwards on the sheep shit slicked floor.

What a day. What an absolute, bona fide bastard of a day it had been.

He'd been beaten, kidnapped, shot at, and had come danger-ously close to catching a bit of *Loose Women* on ITV.

As he lay there, bruised, bleeding, and half-mangled inside a truck full of sheep shit, he thought that—even for him, even by his usual standard—this was something of a personal low. This, he thought was rock bottom.

But, he was wrong.

CHAPTER FIVE

HOON HAD no idea how long the truck had continued driving. Long enough for his bladder to build up quite the head of steam, though. By the time the engine shuddered into silence and the back doors were unlocked, he was desperate for a piss.

"Alright, lads?" he asked, as the two youngest Irishmen caught him by the arms and heaved him to his feet. "Any chance I could nip to the bogs before we do whatever it is we're—"

The reply came in the form of a right hook to the face. For a moment, everything flashed a bright, brilliant white, then unconsciousness, which had been lurking around the fringes of his mind like a paedo at a playground, saw its chance to strike.

The next while passed as a series of static images. Leering faces breathing clouds of icy mist. Gullies of blood. Animal carcasses suspended from the ceiling.

It was the cold that finally roused him. It stabbed at his skin and formed crystals inside his lungs. His whole top half felt like it was submerged in sub-zero water.

His bottom half was a lot warmer. And, on the plus side, he no longer needed to pee.

He wasn't quite standing on the floor. The toes of his boots brushed against it, skiffing the surface, able to take only the tiniest fraction of his weight.

The rest of it was supported by his arms, which were now wrenched above his head, a rope around his wrists suspended from a hook that hung from a rack on the high ceiling. His shoulders burned, even in the cold. The whole length of his arms, in fact, and as he fully roused, a cry of shock and pain burst from his chittering lips.

"Ah. You're awake. Great."

He recognised the voice. It didn't have the same anxious wobble to it as earlier, but there was no mistaking it.

"I take it you've no' really lost your fucking ostrich, then?" he spat as a woman in a fur-lined coat stepped into view from beside him.

Suranne, or whatever the hell her real name was, smiled up at him through the steam from the cup of hot liquid she held in her gloved hands.

"No. No, I haven't," she admitted. "In fact, confession time, I don't actually have an ostrich to lose." She put the back of a hand to the side of her mouth and whispered loudly. "It was a clever ploy."

"It was a fucking weird ploy, is what it was," Hoon spat back.

He was buying time, keeping her talking, giving himself an opportunity to... what, exactly? Backflip off this fucking hook? Aye, he couldn't see that happening.

His head was still clearing, though. Maybe there was another way out of this. He just needed time to think.

"We didn't want to just grab you from the boat. Too many witnesses. Too much potential for mess," Suranne explained. "So, I thought it'd be fun to send you on a little quest."

"But why a fucking ostrich?" Hoon asked.

She smiled at that. It was quite a friendly smile, all things considered, with only the faintest whiff of cruelty about it.

"Just thought it was funny," she replied. "Well, no. Not *just* that. I also wanted to prove a point."

"And what point might that be?"

The smile remained, but the cruelty to kindness ratio shifted a little. "That everyone has their price." She took a sip of her hot drink and smacked her lips together. "See, if I'd asked you to look for a missing child, or whatever, then you could tell yourself you were doing a good deed. You were being a hero. But retrieving an ostrich stolen for the value of its spunk? There's not much heroic about that, is there, Bobby?"

"Don't call me Bobby. Nobody fucking calls me Bobby."

"Yes. Well. They do now," she informed him.

"You didn't speak to Gabriella, did you?" he asked. "This was nothing to do with her."

"Guilty!" Suranne confessed. "But I knew mention of her name would get you all fired up. A friend of Gabriella's is a friend of yours, right?"

"Probably not. I'd imagine half her pals are all insufferable London arseholes like you."

"Oh, almost certainly not like me," Suranne assured him.

"You don't know where they are, do you?" Hoon asked, and he felt confident enough in the reply to grin at her. "You don't have the first fucking clue where they're hidden."

Suranne shrugged, though it was hard to tell given the size of her coat. "I don't care. They're an irrelevance," she said. "Don't get me wrong, I'm sure there are others in the organisation working to find them. They do love to tie up all their little loose ends. But me? I have no interest in where they are. Good luck to them, I say." She blew on her drink, then sipped. "I suspect they'll need it."

The pain in Hoon's arms was becoming unbearable now. What he wouldn't give to be an inch lower. Just an inch, so his feet could shoulder some of the burden.

Fuck it. If they were going to kill him, better to just get it over with.

"Aye, very good, sweetheart," he said. "Mind just shooting me in the fucking head and getting this over with? I've listened to enough self-satisfied smug bastards in my time, I don't have the fucking energy to sit through another one."

A punch struck his kidney area like a jackhammer. Unready for it, his roar echoed around the cold, cavernous room, only muffled by the rows and rows of hanging pig flesh.

His attacker said something, but his accent was too thick, and Hoon's brain too lit up with pain to be able to understand a word of it.

"That's enough," Suranne snapped. She shot a look past Hoon which was laced with venom. "Put your hands on him again, and I'll have them removed. Permanently. Is that understood?"

The reply was a low, indecipherable grunt of deference. Over the sound of his own raw, ravaged breathing, Hoon heard his attacker shuffle back.

"Sorry about that, Bobby. He's not happy with you. It seems you got half his father's face shot off."

"Aye, well," Hoon wheezed. "Good enough for him."

He listened, but the young Irishman didn't take so much as a step towards him. Suranne's warning had been taken to heart, then. That meant she either had a lot more muscle knocking about nearby, or was enough of a danger herself that even that thick fuck knew better than to disobey.

Neither was particularly good news for Hoon.

Suranne smiled, took another sip of her drink, then gestured to him with a tilt of the mug. He caught a glimpse of wee marshmallows melting in the chocolate coloured liquid, and the sight of it somehow made the air feel even colder.

"Look, I get it," she said. "I understand why you think I've brought you here to kill you."

"What, with the whole being beaten and hung from a fucking meat hook thing?" Hoon asked. "Aye, that did make me wonder, right enough."

"This is just to focus your attention, Bobby," she continued. "Now, don't get me wrong, there are a lot of people in my organisation—a *lot* of people—who do want you dead."

"There's a lot of people in general who want me dead," Hoon told her. "That's just my winning fucking personality at work."

"Oh, I quite believe that," Suranne said. She failed to suppress a dry little laugh. "Although, there's someone you'll meet in a moment who wants you dead more than anyone. But those people—the ones in my organisation—they're not like me. You know why? You know what they lack?"

"Tits?" Hoon guessed.

"Ha! Well, often, yes," Suranne said. "Vision. That's what they're missing. Vision." She pointed to him with the mug again. "I think you and I share that trait, Bobby, don't we?"

"Aye, well, you'll no' be saying that once I chew your fucking eyes out of your face," Hoon retorted.

"No, I'd imagine I'd be saying, 'Waaaargh! Stop it! It hurts!'" Suranne declared, flailing her head around for good measure.

She giggled at her own joke, like it was up there with the greatest comedy moments of all time. Hoon watched her, not a flicker registering on his face.

"Not literal vision," she clarified. "Not physical. Big picture thinking, I mean. You and I, we're plotters. We're schemers. We're—dare I say it?—*dreamers*."

Hoon puffed out his cheeks, and a roll of white mist came drifting out through his shivering lips. "I think you've got me confused with some other bastard. Me? I'm more your act-on-gut-instinct type of guy. Like when I floored that fat Mick fuck back at the farmhouse, and smashed up the old boy's face."

Still not a movement from behind him. Not a sound.

Whoever this woman was, for whatever reason, she wasn't someone to mess with.

All the more fucking reason to do so.

"And, to be honest, I think you're giving yourself a wee bit too much fucking credit, too, sweetheart. I mean, there must've been a hundred and one ways to get me on my own. The ostrich thing is just fucking weird."

"Worked, though, didn't it?" Suranne laughed. "And, God, I don't know. Why be predictable? Jumping you on the way back from the pub, shoving you into the back of a van, or whatever? It's dull, isn't it? It's so *ordinary*." She took a step closer, but remained beyond the reach of his legs. "What you'll come to learn about me, Bobby, is that I'm *anything* but ordinary."

"You look pretty fucking ordinary from where I'm dangling, doll," Hoon told her. "I won't even manage an angry wank over this later. It'll just be hanging there limp and totally fucking lifeless. Which, by the way, is how I see your story ending. Just for the record."

She laughed at that, a genuine, trilling giggle that might, in wildly different circumstances, and to an entirely different man, been infectious.

"You're a lot of fun, Bobby," she said. "That's why I wanted to speak to you directly. Why I wanted to make you an offer."

"If it's a quick death you're offering, sign me fucking up," Hoon said. "Better that than keep listening to this shite."

Suranne studied his face while swirling what was left of her hot chocolate around in the mug. She knocked it back in a single gulp, and tossed the mug onto the floor behind her.

"Let's get serious now, Bobby," she suggested. "Let's talk this out. See, there are two paths before you right now. The first path —the left path, if you're a visual thinker like me—is paved with gold. There are flowers—do you like flowers?"

Hoon hung there, saying nothing, not giving her the satisfaction of a response.

Finally, she shrugged.

"Maybe not flowers. But, I don't know, whisky, or porn, or deep-fried *Mars* bars, or whatever it is that floats your boat. The point is, it's a good road. It leads to nice places, and positive experiences. It's like the yellow brick road in *The Wizard of Oz*."

Hoon grunted. "Aye, well, I'm no' really into singing midgets."

"Dwarfs," Suranne corrected. "You can't call them midgets. Midgets is offensive."

"Fuck me, if that's the most offensive thing I've said since I got here, I'm seriously fucking letting myself down."

For a moment, Suranne looked almost irritated, but she recovered quickly. "The point is, Bobby, that's a good road. The left road. That's the one I'd recommend. Because, see, the other road? The right road? Well, that's the *wrong* road. That road is covered in broken glass and spiders."

"Sounds like my fucking living room," Hoon said. "Suits me down to the ground."

She ignored him. Pressed on. "That road doesn't lead to nice places, and it definitely doesn't lead to positive experiences." She looked past him to the part of the warehouse that he couldn't see, and made a brief beckoning motion with her head. "Do you want to see where that road leads, Bobby?"

There was a grunt somewhere behind him. Low. Animal. Something wheezed as it heaved itself closer, step by shuffled step.

"Do you want to see who's waiting for you at the end of that road?"

"Aye, go on then," Hoon said, bluffing it with the bravado.

The truth was, there was something about those sounds behind him—something about the plodding inevitability of it— that was making his heart race faster in his chest.

And, considering it had been going like a fucking humming

bird on speed since he'd woken up, that was really saying something.

"You may remember I mentioned someone who hated you more than... well, than pretty much anyone," Suranne said. She shot a look in the direction of whoever was approaching from behind, then took a couple of wary steps to the side, like even she didn't want to get too close. "I'm going to introduce you now. Or, reintroduce you, I suppose, since I'm told the two of you are already acquainted."

Hoon managed to turn his head just enough to see the figure shambling into view on his left side. Like Suranne, the new arrival wore a thick coat, though the hood was raised, so Hoon couldn't get a clear view of the person inside it.

There was something about the shape, though, even beneath the layers of clothing. Something about the movements...

No. It couldn't be. That wasn't possible.

Hoon had killed him. He was sure of it.

But then, even after the fire, they'd never found his body.

The figure stopped in front of him, head lowered as if admiring Hoon's boots. Hands were raised to push back the hood. Before they did, Hoon saw that they wore gloves. These gloves weren't like Suranne's thick woolly numbers, though. They were thin. Blue. Rubber.

The hood was pushed back, revealing a face as nightmarish as it was familiar. The nose was a mangled stump of scar tissue, the nasal cavities open and exposed in a way that resembled a skull. The cold air of the warehouse meant there was a continuous swirl of misty white around the stump, where his breath rasped in and out through the elongated nostrils.

He hadn't looked a picture of health when Hoon had first met him, with his paper-thin skin and horseshoe of brittle white hair circling his bald head. In hindsight, though, compared to now, he'd looked like a fucking Olympian.

He stood a few inches shorter than Suranne, and yet his presence—the threat of him—filled the warehouse.

"I'm told the Professor and you go way back," Suranne said. "Not told by him, obviously. He doesn't talk now. Not after... Well, why don't you show him?"

The Professor maintained eye contact as he slowly undid the zip of his coat. He had a scarf on—a jolly red and yellow thing that looked completely out of place on him—and he continued to eyeball Hoon as he carefully unwound it.

"Oofyafucker," Hoon muttered. He hadn't meant to, but the sight of the scarring on the other man's throat and neck drew it out of him.

It had been a broken piece of chair leg that Hoon had used. He'd jammed it right through the twisted bastard's neck, all the way from one side to the other.

He should've been dead. It should've killed him. That had certainly been Hoon's intention at the time.

"We got to him quickly," Suranne explained, as if reading Hoon's thoughts. "It was touch and go, but he's a very valuable asset, and so we pulled out all the stops. Do you know what makes him such a valuable asset, Bobby?"

"Is it his winning personality?"

"Not exactly, no. Nor is it his dance moves, though, hard as it may be to believe, he's got those to spare. But, no. What makes him valuable is that he's a man with some very special talents. Some say he's gifted, and having watched him work, I'm not about to disagree. Those talents make him a unique asset to our organisation," Suranne said. "And, I think you could be, too."

Hoon laughed. Like his reaction to the sight of the Professor's throat, it was entirely involuntary.

"This must be a fucking wind-up," he said. "This is the ostrich thing all over again, isn't it?"

"Not at all. It's not often I'm wholly serious, but right now, I am. See, those roads I mentioned, one of them is an opportunity.

One of them leads to success, whatever that might look like to you. Wealth, yes, but other things, too. Power. Respect. And women, of course. If you want them. Or men. Any size, shape, or colour." She chewed her bottom lip like she was biting back a smile. "Or age. We don't judge. Whatever your definition of success might be, that's out there. That's along that left-hand road. Take the road on the right, however..."

"And Skeletor's illegitimate bastard offspring there buggers me through the eye sockets with a pool cue," Hoon spat. "Aye, I get it. Let's just assume the answer is a big fucking, 'Thanks, but no thanks,' and get the next bit over with, will we?"

Suranne didn't seem to be the least bit put out by his response. She shot the Professor a look, and pointed past Hoon, either dismissing him, or sending him to fetch his tools, Hoon couldn't decide which.

Either way, the creepy noseless bastard pulled up his hood and went scuttling off, his breath wisping the air as he passed.

"It's a big ask, I appreciate that," Suranne told him. "I mean, it sounds crazy. We've tried to kill you, for Christ's sake! I don't even know how often. Too many times to count! And yet, here you are! Some might say that means our organisation is inept, but I *know* that's not the case. So it can only mean one thing— you're an impressive specimen, Bobby. You're something quite remarkable. And there is *always* room for remarkable people on our side of the fence."

"Your side of the fence?" Hoon sneered. "Is that the side with all the fucking child rapists and sex traffickers on it?"

"Among other things," Suranne said. "And, look, I want this to be an honest and open relationship, Bobby. I don't like those things. I don't approve. Let kids be kids, I say, don't... whatever. You know?"

"Well, whoop-de-doo to you, doll. You angling for a fucking humanitarian award, or something?"

"Every organisation has its problems," Suranne replied.

"But you can't change them from the outside. Work with me. A man with your skills, you'll soon rise through the ranks. Then, you can help me reshape things. A whole new organisation. A whole new Loop. Under new management. You can make a difference to the world."

She looked past him again, but quickly averted her eyes from the horrifying face of the man staring back at her.

"Or the Professor can make a difference to you. A number of differences, I'm sure. None of them welcome." She held a hand up before Hoon had a chance to reply. "Don't answer yet. There's too much testosterone in the room. Think about it. Take a few days. We'll find you."

Hoon wanted to tell her where to shove her few days. Part of him wanted to let the Professor run riot on him, so he could hold eye contact with the snooty cow all the way through, and show her he wasn't for turning.

A much bigger part of him knew that, as ideas went, this one was fucking demented, and so he played along.

"Fine. You can come to the boat. You know where it is. I'll be fucking waiting."

Suranne's whole face pulled down into an apologetic sort of frown. "Uh, yes. Well, maybe. We'll see," she said, then she gave a wave of a hand.

Chains rattled. The pressure on Hoon's arms eased, and his weight landed on his feet. They weren't ready for him, though. His legs gave way. He hit the freezing floor as a bundle of clothing and pain.

The room spun around him. He tried to stand, but not a part of him obeyed. Not yet. Not this soon.

His arms felt dead. Heavy. The blood frozen in his veins. His legs were folded beneath him like a broken doll's. He couldn't feel them properly, but he could see them, and he wasn't a big fan of the angle they were positioned in.

Nothing broken, though, he reckoned.

Lucky. Lucky old man.

He insisted that his body pay attention to him. Willed it into submission enough that he could shuffle himself into a sitting position, and raise his head to look around.

Suranne, the Professor, and whoever else might have been there in the room with them, were gone. The only reminder of them was the empty mug on the floor, and the faint, distant rumbling of an engine starting up, too far away for him to catch up to, even if his limbs were all functioning properly.

OK, he took back his thought from earlier. *This*, he reckoned, this was rock bottom. Beaten, exhausted, smeared in sheep shit, and lightly steaming from his own pish, with a deranged, mute, skeletal-faced torturer gunning for him—this was as bad as it could get, he thought. Surely to fuck?

And yet, once again, he was sadly mistaken.

CHAPTER SIX

"THE COCKRAGS," Hoon announced, as he watched the fire consuming the boat, and everything in it. "The weasel-eyed fucking cockrags!"

The heat, even from this distance, was intense. He'd come straight here from the icy chill of the meat locker, and his skin didn't know what the fuck was going on. From the way it stung, though, it was clear that it disapproved.

A pair of neighbouring nosy bastards came creeping towards him, their black outlines like cut-outs in the flames.

He couldn't remember their names. Or, more accurately, had never bothered his arse to learn them. They weren't exactly motoring towards him at speed to begin with, but when they saw the state of him, they both slowed further. It was impressively synchronised, like they shared one conjoined mind.

Which, even in his limited experience of them, he reckoned they might well do.

They stopped about fifteen feet away, having jointly come to the same conclusion that this was quite close enough.

"I say!" the wife called to him. "Have you suffered an injury?"

She had that *mouth full of plums* accent that was generally an indicator of the aristocracy, but neither the wealth nor the breeding to justify it.

The husband's accent was a few rungs down the social ladder, but very much striving upwards.

"Have you been in an accident?" he asked.

"Jesus. What are you two meant to be, a fucking no-win, no-fee claims company?" Hoon ejected. "I'm fine."

"Oh. Well. Jolly good," the wife replied. She looked back over her shoulder, and the light from the flames picked out the concerned expression on her face. "Your, uh, your boat..."

"It's on fire," the husband finished.

Hoon couldn't even summon the energy for sarcasm. Shame, really, because this pair had more than earned it with that fucking statement.

Instead, he just sighed, nodded, and said, "Aye, I see that, right enough."

They all watched the flames leaping to the sky, and listened to the *crash* of collapsing wood as the upper deck fell into the one below.

The sirens were getting closer. Maybe they were headed here, after all.

"Did you leave something on in the galley?" the wife asked him.

"No, did I fuck," Hoon replied, and the abruptness of it made the woman shrink back in horror.

"Either of you see anyone fucking about nearby?" he asked.

The couple both shook their heads. The synchronisation was uncanny.

"Uh, no. No, nobody. Not that we saw," the husband said. "Sorry."

Hoon dismissed the apology with a half-shrug, then went back to watching the fire.

He wasn't too concerned about the boat itself, truth be told.

It had served a purpose for a while, but there were plenty of other places he could stay. What he was more concerned about was the stash of firearms he'd secreted aboard, not to mention the envelope full of cash that Suranne had given him.

Of course, they had probably taken the money back before torching the place, anyway.

There wasn't much else of value on board. Some clothes. A rucksack. A selection of knives and some brass knuckles. Nothing that couldn't be replaced.

In fact, aside from the guns and the bundle of cash, the most valuable thing on the boat was probably the assortment of—

A *boom* erupted from the lower deck of the boat, scattering most of the onlookers. A ball of blue flame rolled upwards, like the toxic belch of some ancient fire god.

"Well," Hoon muttered. "There goes the whisky."

Once the inferno had died back again, the nosy bastard neighbours both turned back and sized him up.

"Are you sure you're alright, old boy?" the husband asked. "You look like—"

"Like I've had the shit kicked out of me, then pissed myself?" said Hoon. He began limping towards them, and they both practically threw themselves in opposite directions to get out of his way. "Aye, well, you're not too far off the fucking mark there."

They reunited behind him and watched as he laboriously made his way to the edge of the towpath, dropped to his knees, then began digging at the base of a tree.

"What on Earth's he doing?" the wife whispered.

"I don't have the foggiest, dear," her husband replied.

They both retreated a step or two when Hoon stood up, now clutching a black bin bag that had been tightly wrapped in brown tape so it resembled a sort of squared-off rugby ball.

Hoon grimaced and groaned with every step as he plodded his way back towards them. They stood aside again, but this time stuck together, shoulder to shoulder. Their gazes fell in unison to the package he carried under his arm, both of them regarding it with the sort of fascinated horror usually reserved for videos of invasive medical procedures on *YouTube*.

"Either of you two got a phone I can have?" he asked, stopping right beside them.

The wife kept her eye on the package. The husband broke ranks and met Hoon's eye.

"Um, sorry? A phone you can use, you mean?"

"No. A phone I can have?" Hoon reiterated. He tick-tocked his gaze between them, like this was a perfectly reasonable thing to ask, and they were the ones being the arseholes about it.

"Uh, well... No," said the husband. "No, I'm afraid not, sorry."

Hoon scowled. "Well, thanks a fucking bunch. Big fucking help you two are," he informed them, then he went limping past, back along the towpath, as his home for the past few months slid sideways into the river.

"You, uh, you should really wait for the authorities to arrive," the wife called after him.

Hoon didn't bother to look back. With the way his neck and shoulders were feeling, he didn't know if he had it in him to turn that far. "Aye," he agreed. "I really should."

And with the heat of the fire warming his back, he pressed onwards down the path.

———

The pub was quiet when he arrived, and became even more so when he dragged himself in through the front door. Heads turned to look at him. Glasses stopped halfway to mouths. Had there been a record player, it would almost certainly have scratched into silence.

He'd become a reasonably familiar face at the local watering holes, though had been careful to never frequent the same place more than two nights in a row. He'd also made a point of limiting his conversation to a few choice phrases, the most common being, "Same again, John," despite the fact that none of the barmen at any of pubs went by that name.

It wasn't that he wanted to be thought of as some enigmatic mystery figure by the other punters. Quite the opposite, in fact. He didn't want them to think about him at all.

Which was why, despite the shock at his appearance, there was no outpouring of concern or offers of help. The moment of silence passed, the heads turned away, and the low murmur of conversation quickly resumed.

He hobbled to the bar. The big lad with the broad, honest face was working tonight. He instinctively reached for a shot glass, then appeared genuinely dumfounded when Hoon declined it with a wave.

"Just need to use the phone, son."

"Um... Oh. Right. Yeah. No problem. It's there. At the end of the bar."

Hoon knew that. He'd spent the first few nights in each new establishment mapping the layout in his head. This place was an old-fashioned boozer, full of dark wood that still, all these years after the smoking ban, gave off the smell of nicotine and tobacco.

There were eight tables, twenty-four chairs, plus benches along two of the walls. The seating was mostly upholstered in faded reds and golds, aside from a couple of replacement chairs that had no fabric on them at all.

The pub had two bathrooms—a large gents, with three urinals, two stalls, and a window just about large enough to climb out of in an emergency, and a smaller room with a single toilet and sink that served as both the ladies and the disabled bathroom. That one didn't have a window, and so not only were women short-changed on the facilities front, they were also shit out of luck if they needed to make a quick exit.

A hatch behind the bar led down to the cellar. Hoon hadn't made it down there, but had seen a barrel lift on the street outside, so knew there was more than one way in and out.

From his usual seat at the bar, the mirrors afforded him a clear view of the front door and most of the windows. The rest of the windows and the bathroom doors he was able to watch from the corner of his eye, so if danger had ever come calling, he would be ready for it.

Given all that—given the time he had spent studying the place—he had a firm understanding of *precisely* where the payphone was.

What he didn't have was any money to pay for it. Somewhere between the farmhouse and the warehouse, his wallet and phone had been taken from him.

Fortunately, he'd memorised all the numbers he was likely to need.

"Any chance I can borrow ten-pee?" he asked as he limped over to where the phone sat waiting.

"Eh, are you alright?" the lad behind the bar asked.

"Oh aye, just fucking dandy, son. Shitting rainbows here," Hoon snapped back. "Ten-pee. Can I borrow it?"

"What for?" the lad behind the bar asked.

"For the phone box. I need to make a call," Hoon said.

"Phone box is a quid," the barman informed him.

Hoon physically recoiled at this revelation. He glared pure hot outrage at the payphone sitting on the end of the bar, like it had just made some particularly disparaging comments about his mum's weight and sexual history.

"A quid? A fucking quid?! It's the UK I'm calling, no' the far reaches of outer fucking space!"

The barman shrugged an apology. "What can I say? It's a quid."

"Well, can I borrow a quid, then?"

"For the phone?"

Hoon tutted. "No, son, so I can go get a shopping trolley and go fucking joyriding down a big hill."

The barman's face was a blank canvas of confusion.

"Jesus Christ," Hoon muttered. "Aye, for the phone. *Of course*, for the phone."

The old till *bee-beeped* as the barman prodded a button, and the cash drawer practically assaulted him in its rush to spring open. He plucked a coin from the tray, then hesitated.

"Wait, are you going to give me this back?"

"Probably not," Hoon admitted.

With a sigh, the lad replaced the money, shut the drawer, then fished in his pocket until he found a pound coin. With a *clack* he slapped it down on the bar beside the phone.

"You're a fucking hero, son. Get yourself a drink on me," Hoon said, picking up the coin and shoving it forcefully into the phone's slot like he was trying to make it choke. "You'll have to pay for it yourself, mind you, I'm skint."

"Very generous of you," the barman muttered, then he headed off to the far end of the bar, where one of the regulars was waving a crumpled fiver.

Hoon waited until the lad was out of earshot, then punched in the number and listened to the *burring* of the ringtone.

"Come on, come on, be in you bastard," he whispered, adjusting his grip on the package that was still tucked beneath one sweat-ringed armpit.

The phone continued to ring out. Hoon closed his eyes and clenched his jaw. If it wasn't answered... If he wasn't home...

There was a click from the other end. Hoon straightened, and spoke before the person on the other end had a chance to.

"Hello? Miles? That you?"

From the other end of the line, there was a long, pregnant pause.

"Rhetorical fucking question," Hoon said. "I know it's you."

Down the phone, Miles Crabtree sighed. When he spoke, his voice was a disorientated mumble.

"Hoon? That you?"

"Were you fucking sleeping?" Hoon asked him.

"Yes. I was," Miles said, not bothering to hide his irritation.

"It's no' even ten o'clock, for fuck's sake," Hoon told him. "What are you, a fucking infant?"

"What do you want?" Miles asked. He yawned, and seemed to waken a little. "What's wrong? Has something happened?"

Hoon caught his reflection in the mirror behind the bar. The haggard old bastard who gazed back at him looked like he had both seen a ghost and currently *was* a ghost himself.

"Aye. Aye, you might say that," he replied. He pressed the heavy package to his side, and glanced around to make sure no one was listening in. "I'm going to need you to come pick me up..."

CHAPTER SEVEN

MILES CRABTREE HAD INSERTED himself into Hoon's life at a particularly inopportune moment a couple of months previously, and so Hoon had absolutely no qualms whatsoever about returning the favour, even if that involved painting the passenger seat of his car in sheep shit and blood.

Crabtree worked for MI5. At least, he had done when Hoon had met him, though given the number of rules and laws they had broken together, it was unlikely he had managed to retain his position with the security service.

After what they'd done, in fact, it was unlikely he'd even be employed as a security *guard*. And even Hoon had managed to get a job doing that, albeit for a period of time so short it was likely now mentioned in the record books.

Hoon had offered only the bare minimum information on the drive to Miles' flat, and Miles, to his credit, hadn't pushed him for more. As a result, most of the journey had been spent in silence, aside from a few seconds when Miles had attempted to play a *Simon & Garfunkel* CD, and Hoon had immediately switched it back off.

Miles lived in a two-bedroom ground floor maisonette somewhere just east of Brixton, with its own private entrance and a garden out back about the size of a midge's bollock. The inside felt shabby, like it was in need of a deep-clean and a lick of paint.

Hoon got it, though. Knowing what he now did about Miles, he understood why it had all been left this way, right down to the grubby, toddler-sized handprint low down on the living room wall. The furniture had been arranged around the mark, making it the focal point of the whole room. The whole house, maybe.

"Right, so, you want to get cleaned up?" Miles asked once the front door was safely locked and bolted. "I'll stick the kettle on, then you can tell me what happened."

"What?" Hoon looked down at himself, then shook his head. "No, it's fine, I just need you—"

"Bob," Miles said, cutting him off. He indicated a door on Hoon's left. "Go shower. Towels are in the basket. I'll get you some clothes."

"Fuck's sake. Fine," Hoon said. He thrust the tape-wrapped bag into Miles' arms. "Look after that, but do *not* fucking open it."

———

The shower had taken longer than he'd intended. Getting undressed had been a laborious, occasionally agonising task, and the simple act of lifting his legs over the edge of the bath had been a test of both physical and mental endurance.

The water, when he'd first turned it on, had been like an angry torrent of ice shards against his bare skin, and he'd been forced to flatten himself against the tiled side wall like he was shimmying along a window ledge several storeys above the ground, while involuntarily making a sound like a howler monkey in mourning.

A panicky wrench of the control knob had almost scalded the flesh right off his bones, and most of the following minute had been spent making tiny, almost imperceptible adjustments to the dial like he was some sort of Victorian safe cracker.

Eventually, he managed to get the water to an acceptable temperature and had stood there with one hand against the wall, letting it cascade over him. Head lowered, he'd watched the clear running liquid be polluted by all the blood, shit, and smoke that he'd acquired over the previous few hours. It felt good to be rid of it. He just wished the assortment of injuries he'd picked up during the same period could be disposed of quite so easily.

Despite his earlier urgency, Hoon had spent twenty minutes or more just standing there, letting the water lick his wounds. The heat was helping his shoulders, at least. The muscles there no longer felt like they'd been twisted into knots.

The pain would come back once he was out and moving around, of course, but he allowed himself some time to enjoy the respite while it lasted.

But not a lot of time. Not too much.

The water ran freezing again for the final half-second after Hoon turned the knob to switch the shower off. It hit him like a jolt of strong coffee, and he clambered out over the edge of the bath far easier than he'd got in.

At some point, Miles must have snuck in and left a bundle of clothes sitting on top of the wicker basket that stood just inside the door. The underwear and socks were both new—Miles had made a point of leaving them in their packaging—though the grey t-shirt and navy blue jogging bottoms looked well worn.

Hoon took a towel from the basket and dried himself, then pulled on the clothes. They weren't a great fit—the t-shirt was tight and the trousers were short—but they weren't slathered in sheep shit or yellowed with piss, so they were still a major improvement on those he'd taken off.

He was about to leave the bathroom, when he caught a glimpse of himself in the mirror above the sink. The steam from the shower had blurred the glass, and the shape that looked back at him seemed monstrous and deformed.

Taking the edge of the towel, he gave the mirror a wipe. The face he saw then was less grotesque, but not by much.

"Fuck it," he announced, and he pulled open the bathroom cabinet.

————

"You've shaved," Miles said, when Hoon finally dragged himself out of the bathroom.

"Well spotted," Hoon said.

"Presumably with my razor?"

"Correct," Hoon said. He threw his wet towel down on the couch. Miles immediately picked it back up again.

"Did you at least clean it afterwards?"

"I ran it under the tap, if that's what you mean," Hoon replied.

That wasn't what Miles meant. Not exactly. He had been hoping for something a bit more thorough than a quick shake under running water, but decided that now wasn't the time to make an issue out of it.

"Have a seat," he said, heading through to the adjoining kitchen and bringing the wet towel with him. He called back over his shoulder. "I've made tea."

"I'll have coffee, if it's going," Hoon replied.

"At this time of night?" Miles called back, and he sounded downright horrified by the very prospect.

"It's barely fucking half ten," said Hoon.

He heard Miles muttering and the kettle being clicked back on, then slumped onto the couch. It was a wood and wicker framed thing, with big colourful, flower-patterned cushions that would have been more at home in a conservatory than a living room, he'd have thought.

The coffee table that had been placed in front of it was made of the same materials—minus the fabrics and foam—and Hoon was starting to see a real running theme to the place's aesthetic.

"What's with all the fucking wicker?" he asked.

"What do you mean?" replied Miles, still busy in the room next door.

"Doesn't matter," Hoon told him, then he stretched forward and picked up the tape-wrapped package from where it had been sitting on the table.

It had been an afterthought, really. A last-minute contingency plan in case anything like today's events should ever happen. He'd set up a few other such contingencies around the city, but this one he'd put in place a week or more after those, after waking in the early hours with worry worming away at the insides of his head.

"Coffee. Help yourself to milk and sugar," Miles said, setting a tray down on the table.

It was a wicker tray, and it required a lot of self-control on Hoon's part not to pass comment.

"I'm fine with it as it comes," Hoon said, taking the closest mug and swallowing down a big gulp of the tarry black liquid. "Fuck!" he wheezed. "That's hot."

"Of course it's bloody hot. You just heard me making it," Miles said.

He lowered himself into the room's only armchair—a companion piece to the couch, but with different flowers on the cushions—and took the second mug from the tray.

"Well?" he prompted. "What happened?"

"A lot. A lot fucking happened," Hoon said. Then, taking a somewhat less gung-ho sip of his coffee, he started to explain.

While Hoon talked, Miles said very little, only occasionally interrupting to clarify some small point or detail. For the most part, he sat back, eyes widening in surprise at first, then narrowing as concern became the primary emotional response to Hoon's story.

He did like the ostrich bit, though.

"And she said they're looking for them? For Gabriella and Welshy?"

"Aye," Hoon confirmed. "I mean, she said she wasn't, personally, but some fucker is."

"Presumably, that extends to Greig and his family, too."

Hoon nodded, the thought already having occurred to him. Greig was a young lad, just starting out in life with his missus and wean. Initially, Hoon had used him to get closer to finding Caroline, the missing daughter of an old army pal, but he'd come to like the lad. Or... tolerate him, anyway.

Still, he'd been involved with the international criminal organisation known as the Loop when Hoon had first met him, and Hoon consoled himself with the fact that, had he not forcibly inserted himself into the lad's life the way he had, Greig would probably be dead already.

Gabriella and Welshy, though? Their involvement in all this was solely his doing. It was thanks to him that they'd become targets. Thanks to him that their whole life had been turned upside-down, and they'd been forced into hiding, taking Welshy away from the doctors and nurses who had been caring for him for years, and Gabriella away from the small network of support she'd built up around them both.

That was all Hoon's doing. That particular shitshow was all on him.

"How are they?" he asked, even though he'd promised himself that he wouldn't.

"Greig and his family?"

"Eh, aye. Aye. Well, them and..." He aborted the rest of the sentence, then shook his head. "Forget it. Forget I asked. Need to know only."

"You can know how they're doing," Miles told him. "How *she's* doing. There's no harm in that."

The look Hoon returned was a dangerous thing, the glare of a wild animal backed into a corner. "Aye," he said. "There is. I just... I need them to be safe. All of them."

"They are. I give you my word on that, Bob. Whatever that's worth to you."

Hoon's grunt had a disparaging ring to it, but he didn't question the other man any further. The fact was, Miles was one of a handful of people over the years to have earned a bit of Hoon's trust. Not a lot, mind you—the bastard had lied to him repeatedly in the past—but enough.

Just.

"This woman. This *Suranne*. Any idea who she really is?" Miles asked.

"The fuck d'you think I'm here for?" replied Hoon.

Miles shrugged. "Because you need a bed for the night?"

"No. Well, aye, wouldn't go amiss, right enough," Hoon confirmed. He patted the couch. "This'll do fine."

"Oh, good. I'm so glad. And you're welcome."

"Sarcasm doesn't fucking suit you, son," Hoon told him. "You still with MI5, or did they sling you out on your arse?"

Something about Miles' face altered. The actual movements were imperceptible, but the change was immediately apparent. He now wore the look of a man living in dread of what was going to happen next.

"I'm still with MI5," he said. "Barely, I should add. And not in the same role. So, whatever you're going to ask, I almost certainly don't have the clearance to—"

"I need you to help me find out who that bitch was," Hoon interrupted.

"Right. So, I *definitely* don't have the clearance to do

that," Miles informed him. "I've been allowed to keep control of a couple of projects—your friends' security situation, for one—but otherwise, I'm now in a mostly... admin-based position."

Hoon stared back at him, not blinking. "What?" he muttered. "You're a fucking secretary?"

"No, I'm not a secretary! I'm in an administrative supporting role."

"Which is a fancy fucking way of saying secretary," Hoon assured him. "I don't care what the fuck they've called it on the job description, that's a secretary."

"No, it's—"

"Do you do filing?" Hoon asked, shutting the objection down.

Miles shifted his weight in the chair, like the big floral cushion had suddenly become as uncomfortable as it was garish. "Sometimes."

"Answering phones?"

"Only sometimes."

Hoon snorted. "Aye, only when it rings, you mean? Does the role require a range of what might be described as 'secretarial skills?'"

Miles sighed. "Fine. I'm a secretary," he admitted. "Hence why I don't have the same access and authority as before."

"What the fuck are you talking about? Any office I've worked in, the secretaries run the fucking show. Access? Secretaries have got access oozing out of their arseholes."

Miles frowned. "I don't know what that means. How would that help?"

"Cut the fucking backchat, son," Hoon said, leaning forwards so suddenly the wicker base of the couch let out a worrying *crick*. Worrying for Miles, anyway, Hoon couldn't care less. "I want to know who this woman is, and I want to know how I can find her. I want her full fucking address and postcode.

We'll see how she likes someone rocking up at her gaff without warning. My suspicion is *no' very fucking much*."

"Look, even if I wanted to help... And I do," Miles said. "But, also, I don't. But even if I did, I can't find her based on what you've told me. She doesn't sound like any of the Loop bigwigs we were previously aware of. From what you said, she sounds like a bit player trying to make a play for the big leagues. She might not even be on our radar."

Hoon gave the other man both barrels of a particularly intense eyeballing. Miles, to his credit, held the stare.

"I wish I could help you. I do. But I don't know who she is."

A thought struck Hoon then. Miles watched it happening in real-time, and saw the moment when one corner of Bob's mouth curved upwards into a grin.

"Maybe not," Hoon said. "But we know a slippery little bastard who will."

CHAPTER EIGHT

GODFREY WEST HAD GROWN to dread these days. He never knew when they were going to happen, but he had started to develop a sense, at least, of when to expect them. He'd note a downturn in his mood over breakfast one day, or some raised irritation levels if the book he'd requested from the library hadn't been delivered to his cell, and he'd know. He'd know, without anyone having to say a word to him, that he was being moved again.

They were concerned for his life. That was what they told him. He knew that wasn't true, of course. They were concerned about his testimony. They wanted the information that he had, and as long as he continued not to give it, they had no choice but to keep him alive.

Even so, he was amazed he had lasted this long. The Loop had operatives everywhere. Even with him being constantly shifted around all over London and the southeast, they had to know where he was. They *had* to.

If the shoe was on the other foot—if he had been worried about someone betraying his confidence—he'd know where to find them. And, soon after he had, nobody else would ever have been able to find them again.

He'd been a relatively high-ranking member of the organisation. Not on the global scale, perhaps, but he'd been among the movers and the shakers of the UK-based operations. He'd built up quite a little black book of names—celebrities, politicians, even royals—which he'd had the foresight to keep locked up inside his head, to prevent it falling into the wrong hands.

Unfortunately, this information had also made him a target. Godfrey trusted himself to keep his mouth shut. The rest of the Loop, however, would not.

He felt the cloth bag over the head was unnecessary, but they always insisted. It made the walk through the corridors to the waiting armoured vehicle that much more difficult. Fortunately, he always had at least one burly guard shoving him along, speaking only to bark directions, or orders to "Stop," or "Step down," or "Stop with the fucking humming!"

Once inside the van-sized vehicle, he'd be sat down in a metal and plastic chair facing the back doors with his arms and legs secured in place like he was Hannibal Lecter. It was good that they were afraid of him, he thought. He did enjoy that. But some of the journeys took hours, and the accompanying guards were never willing to scratch his itches.

Today had been no different than any other transportation day, aside from the fact that today's escort had been even less talkative than usual. He had been positively monosyllabic, in fact, directing Godfrey's progress from the cell to the van with a lot of shoving and just the occasional grunt.

Once Godfrey was strapped in, he tried to listen to a whispered conversation that took place just outside the armoured vehicle, but the cloth hood and the reinforced metal walls made it impossible for him to make out any of the details.

A few seconds later, he heard the thudding of a guard—just

the one this time—climbing into the back of the van and pulling the doors closed.

Interestingly, there was no click of a seatbelt this time, he noted. It could have coincided with the engine firing up, he supposed, but it would have to have been bang-on that moment for him not to have heard it.

It was true what they said, he'd found. Remove one sense, and the others adjusted to compensate. Or maybe you just paid more attention to those you had left.

The van rumbled forwards, rocking him around as its wheels found the same potholes they had encountered on the way here. The restraints dug into his wrists and ankles, fastened more tightly this time than they had been on any of the previous journeys.

Godfrey sat up straighter. Squared his shoulders. Set his jaw.

He had made peace with this. He had known this moment was coming.

"Are you at least going to take the hood off?" he asked. "So I can look into your eyes when you pull the trigger?"

"Pull the trigger?"

The accent caught him off guard, but before he could place it, the bag was wrenched from his head, and he winced in the sudden blinding brightness of the overhead lights.

He recognised the man in the guard costume immediately, even with his black eye and bruises.

Not the Loop, then.

Someone arguably worse.

"You'll fucking *wish* that I was here to shoot you," the man in the guard outfit hissed. "You'll be creaming in your fucking Y-fronts at the thought of a bullet through the head by the time I'm done with you, you frog-eyed box of dog tits."

Chief Superintendent Deirdrie Bagshaw of the Metropolitan Police, sat in an unassuming unmarked car, on an unremarkable street in South London, watching an armoured truck go trundling past, picking up speed as it went.

Her face was tight, her mouth puckered like she'd recently been forced to consume something bitter or sour.

"I'd say I hope you know what you're doing, but obviously you don't," she remarked, watching the transporter get smaller in her car's wing mirror.

Beside her, in the passenger seat, Miles nodded his head in agreement. "Obviously. But he can be weirdly persuasive."

Bagshaw shot him a sideways look. "Scary, you mean?"

Miles let out a laugh of exactly one syllable. "That, too. But, we've been getting nowhere with West for months. Maybe he'll find something out."

"Or maybe this whole thing will blow up in our faces," the Chief Superintendent countered. "And we'll both be out of a job."

"Or in jail."

Bagshaw sighed. "Yes. Or in jail."

"But no. It'll be fine," Miles assured her. "I have faith."

"Well, that's good," the police chief replied. She pressed the button that started the ignition, indicated right, and pulled a U-turn in the road. "At least that makes one of us."

———

Hoon had never been the sort of man to mess around with To-Do lists. He'd never bothered with shopping lists either, for that matter, and had never so much as entertained the thought of writing up a bucket list.

The only list he did keep—and one he updated frequently—was his *Shit List*. This was an ever-growing, always changing list of all the people he actively despised and wished harm upon. It contained almost half of all the people he had ever met, but somewhere near the top, above even certain members of Hoon's own immediate family, sat Godfrey West.

He'd earned his high placement several times over, partly due to his sex-trafficking, murderous ways and his loyalty to a worldwide organisation of bastards, but mostly because he had just one of those fucking faces.

Every line of it, every contour had been put there solely to get under Hoon's skin. The way his eyebrows moved, the way his nostrils flared, even the pigmentation of his tan—all of it appeared to have been designed to trigger some deep emotional response in Hoon that straddled the line between 'hatred' and 'revulsion.'

And now, here the fucker was, strapped to a chair in a moving fortress.

And very much alone.

"Alright there, Godfrey?" Hoon asked. He knew West had referred to himself as 'the Eel,' while a free man, but he wasn't going to give him the satisfaction. Also, it was a bloody ludicrous nickname. "Bet you weren't expecting to see me again, eh?"

"I'm sorry? Do I know you?" West asked in his refined South African accent. The question earned him a big fat grin from the man in the helmet and stab-proof vest.

"Aye, you go ahead and play coy, son," Hoon told him. "We'll see how far that gets you."

"Driver! Driver, I need some help back here!" Godfrey called.

Hoon's smile widened. "I wouldn't waste your time. Intercom's turned off. Couple of friends of mine pulled in a few favours."

West smiled back in defiance, but he was clearly shiteing himself, Hoon could tell. He'd looked like a well put together guy back when Hoon had first met him, but swap his tailored suit for some baggy grey jogging gear, and he lost a lot of his polish.

Mind you, the suits hadn't been the most notable thing about his attire.

"They still letting you wear the big nappies?" Hoon wondered aloud. He scrunched up his face and shook his head. "Fucking weird that, I have to say. I didn't even know it was a thing, but after I met you, I looked it up. Loads of you weirdo bastards out there, all fucking nappied up to the hilt, and sucking on dummies. What's the fucking appeal of that?"

West kept his smile fixed in place, but it was an unconvincing facade. "You wouldn't understand."

"Aye, well, I'll no' fucking argue with you there," Hoon said.

The sound of the transporter's engine grew louder as the vehicle headed up an incline. Hoon held onto his chair to keep his balance, and waited for the volume to drop before speaking again.

"I'm told you've been very good at keeping all your wee secrets, Godfrey. You've no' been answering questions."

The bastard's smile widened, and finally became real. "No comment," he said.

Hoon chuckled. "Aye, very good. But, see, there's a big difference between the people who usually interview you and me, Godfrey. Do you know what that is?"

"Cirrhosis of the liver?" West guessed.

"You're funny," Hoon told him. "But, no. Well, no' just that. Them and me, Godfrey, we've got different methods. Them and me, we play by different rules."

The rumbling of the truck speeding up masked West's laughter.

"Let me guess, unlike them, you're willing to resort to torture?"

"Resort? Fuck *resort*," Hoon said. "It's my go-to first option. Amazing how quickly folk'll rattle off answers to your questions when you start poking things up them, or lopping bits off. They start spitting them out like bullets out of a fucking machine gun. It can really free up the whole rest of the day, that."

Hoon slapped his hands on his thighs and let out a big, dramatic sigh.

"Sadly, I promised those friends I mentioned that I'd leave you in one piece, so I'm no' here to torture you, Godfrey. Disappointing as that is. I'm just here to talk to you. I'm hoping you can help me with a wee concern I've got."

"Well! This should be fun!" Godfrey replied. "I mean, I think we already know what the answer's going to be, but let's give it a go, shall we?"

Hoon nodded. "I like the attitude. Positive. Good," he said. He leaned forward, and locked eyes on the bastard in the chair. "A lassie turned up at my place yesterday. Thirties, I'd say. Brown, maybe dirty blonde hair. Hazel eyes. Five-six, five-seven. Called herself Suranne. You know her?"

Throughout the description, West's face had not changed one iota. The smile was still plastered on there, his eyebrows both raised in gleeful surprise.

"Nope," he said. "Not a clue."

"Don't rush, Godfrey," Hoon told him. "Take your time."

"Don't need to. I don't know her," West said. It was his turn to lean forwards, as far as the restraints would allow. "Or *do* I?" he asked in a stage whisper, then he winked and sat back in the chair.

On the list stowed away in Hoon's head, Godfrey West moved up three places.

"She was hanging around with four Irish lads. Probably not for their wit or conversational skills," Hoon continued. "She had another of your creepy fucking Loop pals there, too. Don't know his real name, but he calls himself 'The Professor.' You heard of him?"

The subtle changes to West's expression answered the question for him.

"Aye. Sounds like he's a big rock star with you weirdo fucks," Hoon said. "Enough that they gave him a whole new fucking throat, by the looks of him. Skimped on the nose, mind. Have you seen him? Recently, I mean? He looks like a skeleton's *Tinder* photo."

He crossed one leg over the other, rested an elbow on the knee, then his chin on his clenched fist. It was a friendly, relaxed sort of gesture. Chatty, almost. And yet, given the situation, there was something deeply disconcerting about it.

"So. The woman. Who is she?" Hoon pressed.

The transporter's brakes *hissed* and let out a series of mouse-like squeaks as it slowed to a stop at a junction.

"How is your friend's daughter doing?" West asked. "Caroline, wasn't it? I told you I didn't remember her. That I didn't know her." He made a sound deep in his throat. A little groan that made all the hairs on the back of Hoon's neck stand on end. "But I knew her, alright. She and I got *very* well acquainted during her time with—"

A punch to the face ended the sentence before he could. His head snapped back and hit the metal wall behind him with a solid *thunk* that hopefully hurt him even more than the jab had.

West blinked away tears, licked blood from his burst lip, then grinned again, showing his shiny red teeth.

"It's never far away for you, is it? Violence?" he said. "It's instinctive. It's built-in."

"Answer the fucking question," Hoon told him, sitting back down. "The woman. Who is she?"

"I don't know," West replied. "She could be one of hundreds. Thousands. *Tens* of thousands. It's like assuming all Catholics know each other. Or all plumbers. You don't grasp the scale of it. Your little animal brain, it can't begin to comprehend what you're dealing with."

The blood continued to seep from his split lip. He pressed his tongue against it, and let it linger there while he looked Hoon up and down.

"You think everyone's safe, don't you? That's why you're still doing all this. You think you've got nothing to lose. But you have. Whether you know it or not, you have. They'll find it. No matter how hard you try to hide it all away, they'll find what you love, and they will take it apart, and they will make you watch."

"Don't you fucking worry about me, pal," Hoon told him. "I've put things in place."

"Ah, so there *is* someone," West said, and this time, there was no disguising his laughter. "And you've put things in place, have you? You've got a contingency plan? Let me guess, you've told them you have information about them. About their more... publicity adverse members, perhaps? You've told them that if anything happens to anyone you care about, you'll leak it. You'll go public. Expose them. Does that sound about right?"

Hoon said nothing.

West tutted and groaned, like he had some very bad news to share.

"Yes. That's not going to work. You see, the Loop has been around for decades. Centuries, possibly. You think people haven't tried blackmailing them? You think people haven't tried *exposing* them, even? It's happening now, somewhere. Right now. On the internet. I guarantee it. Look it up, if you don't believe me. Look it up, and I guarantee that somewhere—on some social media account or other—someone is spilling the beans. Someone is shouting about all the terrible things we're doing."

He shrugged and shook his head. It almost looked remorseful, like he was apologising for the hard truth of the matter.

"But nobody is listening," he continued. "Because we do not

want them to listen. Because we do not *allow* them to listen. We control the narrative. We decide who knows what. You can go as public as you like, make as much noise as you want, share whatever information you have. No one would listen. And, if they did, none of it would stick. Even if you did know something which, let's be honest, we both know you don't."

Hoon scraped his teeth across his bottom lip. A delaying tactic. This was not going how he'd hoped.

"Aye, well, joke's on you, pal," he said. "They might not care that I've got information, but I'm sure they care where I got it from. I told them you spilled your guts. You gave up everyone. So, looks like we're both in the shit, eh?"

"Oh. Wow." Godfrey tilted his head back and laughed. It wasn't for show this time, but was a genuinely amused response.

"What the fuck's so funny?" Hoon demanded.

"You have no idea. Like, none," Godfrey chuckled. "You're so out of your depth it's unbelievable. My death warrant was signed the moment I got arrested. Nothing to do with any threats from you, nothing to do with any attempts to blackmail them. The second those cuffs went on me, I was a dead man."

He straightened himself up again and licked more blood from his chin. His lips smacked together like he was savouring the final remnants of his last meal.

"They don't care about your threats. They only care about loose ends. If the Alphas haven't already killed whoever it is you're trying to protect, then they will. Soon. That's not a threat. I'm not in a position to issue threats. It's a statement of fact."

"The Alphas? Who the fuck are the Alphas? Some right-wing basement-wanking involuntary celibate fucks?"

"No. Not that."

"Who, then?"

West filled his lungs with a long, slow breath through his nose. He closed his eyes, making the most of the experience.

When he opened them again, Hoon saw something new lurking there behind them.

Fear.

"You're about to find out," he said.

Hoon frowned. He tensed, and though over thirty-six hours had passed since his beating at the hands of the Irish lads, his muscles screamed in protest.

"What the fuck are you talking about?" he demanded.

"Traffic lights don't last this long," West said. "And I heard the driver's door shut thirty seconds ago."

It took a moment for the pieces to fall into place. It was the roar of an engine that finally hammered it all home.

Not this vehicle's engine, though. Another one. Bigger. More powerful.

And speeding in from the right.

Hoon grabbed for his seatbelt, heaved at it, fumbled with the clasp.

Godfrey West closed his eyes.

And the sound of thunder followed.

CHAPTER NINE

LATER, he would remember the sound.

It was a sound unlike anything he'd ever heard before. Or almost anything.

There had been one other like it. A roadside IED, back in the Gulf. An explosion that had torn his best mate in half before his eyes. Even now, all these years later, the memory of that sound hadn't diminished. It, along with every other detail of that moment, was permanently etched on every atom in Hoon's brain.

On a purely acoustic front, though, the sound inside the armoured car had been much, much worse.

It was the sort of sound, he thought, that would herald in the end of the world. There would be no trumpets or chorusing angels, just the screeching, rending, explosively kinetic catastrophe of noise that had erupted inside the vehicle.

Later, he would remember the sound.

What he would not remember—what he would have no sense of whatsoever—was anything that happened next.

Right now, he remembered nothing. *Knew* nothing. Nothing but darkness stretching out on all sides. An ocean of icy black, crashing against his bare skin. Pulling him down. Swallowing him whole. Filling his lungs with its long, probing fingers.

He tried to scream, but his body wasn't his to control. Tried to fight, but his muscles wouldn't respond. All he could do was float downwards into the dark, into the smothering filth and sediment of it.

Somewhere far off, as they always did, a siren sang.

CHAPTER TEN

LIGHT PRESSED its thumbs into his eyeballs, forcing them closed and drawing a slur of pain from his cracked and shrivelled lips.

He retreated back down into the dark. It was safer there. Nothing could hurt him.

He didn't remember the sound. Not yet. But then, he didn't yet remember anything. Not the van. Not the man in the chair. Not where he was, or how he'd wound up there.

All he knew was this moment. Now. And a thoroughly fucking unpleasant one it was, too.

Even in the darkness, he was starting to feel things. A lot of things, in fact, and none of them good.

Either he was suffering from the worst headache he'd ever had, or someone was sledgehammering his skull with reckless, wild abandon.

His tongue felt like it had merged with the roof of his mouth. They eventually separated with a sound like the scraping of sandpaper, and the effort stole his breath away, and set the darkness spinning around him.

He wanted to run through his usual diagnostic checks, but

couldn't remember what that entailed. Better to just lie here. Better to just wait. Better to just hope that the darkness came back to claim him for its—

No. Fuck that. The headache wasn't going to give him the peace.

He forced his eyes open a crack. The light rushed to close them again, but he stood his ground, eyelids flickering, letting his pupils adjust to what he now realised was quite a dim glow.

Gradually, the world blurred into focus.

He saw a tiled ceiling, polystyrene and pocked with holes.

He saw the metal rail at the foot of his bed, a clipboard hooked over it.

He saw a little bald fella with a straggly white beard vaguely waving to him from across the room. He vaguely waved back, then looked down at his hand like it was an old friend he hadn't expected to run into.

The old man seemed momentarily pleased with the wave, then his head sunk back onto his pillow and he let out a strangled breath, as if it had taken all his energy reserves just to make that small hand movement.

He looked dog rough, the poor bastard. Although, if he thought about it, Hoon probably felt worse than the other guy looked.

"Where am I?" Hoon asked.

Not out loud, although that had been his intention. He swallowed so he could try again, then realised there was something blocking up half of his throat. He brought a hand up and fumbled at his face, then let out a grunt of alarm when he found the tube that had been inserted up his nose.

With the same hand, he felt along his arm, until he found the cannula taped to the big vein on the back of the other hand, and a second, thinner tube, that hooked him up to a drip bag hanging from a stand beside his bed.

"The fuck?" he slurred. It came out all drool and consonants, but was enough to arouse the interest of the old man in the bed across from him.

He raised his head again, gave another of his now-trademark waves, then flopped back onto the pillow, well and truly spent.

Hoon knew how he felt. He'd barely been conscious for a minute, but already he could feel sleep anchoring itself to him. Getting its hooks in. A wee bit of shut-eye would be lovely. A wee doss would see him right.

But, no. Instead, he tore the needle from the vein in the back of his hand, grabbed at the tube taped to his face, and—

"Jesus Christ, Bob. What are you doing?"

Miles' voice came from somewhere back and to the right. He appeared in Hoon's peripheral vision, grabbing for his hands to stop him yanking the tube out. From his dazed expression, it was obvious that Miles had been sleeping, too, although his seemed to be your everyday normal snooze, as opposed to whatever head trauma Hoon had found himself the victim of.

It was then that he remembered the noise. The thunder. The explosion. The sound of something heavy being walloped at high speed by something even heavier, as heard from the inside.

It had been deafening. Terrifying. It had ripped him from the here and now and whisked him back to somewhere far away. To some time long ago.

And the noise had brought movement. He remembered that now, too. Parts of it, anyway. A sudden, uncontrollable lurch, his body flung around in his chair, the seatbelt cutting into his neck between where the stab vest ended and the helmet began.

It had felt catastrophic, the noise, and the motion, and the pain. There had been nothing loose in the back of the transporter—nothing to fly around or hang in the air like time had stood still, while the transporter itself rolled and crashed around it.

There had just been him.

Wait. No.

There had been someone else.

He realised that Miles was talking to him, but there was a rushing in his ears like falling sand, and he didn't have a clue what the MI5 man was saying. He chose not to worry about it, and instead tried to remember who'd been there with him.

Not someone he cared about, he didn't think. Although, to be fair, that would be statistically unlikely. But someone important. Someone he...

Fuck. Aye. That bastard.

Even through the Swiss cheese of his memory, he pieced it together. Christ, had he really been that stupid?

"...you even listening?"

The tone of Miles' voice was becoming annoyingly insistent now, and Hoon had no choice but to pay attention.

"I said, are you OK?" Miles asked again.

"Do I fucking look OK, you bat-eyed tub o' fudds?" was what Hoon wanted to say, but the tube down his throat prevented him even attempting it, so he settled instead for a half-choked, "No."

"Do you want me to get someone? A nurse, or a doctor, or...?"

Hoon almost wanted to hold on to see what that third option was going to be. A cleaner? The canteen staff? The wee goblin-man in the bed across?

He managed another, "No," then, before Miles could intervene, grabbed the tubing that was inserted up his nose, and rid himself of the whole lot in a series of long, nauseating pulls, each one accompanied by a cringing whine of horror from the man in the chair beside him.

The final few inches triggered his gag reflex, and he coughed and retched as it left his throat. With a gargle of triumph, he let the tube fall off the side of the bed, and Miles danced his feet sideways to avoid it hitting his legs.

"You're not supposed to do that," Miles said. There was a haunted look on his face, like the last few moments had been among the most traumatic of his life. "You could get into trouble."

"'Smy fuckin' throat," Hoon whispered, because that was pretty much all he was capable of. "Where am I?"

"You're in the hospital," Miles told him.

"I fucking guessed that much. Why? What happened?"

"You don't remember?" Miles asked, leaning forward until he came back into view. He had stubble on his chin and halfway down his throat. Hoon was pretty sure he'd been clean-shaven the last time they'd spoken.

Shite. This was worse than he thought.

Hoon did remember. Some of it, anyway. Enough.

But he wanted to be wrong. He wanted to be told he'd imagined it. Or, at the very least, that it had been a terrible accident. A mistake. Wrong time, wrong place.

Even if Miles had told him that, though, he wouldn't have believed it. He couldn't. It would've been far too big a coincidence, and if there was one thing he'd learned during his years as a copper, it was that genuine coincidences were few and far between.

And one this size would be bloody miraculous.

"There was a truck," Miles said.

He left it there for a few seconds, like he was hoping it would be enough of a prompt for Hoon to fill in the blanks.

When Hoon said nothing, he sighed, massaged his temples with the tips of his fingers, and continued.

"There must have been... I don't know. An arrangement. The driver of the armoured car, he stopped at a junction. Overshot it a bit, so he was blocking a lane of traffic coming from the right. So the witnesses said, anyway. We were following behind, but stuck at other lights, so didn't see it happening." He sucked in his bottom lip. "Heard it, though. Sounded nasty."

The details were still vague, but Hoon was pretty confident that it hadn't been a barrel of laughs.

"Anyway, the driver, he, eh, he got out. Made a run for it. Then, the next thing... bang. The truck hit you. Rolled you over. You took quite a hit to the head. If you hadn't been wearing the helmet and body armour..."

"What about West?" Hoon asked. "He make it?"

Miles shook his head. "No. Can't say it was even touch and go. The impact snapped his neck."

Hoon grunted. "That sounds upsettingly quick and pain-less," he croaked.

"What about the driver of the truck?" Hoon asked.

Another shake of the head from the MI5 man. "Killed in the crash. Airbag was disabled and seatbelt had been tampered with. They're trying to identify him but, well, there's not a lot left to go on."

"Bagshaw going to keep us posted?" Hoon asked.

"Deirdrie?" Miles' chair creaked as he shifted his weight. "Uh, no. She's not being informed."

Hoon's forehead furrowed, which made lots of little marbles of pain go rolling around inside his skull. "Why the fuck not? She's a chief superintendent."

"She's on suspension pending a full investigation," Miles explained.

Hoon groaned. "For helping me get close to that bastard?"

"Yes. They've been looking for an excuse, and this handed it to them on a plate," Miles confirmed.

"Fuck. She was a good asset," Hoon said.

Miles tutted. "And a lovely person. She doesn't deserve this."

Something about the way Miles said it made Hoon take note. Something about the emphasis on the word 'she,' that implied while she might not deserve it, someone else did.

"They've canned you, too?" he asked.

Miles smiled, but it was an empty gesture. "Suspended. Pending investigation. Like Deirdrie. Different organisations, same rules."

"Shite. Sorry," Hoon said, and for once, he almost sounded genuinely contrite.

"No apologies necessary," Miles said. "I knew what I was getting myself into. I accepted the risks. I just..." He sighed. "I just wish I knew how those bastards knew where West was going to be. Moving him is a tightly controlled operation."

"You said the driver was dodgy," Hoon reminded him. He was clutching at straws. Hoping he was wrong.

But knowing, more surely than he knew anything, that he wasn't.

"Drivers never know where they're going until he's loaded up and they're on the move," Miles explained. "Details are programmed into the satnav. No phones. Secure channel, radio contact only. There shouldn't be any way that—"

"It was me," Hoon rasped.

Miles smiled. It was a confused, vacant sort of smile, like someone pretending to be in on a joke that had soared miles above their head.

"What do you mean?" he asked.

Hoon grimaced and shuffled himself further up the bed on his elbows. Several wheezing, breathless moments later, when he'd recovered from the effort, he was able to continue.

"All that shite. Her saying they wanted me to join them," he said. "She knew. She knew I'd go and ask him about her, try and figure out who she is. I led the bastards right to him. The fuckers used me."

"They also nearly killed you."

"They should be so fucking lucky," Hoon muttered.

Miles stood up and retrieved the chart from the end of the bed. "No, I mean they nearly killed you. It was touch and go there for a while. Like I said, if it wasn't for the helmet..."

"How long?" Hoon asked.

"How long what?"

"How long was I out for?"

"Long enough."

That wasn't enough of an answer.

"How long?"

Miles returned the clipboard to the hook on the foot rail, then glanced over at the old man in the bed opposite and returned his little wave.

"About a day," he said, not meeting Hoon's gaze. He didn't need to. He could feel it boring into him.

"A day? What do you mean? I've been out of the game for a whole fucking day?"

"Actually..." Miles checked his watch. "More like thirty-six hours. Like I said, you were in a bad way." He turned back to the man in the bed. "And a lot's happened while you were out of action. If you weren't already lying down, I'd tell you to take a seat."

"That sounds a bit fucking ominous."

"Uh, yeah," Miles said. He sat down again, being careful to step over the trailing plastic tube that had, until recently, been deep inside Hoon's innards. "Yes, I suppose it does."

Before the MI5 man could explain any further, the swing door to the ward was opened, and a strikingly tall dark-skinned nurse entered wearing a smile that very quickly turned upside-down.

The door *thu-thunked* closed again, and the nurse was suddenly right up in his face.

"What's this you've done now?" she demanded. She sounded like she had stepped off the boat that morning. The boat in question having sailed down the Tyne from Newcastle. "Who took out your feeding tube, pet?"

"He did," Hoon said, nodding at Miles.

Miles gawped in horror at the nurse, who short him a fierce, fiery look.

"What? No! No, I didn't. It wasn't me. It was..."

"We know fine who it was," the nurse said, giving Hoon a mostly playful but still firm slap on the back of the hand. She picked the hand that had recently had the needle in it, he noted, so it stung like a bastard. "We saw him on the camera. Silly bugger, you could've done yourself real damage."

"Aye, well, least I'm in the right place," Hoon said. "Now, d'you mind, sweetheart? We were having a fucking conversation here."

The nurse didn't miss a beat. She picked up his wrist, took out her watch, and set about checking his pulse. "You're not here for chit-chat, Mr Allcock. You're here to recuperate."

"Mr Allcock? Who the fu—?" Hoon began, then he spotted the urgent look and shake of the head from the man in the chair by his bed, and abandoned the question before he could fully ask it.

"Hush now," the nurse told him. "I'm counting. Then, I'll get the doctor. Let him know you're awake."

There were three groups Hoon knew better than to argue with—nurses, Geordies, and women. Since he'd hit the hat-trick, he kept his mouth shut and waited for her to finish, then only barely protested when she pulled down his bottom eyelids and shone the torch into each of his eyes in turn.

"Can you tell me your name?" she asked, once she'd finished with the physical checks.

"Not a fucking clue, sweetheart," Hoon said.

He did know his name. What he didn't know was Mr Allcock's.

"Date of birth?"

"Nope. Nothing," Hoon said. "You should probably get a doctor, eh? Sounds to me like I've smashed the old fucking noggin up good and proper."

The nurse's eyes narrowed like she had a sense she was being played, then she tutted and turned away, telling him she'd be back as soon as she could, and warning him not to do anything else stupid in the meantime.

Hoon waited until the door had swung closed again, then started to sit up until a sharp sting of pain in his crotch made him suddenly freeze like time itself had stopped.

"The fuck was that?" he hissed through the side of his mouth. Even as he asked the question, though, he was already figuring out the answer. "Have I got a fucking catheter in?"

"I haven't looked," Miles said. "Though, judging by the big bag of piss at the side of the bed, I'd say it's probably quite likely."

"Right. Oh. Fuck. *Fuck*," Hoon said, very gingerly lying back down. "You'll have to pull it out."

"What?! I'm not pulling it out," Miles protested. "The nurse will do it."

"We're no' hanging about until she gets back," Hoon said. "We're getting out of here."

"*What*?!" Miles yelped again, but at a higher pitch than last time. "We can't. You're injured."

"I'm fine, apart from the fucking hose up my bellend." He threw back the covers, revealing a fetching hospital gown, and a thin rubber tube extending from the bottom of it. "Grab that and pull it. Fucking gently, though!"

"I can't... I'm not going to..." Miles said, but he knew he was fighting a losing battle.

He glanced at the door, in the hope that the nurse might come storming through, but while he could hear voices and foot-steps, they were all distant, busy elsewhere.

He looked over at the old man in the bed opposite, who was watching events in rapt fascination. The old man waved again. Miles returned it, half-heartedly.

"Fucking hurry up," Hoon barked. He shuffled closer to the edge of the bed, presenting the hose.

"I can't believe I'm doing this," Miles muttered. He wiped his hands on his trousers, like he could pre-emptively clean off all the things he hadn't yet touched, then took hold of the tubing.

"Right. Easy," Hoon whispered. "Take your time. Slow and steady wins the fucking—"

He let out a cry of pain, and jack-knifed into a V-shape on the bed. Miles immediately released his grip and raised his hands like he was surrendering to an invading army.

"I'm sorry! I'm sorry! That wasn't me! I barely touched it!"

Colours danced before Hoon's eyes. He gestured wildly in the direction of the bag of urine hanging by the bed. "Check the fucking instructions!"

Miles leaned sideways in his chair, his eyes darting left and right as he scanned the text on the side of the bag. "There aren't any instructions!" he said. "It's just a load of stuff about disposing of piss."

"Well fucking Google it!" Hoon cried.

As Miles fumbled for his phone, the old boy in the opposite bed got in on the action. "You just cut the wee knob bit off."

Hoon's stare of outrage probably set the poor old bugger's recovery back by several days. "I beg your fucking pardon?" he demanded. "There's nothing fucking wee about it."

"On the thing. The wee balloon bit," the old man said, gesturing with the same level of vagueness as his earlier waves.

"What wee fucking—?"

"Found it," Miles announced. "What do I do with it?"

"Just pop it," the old man said. "It releases the pressure at the other end, so you can then pull—"

"Alright, we don't need the fucking science lesson!" Hoon told him. He gave Miles a nod. "You heard him. Pop it."

"With what? I don't have anything to pop it with!"

"Use your fucking teeth, then!"

Miles recoiled in disgust. "I'm not using my teeth!"

"You can use my teeth," the old man suggested.

Hoon scowled. "How in the name of Christ are we meant to...?" he began, then he saw the upper set of fake gnashers being held aloft like they were the fucking Lion King. "Go! Get them," he ordered, which earned another pained groan from Miles.

"I don't want to touch his false teeth!"

"Well, then you'd better hurry up and get fucking chewing!"

Miles made a sound like he was being strangled, then got to his feet. "I really wish I'd never met you sometimes," he muttered, then he scurried across the room, and—with one finger and thumb—accepted the offered top teeth of the gummily grinning pensioner.

CHAPTER ELEVEN

"RIGHT NOW, pet, I've got the doctor here to check you over," the nurse announced, pushing open the door to the High Dependency Unit room.

She stopped at the curtain that had been drawn all the way around the bed, and brought her ear closer to it, listening in.

"You decent, Mr Allcock?"

Behind her, the doctor, an Indian man as short in stature as he was in patience, cleared his throat and checked his pocket watch. He gave a nod to the old man in the room's other bed, acknowledging his wave.

"Mr Allcock? Don't mind me, pet, I'm coming in," she said.

She popped her head through the curtains. The doctor looked taken aback by her ejection of surprise.

"Problems, nurse?" he asked.

"Aye." The curtains parted to reveal an empty bed with the uppermost set of some ancient false teeth lying on the sheet where the patient should have been. "You could say that."

Across from the door, on the opposite side of the room, the cool night breeze blew in through an open window.

―――――

Hoon lurked in the bushes, head down, bare arse presented to the world through the gap in the back of his gown. The ground floor room had been a stroke of luck. High bloody time he'd had one of those.

There had been a square of grass outside, penned in on three sides by other wards and corridors. On the fourth side, a head-high brick wall had required a bit of teamwork to get over, and if Miles had looked haunted by the sight of Hoon wrenching out his feeding tube, it was nothing compared to how he looked after boosting him to the top of the wall in his open-backed hospital garment.

There had been some scrambling, some swearing, and a few hurled insults, but eventually Hoon had managed to give Miles the assist required for him to heave himself over the wall, too.

They'd both landed clumsily on the other side, their falls broken by a dispiritingly prickly hedge before they rolled down onto another strip of grass, this one much less well maintained than the last.

From there, they'd figured out the route to the car park. Miles had led the way, stopping every minute or so to let the struggling Hoon catch up. They'd kept to the shadows where possible, ducked under windows when necessary, and less than quarter of an hour after Miles had screwed his eyes shut and pulled out Hoon's catheter, they reached the edge of the road across from where Miles had parked his car.

Even at this time of night, the road was busy, with a constant flow of traffic moving through the hospital grounds. A man limping across it in a hospital gown and bare feet was likely to draw some unwanted attention, and so Hoon had waited, crouched in the foliage, while Miles had gone to bring the car around.

He shivered, the thin medical smock doing very little to

keep out the cold. Especially around the back. It was more than the chill that was making him shake, though. His body was mounting a protest. He shouldn't be here, it was telling him. Having been unconscious for over a day, he should be lying in bed, taking whatever medical intervention came his way. Where he should *not* be was semi-naked in a bush at the back of a hospital. It was being quite clear on that point.

And yet, here he was.

Less than two years ago, he had been a detective superintendent in Police Scotland. Now, he was a man with his arse in a conifer.

How the mighty had fallen.

He spotted Miles' car through a gap in the hedge, and watched it slowing to a crawl as it drew closer. Hoon waited until it was almost alongside him, then pushed free of his cover and emerged onto the road right beside the vehicle.

The brakes were applied with a rusty-sounding rasp. Hoon pulled open the back door, tumbled inside, then closed it again behind him.

"Go, go, go," he urged, lying as flat as he could to avoid being seen.

"I don't think anyone's chasing us, or anything," Miles told him, but a dunt to the back of his seat stopped him from arguing any further. Instead, he heaved the gearbox into first, carefully checked all three mirrors, and pulled away from the kerb.

When he had safely rejoined the flow of traffic, he angled his rearview mirror so he could see Hoon on the back seat.

"Right, where are we going?" he asked.

"Can't go to your place," Hoon said. "They're obviously watching it."

He struggled up into a sitting position, his chest heaving, his pulse racing like he'd just finished a hundred-metre sprint. His body's silent rebellion was continuing and was now manifesting itself as a skull-splitting headache and a rising sensation of nausea.

He stole a look out the back window, still not convinced that nobody was following. There was nobody obviously tailing them, though, and so he faced front again before the nausea had a chance to worsen any further.

"So, any suggestions?" he asked. "Can't go to my place, since the fuckers burned it to the... Well, no' the ground, exactly. To the bottom of the fucking sea."

"River," Miles corrected.

Hoon scowled. "Oh aye, let's us just sit here splitting fucking hairs, will we? Like we've no' got bigger fish to fucking worry about."

The word escaped Miles' lips before he could stop it. "Fry."

"What?"

"Bigger fish to..." Miles shook his head. "Doesn't matter."

"What the fuck was up with calling me 'Mr Allcock,' by the way?" Hoon demanded. "Was that a fucking dig at me?"

"What?" Miles adjusted his mirror again until he found Hoon's face. "No. That was the name of the guard we swapped you with. Richard Allcock. Made sense to keep up the charade."

"Fuck off!" Hoon cried, with such emphasis and volume that Miles jumped, jerking the wheel a little and weaving the car towards the centre line. "No fucking way is he called that. *Richard Allcock?*"

Miles gripped the wheel more tightly. "He is. Why? What about it?"

"That's no' his fucking name!"

"It is!" Miles insisted.

Hoon shook his head. "Nut. Is it fuck. No way. Nobody's calling their wean *Dick Allcock.*"

Miles said nothing as they approached a roundabout. He took the right lane, and it was only once he'd turned off at the third exit that he replied.

"Hadn't even thought of that. That's grim, right enough," he admitted, sucking air in through his teeth. "Poor guy must've had a hell of a time in school."

"He wouldn't even have survived his first fucking day at my school," Hoon said. "Years later, he'd still be spoken about in whispered legend. The kid who'd cringed so hard he'd fucking imploded." He tutted and looked out at the passing lights of the city. "Dickie fucking Allcock."

They continued on in silence for a minute or more, each one tangled up in their own thoughts. Miles flexed his fingers on the wheel, stretching them out to their full span, then tightening them again. This did not go unnoticed by the man behind him.

"What's wrong?" Hoon asked. "I mean, aside from the fucking obvious?"

"What? Um, nothing."

Hoon sat forward so he was half-wedged through the gap between the two front seats. "Bollocks. There's something," he said. "There's something you're not telling me."

"No. No, there's nothing, there's..." Miles abandoned his denial and huffed out a big sigh. "There is something, yes. I wasn't sure how to tell you, because I wasn't sure how you were going to take it, and I don't know what, if anything, you're going to want to do about it."

Hoon waited for approximately four-fifths of a second before barking out a reply. "Well, spit it out, then. What the fuck is it? What is it you're no' telling me?"

"It's, um..." Miles met Hoon's eye in the mirror. "It's Welshy. He's in a bad way, Bob."

"Aye, that's no' exactly news. Poor bastard's fucking bedbound."

"No. I mean, yes. Obviously, but that's not..." He sighed. "He's getting worse."

"Worse? What do you mean?" Hoon asked. "How much

worse are we talking?" He caught the look in the mirror. The apology. "Aw... fuck."

Hoon flopped back, leaned his head back, and looked at the fabric roof lining above him.

"I don't think the move helped," Miles told him. "But he was deteriorating prior to that, according to his records. Without the move, he might've had another few weeks."

"Another few weeks? Fuck. How long has he got?"

Miles stared ahead, following the red tail lights of a taxi in front. "They think... They say... It could be any time."

Hoon clutched at his head like he was trying to stop it cracking open. "Aw, no. Aw, fuck. Welshy." He sat forward again. "You know where he is, aye?"

Miles turned and shot a look back over his shoulder. "Well, yeah, but..."

"But what?"

"But you said you didn't want to know. You told me not to tell you. Ever."

"Aye, well, now I'm changing my mind," Hoon said. "Take me there. I want to see him."

"No, I understand, it's just that you told me that under no circumstances was I ever to—"

"Miles!" Hoon barked, and the driver almost lost his grip on the wheel again. A quick check in the mirror told him that it would not be wise to argue further with the man in the back. "Take me to Welshy," Hoon instructed. "Right. Fucking. Now."

———

They stopped at a big supermarket on the south-western outskirts of the city. Miles went inside to grab some painkillers, trainers, and a set of clothes that wouldn't make Hoon look like he'd recently escaped from a hospital. Which, of course, he had.

While Hoon got himself dressed in the back seat, Miles

filled up the car's tank at the supermarket's on-site petrol station.

When he went inside to pay, he returned to find Hoon on his hands and knees behind the car, craning his neck to better see the underside.

"What are you doing?" Miles asked. There were a couple of other people at the petrol station, hoses in hand, watching Hoon crawling around on the forecourt. "People are watching."

"I don't give a fuck what they're doing," Hoon said. He squinted into the darkness beneath the car, and ran a hand along the bottom of the chassis. "I'm checking nobody's tracking us."

"They aren't," Miles assured him. "I sweep it every couple of days."

"And did you sweep it today?" Hoon asked.

"Yes. I swept it today," Miles said. "After watching you getting pulled from that wreckage, I swept it about half a dozen times. It's clean."

"Aye, well," Hoon grunted, pulling himself up on the bumper. He brushed his hands together, then wiped them on his new, slightly oversized jeans. "It had fucking better be."

They got into the car, Hoon now in the front passenger seat, rather than hiding in the back. Miles clipped his seatbelt on, made a microscopic adjustment to his mirror, and then started the engine.

"You bring that package I left with you?" Hoon asked.

Miles turned his head to look at him. "Yeah. It's in the boot." He sighed. "You're going to want it, aren't you?"

"Well, I'm no' asking for the good o' my fucking health."

With a tut, Miles shut off the engine, unclipped his belt, and opened the door again. Hoon sat facing forward, his fingers tapping out an impatient rhythm on the dashboard, while Miles opened the boot, fished out the tape-wrapped package, then slammed the lid back down again.

He returned to the car a moment later and dumped the parcel into Hoon's lap. "There. Anything else?"

"Did you get me that phone I asked for?"

Stretching, Miles grabbed one of the bright orange supermarket carrier bags from the back seat and dumped that on Hoon, too. "There. Basic, like you asked for."

Hoon didn't bother to check that bag. "And did you get me credit?"

"Yes, Bob. I got you credit," Miles said, his irritation clear. "There's a ten-pound voucher in the bag."

"A fucking tenner?" Hoon spat. "Is that it?"

"Well, I didn't know how much you needed!"

"More than a fucking tenner, that's for sure," Hoon replied. "What the fuck do you think I'm planning on doing, making a five-second call to myself?"

Miles started the engine again. "That doesn't even make sense," he muttered. He grasped for his seat belt, clipped it in, then pointed to the design on the front of the T-shirt he had bought in the store. "That is absolutely appropriate, by the way," he remarked, then he crunched the car into gear, and pulled away from the petrol station.

CHAPTER TWELVE

HOON STOOD JUST inside the front door of a ramshackle old farmhouse somewhere within spitting distance of Yeovil in South Somerset, where time seemed, for the moment, to be standing still.

Miles was talking, but he wasn't hearing him. Not really. The sounds, maybe, but not the words. His attention was instead focused solely on the woman standing at the other end of the hall.

He'd known her for years. Technically. He'd first met her a lifetime ago, when Welshy had introduced her as his girlfriend. One look at her long legs, deep tan, and dazzling smile, and Hoon, like all the other lads from their troop, had been insanely jealous.

She'd been all floral skirts and Spanish accent back then, and had seemed to dance through the world without a care or worry, her auburn hair tumbling in curls around her head like it was moving in slow motion.

How Welshy had managed to land someone like her was always a hot topic of debate. It wouldn't last, they all agreed.

Ugly bastard like him? No way she was sticking around when the going got tough.

But here she was, well over two decades later. Sticking around.

And the going had never been tougher.

"Gabriella," Hoon said, giving her the sort of nod that might usually be reserved for work colleagues you weren't particularly fond of.

Her brow creased, like the greeting—or lack of it—had confused or hurt her. Her once smooth, blemish-free skin, had picked up its share of wrinkles over the years, and even when she relaxed her frown, the creases lingered a while.

"Bob," she said. She pointed to his chest, and a smile tugged at the corners of her mouth. "I like the shirt."

The rest of her may have aged, but the smile hadn't. The smile was twenty years younger and, God help him, when it was pointed in his direction, so was he.

He looked down at the T-shirt. From his perspective, it showed an upside-down picture of *Mr Grumpy* from the *Mr Men* children's book series. A caption above the image of the scowling rectangular figure read, 'I Had Fun Once,' while another below concluded, 'I didn't like it.'

"Aye. This fudd thought it was funny," Hoon said, jabbing a thumb in Miles' direction.

"It is funny," Miles insisted.

From the way her smile widened, it was clear that Gabriella agreed. Her legs carried her forwards, slowly at first, then faster. She stopped just short of throwing herself at Hoon, and they spent a few awkward moments positioning themselves for the most stilted and uncomfortable hug in history.

"It's good to see you," she told him.

"Aye. Eh... thanks," Hoon said.

A wee voice in his head chastised him. *Thanks? For fuck's sake...*

"I mean, you too," he added.

"Is it safe, though?" Gabriella asked, her eyes darting to the door the two men had come in through. "You weren't followed?"

"It's OK. Coast's clear," Hoon told her. "Nobody followed us."

She relaxed a little at that, and for a moment, she rested a hand on his arm. It didn't linger for long, but Hoon could still feel her touch even after she turned away.

"You'll want to see Welshy," she said.

"How is he?" Hoon asked.

She didn't say anything, and yet a shake of her head said *everything.*

"Is it OK if I, eh... go say hello?"

"Of course. That would be lovely," she said. Despite her best efforts, there was no way to miss the wobble in her voice. "Just... don't expect to get much out of him."

———

This had been a bedroom once. A child's, judging by the bright blue and yellow paints that adorned the walls, and the zigzag patterned carpet that made the floor seem to undulate unpleasantly as Hoon stepped over the threshold.

Technically, it was still a bedroom, though only in as much as there was a bed in it. Where the other furniture should have been, there was equipment. Bleeping and wheezing and clicking medical equipment, keeping the room's sole occupant hovering just this side of the abyss, tethering him to life with pipes, and tubes, and cables, and wires.

It wasn't a bedroom, it was an elaborate machine built to cheat death, or at least delay it a while.

And there, at the heart of it all, lay Gwynn 'Welshy' Evans, one of the best friends Hoon had ever had.

And one of the only true ones.

Hoon had been braced for this. Welshy had been in a bad way when he'd last seen him, but it was immediately obvious that he was worse now.

It had been a stroke and some subsequent complications that had confined him to bed, and locked his mind away inside his broken body. He had been confused most of the time, yes, but there had been glimpses of him through the windows of his eyes. Moments of recognition and of recollection. Flickers of the man he had once been.

That man, Hoon knew as soon as he stepped into the room, was almost certainly gone now.

He seemed shrunken there in the bed, like old fruit dried out by the sun. The pillows propped behind his head looked enormous by comparison. He'd been a big lad, strong and imposing, but Hoon could've carried what remained of him in one arm.

And he would've done, too—for as long and as far as the bastard needed.

Assuming you could ignore the looming spectre of Death, it was just him and Welshy there in the room. Gabriella had said she'd give him a bit of time, and Miles had gone to put the kettle on.

Hoon stood there, just inside the door, his mouth open, but no sound emerging.

It was a relatively new experience for him, being lost for words. Usually, they came freely and easily—often too much so, and sometimes even when he'd rather they didn't.

After a few seconds of standing there, not sure what to say, instinct kicked in.

"Alright, ya lazy prick?"

He stepped further into the room, closer to the bed, and spotted the bag of liquid that hung from the side of it, such a deep shade of yellow it was almost brown.

"Don't fucking envy you that, pal," he remarked. "Was stuck with one of them myself earlier. No' a big fan, I have to say."

Another step further from the door. Closer to the bed.

Welshy's eyes were closed, the lids flickering like he was trapped in some terrible nightmare. Whatever it was, Hoon was sure it could be no worse than the one waiting for him if he woke up.

"You look..." Hoon began, then stopped.

He looked *what*? Nice? Well? Like he was making the most of a bad situation? None of those applied, and they'd known each other too long, gone through too much, to piss about with niceties.

"Like a bag of shite," Hoon concluded.

He was right by the bed now. One of Welshy's hands was just a few inches from his, but he couldn't bring himself to bend down and touch it, for fear that the skin might tear, or the bones shatter in his grip.

There were no words. That was the problem. Try as he might to find them, there were no right words for this moment. Nothing he could say that would reach into the dark pit Welshy had found himself in, and flick on a light for him. Words of encouragement or comfort meant nothing to him now. He was beyond that. Beyond everything but the final journey itself.

Hoon's throat tightened. His eyes itched. Welshy had been a bloody good soldier. This wasn't the right sort of death for a man like him. He deserved to go out with a bang. To go out spitting and swinging at the world. He'd been owed a warrior's death.

The slow, degrading one he was being given was anything but.

There was a knock at the door behind him, soft and inquisitive. Hoon quickly rubbed his eyes with the palms of his hands, cleared his throat, then turned to find Miles peeking through a crack in the door.

"Uh, tea's ready," the MI5 man said. "Gabriella's asking if you're hungry. She was going to make some toast."

"Was she going to put some cheese on it?" Hoon asked.

Miles frowned. "Um, not that she mentioned."

"Well, you might want to go and fucking suggest that," Hoon replied, then he turned back to the man on the bed as Miles closed the door again. "You no' got that lassie trained properly yet, Welshy? Who offers up plain fucking toast? Is she wanting rid of us, or something?"

There was, predictably, no reply. No reaction. No response.

Hoon moved to place his hand on his old pal's, but there was an invisible force field there, keeping them apart, stopping him from following through with it.

It wasn't fair. None of it was fair.

It wasn't right.

But it was what it was.

"Ah, fuck," Hoon whispered, then he ran a hand down his face, took a moment to compose himself, and turned to the door.

———

Miles and Gabriella were leaning on the breakfast bar and chatting away like old mates when Hoon joined them in the kitchen. He didn't know why that annoyed him so much. Miles had protected her. Welshy, too. He had earned the right to be friendly with her. He'd been her only real contact in the last few months—the only one who knew who she and Welshy really were. Hell, he probably knew her better than Hoon did by this point.

Hoon's eye twitched as that thought occurred to him.

OK, so *that* was why it annoyed him so much.

"So, this is where you've been hiding," he announced, inserting himself into their conversation.

He gave the kitchen a critical look, like he was a designer on a TV home makeover show. The room's fixtures were dated, but in that 'built to last' way that meant they had probably been back in fashion at least twice since first being put in.

"Not bad, is it?" Miles said.

Hoon grabbed a drawer handle and tested it with a shake. He appeared genuinely disappointed when it didn't snap off in his hand.

"Aye. It's alright, I suppose," he conceded.

Gabriella met his eye across the breakfast bar. "Is Welshy OK?"

Hoon puffed out his cheeks. "I mean... compared to what?" he asked. "He's asleep, if that's what you mean."

Gabriella's look of relief indicated that this was about the best they could hope for these days. She smiled at Hoon. It was a kind, gentle thing, and he realised that she was consoling him.

Despite everything, *she* was consoling *him*.

Just like twenty-odd years before, Hoon found himself wondering how Welshy had managed to land someone like Gabriella. It didn't matter now, of course. Whatever the explanation, he was just glad that he'd had her taking care of him.

"You look like shit," she told him, and he managed a laugh at that. Having seen his reflection, he was in no position to argue.

"Aye, you're no' wrong there," he said.

Gabriella's gaze traced the slowly healing cuts on his face, and the deep red welt on the side of his neck. "What happened?"

Hoon puffed out his cheeks. "Eh, couple of kickings, a kidnapping, and a car crash," he said, rubbing a hand on his chin and staring off into space. "I think that's about it."

There was concern in the look she was giving him. He was quietly pleased about that, though he'd never, even under torture, confess to it.

"Don't fucking worry about me," he told her. "I'm like a fucking rubber ball me."

Miles chuckled. "What, you mean you always bounce back?"

Hoon tutted. "No, I mean I'm completely fucking spherical and live in a child's pocket. Course that's what I fucking mean, it doesn't need spelling out."

"I think something's burning," Miles remarked, grateful for the opportunity to change the subject.

It took a moment for the words to filter through, then Gabriella leapt for the old cooker and rattled the grill pan out from under the heat.

Four slices of bread had lightly charcoaled around the edges, but the rest was protected by a bubbling morass of gloopy yellow cheese. She slid them all onto a large plate that she'd had on standby, then placed it on the worktop between them.

Hoon nodded his approval. "You told her about the cheese, then?"

"Yes, he did," Gabriella said. She *thunked* salt and pepper cellars down on the breakfast bar beside the plate. "But it was already in hand. I'm hardly going to give you just plain toast, am I? I'm not an animal."

Hoon dumped a generous helping of salt and pepper on one of the slices of bread, then picked it up and folded it in half, squidging the cheese together. "Never fucking doubted you for a moment," he told her.

He took a big bite and chewed, visibly and audibly savouring the taste. His mouth was still mostly full when he shot Miles a sideways look.

"Now, correct me if I'm fucking wrong, but did you no' mention something about the kettle...?"

CHAPTER THIRTEEN

ONCE THE TOAST WAS EATEN, and the final extra slice divvied up between them, they retired to the living room with their teas and coffees.

Stepping into the room was like stepping back in time. Whoever had furnished it either had an eye for antiques, or hadn't gone furniture shopping in a very long time. Judging by the general shabbiness of everything, Hoon was leaning towards the latter.

Gabriella sat on the couch, the red fabric of the seats worn all the way down to the weave. Hoon and Miles each took one of the wooden-armed armchairs, positioned either side of the fireplace. The single concession to modern living in the place was probably the only unwelcome one—the fireplace having been blocked off, and a shitty wee electric bar-fire shoved there in its place.

The walls were adorned in floral patterns and flocked leaves. A narrow shelf ran all the way around the top of the room, and played home to maybe fifty or sixty little cow and sheep ornaments. Hoon hoped they had come with the house and weren't Gabriella's, or he'd have no choice but to revise his otherwise positive opinion of her.

Hoon was still taking in the details of the room when Gabriella decided the time had come to get down to business.

"Don't get me wrong," she began, which was never a great opener. "It's good to see you. But why are you here? Has something happened?"

"Who are you asking, me or him?" Hoon said, indicating Miles with a nod.

"You. Obviously. Miles comes round to check up every couple of weeks," Gabriella replied.

Hoon's eyes were drawn to the man in the other armchair. Oh, *did he now?*

"Aye, fair enough," Hoon replied, turning his attention back to Gabriella. "I'm here because... well..."

It occurred to him that he hadn't thought through what he was going to say. How he was going to explain it all to her.

Fortunately, he'd underestimated her once again.

"We're in danger, aren't we?" she said. "Your plan to keep those people from coming after us, it hasn't worked. That's why you're here. Isn't it?"

"Pretty much," Hoon conceded. "That's... eh, aye. That's pretty much nailed it, right enough."

"But they don't know where we are. Do they?" This time, she aimed the question at Miles. "You said nobody knew but you."

Miles, who had been halfway through a big gulp of tea when Gabriella had turned to him, now quickly swallowed it down. It was still hot, and he winced as it slipped down his throat.

"Um, yes. Yes, that's... what I said. And they didn't."

"They didn't?" Gabriella said, sitting more upright on the couch.

"Don't. They *don't* know where you are," Miles corrected.

"Yet," added Hoon. "They don't know *yet*."

Gabriella stared at them both in turn, her expression turning from confusion to impatience. "Well? Is one of you going to explain?" she demanded. "Or do I have to guess?"

Miles lowered his eyes, not quite able to bring himself to look at her. "I've, eh, I've been suspended from duty," he explained. "My caseload... everything I've been working on... it'll be handed over to another officer to deal with."

There was a lot to unpack in that statement, and Gabriella eyeballed him as she did just that. Hoon could practically hear her brain whirring, racing ahead, considering all the ramifications of the words that had just come out of Miles' mouth.

"Which other officer?" she eventually asked.

Miles rubbed his temples with a finger and thumb of the same hand. "I wish I knew. I've requested a colleague I think I can trust..."

"Who you *think* you can trust?!" Gabriella yelped.

"No. No, I mean... I know I can. She's solid," Miles insisted. "But I don't know if they'll use her. They could give it to anyone."

"So, what are you saying?" demanded the woman on the couch.

When she got angry, her native accent became stronger, like the real her was battling to get out. Right now, she might as well have been finishing every sentence with an, 'Olé!'

"Are you saying that someone could be heading here now to kill us?"

"No. No, definitely not," Miles assured her. "Everything's encrypted. I made sure of it."

"And they can't break the encryption?" Hoon asked.

"No." Miles shook his head, then swallowed. His eyes darted around the room, as if looking for an escape route. "I mean... unless they really try."

"Oh, fucking great!" Hoon ejected. "So, as long as these Alpha fuckers are a shower of half-arsed bastards, we'll be fine."

Miles didn't reply to that. Not in words, anyway. His hand crept to his mouth, though, and much of the colour drained from his cheeks.

"Alpha fuckers?" Gabriella asked. "What are Alpha fuckers?"

"No, they're not called 'Alpha fuckers,'" Hoon replied. "Some guy I spoke to mentioned them. 'The Alphas.' Some sort of fucking, I don't know, clean-up crew."

Something was lost in the translation, and Gabriella frowned. "They're cleaners?"

"No, I don't mean—"

"They're contract killers," Miles announced, his voice muffled by the hand that was now clamped over his mouth like he was worried someone might try to read his lips.

Hoon sighed. "Aye. Aye, they fucking would be."

"You sure that's what he said?" Miles asked. "I assume this is West we're talking about? You're sure he mentioned the Alphas?"

"Aye. Deffo. Why?"

"Shit. *Shit.*"

"Keep your fucking hair on. What's the problem? Who are they?"

Miles unstuck the hand from his face, picked up his mug from the coffee table, and ushered it shakily towards his mouth. He took a big, steadying slurp before replying.

"I mean, officially, we don't know," he said. "The agency, I mean. We've only heard rumours about them."

"Rumours?" Gabriella asked.

Miles met her gaze. "Horror stories, really. But, we've never been able to confirm their existence."

"So, what are the fucking rumours, then?" Hoon demanded. "What are we dealing with?"

"Um... I suppose it depends on which rumours you believe," Miles said. The hand holding his mug was still trembling when he set the tea back on the table. "Broadly, though, they have enough elements in common to paint a picture."

"Never mind painting a fucking picture, son," Hoon urged. "Just use your fucking words."

Miles exhaled and put both hands on his thighs. "I suppose 'cleaners,' is a pretty apt description, really. When threats or diplomacy fail—when the Loop's usual mechanisms of black-mail or intimidation don't get results—then the Alphas step in."

"So they're like, what?" Gabriella asked. "Problem solvers?"

"Problem eliminators," Miles corrected. "They're like the Loop's own SAS. Highly trained killers—ex-special forces, mainly, most of the rumours agree on that. They get pointed at a target and don't stop until they've wiped every last trace of it out of existence. The target, their families, friends, anyone who was in regular contact with them."

"Bollocks," Hoon said. "You can't go massacring some fuck-er's whole contact list without people noticing."

"That's where the rest of the Loop comes in," Miles explained. "They do damage limitation. They stop the stories getting into the media, they curtail any police investigations... Or they make it all look like an accident. A floor collapsing at a wedding reception. A plane crash. Whatever, they use their resources to cover it up. No loose ends."

He gave that a moment to sink in, before continuing.

"They can murder whole families—whole lineages—and make it so that nobody bats an eyelid."

Gabriella sat back into the couch, letting the cushions wrap themselves around her like a comforting hug. By the looks of her, she needed one. Her face, despite her naturally darker skin tone, had turned almost the same shade as Miles'.

"And they're coming for us?"

Both of the room's other occupants were looking to Hoon to answer that question. He tried as best he could to shrug it off.

"Maybe. I don't know," he said. "I mean, West reckoned they were, but what the fuck did he know? They killed him, it's no' like he was still in the loop. I mean, the figure of speech loop, no' the fucking Loop loop." He scowled. "What a stupid fucking name for an organisation, anyway. *The Loop*. What sort of monobrow shit-for-brains creative fucking vacuum of a human being came up with that?"

Miles stood up suddenly, and sidled to the window. The farm was surrounded on all sides by open space, and the light from the windows barely made a dent in the darkness. There was nobody right outside, but there could be dozens of them standing there just thirty feet away, and there was no way he'd even know.

"He'd have known procedure," the MI5 man said, keeping his voice low. "He might not have been involved in that particular conversation, but he'd have known what they'd be discussing. He'd have known what they'd decide."

Gabriella pulled her feet up onto the couch, like it was some sort of fortress that might protect her.

"You said you weren't followed," she whispered. "You said nobody was coming."

"And they aren't," Hoon said. He joined Miles at the window, and pulled the curtains shut. "Nobody tracked us here. Nobody knows where you are. I don't know what's going to happen, but right now, you're safe."

Gabriella's eyes were wide. Wet. "You promise?" she asked.

"Aye. I promise," Hoon said.

"You can't promise that," Miles countered. "You don't know that for sure."

Hoon glowered back at him, and the room itself seemed to darken around him. He slapped a hand on Miles' shoulder and escorted him into the hall. "Miles. Mind if we have a wee word in the kitchen?"

Gabriella sat huddled on the couch, listening to the murmur of conversation from the room next door. It was quite a one-sided conversation, she thought. She couldn't make out the words, but the sentiment was pretty clear.

As the dressing down continued, she slowly stood up and crept over to the window, parting the curtains just enough to look out.

She had grown used to the ring of darkness that surrounded the house every night. It had worried her at first, but she'd soon become accustomed to it.

Tonight, though, was the first time it scared her.

She jumped when the door opened behind her. "Right, that's us agreed, then," Hoon said striding into the room with a cowed Miles trotting behind him. "There's no immediate danger. Even if they're fucking savants, it's going to take days to crack all the snidey wee fucking codes fannybaws here put on your address."

"He means the encryption on the files," Miles translated.

"I said what I fucking meant," Hoon bit back. He hesitated, replaying the sentence. "Or... I meant what I fucking said. Either way..." He made a typing motion that, while brief, somehow managed to convey his utter disdain. "You're a snidey wee fucking code goblin, and don't you forget it."

Gabriella pulled the curtain back into place, blocking her view of the darkness surrounding the house. "But they will crack it? Eventually, they'll find out where we are?"

Hoon wished there was a way to sugarcoat it. He didn't often hold back, but he wished he could here. He wished he could spare her the truth.

But she deserved that from him, if nothing else.

"Aye," he confirmed. "Aye, they'll find out."

Gabriella ran both hands through her hair, then gripped it,

like she was trying to rip it out of her scalp. "And then they'll come. And they'll kill us. They're going to kill us, aren't they?"

"No. No, they won't," Hoon said, crossing to her and placing his hands on her arms. He guided them down to her sides. "I'm no' going to let that happen. I'm going to look after you, alright?"

"And what about the others?" asked Miles.

With some reluctance, Hoon released his grip on Gabriella and turned to the MI5 man. "What?"

"Your little boxer friend. Greig. Him and his family. They're loose ends. They'll get their details, too." Miles groaned and sat back down in his armchair, rubbing his forehead like he might be able to deter an oncoming migraine. "God. They've got a baby."

Gabriella's face became a mask of horror. "They won't kill a baby!" she yelped, but her conviction quickly left her. "They won't, will they?"

"No loose ends," Miles muttered.

"Yes, but a *baby*?"

Hoon paced the floor. Partly, this was to help him think, but his muscles had begun to seize up after the hammering they'd taken in recent days, and getting a bit of movement into them would help delay the pain a little longer.

"Right. Fuck. Aye," he said, then he repeated the same three words again twice, each time in a different order, and punctuated by an about-turn when he reached the limits of the floor space.

He finally stopped right in the middle of the room, and turned to face the others.

"So, here's the situation as I see it," he announced. "We've got a ticking fucking clock going on these bastards getting the addresses. When they do—tomorrow, the next day, whatever—they're going to come after Gabriella and Welshy, and they're going to go after Greig's family."

"And kill us," Gabriella added, just to hammer it home.

"Aye. Well, fucking try to, anyway," Hoon said.

"I'd imagine you and I are pretty screwed, too," Miles added.

"Oh, fuck, aye. Never in any doubt," Hoon agreed, then he staggered back a step when a thought struck him like a physical blow. "Fuck. Wait a minute, wait a minute. Caroline. Bamber. What about them? She knows more than anyone. She was right in amongst it. They must be in the fucking firing line, too?"

"Um... I don't know," Miles admitted. "She's at home. Most of the women you freed are at home. Nothing's ever happened to them."

Expressions of confusion and relief both battled for supremacy on Hoon's face. In the end, they were both wiped away by a scowl of suspicion. "That doesn't make any fucking sense."

"They, uh, they don't tend to know much," Miles explained. "Their movements are controlled. And the drugs do a number on them. Even before you came along, some escaped. Survived, I suppose. They couldn't even give us a description of anyone, much less a name."

Hoon didn't want to think about the ramifications of that explanation. He didn't want to dwell on everything that might've happened to Bamber's daughter at the hands of those evil bastards.

He didn't want to, but he couldn't help it, and he was forced to take a seat before his legs gave out from under him.

"Right. Well, that's something," he muttered, shutting down his swelling rage. "So, just us here and Greig's family to worry about."

"Yeah," Miles said. "Unless..."

"Unless what?"

Miles shifted in his seat. "I mean, I doubt they'd go after her. She's too high-profile."

"Who's he talking about?" Gabriella asked Hoon.

"Deirdrie?"

Miles nodded.

Gabriella looked from one man to the other.

"Who the fuck's Deirdrie?" she asked, then something clicked into place. "Wait, is that the policewoman? They won't go after her, will they? She's high-up. Isn't she, like, the chief of police, or something?"

"Chief superintendent," Hoon said. He shook his head. "No, too bold a play."

Miles stared back at him, clearly not convinced.

"You're not really fucking telling me they'll try and kill her, are you?" Hoon demanded. "She's lasted this fucking long. And no fucking way the polis aren't going to be all over it if someone takes her out. Papers can't tuck that one away on page twelve."

Miles still didn't look like he was finding Hoon's argument entirely persuasive, but he shrugged and shook his head. "No. Probably not," he agreed. "But maybe we should call her or something. Just to keep her up to date."

Hoon nodded. "Aye. A wee fucking heads-up can't hurt," he admitted. "You got her mobile number?"

Miles reached into his pocket for his mobile. "Yeah, it's in here."

Hoon sat forward and jabbed a finger in the other man's direction. "Wait, is that your fucking phone? Is that your *actual* fucking mobile phone?"

"No. Of course not," Miles said, shooting Hoon an insulted look. "That's back at the flat. This is an unregistered pay-as-you-go. You know, like the one I bought you that I doubt you're ever going to pay me for? But better."

"Good. I thought I was going to have to fucking stamp you to death there," Hoon said, sitting back in the chair. "Right, scribble down her number, then go get your jacket on."

Miles looked up from the phone and glanced at the old

grandfather clock in the corner. "It's one in the morning. Why am I getting my jacket on?"

"Because someone needs to go get Greig's lot and bring them here," Hoon explained. He grinned at the look of dismay on the other man's face. "And you're the only one who knows where the fuck to find them."

"What? You're just going to gather everyone here?" Miles asked. "That's your plan? Make life easier for them? Give them one target instead of two?"

"You got any fucking better ideas?"

"Yes!" Miles yelped.

"Great. We're all ears," Hoon said, crossing his arms and sitting back in the chair.

The incredulous look on Miles' face gave way to a sort of weary resignation. "I mean... I don't have any *right now*. But that doesn't mean..." He sighed and stood up. "Fine. I'll get my jacket."

"Good lad," Hoon said. He called the MI5 man back just as he reached the door. "Oh, and Miles?"

"Yes?"

"If anyone follows you back here, I'll kill you my-fucking-self."

Miles looked back at him just long enough to confirm that he was serious, then tapped two fingers to his forehead in salute, and sidled out into the hall.

CHAPTER FOURTEEN

CHIEF SUPERINTENDENT DEIRDRIE BAGSHAW couldn't sleep. This in itself wasn't unusual. She'd always been a night owl—she'd loved the late shifts when she was back on the beat, and though those years were long gone, her body clock had never quite fully readjusted.

Most nights, she'd be sitting up going over paperwork until two, maybe three o'clock, then would force herself to turn in for the night, in order to mitigate the foul mood that the early morning alarm always brought with it.

Tonight, though, she had no paperwork to sift through. No work of any kind, in fact. For the first time in as long as she could remember, Deirdrie Bagshaw was at a loose end.

She'd even resorted to putting on the television. She couldn't recall the last time she'd done that. Long enough ago that it had taken her a full two minutes to find the button on the remote that turned the bloody thing on, anyway.

There had been a crime drama on ITV. It was utterly absurd, and had wound her up within moments. Clearly, whoever had written the thing had never worked on the force. Or, for that matter, done an ounce of research.

She doubted he'd even met a policeman.

There was nothing of interest on any of the BBC channels, though this was hardly surprising. Half-one in the morning wasn't generally considered a peak viewing time, and most people tuning in now would be too pissed or too exhausted to have retained any critical faculties.

She settled on a repeat of a cooking show on Channel 4. It had Jamie Oliver in it, and was being signed for the deaf. Judging by the apparent venom the signer was putting into her movements, it was clear that she was no more a fan of Oliver than Deirdrie was.

Still, for all his faults, at least Jamie Oliver had never demonstrated a complete disregard for police procedure in any of his programmes, so this was still better than the offering on ITV.

He was cooking lamb, flavoured with Moroccan spices, and served on a bed of something that looked a bit like rice, but probably wasn't. Not *normal* rice, anyway. Jamie Oliver no doubt thought himself too good for normal rice. It would be cauliflower rice, or chunky lemon couscous, or something equally far removed from a microwaveable bag of *Uncle Ben's*.

It looked tasty, though. The lamb more so than the rice-like substance it was resting on. Deirdrie hadn't been much in the mood for dinner, and had made do with a couple of hard-boiled eggs that she'd sat and peeled, one by one, at the little fold-out dining table in the corner of the living room.

There was a dining room across the hall—her police salary had brought her certain comforts, and she'd got onto the housing ladder before the London property market went berserk—but she only used it when she had friends round, which meant she rarely used it at all, and even less so in recent years.

Her stomach rumbled. She tried to distract herself from it by watching the little woman doing the sign language in the corner. Deirdrie didn't know much about British Sign

Language, but she was fairly sure that the signer was calling Jamie Oliver a wanker. Certain hand gestures were universal.

The hunger kept nagging at her, though, and when the TV chef pulled some freshly baked bread from some sort of clay oven thing, she knew she couldn't put it off any longer.

After a couple of goes, she managed to heave herself up from the depths of her armchair. She had just turned towards the hallway when the screen of her mobile lit up, and it shuddered across the coffee table on a wave of vibrations.

She placed her hands on the hips of her dressing gown and stood there staring down at the phone. The caller wasn't in her contacts, so no name flashed up on the display. Instead, it showed a mobile number, but not one that she recognised.

It took her a few moments to make a decision. She pulled the belt of her robe tighter around her middle, then reached down and picked up the phone.

"Bagshaw," she said with a clipped, well-practised irritability that was usually effective at deterring time wasters.

She recognised the voice on the other end from its first guttural syllable.

"Deirdrie," said Hoon. "You're awake."

"Yes, well, I am now," Bagshaw said. She picked up the telly remote, searched for the volume button, then abandoned the quest and headed quickly towards the kitchen, instead. "You shouldn't be calling here. There's an active investigation."

"Aye, so I hear," Hoon replied. "And I'm fine, by the way. Thanks for fucking asking."

"I didn't ask," Deirdrie pointedly reminded him. It was cold in the kitchen, and she pulled her robe more tightly around herself, then closed the window. "Right now, you may be surprised to learn, your welfare is not high on my list of concerns."

She opened the fridge, letting the light spill out across the small, but fastidiously neat kitchen. The fridge itself was just as tidy and well organised. This wasn't difficult, though, when the contents were made up of a single container of milk, another of cranberry juice, and a tub of mixed salad from the deli counter of the supermarket around the corner.

Calling it salad was being very generous, too. Half of the tub was filled with sweetcorn and croutons, and the rest was mostly bright red bits of beetroot and chunky coleslaw. A solitary cherry tomato sat balanced on top, so the whole thing vaguely resembled a clown that had recently been involved in an industrial accident.

"Aye, well, fortunately for you, your fucking welfare is a concern of mine," Hoon said.

Bagshaw passed the phone from one hand to the other and swapped ears, freeing her up to reach in and take out the tub of pureed clown face.

"What are you talking about?" she asked, giving the tub an experimental sniff.

It wasn't out of date, she knew that. But something about that particular combination of ingredients was giving her cause to hesitate. She'd piled it all in without much thought at the time, and the beetroot juice had seeped into everything else, so none of it looked particularly appealing.

"Look, don't take this as fucking gospel," Hoon told her. "But something West said before we were walloped by that fucking lorry—"

"You're phoning to tell me I could be in danger," Deirdrie said, finishing the sentence for him.

She slid the salad back into the fridge, in the hopes it might look better in the morning, and then picked up the apple juice carton. It was disappointingly light, and a quick shoogle of the container resulted in only the faintest of sloshing sounds from what was left of the liquid inside.

"Aye. Aye, exactly," Hoon said.

"Well, thank you for your concern," Bagshaw told him. "It's noted."

"You don't sound too worried," the voice in her ear replied.

Deirdrie shrugged and closed the fridge, plunging the kitchen back into near darkness. "As you know, danger comes with the job," she said, shivering in the cold. "It's never far away. I've faced it before, and I'm sure I'll face it again. Right now, my concern is keeping my job. So, if you don't mind, I'm going to say..."

Her voice trailed off into silence. The floorboards creaked beneath her as she shuffled around on the spot.

"You're going to say what?" Hoon asked.

She didn't answer. She daren't.

The kitchen window.

She hadn't opened the kitchen window.

The door stood half-open. She held her breath, straining to listen above the mockney ramblings of the TV chef still blaring out from the living room.

Somewhere, along the hall, a shadow moved.

"Bob," she whispered, slowly sliding a large knife from the block on the worktop beside her. "Someone's here."

CHAPTER FIFTEEN

HOON GOT up from the seat like he had been fired out of it. He was alone in the living room, Gabriella having gone through to sit with Welshy for a while, so there was nobody there to see his dawning horror.

"What do you mean? Who's there? Are you sure?" he asked.

There was no answer except the unsteady rasping of Deirdrie's breathing, and the rustling of fabric as she moved through the house.

"Get out," Hoon urged. "Get to the door, and get out, now."

No reply. No reaction.

"Deirdrie, are you fucking listening? Get out of there. Get the fuck out of the house before—"

Her shouts cut him off. It was loud and up close at first, then became more distant, like she was moving away from the phone.

"Get out!" she cried, mirroring Hoon's own warning. "Police! This is private property! I've got a knife! Get out now, or—"

The sentence ended in a sound that made Hoon think of wet, gristly things. He called her name, shouted to her, but heard only a series of short, rasping gasps.

After that, there was silence. He listened to it, pressing the phone hard against his ear, trying to detect any signs of life above the sound of his heart hammering away inside his chest.

There was a voice in the background. Far off. TV, maybe.

And then, right at the fringes of his hearing, there was another sound. Footsteps padding on carpet. Floorboards groaning under someone's weight.

He heard the phone being picked up, the rustling sound as it was turned over in a gloved hand. There was something animal-like about the breathing that came next. It was a snuffling sort of wheeze. Hoon recognised it, and the image of a man with a scarred throat and no nose was suddenly right there in his mind's eye, glaring pure hatred at him.

"The fuck have you done?" Hoon asked.

The breathing became faster. Became a giggle of laughter, rising in pitch even as the phone was passed on to someone else.

"That you, Mr Hoon?"

Suranne. Or whatever her name was.

"What the fuck have you done to her?"

"We've done what we always do. We've tidied a loose end," she replied.

"I'll fucking kill you for that," Hoon told her. The warning wasn't said with any particular venom, just a level of matter-of-factness that made it all the more chilling.

Suranne, however, didn't seem remotely fazed. "Don't go blaming me for this," she said. "You dragged her into it all. She had a long career. And the reason for that is that she never allowed herself to become too aware of our activities. She avoided getting herself involved. Until you came along, and dragged her into it. Her suicide is on you."

"Suicide? What are you...?" Hoon began, before he twigged. "Of course."

"Disgraced, suspended from the job she dedicated her

whole life to," Suranne continued. "Inevitable, really. Tragic, but inevitable. She'll be sadly missed, I'm sure."

"You won't fucking get away with this," Hoon said.

"Yes. We will. We always do," the woman on the other of the phone said, before switching subjects. "Have you had time to consider my offer?"

"There was no fucking offer," Hoon told her. "It was a setup. You used me to get to West."

It was Suranne's turn to laugh now. Hers was not the same sickening giggle as the Professor, but something light that trilled off her tongue. In other circumstances, it might have sounded quite charming. Right there and then, though, it made Hoon's skin crawl.

"Well done. You figured it out," she told him. "Ironically, that does almost make me want to offer you a position with us. Is that crazy? But, I suspect I could guess your answer."

"What, 'Ram it up your fishy hoop, you badly-aimed wad of ejaculate,' you mean?"

There was just a moment of hesitation from down the line.

"OK, so I wouldn't have guessed it word for word, maybe, but I could predict the general gist of it," Suranne replied.

Hoon glanced back over his shoulder at the door, and lowered his voice. "Listen. It's me you want. Forget everyone else, and I'll turn myself over to you. You can do whatever the fuck you like to me, just leave the others out of it."

There was silence from the other end of the line. Hoon held his breath. Was she actually considering it? Would she actually agree to the offer?

And could he trust her, even if she did?

"Sorry, was wiping away a tear there," Suranne said, and Hoon knew from the exaggerated *sniff* of emotion that she was mocking him. "Lovely offer, Mr Hoon. Far nobler than I'd have given you credit for. I thought men like you had died off long ago, if they ever even existed in the first place. But, no. That's not a trade I'm prepared to make."

"You're making a big fucking mistake here, sweetheart," Hoon told her. "Believe me, you want me to come quietly. It's that, or I rip all you fuckers a new arsehole. Aye, and I don't mean individually, either. I mean one big fucking *collective* new arsehole between the lot of you."

"That would be quite something," Suranne said, and she was laughing again. "But here's what's actually going to happen, Mr Hoon. We're going to come for you, like we came for the late Chief Superintendent—may she rest in peace—and we're going to do what we did to her, only much less quickly. We're also going to kill anyone we think there's a *chance* you might have told about us. That means the lovely Gabriella, her poor suffering husband, our mutual friend Miles, and anyone else we think might pose even the vaguest threat to our organisation."

"Aye, well, good fucking luck finding us."

The laugh came again. The hairs on the back of Hoon's neck all stood on end at the sound of it.

"Oh, Mr Hoon. I thought you were smarter than that," she replied. "We already know where you are."

Hoon's stomach felt like an icy hand had just gripped it and squeezed.

"Bollocks you do."

"Don't believe me?" Suranne asked, and he could hear the grin in her voice. "Go look out the window."

Hoon's gaze shifted to the curtains, closed against the darkness outside. From Welshy's room, he heard the low murmur of Gabriella's voice, offering her husband words of comfort.

His feet moved on their own, plodding him, step by step, towards the window.

"What do you see?" Suranne asked.

Hoon stretched out an arm and, with two fingers, parted the curtains just enough to see through the gap. The first thing he saw was his own beady eyeball staring back, but then he looked through the reflection as far as the spilled light from the farmhouse allowed.

He let the curtain fall back into place. "I see fuck all, because you're not here," Hoon told her. "Because you don't have the first fucking clue where here is."

"Or maybe we're on our way there right now," Suranne suggested. "Maybe even as you and I speak, death is tightening its noose around you all. Perhaps there will be a creaking of a floorboard ten minutes from now. A tapping at the window in an hour. Because, what separates you and me right now is not distance, Mr Hoon. It's time. That's all. An ever-decreasing period of time. Tick-tick-tick-tick-tick-tick-tick."

Hoon tutted. "You pricks do love the sound of your own fucking voices, don't you?" he told her. "Is there a fucking training course you all get sent on? *Mediocre Villain Monologues* one-oh-fucking-one? You want me, sweetheart, fucking bring it on. I'll be waiting."

He pressed the button that ended the call, then shut off the phone and removed the battery from the back. Given that he'd called Deirdrie's mobile, it would've been almost impossible for them to run any sort of trace on the call. But, stupidly, they had his number now. All it would take was a contact within the network, or someone with the authority to request the data from them, and they'd be able to get a general location.

Given that there was fuck all else for miles around, finding the farmhouse from there wouldn't exactly be a challenge.

"Fuck!" he hissed, squeezing the phone so hard the plastic casing gave a *crack*. "Stupid fucking fuck-fuck-fucking fuck! *Fuck!*"

"Everything alright?"

Hoon wheeled around to find Gabriella standing in the door. She looked worried. Hardly surprising, given the way he'd been swearing and slamming the heel of his hand against his forehead.

"Eh, fine. Aye," he said. It would've fooled no one, and Gabriella was smarter than most.

"It doesn't look fine," she said.

"It's nothing. Don't worry about it," Hoon insisted.

He suddenly felt claustrophobic standing there with her in the living room, and Gabriella stepped aside when he hurried past her into the hall. He continued on into Welshy's room, and she stuck close behind.

"Bob. What is it? What's happened?" she asked. "You're scaring me."

"I fucking told you, it's nothing," Hoon said.

He looked down at Welshy lying in his bed, fenced in by the railings, and kept alive with oxygen, feeding tubes, and drips. Just a few hours ago, that had been Hoon, too. He'd endured it for a few hours at most, and wouldn't wish it on his worst enemy.

OK, no, that wasn't true. There were plenty of people he'd wish it on, and much worse, too.

But not on someone he cared for. And certainly not on a man he thought of like a brother.

Welshy's hand still lay there, palm upwards, fingers curled in like the legs of a dead spider left to dry out in the sun. He wanted to take it in his. He wanted to hold it, and offer whatever comfort he could.

But his body wouldn't let him. His hands refused to move.

"They killed her," he said, still not looking back over his shoulder.

"Who?" Gabriella asked. She let out a sound like a startled bird. "The policewoman?"

"Aye," Hoon confirmed. "While I was on the phone."

"Oh, God. Oh, Jesus! What do we do? Do we call someone? I mean, we have to call someone."

Hoon shook his head. "No point. There's nothing anyone can do for her now."

"Oh. Shit. God. That's... I don't know what to say."

Gabriella flopped down into the wingback armchair that had been placed beside the bed. There was a pillow on it, and a creased blanket hanging over the back. Hoon could picture her sleeping there most nights, ready to help Welshy with whatever he needed, or just enjoying being as close to him as current circumstances allowed her to get.

There was another chair in the corner—a rickety-looking dining chair that currently served as a surface on which to stack folded sheets and pillow cases. Hoon transplanted those onto the floor, then brought the chair over so it was at the side of the bed, nearer the foot end, and facing Gabriella's at the head.

"There, eh, there's something else, too," he said.

Even those words terrified her. He could see how they filled her with dread. He should tell her, of course. He should let her know how he'd messed up. But she'd worried enough for one night.

And, if he was being honest, he couldn't bear the idea of her thinking less of him.

It would take time for them to run the trace. Hours, at least. They wouldn't be coming tonight.

Let her have tonight, at least.

"They're going to make it look like suicide," he said.

Gabriella's eyebrows came together. Clearly, this hadn't been the follow-on she'd expected.

"Oh. That's horrible," she said. "Did they say anything else?"

Hoon shook his head. "Nothing worth losing any sleep over."

"Sleep? What's that again?" Gabriella asked, and they shared a smile.

"Aye. Can't imagine you get a whole lot of that," Hoon said.

"Less here than before," Gabriella told him. "Especially in the last few weeks."

Hoon watched her reach out and place her hand on her husband's, in the way he hadn't been able to bring himself to do.

It had been one thing doing it back in Gwynn and Gabriella's house. Even then, despite everything that happened to him, the man in the bed still at least resembled Welshy. The version of him lying there now, though, could not have been further away. He was a cruel mockery of Hoon's old friend. A brutal fucking satire of everything he had been.

"What are the doctors saying?" Hoon asked, averting his gaze from the show of affection.

"They, um, they don't know if he's in pain," Gabriella said, and the way her throat tightened around the words almost broke Hoon's heart. "He's on morphine for it. But they don't know if they're stopping the pain completely, or if he's still..."

She choked on the rest of the sentence, and looked straight up at the ceiling, hiding her tears.

"It's OK," Hoon assured her. It wasn't, of course. Everything was pretty far removed from OK.

"I just... I just can't stand the thought of him hurting and not being able to tell us," she managed to say, forcing out the words.

Hoon stole a sideways look at the man in the bed. "No. No, of course not," he said. "But he's out of the game. He's not suffering. Not now."

He didn't believe that. Not really. But those were the words she needed to hear.

Gabriella wiped her eyes on her sleeve, sniffed noisily, then nodded her thanks. When she spoke again, her voice was back under control, the emotions that had threatened to overcome her now forced back down again.

"They're saying it's just a matter of time now."

Hoon gave a slow, solemn nod, thinking back to the last thing Suranne had said to him on the phone.

"Aye. I suppose everything is, in the end," he remarked. The chair beneath him groaned as he tried to get comfortable in it. "Mind you, if anyone's going to fucking drag it out, it's that bastard there. Did he still do that thing where he'd get you to put your hand on his forehead to check his temperature if he had so much as a fucking runny nose?"

Gabriella laughed so sharply that tears leaped back to her eyes. "Yes! God. All the time! I bought him one of those digital thermometers in the end. The one you point at stuff and it tells you the temperature."

Hoon snorted. "Bet he didn't fucking believe that, either."

"He didn't! Took it back twice, convinced it must be broken."

"Aye, that sounds about right. He'd always get us to do the hand on forehead thing, and we'd always say the same thing. 'Of course you're hot, ya prick, you're in a fucking desert.' He was never bloody happy with that, though. Went round asking every other bastard to have a feel." Hoon chuckled. "I'll be honest, some of the boys started thinking it might be a weird fucking sexual thing."

"Well, it wasn't one he ever shared with me!" Gabriella laughed, then it fell away into something awkward and uncomfortable. "Sorry. Too much information."

Hoon pulled a face that he hoped would dismiss her apology, reassure her that she hadn't said anything out of turn, and salvage what was left of the conversation. Given how late it was, though, and considering the day he'd had, that was quite a lot to ask from one facial expression, and he instead pulled a sort of grimace of amusement that only served to make the whole situation feel that much weirder.

Shite.

He slapped his hands on his thighs, signalling that the time had come for him to go... elsewhere. Exactly where didn't really matter, he just knew he had to get out of the room before anyone cringed themselves to death.

"Mind if I use your shower?" he asked. "Between one thing and another, it's been a rough couple of days. Be good to get cleaned up."

"Of course," Gabriella told him. "It's down the hall. Grab a towel from the pile you chucked on the floor."

"Nice one, ta," Hoon said. Getting to his feet, he took the top towel from the bundle.

"I should warn you, though," Gabriella told him. "At this time of night, it's not going to be particularly hot."

"No bother," Hoon said. He slung the towel over his shoulder. "I'm sure it's nothing I can't handle."

CHAPTER SIXTEEN

"FUCKING JESUS FUCK!"

Hoon's body spasmed in the flow of water like he was being zapped with an electrical current. When he'd been in Miles' shower—whenever the hell that had been—he'd been convinced that the initial blast of water couldn't get any colder.

He realised now that he had been very much mistaken.

He wasn't even convinced the liquid coming out of the shower was actually water. Surely water became fucking solid at this temperature? The substance currently turning his skin blue had to be something with a far lower freezing point. Alcohol, maybe.

He should be so lucky.

Unlike the shower in Miles' flat, this one didn't appear to be getting any warmer. Hoon had been hoping to stand under the flow of the warm water for a while, letting it ease the tension in his muscles, but the icy torrent was doing precisely the opposite, and he could feel his limbs stiffening with every second that passed.

He scrubbed himself as best as he was able, then fumbled with the taps until the water shut off with a series of worrying clanks and burbles that seemed to travel up the walls and through the rest of the house.

He stood there for several seconds, listening, half-expecting the ceiling to come crashing in, but then the cold got the better of him and he climbed out, snatching his towel from the sink where he'd left it balanced.

"Fuck's sake!" he ejected when he unfolded what he now knew to be a hand towel. He rubbed himself vigorously with it, trying to chase away the chill. Then, when all his many aches and pains voiced their protests, he eased off on the pressure a little, and shivered his way through the rest of the drying procedure.

Mr Grumpy scowled at him in the mirror as he pulled the T-shirt back on. Miles had picked him up a couple of sets of clothes, but given that he'd only been wearing these for a few hours, it felt like far too soon to change them.

Besides, he'd seen the other T-shirt. It was a bright yellow monstrosity with the face of *Tweety-Pie* on the front, and, 'I tawt I taw a puddy cat!' emblazoned across the shoulders in bold red print.

Mr Grumpy, puckered faced wee arsehole that he was, was much more up Hoon's street.

Once dressed, Hoon left the bathroom. He reached up to click off the extractor fan, which he reckoned had some brass neck to even turn itself on in the first place. There had been no steam extraction required, because there had been no steam *to* extract.

He took a moment to call the ventilation system a prick, as if the lack of hot water was somehow its fault, then he padded along the corridor in his socks, and leaned his head back into Welshy's room.

"Aye, you weren't fucking kidding about the water," he began, then he stopped when he saw Gabriella all scrunched up in the big armchair, eyes closed, breathing lightly.

She'd made the best of it, but she didn't look comfortable. She couldn't be. Nobody could spend the night contorted into that position and wake up without crippling pain.

He sat his shoes down beside the bed, then bent, hooked his arms under the sleeping woman as best he could—being careful not to accidentally grab hold of anything inappropriate—and hoisted her up out of the chair.

She murmured something, but her eyes remained closed as he carried her out of the room.

They did open momentarily when he *thonked* her head against the door frame, but the flash of panic in them faded quickly when she saw him looking down at her, hushing her back to sleep.

It took him a few tries to find her bedroom. Because of the narrow hallway, he was forced to sidle, crab-like, up and down it, dunting doors open with a foot and then sort of twisting himself inside in a way that avoided walloping her skull off anything else.

"You're heavier than you fucking look," he whispered as he finally shuffled, knees bent, into her bedroom. He deposited her onto it not with a smooth and gentle descent, but with a grunt of relief and a drop from several inches.

To his amazement, she remained sleeping throughout, and barely stirred when he pulled the quilt across her.

He hung off a second to make sure she wasn't going to wake up, then rubbed his hands together. "Right. Must be a fucking drink somewhere in this place."

He hunted high and low, but the best he could find was a half-open bottle of cheap red plonk on top of the fridge. Judging by the dust on it, it had been sat there for a while.

"Any port in a fucking storm," he muttered, then he took the bottle, plucked an upturned mug from the draining board by the sink, and returned to Welshy's room.

The armchair wasn't as comfortable as it looked. The bottom sloped dramatically backwards, and the back was fixed at exactly the wrong angle. If Gabriella spent her nights sleeping here, it was a wonder her spine wasn't kinked like a question mark.

"Alright, Welshy, son?" Hoon asked, loading his mug with the wine. He screwed the cap back on the bottle, but loosely. No point in kidding himself.

Welshy, to nobody's surprise, said nothing. His eyes were closed, the lids still fluttering. The way they moved made Hoon think of sandstorms and heat, and of months fighting side by side.

"Aye. Long fucking time ago," Hoon remarked. He knocked back a glug of the wine, and his face screwed up so tightly it looked like his mouth was a black hole, sucking the rest of his features inside. "Jesus fuck!" he hissed when the initial shock of it had worn off. He reached down the side of the chair, picked up the bottle, and studied the label. "That's alright, that, actually. It's no' bad."

He set the bottle back on the floor, raised the mug in a toast to the man on the bed, then settled into the chair as best as its demented design would allow.

"Better than some of the stuff we used to drink, anyway," he said. "Mind some of that shite? Fucking paint stripper in a novelty bottle. And that was in this fucking country, never mind the stuff we had abroad."

He chuckled and adjusted himself in the chair, still searching for an acceptable position.

"Here, d'you mind that stuff Bamber got us that time? Off that Kuwaiti fella with the two big teeth. The fangs. Mind?"

Welshy remained motionless, neither confirming nor denying his memory of the event.

"Swapped him two days' rations for it, and it turned out to be a big bottle of piss!" Hoon's laughter grew in volume, peaked, then fell away again. "Mind you, I wish I hadn't volunteered to try it first."

He took another sip of the wine, like it might wash away the taste of decades-old urine.

"Wouldn't fucking change it, though," he said, and there was no trace of the laughter left now. "Aye, I'd swap the bottle of piss. Maybe one or two other things. But in general, I mean. Even after everything we saw." He looked down at his mug and gave the red liquid a swirl, watching how it licked up the sides of the white porcelain. "Even after some of the things we did. I wouldn't change it."

He readjusted himself again, finished the rest of his drink, then burped and shook his head.

"Actually, no, I'm talking shite. I'd change fucking loads of it, actually," he decided. "But you, me, Bamber. Jesus, even Chuck, evil wee bastard that he turned out to be, I wouldn't change those times. What about you?"

He filled his mug while waiting for a reply he knew wouldn't come.

"No, thought not," he said, toasting the man in the bed for a second time. "Cheers!"

His gaze crept to Welshy's hand, still lying there on the bed. Since Gabriella had held it, the fingers were now open wider, like they were welcoming his touch. Pleading for it.

Hoon looked away to the walls, the floor, the ceiling. Anywhere but that hand. Anywhere but the shrunken prison of a body that had locked away his best mate.

He knew why it was so difficult to look at him. Why it was so hard to see him like that.

It wasn't because of his physical appearance, drastically altered as that was.

It was because he'd promised. They'd each promised the other, in fact, after a sniper bullet had taken a chunk out of the spine of a US Marine right in front of them. They'd dragged him into cover, but Hoon could still remember how he'd screamed that he couldn't feel his legs. How his arms had trailed through the dirt, grit and rocks wearing down the skin on the backs of his hands until the sand ran with blood.

He hadn't noticed.

He was evac'd out by chopper an hour or two later, once the area was locked down, but it was months down the line when Hoon and Welshy heard how he was doing.

Near-total paralysis. Cared for twenty-four-seven. Poor bastard couldn't sleep without a hose in his fucking lungs.

And they'd promised, the two of them, that neither would let the other get into that state. If it came to it—if it was a choice between spending the rest of their lives like that, or ending it all —they'd each help the other on their journey. They'd fulfil the other's wishes, no matter the consequences.

And now, all those years later, here Hoon was, sipping wine at Welshy's bedside.

Time and circumstance had made a liar of him.

It was different, of course. They'd been young men back then, and the thought of spending fifty years in a motorised chair had been much more terrifying than death.

People changed. As you got older, you started to see the world differently. To want different things. It was not beyond the realms of possibility that one of the things Welshy no longer wanted was to have a bullet fired through his forehead at point-blank range.

He had Gabriella, after all. They'd built a life, and lived it well. Who the fuck was Hoon to come in thinking he had any right to interfere in that? A half-pissed promise made on a battlefield decades before had no authority here.

And yet, Welshy's dead spider of a hand lay there on the bed, taunting him for his cowardice.

CHAPTER SEVENTEEN

HOON HAD JUST POLISHED off the last dregs from the wine bottle when he heard the *clank* from outside. Close by. Right by the house.

He was on his feet even before the sound had fully registered. Welshy's room was lit by a small table lamp near the bed. Hoon searched for a switch to turn it off, then yanked the cable from the wall, instead, plunging the room into darkness.

Something scuffed around outside, like someone was walking along the side of the house, hugging close to the walls.

Shite.

He thought back to what he'd done with the package that he'd dug up from the banking beside the boat. Had he brought it inside? Was it still in Miles' car? He'd been so distracted at the thought of seeing Gabriella that he couldn't remember.

The curtains were closed, so nobody out there would be able to see in. Of course, it also meant he couldn't see out. He could hear, though, and there was definitely movement going on out there. Slow. Deliberate. Secretive.

He poked his head around the door frame and into the hall. The front door stood at one end of it, the world beyond only visible through the dunkles in the patterned glass. He studied the darkness beyond the door, but saw nothing to indicate anyone was out there on the step.

After a quick glance in the opposite direction, he ducked across the hall and into Gabriella's room. She was still asleep. That was the first thing Hoon noticed. The second thing he noted was the window, the curtains thrown wide. His own startled reflection stared back at him, but through it—for a second, maybe less—he saw movement.

Gabriella cried out in fright as he threw himself on top of her, bundling them both off the bed and onto the floor beneath the window.

"What the fuck are you doing?!" she started to bellow, until Hoon's hand clamped over her mouth, and he pressed a finger against his lips.

He raised his eyes to the window above them. Gabriella took a second to catch on, then nodded her understanding.

"Do you have a gun?" Hoon whispered.

She shook her head. "No. Don't you?"

"Not handy," Hoon admitted. "Have you got knives in the kitchen?"

Gabriella scowled at him. "Of course I've got knives in the kitchen! Kitchen knives."

"Alright, alright. Sorry I fucking asked," Hoon muttered.

He popped his head up above the window ledge, spent roughly two-fifths of a second checking the coast was clear, then caught her by the arm and launched them both, heads down, through the bedroom door and out into the corridor.

"In there," he ordered, shoving her into Welshy's room. "Stay down. Stay quiet."

He started to pull the door closed, but Gabriella grabbed for it, stopping it shutting all the way.

"Wait! Where are you going?" she whispered.

"I'm going to fucking sort this," Hoon told her. Then he gave another tug on the door handle, wrenching it all the way shut.

He hesitated for a moment, one hand on the door, then went striding up the hall and into the cluttered kitchen.

Most of the spaces in the knife block on the worktop were empty, but two handles jutted upwards like Excalibur from the stone. He pulled them both out, triumphantly, then groaned when he realised he was holding a bread knife and a sharpening tool.

"For fuck's sake," he grumbled, tossing them onto the worktop. He tore open a couple of drawers but found mostly spoons, an unreasonable amount of tinfoil, and a balloon whisk. "Knives. Knives, where's the fucking knives?!"

His eyes fell on the sink, the basin full of dirty, stagnant water. He thrust a hand in, and after a bit of rummaging, found the handle of what turned out to be a particularly long and lethal-looking blade.

That would do nicely.

There was a back door leading out from the kitchen. He took the old key from the lock, opened the door, then stepped out with the knife raised at head height. Prime stabbing position. Pity any poor bastard who got in the way of that downward blade trajectory.

He secured the door behind him again, and buried the key down in one of his pockets.

And then, he waited, breath held, tucked into the doorway so that he would be all but invisible to anyone approaching close to the walls on either side.

There, he listened. A light evening breeze rustled the overgrown grass. A wooden wind chime *thonked* out a tune somewhere around the front of the house. He was glad he had the knife, because he'd be cutting that fucking thing down at the first available opportunity.

He couldn't hear anything else. Nothing out of the ordinary, at least. He risked emerging from the indent of the door, and was immediately blinded when a security light at the back of the farmhouse ignited, firing ten thousand lumens of concentrated light straight to the back of his eyeballs.

"Fuck's sake!" he hissed, shielding his eyes and scampering around to the side of the house where he wouldn't make for such an obvious target.

Spots danced in front of his eyes, completely eliminating any chance of being able to see into the darkness. He kept low, feeling his way around the building, the knife now held at his side, primed to deliver an upward thrust that would be equally, if not even more unpleasant than the downwards version.

He was nearing the front of the building when he heard the faint *clank* again, even over the racket of those bloody wind chimes. He pressed himself in tight against the rough stone wall, shuffling sideways until he was as close to the corner as he could get while still remaining in cover.

There was definitely movement. Someone creeping through the undergrowth towards him. Getting closer. Closer.

Hoon held the knife ready as the rustling grew louder. Nearer.

Any second.

Any moment now.

He made a grab just as the footsteps rounded the corner, and almost tripped over a startled fox that quickly shot away from him, its ears flat with fear. It stopped and turned long enough to shoot him an indignant look, then went running off, tail bobbing until it was swallowed by the darkness.

"Bastard," Hoon wheezed.

He scanned the shadows for the fox for a few moments, then continued around to the front of the house. An old metal bin—the sort that played home to that angry wee green bastard on *Sesame Street*—lay on its side, its contents spilled out across the path.

Hoon tucked the knife into his waistband, then realised that this probably wouldn't end well, and took it back out again. He sat it on the ledge of what he thought was Welshy's window, then rapped on the glass.

"It's fine. Nothing to worry about. Just a fucking fox," he announced.

A moment later, the curtains swished, and Gabriella's face was revealed, looking significantly less stressed than it had a few moments earlier.

"A fox? Is that all?" she asked, her voice muffled by the window pane. "You catapulted me out of bed for a fox?"

Hoon grunted out something like a laugh. "It was quite a big fox, if that makes it any better?" he asked.

And then, reflected in the glass, a set of headlights blazed in the darkness. He saw Gabriella draw back. Heard the sound of four doors closing. Felt the bottom fall out of his world.

The gunfire started before he could move. Flames spat at him from the ocean of black. Even over the roar of it, he heard glass shatter, and stone crack. He heard Gabriella scream. Saw leering faces picked out in the glow of muzzle flashes.

Felt burning lead tear through his body, ripping it apart, chewing him up, reducing him to nothing but gristle and meat, and raw, bloodied bone.

―――

He woke up punching at the air, crying out with imagined pain, and with a fear that was only too real.

He was half sitting, half lying on the floor, like the chair had rejected him. The wine bottle and mug both lay tipped over beside him, a dribble of red dotting the carpet.

His hands trembled as he scraped the palms across his head and down the back of his neck so he could massage the knot of tension that had bunched itself up there.

"Fucking hell," he remarked, for the benefit of nobody but himself.

He listened then—not for movement outside, but from inside, in case he'd wakened Gabriella with his shouts.

Nothing stirred in the house. The only sounds were those of the machines keeping Welshy tethered to this plane of existence.

With some effort, Hoon dragged himself back up onto the uncomfortable armchair. Closing his eyes, he slowly brought his breathing back under control.

It had been a dream, of course, but at the same time, it had all felt so real. The look of panic on Gabriella's face as she realised what was about to happen. The pain of the bullets punching holes through his flesh. The grim acceptance that this was the end, and there was nothing he could do about it.

It had all felt real, yes, but not only that. *Worse* than that.

It had felt inevitable.

He opened his eyes, and let out another big, slow breath.

And that was when he noticed that Welshy was watching him.

"God. Alright, mate?" Hoon said, forcing some levity into his voice. "Didn't see you were awake."

Only one of Welshy's eyes had opened, the other half of his face almost completely unresponsive since the stroke that had condemned him to this existence. It seemed to tremble in its socket, like the muscles holding it in place had become too slack and too weak to keep it steady.

A sound emerged from somewhere deep in Welshy's chest, fading as it fell from his dry, motionless lips. It was a sound that, on its own, meant nothing.

Combined with that look, though, and with everything Hoon knew about the man in the bed, it spoke volumes.

Hoon ignored it. Pretended he hadn't heard.

"They, eh, they looking after you alright, mate?" he asked.

He maintained a smile, pinning the lie to his face. "Gabriella says the doctor and nurses come in and out to see you. That's, eh..."

The eye pleaded with him. Implored him.

"That's good that you've, eh, you've got..."

Hoon couldn't stand it any longer. He broke eye contact, looked away, but found himself staring down at that dead, lifeless hand, all shrunken and curled up.

The sound came again. Higher in pitch this time. More desperate than before, insisting he listen, insisting he hear.

Insisting he act.

Hoon got to his feet, shaking his head, turning away. "Welshy. I can't, mate," he told the door. "I'm sorry. It's not fucking fair. I know. But... I can't."

Another sound. A whimper this time that popped like a bubble on the dying man's lips.

Hoon shut his eyes, but even there in the darkness, Welshy stared back at him. Shaking. Begging.

They didn't know if he was in pain, Gabriella had said. They didn't know if he was suffering.

But they did know. Deep down. Of course they did.

This was so far beyond suffering. This was inhumane. This was Welshy's worst nightmare, built like a prison around him, bricking him up, trapping him inside.

The shimmering eye stared deep down into him.

The hand on the bed called him a liar. Called him a coward.

Hoon hurried to the door, grabbed the handle, started to pull it open, then stopped.

Behind him, machinery bleeped and clicked and wheezed.

They had spoken about this.

They had promised. Made a deal. Sworn an oath.

Whatever it took. Whatever the consequences.

The rest of the house stood in hushed silence, like it knew this moment was significant. Important. Worthy of note.

Gently, like he was moving something explosive, Hoon eased the door closed.

He turned to the bed, and to the twisted-up figure who lay there, dwarfed by the blankets around him.

The journey across the room seemed to take forever. He stopped by the bed, tilting his head so he was looking straight down into Welshy's wide, staring eye. A look passed between them that defied words, or definition.

Another sound made its way out from somewhere within Welshy. It was a sigh of something long overdue.

At last—finally—Hoon took the other man's hand in his own. It felt cold to the touch, like the life that had been in there was already packing up to leave.

Hoon squeezed it. Brought it to his face. Pressed the back of it against his cheek. A tear ran along Welshy's thumb, and trickled up his arm.

The eye watched, unblinking, then slowly crept to the bedclothes piled up on the armchair beside him. It lingered there for a moment, and when it returned to its starting position, Hoon's jaw was set, the lines of his face fixed in grim determination.

Hoon reached down and swept a strand of hair off Welshy's face. He gave the hand another comforting squeeze, then returned it to where he'd lifted it from the bed.

"I fucking love you, man," he whispered.

And with that, he reached for the pillow.

CHAPTER EIGHTEEN

THEY WERE SITTING in the living room when Miles' car pulled up, listening to the slow, rhythmic ticking of the grandfather clock. The sun was streaming in through a gap in the curtains, its fingers having crept several centimetres across the floor since dawn had first broken.

It had been rough on her, of course. She'd all but fallen onto the bed, hugging him, holding him, his skin cold beneath her touch.

She had blamed herself. Condemned herself for not being there to help him. To hold his hand. To just be with him at the end.

It had happened quickly, Hoon told her. It had been peaceful, in the end. If it hadn't been for the readouts of the medical equipment, he'd said, he'd never have noticed Welshy passing.

She had taken some comfort from the lie.

And Hoon had yet another secret he would carry with him to the grave.

She'd cried for a while then. Hoon had stood back by the door while she'd sat in the chair beside the body of her husband, all her months and years of grief bubbling to the surface until she eventually fell quiet, all hollow, and empty, and spent.

Minutes had passed without comment or movement. Then, she'd got up, whispered something in her husband's ear that wasn't meant for Hoon's, and planted a kiss on Welshy's forehead.

She had left the room then. They both had. Four hours later, they hadn't yet been able to go back.

Neither of them had been in the mood for eating, but both had insisted that the other really ought to, until they'd ended up with a big plate of hot, buttery toast on the table in front of them, and no inclination whatsoever to eat any of it.

The tea had been more welcome, piping hot and cloyingly sweet. Even Hoon had eschewed his usual coffee, though he only made it halfway through the mug of milky, sugary *PG Tips* before coming to his senses and making himself a fresh cup of the black stuff.

They hadn't spoken much, just a few aborted attempts at conversation that never amounted to anything. The company was comforting, though. Even Hoon, who prided himself on needing nothing from anyone, didn't really want to be fully alone with his thoughts and doubts right now.

A car door opened and closed out front, momentarily dragging Hoon back to the nightmare from the night before, but then a call of, "It's alright, it's just me," from Miles returned him to the here and now.

The front door was locked, and when Miles knocked on it, Gabriella didn't even seem to notice. Hoon got up, plodded along the hallway, then unlocked the door but didn't open it. He was halfway back to the living room when the handle turned and Miles popped his head around the door frame.

"Uh... Oh. Right. I thought you might, you know, at least have let me in," he said, but by the time he finished, Hoon was already back in his chair beside the fireplace.

The door creaked open, clicked closed, then a series of short, hurried footsteps announced Miles' arrival in the room.

"What's wrong? Has something happened?" he asked, picking up on the mood in the room. "It's not... It's not Gwynn, is it?"

Gabriella nodded, but said nothing. Miles gave a little groan of sympathy, and hurried to join her on the couch. "Oh. God. I'm so sorry," he said. He shot Hoon a quick look. "Both of you. I know how much he meant to you."

"Thank you," Gabriella said. She sounded robotic, like the pouring out of her grief had temporarily drained her of all other emotions, too.

One of Hoon's legs bounced in agitation. He sprang up from the chair again, and ducked his head out into the hall. "Where the fuck are they?" he demanded. "Greig and his missus and kid? Have you left them out in the fucking car?"

"Uh, no," Miles said. "There was a complication."

Hoon wheeled around. "What kind of complication?"

"They, um, they wouldn't come."

Hoon stood there, framed in the doorway, not moving. He stared at Miles like he'd replied in a foreign language, or just made a sound like a big foghorn.

"What the fuck do you mean?" he asked when it was clear that Miles wasn't going to offer any more information voluntarily.

"They didn't want to come. They said it sounded too dangerous."

"Too fucking...?" Hoon stood up. "Not fucking coming is too fucking dangerous! I can fucking protect them. I can look after them!"

Miles raised his shoulders in an uncomfortable *don't-blame-me* sort of shrug. "They weren't convinced by that," he explained. "They said nobody's come after them so far."

"Because no bastard knows where they are!"

"Uh, yeah." Miles scratched the back of his head. "Turns out, they haven't been as strict about staying anonymous as they might have been."

"What's that supposed to mean?" Hoon demanded.

"Cassie—Greig's partner—she, eh, she apparently went and stayed with her mum for a couple of weeks back up in Scotland."

Hoon's eyes almost boggled right out of his head. "Her mum? She went to stay with her fucking *mum*? What fucking part of top-secret witness relo-fucking-cation does she no' understand?"

Miles offered another of the shrugs he hoped absolved him of all responsibility. "Apparently, she's kept in touch with a lot of her old friends online, too."

Hoon threw his hands into the air in frustration. "Jesus Christ. Were you no' meant to be keeping an eye on them?"

"I can't watch them twenty-four-seven!" Miles protested.

"She fucked off for a fortnight!" Hoon shot back. He marched past the other man and threw himself into the armchair. "So, those bastards probably already know where they are!"

"Well, yeah. That was sort of their point," Miles said. He lowered himself into the chair on the other side of the fireplace, but carefully, like he might have to jump to his feet and make a run for it at any moment. "And, thinking about it on the way back, it does sort of make sense. Anyone Greig could identify, they're either dead, or... Well, just dead, I suppose. You saw to that. I mean, yes, the Loop protects itself, but sometimes protecting itself means *not* protecting itself. You know what I mean?"

"Absolutely not a fucking Scooby," Hoon told him. "If my ears could smell, all they'd be getting a fucking whiff of right now is you talking shite."

Miles spent a moment trying to unravel either of those last

remarks, then shook his head. "I mean, they've infiltrated a lot of key organisations—the police, the judicial system—but the Loop isn't a blunt instrument. It's careful. It's precise. If they murder a young family, questions will be asked. Yes, they can probably deflect a lot of them, but why take the risk if they don't have to? They're a global criminal and terrorist organisation, generating revenues in the billions every year. Do you really think that Greig—*Greig*—can do anything that would even remotely harm them?"

"That wee nyaff?" Hoon grunted. "Be like a fucking louse on a giant's tadger," he admitted.

"Well, not quite how I'd phrase it, but yeah. Sure. If you like," Miles said. "Killing a young couple and their baby is high profile, and if there's one thing they try not to be, it's high profile."

Hoon sat back in the chair. He didn't like the situation one bit. He didn't like that someone had disobeyed a direct fucking order from him for starters.

And he liked even less the fact that they were probably correct to do so.

The reasoning made sense. Hoon was a target. The Loop would be coming for him. Anyone around him was at risk of becoming collateral damage.

He stole a glance at Gabriella, still sitting on the couch.

Anyone.

"Aye, well, they might no' be as worried about high profile targets as you think," Hoon said. "I spoke to Deirdrie."

"Bagshaw?" Miles allowed himself to relax fully into the chair, the immediate threat of Hoon's anger blowing up in his face apparently subsiding. "What was she saying?"

"Not a lot," Hoon said. "Too busy being fucking murdered."

A suggestion of a smile played faintly across Miles' lips, like he was anticipating a funny punchline. When Hoon didn't follow up with one, though, it soon evaporated.

"What? You're serious?"

Hoon nodded. "That lassie who said she was trying to recruit me. It was her. Others, too. Fuck knows how many."

"Jesus Christ! Jesus Christ, and they... what? They killed her? While she was on the phone?"

"Mid-fucking convo," Hoon said. "I heard the whole thing."

Miles winced in horror at the very thought of it. "God. And what did they do to her?"

Hoon tutted. "Well, they didn't exactly fucking narrate it!" he retorted. "They weren't giving a blow by blow account, but I got the fucking gist. They say it'll be written up as suicide."

Miles chewed on his bottom lip, staring past Hoon to the wall behind him, like his next lines were written there. He gazed emptily at that empty spot for a while, then nodded slowly. "That makes sense. She's just been suspended. Probably going to get sacked. Disgraced high-ranking officer taking her own life is an easy story to sell."

"If they can get to her and get away with it, they can sure as fuck kill Greig and his family," Hoon pointed out.

"But there was a point to killing Bagshaw," Miles countered. "She had clout. She was respected. There was going to be an investigation. People would listen to what she had to say. She was a threat to them."

"Aye, well, they must think you're a fucking threat to them, too," Hoon said. "Suranne. Our mystery woman, whatever she's called, she mentioned you by name."

Miles sucked air in through his teeth. "I'm guessing not in a positive way?"

"In a, 'We're going to fucking kill that wee prick,' sort of way," Hoon said.

"She called me a wee prick?"

Hoon shook his head. "Naw, that was just me right there. She called you by your name. But, on the other hand, I'm no' threatening to murder you, so swings and fucking roundabouts, eh?"

"Did they mention me?" Gabriella piped up. She didn't look worried about what the answer was going to be, just curious, and even then, only mildly. She might as well have been asking the time, or whether either man had any plans for the weekend.

Hoon briefly considered lying to her, but she deserved better than that.

"Aye," he confirmed. "They did."

Gabriella raised her eyebrows in a half-hearted show of surprise, then nodded her understanding.

"Oh," she said, then turned to the window and stared, like she was somehow able to look straight through the curtains to the world beyond.

"I'm not going to let anything happen to you," Hoon promised, but she no longer appeared to be listening.

"And did they mention Greig?" Miles asked.

Hoon had already been thinking back over the conversation with Suranne to find the answer to that question, so it was on the tip of his tongue when Miles asked the question.

"No. Not by name, anyway."

"There you go, then," Miles said. "I think they should be safe. And, coarse as this is going to sound, with Welshy gone, we've now got options."

Hoon was on his feet before the sentence could stumble to its conclusion. He loomed over the seated man, fists clenched, eyes practically out on stalks.

"What the fuck did you just say?" he hissed.

Miles held both hands in front of himself, like he might be able to hold Hoon back. "I'm just saying! It's tragic that he's gone—really, it is—but it opens up possibilities. We were worried about the Loop finding this place. Now, we don't have to be here when they do."

Hoon's chest started to puff up, like he might inflate and fill the room. Gabriella put a pin in him before he had a chance to react.

"He's right."

Both men turned to look at her. Her focus was on the living room door now, like she could somehow see around the corners of the hall and into the room where her husband lay, now covered with a sheet she'd fetched from the airing cupboard.

"If they're coming here, we should go. We should leave."

Hoon scowled like he couldn't believe what he was hearing. "What, and just fucking leave him?"

"I don't think he's going to mind," Miles said, and this time even Gabriella looked at him like she might punch his lights out.

"We call an ambulance first. We get him taken somewhere safe."

Miles smiled weakly. "Or that, yes. We could absolutely do that."

"And then we go," Gabriella said. "We pack up, we move out, and we go."

"I don't think there's a desperate rush," Miles said. "The files are pretty heavily encrypted. It could be a few days before they even find them, then it's going to take time for them to access the information."

"Eh, aye. Aye, about that." Hoon scratched the back of his head. The sound of it resonated around the suddenly silent living room. "It might be a wee bit more pressing than you think..."

CHAPTER NINETEEN

MILES WAS PACING back and forth now, occasionally pausing to bury his face in his hands or make pained, groaning noises like he was in the late stages of labour.

"So, they have your phone number. Your new number," he said. "They have that."

These weren't questions, Hoon knew. They had been questions the last few times Miles had said the words, but now they were statements. Or accusations, maybe.

"Aye," Hoon confirmed.

"Which means they can get onto the network, find out which base stations you connected to, and get a pretty good idea of where you called from."

"That's about the fucking size of it, aye."

Miles flinched. "And you didn't think them getting your number might be an issue? It didn't *fucking occur* to you that this might happen?"

"No, it fucking did not," Hoon retorted, with far more venom than Miles had been able to muster. "I wasn't fucking phoning them, was I? I was phoning Deirdrie. How was I to know she'd be inconveniently murdered halfway through the fucking conversation?"

Miles paused in his pacing again. "You can withhold your number. You know that, right?"

"I'll withhold your fucking number in a minute, if you keep talking to me like that," Hoon shot back.

"What does that...? What does that even mean?" the MI5 man cried.

Hoon launched himself onto his feet. "Keep going pal, and you'll fucking find out what it— Oh, fuck knows. I don't fucking know what it means!" he admitted, albeit with way too much aggression for it to be taken as any sort of an apology. "It just felt like the right fucking thing to say at the time!"

"Why are you still shouting at me, then?" Miles yelped.

"Because I always fucking shout!" Hoon bellowed back. "That's just how I fucking speak."

"Jesus Christ!" Gabriella's voice was a shrill screech of exasperation. She got between the men, and shoved them both in the chest, forcing them apart. "Can you two just grow up? You're behaving like children."

"He's the one who needs to fucking grow up, no' me," Hoon replied, but the look this earned him from Gabriella stopped him saying any more.

"Whatever's happened has happened," Gabriella said. "Mistakes were made—"

"I wouldn't call it a fucking mistake, exactly," Hoon countered. "I wasn't to know that—"

"*Mistakes were made,*" Gabriella reiterated. "You can waste time waving your dicks at each other—"

Miles smoothed down the front of his shirt. "I wouldn't say that's what we were doing, exactly..."

"*Or* you can work together to come up with a plan. Because, if you're right—if they know where we are—then they could be on their way here now." She shot a worried look at the curtains. "They could be right outside."

Hoon crossed to the window and carefully parted the curtains. He immediately let out a hissed, "Fuck!" and then let the curtains close again.

Behind him, the room's two other occupants tensed in fear.

"Shit. Are they there?" Miles whispered.

Hoon looked back over his shoulder. "What? Oh. No. Sorry. Just the sun. Fucking bright outside. There's nobody there."

"Jesus!" Gabriella tutted. "I thought they were outside!"

Hoon shook his head. "All clear."

"We should phone the ambulance then," Miles suggested. "Get Gwynn taken care of, then formulate a plan."

"I've already got a plan," Hoon said. "You two fuck off somewhere safe, I let them come to me."

"Ha. Yeah," Miles said, dismissing the suggestion. "But we need a real plan."

"That is the fucking real plan," Hoon said, and his tone suggested that the matter wasn't up for debate.

"What are you talking about?" Gabriella asked. "We're not going anywhere."

"Aye. You are," Hoon insisted. "The one thing we know—the one fucking thing we're sure of—is that these fucking ball-chinned shite-nuggets are coming after me."

"And us," Miles said. "They're coming after all of us."

"Aye, but are they?" Hoon asked. "What you said earlier, about Greig. About how these fuckers operate, it got me thinking. What the fuck does Gabriella know about anything?"

"Thanks very much," Gabriella replied.

"I don't mean general knowledge. I'm sure you could hold your fucking own on *Mastermind.* I mean about the Loop. What could you actually tell anyone that they'd lose so much as a wink of fucking sleep over?"

Gabriella made some sounds that might have been the beginning of an argument, but they didn't amount to anything.

"But what about me?" Miles said.

"What a-fucking-bout you?" Hoon asked, dismissing the question with a sneer. "How long have you been after these pricks? Years. And the only fucking significant thing you've achieved in that time is convincing me to do your fucking dirty work."

"That's not quite how I'd describe it," Miles protested, but Hoon wasn't listening.

"You couldn't lay a fucking finger on them when you still had a job, son. What the fuck are you going to do when you're inevitably let go with no fucking redundancy money or pension?"

Miles tried to laugh that off, but didn't get very far. "They're not going to... They have to give me my pension. I think."

"I'd check the fucking small print on that, son. Ask a man who fucking knows," Hoon said. "But my point is, I've been a pain in their arse, and they know I'm going to continue to be unless they fucking do something about it. You two, though? You two are unnecessary attention. You said it yourself."

Miles' face went through a range of expressions, like he was trying to come up with the perfect counterargument. The fact that he said nothing, though, only confirmed Hoon's thinking on the matter.

"Being around me, that's where the fucking danger is," Hoon said. "Aye, they come here and find you, they might kill the pair of you. But I don't think they're going to come looking. Let's no' fucking kid ourselves here, if they wanted to get to either of you, they could've done it long before now. Gabriella and Welshy were at home for weeks before we shunted them out of there. Miles, for a spy, you're about as clandestine as a fucking drag queen at a Mormon wedding."

"I'm not a spy," Miles corrected, but Hoon dismissed it with a tut and a glare.

"You know what I fucking mean," he snapped. "The point is, these fuckers could've taken either of you out whenever they liked. Greig and his family, too. I see that now. It's fucking obvious. None of you are targets. I don't care what the fuck they say. You're only in danger if you're with me. So you can't be with me. It's that fucking simple."

Gabriella laughed. It was a mirthless, mocking sound, that soon gave way to anger. She prodded Hoon in the chest, forcing him back a step.

"We're not just leaving you. We all go, or none of us do. They're after all of us, not just you."

Hoon studied her face for a few moments, like he was trying to commit it to memory. Then, when he was finished, he looked past her to where Miles had sat on the arm of the couch, his hands slowly rubbing up and down on his thighs like he was trying to fight back pain, or control a panic attack.

"Tell her," Hoon instructed. "Tell her I'm right."

"I don't care what he says," Gabriella cut in. "When you came down the first time, when you came and stayed with us, you promised Welshy. You promised him you'd keep me safe. I heard you."

"That's exactly what I'm doing," Hoon countered. "I'm getting you away from me. That's how you stay safe."

"No. I stay safe by being with you, Bob. Whatever happens, I'm safe with you. I know it. You can keep me safe. You can protect me." She put a hand on his face. Her touch was agony and ecstasy, all rolled into one. "And I can protect you, too," she told him. "We, I mean. Miles and me. Both of us. We can all look out for each other."

Hoon placed his hand over hers. He caressed it, then removed it from his face.

"I can't. I can't do it, Gabriella. I can't protect you if you're with me."

She smiled like she was dismissing the concerns of an anxious child. "Yes, you can! I know you can," she insisted.

Her hand reached for his cheek again. He blocked it. The muscles in Hoon's jaw tightened, like they were either trying to keep words in, or forcing them to come out.

"What, like I protected Welshy, you mean?"

Gabriella frowned. Shook her head. That smile broadened further, becoming something almost patronising. "What happened to Gwynn wasn't your fault, Bob. It was nobody's fault. It was a stroke. It was awful, but there's no way that anyone could have done anything, much less you."

"That's not what I mean," Hoon said, and the words seemed to ring out in the silence that followed.

"What do you mean, then?" Gabriella asked. "What are you trying to say?"

Hoon couldn't look at her. Couldn't bring himself to hold that wide-eyed, questioning gaze. He picked a spot on the carpet, instead.

"You're right," he said. His voice was a low rumble, like distant, far-off thunder. "I did promise him I'd look after you."

"I know. I heard."

"No. Long time ago. Well before any of this shite. Back in the day," Hoon told her. "He said that if anything happened to him out there, that I—well, me and the boys—had to make sure you were OK. Daft bastard had only been seeing you for a few weeks, but he was already all the way sucked in. Marriage, kids, he was talking about it all. We took the piss, of course, but he didn't care. He loved you." Hoon summoned the strength to glance at her, just for a moment. "From the first fucking moment he met you."

His eyes were directed back to the carpet again, and he ran a hand down his face, composing himself. Preparing himself for what came next.

"Anyway, he made us promise. He made us fucking swear that we'd make sure you were looked after if anything happened to him. If he died out there, we were to make sure you were alright."

"There you go, then!" Gabriella practically cheered. "You promised. You can't let him down."

"But he made me promise something else, too," Hoon continued. "This one was just me."

A floorboard creaked as Miles shifted his weight and looked towards the hall. He made a sound—an utterance—that told Hoon he'd figured it out.

That he knew precisely what had happened in the night.

What Hoon had done.

"You don't worry too much about dying when you're out there," Hoon said. "I mean, aye, you do. But the longer you're out there, the more shit you see. And the more you see, the more you realise that there are things that can happen to you that are worse than death—a lot fucking worse—and you worry about that stuff more."

Confusion was still written on Gabriella's face, but she had backed up a step. Maybe two. Her smile had still been hanging in there, but now it fell away completely.

"I don't... What are you saying, Bob?"

Hoon swallowed. Met her eye. "I think you know."

"Tell me," Gabriella insisted.

She was going to make him say it. She was going to drag the words out of him, either because she didn't believe the dark roads her imagination was taking her down, or because she wanted to force his confession. Needed to hear the words for herself.

He owed her that much, at least.

"I killed him," Hoon said. It was quiet and matter-of-fact, like an off-hand remark about the weather.

Gabriella's eye darted left and right in tiny increments, searching his face for something that he knew she'd never find.

"What?" she asked, a note of disbelieving laughter accompanying the word. "What do you mean? What are you saying?"

"I killed Welshy," Hoon said. His voice almost cracked. That wouldn't do at all. He reinforced it, until it sounded hard and cold. "While you were sleeping. I killed him."

Gabriella let out that little note of laughter again, and looked round at Miles, like she was expecting him to deliver the punchline. Instead, he followed Hoon's lead and averted his gaze, avoiding the widow's eye.

"You... killed him?!" Gabriella spluttered, wheeling back to face Hoon. "You... What do you...? You killed Gwynn?!"

"He asked me to," Hoon told her.

She lashed out at that, slapping him on the upper arm, eyes blurring with tears. "How the hell could he have asked you to?! He couldn't speak!"

"Not tonight. A long time ago," Hoon said.

"What, back in the fucking day?" Gabriella cried, hitting him again after almost every word.

"Aye. We made a pact," Hoon said. He didn't try to avoid her slaps. He deserved them all. "We wouldn't leave each other suffering."

"A fucking *pact*?!" she screeched. "That was decades ago! You were *children*! How dare you? How fucking *dare you*? You don't know what he wanted now! You don't *know*."

Her stare burned into him like a welder's torch. He summoned the strength not to look away. "Aye," he said. "I did."

She held him there, fixed in place by her stare for several speechless moments, then looked him up and down as if seeing him—truly seeing him—for the very first time.

And then, out of nowhere, a big right hand cracked him across the jaw. He saw it coming in time to react and, more importantly, in time not to. He rolled with it, turning his head away.

When he turned back, she was running from the room. Running from him.

"Jesus, Bob," Miles muttered. He started towards the door, but Hoon caught him by the arm.

"Leave her. Give her a minute," Hoon instructed.

"She's upset!"

"Of course she's fucking upset! I just told her I killed her husband. What do you expect her to be doing? Cartwheeling across the living room? Breaking into fucking song?" Hoon barked. "Luckily, being upset's no' a fucking terminal condition. Being here when them Loop pricks turn up, though, that will be. So, you need to get her out of here, pronto."

Miles shook his head. "We're not just leaving you, Bob. We'll all go, hole up somewhere, and put our heads together. We'll make a plan."

"I've got a fucking plan," Hoon told him.

"Waiting here until they come and kill you isn't a plan!"

"Aye, it is," Hoon insisted. "But it's a shite plan, hence why I'm no' fucking doing it."

"Oh. Right. So... what? You've got a different plan?"

"Don't sound so fucking surprised! Course I've got a different plan! I've got about five different plans, I'll have you know. Not fucking one of which involves me hanging about here until that *Argos* catalogue of arseholes turns up and shoots some exciting new holes in my face."

"Right. OK. So... what's the plan, then?" Miles asked. "What are you going to do?"

"I'm going to kill them," Hoon explained. "I'm going to kill every fucking last one of them."

"That's... not a plan."

Hoon shrugged. "It's a nugget of a plan. I'm going to wing

the rest." He pointed to the house's phone, standing on a table in the corner. "Now, get a fucking ambulance sorted for Welshy, then I'm going to need you to do three things for me."

The MI5 man looked worried. It was unusual for Hoon to ask for help. On the few occasions that he had done so in the past, it had rarely ended well for Miles.

"What three things?"

"I need you to go get that package out of your car. I need you to find me a map—your phone will do," Hoon told him. He didn't turn to look at the living room door. He didn't even acknowledge it existed. "Then, I need you to get Gabriella and take her as far fucking away from me as possible."

CHAPTER TWENTY

THEIR CONTACTS within the police had been very helpful. The phone network, in turn, had been equally as forthcoming with information. The details the network had been able to provide didn't pinpoint the caller's location, but it triangulated it down to a rough geographical area of just a few square miles.

And, as luck would have it, there were less than a dozen buildings covered by that zone. Rule out the shops, the pub, the little primary school, and both churches, and you were down to fewer than five.

A little more research into land ownership, some cursory checks on *Google Maps*, and a bit of common sense, and they narrowed the likely suspects down to just one solitary farmhouse, surrounded by fields, hidden well away from prying eyes.

A safe house, if ever there was one.

They parked both their vans on the grass verge of a nearby side road, then cut through some woods until they reached the fence that marked the boundary of the farmland. From across the furrowed field, they studied the building, binoculars fixed on the windows.

The curtains were mostly drawn, blocking their view of the

rooms beyond. A car sat in the driveway, tucked in close to the front door, like it was on standby for a speedy exit.

Soft plumes of white-grey smoke rose from the chimney, travelling straight upwards through the still, breezeless air, but otherwise there was no sign of movement.

The field was several hundred yards wide, and offered little to no cover. She didn't like it. Too open. Too risky. If someone in there had a rifle and a steady aim—and she knew from his records that Hoon had at least one of those—then they'd be picked off before they could make it halfway.

They headed north through the woods, keeping the house on their left, then banking around behind it, following the line of the trees. The woodland was closer to the house around the back. A minute's walk, maybe less, with some thick foliage and uneven ground providing options for cover.

In a way, this made it more dangerous. Hoon was no fool. He'd know this was the best approach, so if he was watching anywhere, it would be here.

She scanned the rear of the building with the binoculars. Closed curtains. A shut door. No movement but the slow, lazy rising of the smoke.

On her signal, the squads advanced. Fifteen of them, eight from one van, seven from the other, the black of their outfits and balaclavas more suited for night ops than this daytime assault.

But time was of the essence. Hoon had been easy to get to on the boat, but he hadn't been trying to hide then. Now, he knew they were coming. Now, he was on the run.

Or he would be, if he had any sense.

In her encounters with the man, he'd come across as a boorish idiot with a penchant for bad language and sudden outbursts of violence. But he was more than that. He'd risen through the ranks of the special forces. He'd been a detective superintendent of police. He was smarter and more cunning than he first appeared.

Then again, that wouldn't be difficult.

They reached the house without incident. She dished out instructions silently, with points, and looks, and hand gestures.

The squads split up, fanned out, followed her orders. Doors were kicked. Windows shattered. Tear gas bloomed through the rooms of the house.

Masks were lowered. Guns were raised. She made her way around to the front of the house, her weapon held ready, waiting for the shouting to begin and the excitement to kick off. She quite enjoyed these moments of anticipation, but she much preferred the moments that came after. The confrontation and the violence. The glory of victory. The whiff of death.

Give her the storm any day, rather than the calm before it.

Today, though, provided only disappointment.

"It's empty," a gunman in a gas mask informed her, stepping out through the front door. "Nobody's there."

"What, nobody?" she asked, flicking her gaze across the front of the building, then around at the car parked in the driveway beside her. It was a small hatchback, and the patina of grime on the windows suggested it hadn't moved in weeks. The front number plate was missing. Removed recently, judging by the patch of relatively clean paintwork in the spot it should have been occupying.

"Whole house is empty," the man beside her confirmed.

She rolled her balaclava up onto her head and scowled, making no bones about her disappointment. "So... what, then? It's the wrong place?" she asked. "It can't be the wrong place."

"No. It's the right place," the man replied, his voice taking on an eerie echo inside the mask. He presented her with a sheet of paper, neatly folded in half. "We found this in the kitchen."

She unfolded the paper and stared at the words written on it in thick black marker, her expression of disappointment becoming one of irritation.

The words, 'NAE LUCK, YA FANNIES,' taunted her from the page.

She scrunched up the note and tossed it onto the ground, then stamped on it twice for luck.

"You sure you checked everywhere?" she demanded. "Did you look in all the rooms?"

"Yeah. They're gone. Load of medical equipment in one, but the bed's empty. They must have known we were coming."

A frown creased the lines of her forehead. Her lips moved, like she was doing a difficult calculation in her head.

Hoon came across as a boorish idiot.

But he wasn't. Not even close.

She turned her attention back to the car, with its missing front number plate.

She walked around to the back of the vehicle, picking up the pace as she got closer.

The rear plate was gone, too, and the realisation hit her like a bolt of lightning.

"The vans!" she hissed, breaking into a run. "He's going for the fucking vans!"

———

They crashed from the trees beside where they'd parked the vans, and a number of expletives rang out when they discovered that the number of vehicles parked up on the verge had been reduced by fifty percent.

The number plates of the van up front lay discarded on the road, no doubt replaced by those taken from the car.

"The tyres. He's done in the fucking tyres!" one of the soldiers announced, venting his frustration with a wild kick at the slashed and ruined rubber.

"Wait, which one did he take?" demanded another man.

The rear doors of the remaining van were pulled open, and several more expletives rang out at the roadside.

The woman who'd called herself Suranne looked both ways along the single-track road, like she might be able to catch a glimpse of the stolen vehicle disappearing around a bend.

No such luck. The bastard was probably long gone.

Unhooking the radio from her belt, she thumbed the button, and barked out a series of instructions. She had a contingency plan in place for just this sort of thing, of course. She had a contingency plan for most things.

Somewhere, not too far away, four motorbike engines roared into life.

CHAPTER TWENTY-ONE

HOON WHISTLED to himself as he powered the van along the narrow, winding roads of North Dorset, following the signs for place names he'd never heard of. The tune was a relatively cheerful composition of his own. He'd started it below his breath while unscrewing the van's number plates, and it had evolved into something bordering on joyous when he'd found the keys in the glove box, and driven off at speed.

His plan had multiple stages. The fact that he was alive and moving on his own steam right now meant that the first five of these had gone surprisingly smoothly. The next steps should be easier—find a van similar to the one he was in, swap plates, then get back on the road. He just had to be careful to avoid ANPR cameras, or they'd pick up the fact that the vehicle he was driving was not, in fact, the *Citroen C3* that the registration claimed it was.

That shouldn't be too difficult for now, of course. He'd been driving for about three miles, and had met less than half a dozen cars coming the other way. Mostly, the roads he was using didn't allow for two way traffic, so the chances of them being equipped with number plate recognition cameras were slim.

Those chances would increase the closer he got to the bigger towns, of course. Yeovil was just a little way up the map in South Somerset. That would be his best chance of finding a matching van with which to better disguise this one, but a large town also meant police, and if he was pulled over, he didn't think, "Sorry, officer, I was fleeing a top-secret criminal cabal," was likely to be accepted as a reasonable excuse.

Hoon's whistling had just reached a particularly upbeat chorus when he heard the *thump* on the wall behind him. The van was split into two sections—a cab area, with three seats, a steering wheel, and everything else required to make the van move in the direction you wanted it to—and a boxed-in cargo section which took up about eighty percent of the vehicle's available space.

He didn't stop whistling, but lowered the volume until it was little more than a tuneful movement of air between his lips.

The sound came again. Twice, this time, in quick succession. *Thump-thump.*

It was the sound, he realised, of someone knocking.

"Aw, shite," he muttered, his improvised tune dying away completely.

There was someone in the back of the fucking van. Why hadn't he thought to check? Why hadn't he opened the doors and looked inside?

Thump. Thump. Thump.

Hoon slammed a hand on top of the wheel and grimaced through gritted teeth.

"I fucking knew it was going too well," he spat.

Still, there was no real urgency to the knocking. No sense of panic. Whoever was in there probably had no idea that anything was amiss. Or no idea of just *how* fucking amiss things were, at any rate. That meant Hoon still had options. Despite the unexpected passenger, he still had time to think.

A movement in the side mirror caught his eye. Over the

rumbling of the van's engine, he heard the higher-pitched whine of a motorbike approaching fast. It seemed to come from nowhere, but closed in quickly, two wheels tearing up the road.

There was a bend approaching. Hoon started to slow, which only allowed the bike to close in more quickly.

He checked the mirror again. The uneven road made the reflection jump around, but everything about the rider screamed 'danger,' from the angle of his body to the speed at which he was approaching.

He was dressed all in black, which wasn't particularly unusual. What was more unusual was the way he was now steering the bike with one hand, the other reaching for a walkie-talkie he had clipped to his belt.

"Shite," Hoon grunted.

And then, he applied the brakes. The motorcyclist, to his credit, *very nearly* avoided crashing directly into the back of the larger vehicle, as it went from doing forty miles per hour to being completely stationary in the middle of the narrow road with almost no warning whatsoever.

The front wheel managed to just skim by the van's rear bumper, but neither the rest of the bike, nor the man sitting astride it, were so fortunate.

The impact reverberated around inside the van, the mostly-empty cargo area acting like a big amplifier that fired the sound through the wall and into the cab. Hoon crunched the van into reverse, backed up until he felt something *pop*, then pulled forwards again, quickly picking up speed.

In the mirror, the rider grabbed at his thigh, like he was trying to tear something out of his flesh. At first, Hoon thought the man's leg had been impaled on something, but then the rider produced a handgun from a thigh holster, and Hoon weaved sharply to the left as a gunshot rang out, and a bullet whistled past him on the right.

There was another clatter from the back of the van, the

occupant having been fired against the side wall by the sharp and unexpected manoeuvre.

Hoon floored the accelerator, powering towards the upcoming bend. It was a sharp one—not quite a hard right turn, but close—and the van felt like it was going to tip as he swung into the turn, wrenching hard on the wheel.

From behind him, there came another big *thud*, and he imagined that had anyone been watching from the roadside at that moment, they'd have seen the perfect imprint of a human being appearing on the side of the van.

The van's suspension squeaked as the weight shifted back onto all four wheels. There was a crossroads ahead, with a 'Give Way' sign and dotted white road markings indicating that he should stop to check for traffic coming from the left and right.

"Fuck that for a game of soldiers," he announced to nobody in particular, and his foot went to the floor, urging the van to pick up speed.

It responded slowly, the engine groaning like it didn't approve of this course of action. Hoon dropped down a couple of gears, and the low, reluctant grumble became a whining cry of distress. It did the trick, though, and the van leaped forwards, even as the person in the cargo area was sent tumbling towards the back.

Hoon gritted his teeth as he went roaring towards the cross-roads, braced for the possibility of another devastating side-impact, only without a helmet and body armour to protect him this time.

Mercifully, no large vehicles ploughed into him, but as he thundered across the junction, he saw two more motorbikes coming up fast on his left, picking up speed as they caught sight of him.

"Shitey-fucking-shite-fuck!" he spat, changing gear, steering, and trying to reach into the passenger footwell all at the same time.

The package he'd dug up from the river bank was rolling around in there, just enough of the tape torn open for him to have removed a bundle of cash from inside.

Gabriella had refused the money, of course. It had been just about the only thing she'd said to him between when the ambulance arrived and when she climbed into Miles' car.

He'd given it to Miles, instead—forced him to take it—keeping only a few hundred quid to see him through the rest of his plan.

It hadn't been much, just a couple of grand, but it had been the only one of his stashes he'd been able to get to before things had gone to shit.

The other half of the package was still wrapped up, and lay tantalisingly beyond his reach on the floor of the footwell. He stretched for it, fingertips just brushing against the tape, then he was forced to abandon it and grab the wheel with both hands as another bend in the road came racing towards him.

He swore again—the same words as last time, but in a slightly different order—and the van swerved violently from side to side, skirting the very edges of a skid, and rattled the mystery passenger around in the back like a pinball in a scoring frenzy.

Both motorbikes were hurtling up behind the van, growing larger in the right-hand mirror. The road had widened into two lanes here, and even if he managed to *emergency stop* another of the bastards into oblivion, there was no saying he'd be able to get both.

Another turn came up fast. He dropped gears, wrenched the wheel, and the van drifted sideways around the bend, smoke billowing from the melting rubber of its tyres, their squeals almost loud enough to drown out the violent *thumps* and *thuds* from just a few feet behind him.

He checked the mirror to see if the bikes were still following, then ducked when a bullet punched through it, shattering glass and tearing through metal.

"Bastards!" he ejected, then he swerved right across the road until he could catch sight of them in the left-hand wing mirror.

A horn blared directly ahead. Flicking his eyes to the front, he swung left just in time to avoid colliding with a saloon coming the other way, the driver flashing his lights and blasting his horn to demonstrate his contempt.

"Ah, fuck off!" Hoon spat, giving the man the finger as they *whooshed* past each other in opposite directions.

The sudden manoeuvre had rolled the half-wrapped package closer towards the centre console. Hoon adjusted his grip on the wheel, held the van in as straight a line as possible, and made a grab into the footwell.

He cried out in triumph as his fingers finally found what they'd been reaching for, then let out a series of little panicky yelps as the van mounted the grassy verge at the side of the road, and he was forced to hurriedly course-correct.

The package fell onto the middle passenger seat. He slapped and tore at the tape with his left hand, but he'd wrapped it too well, secured it too tightly against the cold, wet soil in which it had been buried.

Give him a pair of scissors and an uninterrupted few minutes, and he might get somewhere. Here and now, though, he had neither of those things. Short of him winding down the window and throwing it at the bastards, the package was not going to prove helpful.

"Right, fine. Fuck it, then," he declared. "We'll do this the hard way."

There was a turn coming up on the right, a wide-mouthed junction connecting this road to another. Hoon swung the van way out to the left, then wrestled the wheel in a full lock to the right, pulled on the handbrake, used the extra space of the junction to spin the van around in a complete one-eighty.

He felt himself start to roll out of his seat, before the belt tightened its grip across his chest, holding him in place. Whoever was in the back of the van was less fortunate, judging by the way their impact shuddered all the way through into the front. They hadn't shouted. Not once. But then, given how violently they'd been tossed around back there, there was a good chance they were either unconscious or dead. Certainly, they'd stopped trying to get his attention by politely knocking on the dividing wall.

If they hadn't realised that something was amiss when he'd first driven off with them, he was confident that they'd at least have their suspicions by now.

The motorbikes came roaring up, one behind the other, staggered on the road just a few feet apart. The rider in front was taking aim with a pistol. The one behind barked something into a radio. Neither was good news, but one was far more pressing than the other, so Hoon made the gunman the priority.

He crouched low behind the wheel, making himself a smaller target, and slammed the accelerator pedal all the way down to the floor. He stuck to the left side of the gearbox, imbuing the van with a sense of urgency this time as it lurched, wheels spinning towards the bikers.

The gunman took the lead, closing in on the right, swinging the pistol around, ready to shoot at Hoon through the side window. Before the bastard had a chance, Hoon swerved and threw the door open. He quickly pulled his arm back in before the impact with the oncoming biker shattered the glass and slammed the door closed again.

Hoon stuck his head through the hole where the side window had been, and looked back in time to see the biker with the gun go sliding along the tarmac, his helmet grinding on the uneven road surface, the chassis of his bike throwing sparks into the air as it bounced, rolled, and finally came to a rest in the ditch.

His feeling of triumph quickly abandoned him when he faced front again, just in time to see arrows warning him of a sharp left turn. This time, two of the van's wheels fully left the ground, and Hoon threw his weight into the bend, desperately trying to counterbalance and stop the van tumbling into a roll.

The outside edges of the driver's side wheels scraped along the verge, chewing the grass and churning the soil. They kept the van from rolling, but as it slammed back down onto all four wheels, the impact jolted the air from Hoon's body in one big, breathless wheeze.

He somehow made the turn, and then saw, just a few feet ahead, another motorbike hurtling towards him. The rider raised a hand like this might offer some sort of protection from the much larger vehicle currently bearing down on him.

It did not.

There was a *crunch* that made all the other impacts seem tame. There was a strangled scream that lasted all of half a second. There was a *pop* below the wheels that turned even Hoon's stomach.

The van skidded, the back end swinging, spinning the whole vehicle around in the opposite direction and, by the sounds of it, *properly* fucking up the poor bastard in the back.

The collision had triggered the van's hazard lights. Hoon sat there behind the wheel, the little red exclamation mark on the dashboard clicking on and off in time with the lights.

On the road, what had until recently been a motorbike, but which could now be described as 'bits of one' at best, lay strewn across the road. There was something else strewn across the road, too, just like the bike, only wetter.

In fact, 'strewn' probably wasn't the right word in this instance. 'Splattered,' would have been more appropriate. 'Smeared,' maybe.

Hoon turned off the hazards, and crept forward in the van

until he was alongside the debris, both mechanical and human. In amongst it all—between a broken carburettor and what might have been a hip—he saw a blood-smeared handgun.

After a quick glance in both directions to make sure the coast was clear, Hoon got out of the van, fished the pistol from the surrounding viscera, and wiped it as best he could on the trousers of the dead man. Considering the state they were in, though, any improvement was negligible, at best.

The gun felt instantly familiar in his hand. *Glock 19*, a more compact version of the *17*, which he'd used extensively over the years. This version was a little less accurate, but more easily concealed. The slightly reduced size made it ideal for plain clothes operations, even if it meant two fewer bullets in the smaller magazine.

He slid the mag from the grip, and was pleased to find it fully loaded. Slotting it back into place, he chambered a round, just as the other motorbike swung around the bend fifty yards or so up ahead.

The bike slowed when the rider caught sight of Hoon standing there in the road between the smouldering carnage and the mangled cadaver. Hoon rolled his head around on his shoulders, stretching the tendons in his neck, enjoying all the little *cricks* and *pops* they made.

The biker twisted his grip. The engine howled. The motorbike shot forwards like it had been fired from a launcher, and Hoon watched, not moving, as the man sitting astride it went for his gun.

Hoon brought up the *Glock,* narrowed his eyes, and squeezed off a single shot. He'd been aiming at a shoulder, but the round found the rider's chest.

He seemed to stop in mid-air, the bike continuing on without him for a couple of seconds, before wobbling and crashing to the ground.

By that point, its rider was already flat on his back, one hand on his heart, motionless but for the blood oozing between his gloved fingers.

Hoon looked both ways along the road, but saw no other vehicles approaching in either direction.

He pointed to both dead men in turn, said, "And let that be a fucking lesson to you," then climbed back into the van, shoved the gun in the glove box, and pulled away from the scene.

Behind him, in the cargo space, the van's forward momentum sent something heavy sliding slowly across the floor.

———

Suranne stood far back from the cordon tape, and the ambulances, and the flashing blue lights of the police vehicles, hidden by the surrounding trees. She didn't know yet exactly what had happened, but the lack of response on the radio, and the burgundy sheen she could see coating the road gave her some idea.

This would be difficult to cover up. Not impossible, of course—nothing was impossible—but it would take time, money, and a lot of resources. If those above her found out, they would not be pleased.

She'd have to make sure they didn't.

"It looks like he got away," one of the men behind her remarked.

"Well, clearly he fucking got away," she hissed, not taking her eyes off the scene. "I want him found. Today. I don't care what you have to do. I don't care what it takes. We find him. And then, we kill him."

She turned to face them, and the whole squad straightened to attention.

"Are we all fucking clear on that?" she asked.

"Yes, ma'am," they said in unison, and as they snapped off their salutes, she went striding past them into the darkening woods.

CHAPTER TWENTY-TWO

HOON FOUND JUST what he was looking for in a supermarket car park just north of Yeovil. The vans weren't an *exact* match—same make and model, different year and trim—but it was close enough. The fact that it was tucked away in a side section of the car park didn't hurt, either, as it meant he was able to swap out the plates without interruption.

That done, he continued on for a few more miles until he spotted a little rural pub called the *Half Moon Inn*. It was located in a village so small it barely qualified as a street, and had a thatched porch, a brick chimney, and an old slate roof that rippled like it was one heavy downpour away from falling in.

It was the sort of pub that people walked their dogs to for a big Sunday lunch. Hoon imagined if he went inside there wouldn't be a single person there who wasn't wearing Wellies and tweed jackets with leather patches on the elbows. It would be a friendly place, he thought. A place where families could go and while away a lovely few hours together, with the sun streaming in through the big windows.

Not really his cup of tea at all. Give him a manky, dark room with puddles of beer on the wobbly tables, and a general understanding that you don't speak unless spoken to, and even then only in words of one syllable.

What this place did have, though, was a private car park that led around the side of the building, walled in so passing cars couldn't see inside.

The van trundled across the pavement and through the entrance, and Hoon continued all the way to the back, then tucked the van in behind a row of glass bottle recycling containers.

He got down from the driver's seat, put his hands on his lower back, and rearranged his spine into something more like its natural position. After a few more stretches of his neck and shoulders, he brought his ear closer to the van's back doors and listened for any sign of movement.

Whoever was back there had spent most of the short journey north *clunking* off the walls, or slipping around on the floor. For a while, Hoon had actually made a bit of a game of it, turning sharply wherever possible, then listening for the satisfying *baduung* of a human torso hitting a metal wall at speed.

It was only when it occurred to him that whoever was in the back might be a prisoner, rather than the horrible bastard he'd assumed them to be, that he decided it might be best to pull over somewhere and check.

He'd passed a couple of parking spots at the side of the road, but they were either packed with other vehicles or too exposed to passing traffic. The car park of the *Half Moon Inn* wasn't the ideal place to check out his mystery cargo, but it was the best option among an otherwise bad bunch.

Glancing around to make sure nobody was sitting in their cars watching on, Hoon rapped his knuckles against the van's back door. "Hello?" he called, raising his voice. The metal body of the van wouldn't make it hard to hear him, but if the poor bastard inside was still alive, then the ringing in their ears would make hearing anything a challenge.

Nobody answered from within the vehicle. No words. No groans. No shuffled movements.

"Fuck it, then," Hoon said. He pulled at the door handle, found it locked, then patted at his pockets, searching for the keys.

When he failed to find them, he returned to the driver's seat and rummaged in the various dookits and indents in the dashboard. Finally, he found the keys in the drinks holder in the centre console, twirled them around on his finger, and slid back down to the ground.

He was halfway to the back when he saw the door standing open.

"Shite!" he ejected, dashing around to the rear of the vehicle. Blobs of blood smeared the walls and floor—not enough to have caused any lasting damage, but enough to have hurt.

A mobile phone lay on the floor of the van, smashed not just beyond repair, but practically out of existence.

Other than that, though, and a couple of small black rucksacks tied with climbing rope to the wall at the opposite end, the van's cargo area was empty.

"Fuck!"

Hoon slammed the door and spun on the spot, searching for any sign of whoever had just done a runner. They couldn't have made it all the way to the car park entrance, and there were no obvious ways into the pub on this side of the building.

His gaze fell on the eight cars, two vans, and a solitary motorbike that currently shared the inn's parking facilities with him, and offered the only possible cover for someone trying to hide.

"Right, cut the shite," he boomed. "I can't be fucked looking for you, and there's only about four fucking places you can be, anyway, so no point in pissing about."

He waited, hands on his hips, listening for a response that didn't come.

"I fucking mean it," he declared. "I'm no' in the fucking mood for this. Come out, and I'll do you the fucking honour of saying no more about this wee fucking transgression you've got going on here."

He waited again.

Still nothing.

He sighed, making sure his impatience was loud enough to hear all the way from the other end of the car park.

"Right. Fair enough. Here's what's going to happen, then. I'm going to count to three." Hoon announced. "If you're no' out by then, I'm going to come and find you. And then—and I promise I'm no' exaggerating here—I will boot you so hard in whatever reproductive organs you happen to possess that they'll be launched out the top of your head and into a fucking geostationary orbit around you. You'll just be stuck watching them hovering in front of you, forever out of fucking reach."

He gave that imagery some time to bed in, before continuing.

"Assuming that's no' a turn of events you're particularly keen on exploring, if I were you, I'd give serious fucking consideration to doing as you're told."

He listened once more, an ear cocked towards the parked vehicles. When still no response came, he shook his head, tutted, and crept forwards as he began to count.

"One."

His boots crunched on the loose gravel beneath them as he closed in on the first vehicle. It was an old *Volvo* estate, parked close and tight to a small *Vauxhall* van with the name of a joinery business emblazoned in faded blue print on the side.

He peeked between them.

Nothing.

"Two," he continued. "I'm getting my fucking kicking leg warmed up here, by the way."

He dropped into a crouch, looking under the vehicles,

searching for feet or some other sign that someone was hiding behind the joiner's van.

Nope.

He stood up, strode to the centre of the car park, and shouted, "Three!" in a tone that made it clear he was officially all out of patience. "Right, well, you'd better kiss goodbye to your bollocks or your minge, because I made a generous fucking offer there, that you've thrown back in my face."

When still no response came, Hoon jogged over to the car park entrance, looked in both directions, then turned his attention back to the parked vehicles. He did the full circuit, checking behind, inside, and under each car and van.

He found no one. Whoever had done a runner when his back was turned, they were gone. And that meant that he needed to be, too.

He wasted a few seconds swearing at the world in general, then returned to his stolen vehicle, opened the driver's door, and clambered inside.

The muzzle of a *Glock 19* stopped him, freezing him mid-climb. His gaze lingered on the gun for a few moments, then raised to the bloodied, nightmarish face of the man holding it.

The Professor had looked like something from a nightmare even before being repeatedly *thwanged* around in the back of the van. Now, with blood oozing from an undetermined number of cuts on his head, a big flap of skin hanging off his left cheek, and one eye swollen completely shut, he looked significantly worse.

In fact, no. Hoon wasn't convinced that he *did* look worse, exactly—it was hard to go any further down from that horror-show of a starting point—but forty miles of smashing off walls certainly hadn't done anything to improve his appearance.

"Jesus fuck!" Hoon spat. "You look like you've been tea-bagged by the Incredible Hulk."

The Professor motioned with the gun for him to get into the

van. Hoon noted that the fingers on the other man's left hand seemed to have had a rather dramatic falling out, and were all facing in different directions, like they couldn't stand the sight of each other.

No way this bastard was driving anywhere. That was good. It meant he'd need to keep Hoon alive long enough to get him to wherever he wanted to go.

A hospital seemed like the obvious choice, but then Hoon guessed the Professor's medical needs weren't generally handled by the NHS.

"Right, what now?" Hoon asked, closing the door and raising his hands.

Presumably, both of the Professor's eyes moved to indicate the van's controls, but as only one was visible, it was impossible to say for sure.

Hoon pressed his foot on the clutch, pressed the start button, and waited for the engine to rumble to life.

"So, eh, that was you in the back, was it?" he asked. "Sounded fucking rough, all that thumping and banging." He offered a smile of consolation. "I really wish I'd known it was you," he said. "I'd have reversed into a fucking wall."

The Professor's breath rasped wetly in through his ravaged nose and throat, little bubbles of blood bursting around his gaping nostrils. He waved the gun at Hoon, giving a little flick to the right which was presumably meant to be an instruction.

"I don't have a fucking clue what that means," Hoon told him. He nodded at the *Glock* as the gesture was repeated. "Doing it again's no' fucking helping. What does it...? Fucking... wiggle waggle? What's that meant to be?"

The Professor grunted. Given the scarring on his throat, even that utterance was just short of miraculous.

Still, Hoon was unimpressed.

"Just fucking going *ugh* at me isn't going to help, is it?" he said. He mimed tapping on the satnav. "Here, what's the postcode of the place we're going? '*Ugh*.' Alright, is that with one fucking U or two?"

The gun trembled in the Professor's hand. The damage to his face made his expressions hard to read, and the pint and a half of blood currently slicking his skin didn't help matters, either. He was either angry, Hoon reckoned, or passing a kidney stone the size of a walnut.

Possibly both.

"I tell you what. I'm going to make this easier," Hoon said.

There was a flurry of movement. The Professor had no way of stopping the gun being torn from his trembling fingers. No way of preventing the hand grabbing him by the back of the head. No way to save himself from the impact of the dashboard.

The sound he made wasn't like an animal, exactly. It was more like the sound of *all* animals, letting rip at the same time. It was a cry of such pain, and shock, and distress that Hoon was sure it would follow him all the way to the grave.

He hoped so, anyway.

"You could've fucking shot me there," Hoon pointed out. He pressed the muzzle of the gun against the Professor's temple with just enough pressure to tilt his head to the left. "It's no' very nice having a fucking gun pointed at you, is it? I bet you're no' enjoying this much, are you?"

The Professor said nothing. Then again, he couldn't even if he'd wanted to.

"Aye, I fucking thought not," Hoon said. He shoved the gun down into the pocket on the door beside him, then pointed to the handle of the one beside the Professor. "Right, out we fucking go," he ordered. "If you think you're getting to sit upfront with me the whole way, you're in for a fucking world of disappointment."

———

Two hours, a rump steak with all the trimmings, and a slice of banoffee pie later, Hoon sat parked up in a layby near a sign announcing that *Queen Camel* lay just a few miles ahead.

It was unlikely, he thought, that the sign was directing him towards an actual camel, royal or otherwise. Instead, it'd be yet another quaint wee English town or village with a stupid name —another Boggy Bottom, or a Bitchfield, or a Bell End. It was probably on a list on the internet somewhere, so humourless fucks the world over could memorise and recite it as a substitute for having any decent banter or personality of their own.

Calling a village *Bell End* was pretty funny, mind you. He'd give them that one.

And there was a place in Orkney called Twatt that he'd always thought about visiting, if only to get a photo of himself next to the sign.

His passenger—or prisoner, more accurately—hadn't made a sound since being bundled into the back of the van. Hoon had secured him to the tie hooks with the lengths of climbing rope, partly so he wouldn't go tumbling across the floor the first time the van came to a corner, but mostly so the creepy bastard couldn't try and escape again.

Hoon hadn't yet decided if the Professor was a complication or a gift from the gods. Before he'd realised he was back there, Hoon's plan had been fairly straightforward. It had involved him returning to London, retrieving all the guns he had stashed around the city, then clicking his battery back into his phone and waiting for the Loop to come after him.

He wouldn't be able to take them all out, of course—they were a worldwide criminal network, after all—but he'd take immense satisfaction in getting rid of the ones that he could.

They'd kill him eventually, of course. But then, they'd kill him eventually, anyway. Better to go out with a bang. Or, better still, several hundred bangs, and a whole lot of blood on his hands.

As plans went, it had been fairly straightforward. 'Elegant' was probably a stretch, but there had been a simplicity to it that he'd enjoyed. *Get gun, shoot baddies.* He'd had an entire military career based on not a whole lot more than those four words.

But things were more complicated now. He had something that the Loop wanted. Something they'd gone to a lot of effort to bring back from the dead, or as close to it as it was possible to get, at least.

That changed things. Maybe killing a bunch of people and then going out in a blaze of glory wasn't the best way for him to end all this. Maybe the day wasn't going to end with him taking several rounds to the head and chest at point-blank range. Maybe there was something else he could do.

Yes. There must be. There had to be. He had a valuable prisoner now, and that meant he had something else, too.

He had options.

He just wished he knew what the fuck they were.

Hoon flexed his fingers on the wheel and kept his gaze averted from the road. Evening was closing in, and a few of the passing cars had already clicked on their headlights so they dazzled him as they approached.

It was unlikely they'd switched them on specifically for that reason, even he had to admit. But, still.

"Arseholes," he muttered, making his irritation at them clear to absolutely nobody but himself.

Options, then. What were they?

"*What can you do with an ugly bastard?*" Hoon sang below his breath, absolutely murdering the tune of the one about the drunken sailor.

The problem was that sitting here at the side of the road in a stolen van that was probably, even now, being hunted by angry armed bastards wasn't particularly conducive to planning. But then, where else could he go? The boat was sunk. The farmhouse was a no-go. They'd surely be watching his house up in Inverness, assuming they hadn't burned that to the ground, too.

Where, then?

Somewhere they didn't know about.

Somewhere he could clear his head, make a plan, and prepare.

And, ideally, where he wouldn't be seen dragging a tied-up bloodied and disfigured older gentleman up the garden path.

The answer crept in at the back of his brain and just sort of sat there, waiting to be noticed. He pretended not to, but it didn't care. It just sat there quietly, like a right smug bastard.

That couldn't be the only option. There had to be an alternative. There had to be somewhere else he could go. Somewhere that wasn't *there*.

Somewhere that didn't involve seeing *her*.

But, if there was, then he was fucked if he could think of it.

"Oh, for Christ's sake," he groaned, massaging his temples in a futile attempt to fend off a stress headache.

There was no avoiding it.

There was only one place left for him to go.

Westward.

CHAPTER TWENTY-THREE

THE DRIVE NORTH took all night. It would've been quicker on the motorways, but motorways meant cameras, and he had no idea if his number plate switch had been spotted yet. With a bit of luck, the owner of the other van would be too thick to notice for a few days, but for all Hoon knew, the police were already hunting for his recently acquired registration, and one ping on an ANPR camera would be all it took to find him.

He'd had to stop a couple of times to have a slash at the side of the road. He had even allowed his prisoner to do the same, though this was mostly because he didn't want the back of the van to be sloshing around with puddles of lukewarm piss.

He'd loaded up with drinks and snacks in a petrol station somewhere just south of Blackpool, and had even bought a first aid kit with which to patch up some of the Professor's injuries. It wouldn't do to let him bleed to death. Alive, he was an asset. Dead, he was just additional hassle, and Hoon'd had enough hassle lately to last him a bloody lifetime.

And to think, all this had started with a fucking ostrich.

The sun was thinking about making a reappearance by the time the van was winding its way up the twisting road alongside

Loch Lomond. A lot of people hated this stretch of road—the sudden twists and turns, the unexpected narrowings, the raw *what-the-fuck-do-I-do-now?* terror of meeting an oncoming bus on a corner.

Hoon, on the other hand, loved it. This, he always thought whenever he came within a wasp's eyelash of hitting a wall, a tree, or an approaching vehicle, was what driving should be like. Forget the dull treadmill of a motorway, where each mile rolled by the same as the hundred before. This—teeth gritted, knuckles white, no two turns the same—*this* was much more his style.

It was still early, though, and traffic on the road was sparse, and he was almost disappointed to reach the Crianlarich bypass without a single skin-of-the-teeth encounter.

His plan had been to have a final rest stop at the *Green Welly* in Tyndrum, but the place was in darkness when the van rolled into the car park. A quick check of the front door told him it wasn't due to open for another three hours, by which point he'd be at his destination.

A niggling doubt that he'd been ignoring for the past four hundred or so miles brought itself to his attention again as he returned to the van. He'd repeatedly told himself that he'd worry about it later, but he was almost all out of later now.

In a couple of hours, he'd be at Westward, a place he hadn't set foot in, in almost twenty years. He hadn't spoken to her more than twice in that time, either, and the few words they'd exchanged hadn't exactly been friendly.

He was travelling all this way and pinning all his hopes on a place where he might not even be welcome.

There were plenty of places that he'd made himself unwelcome over the years, of course, but this was different. None of those other places had *her* guarding them.

Still, there was no point in turning back now. After a quick check to make sure his prisoner was still in the land of the living, Hoon returned to the driver's seat, and pulled up the steep hill that rose towards Rannoch Moor, and through the rugged, sunrise-dappled mountains of Glen Coe.

The road itself here was generally less eventful than the unrolled ball of string that was the one running along Loch Lomond side. Long, straight stretches gave way to swooping bends, with just the occasional sharp turn into a steep climb to keep you on your toes.

The dips and humps of the road could always catch out the unwary, of course, and many an accident had occurred when someone had overtaken, unaware of an oncoming vehicle just beyond the next rise.

And then there was the deer problem. Come the winter, driving at night became a sort of high-speed game of chicken, with each new turn and bend offering a fresh opportunity for one of the bastards to throw themselves in front of your car.

Anyone familiar with the road knew all the dangers to look out for, though, but even to those who drove it every day, the route never became boring, thanks to the landscape it cut through—literally cut through at some parts, with a trench gouged through the mountains themselves—as the road journeyed further north.

From its snow-capped peaks where golden eagles circled, to its thundering waterfalls where tourists *Instagrammed*, there was always something to see, and the landscape drew half a dozen mumbled, *fuck me*s and a spontaneous round of applause from Hoon as he powered through the last leg of the journey.

Fort William was just waking up when he hit the outskirts. On the bypass that ran along the back of the town, he passed the first police car he'd seen since the central belt, and held his breath, waiting for them to either spot his missing mirror, or have his plate flag up on the car's camera.

There was no wailing of sirens, though, and by the time he was through the town and heading towards Corpach, he reckoned he was in the clear.

From there, the remaining forty or so miles passed in a bit of a blur. Getting to the house wasn't easy—that's why she'd bought it—and his memory of which turn-off to take was a little hazy.

There was walking involved—a three or four-mile trek across a worn hill path which he wasn't relishing the thought of even without having to drag his hostage with him. It was that or continue on to Mallaig and hire a boat to get him back to where the house stood tucked away in its own private bay. If he'd been on his own, he might have taken that route. With a bloodied monster-man for company, though, it wasn't really an option.

After a couple of wrong turns, he found the tiny, three-space car park from which the footpath led off. It was empty, but then, as far as he could remember, it always had been. She'd never owned a car, and had always made her way to and from the house on a knackered little powerboat that, for reasons best known to herself, she'd named *The Dirty Slapper*.

The Professor, as expected, proved to be an absolute pain in the arse. He'd tripped and stumbled over almost every step of the four-mile hike, huffing and moaning out protest after whinging protest, until Hoon had been forced to all but drag the bastard behind him across the grass.

Eventually, about an hour later than Hoon had hoped, they crested the rounded peak of a hill, and the wide expanse of Loch Nevis stretched out before them.

Beyond it, on the opposite shore, lay the Knoydart Peninsula, a place often described as Europe's last true wilderness, but which also—and more importantly, as far as Hoon was concerned—boasted a cracking wee community-owned pub.

And below them, right on the edge of the bay where the soil became sand, surrounded by old wooden chalets in various states of disrepair, stood Westward.

———

"Good morning, my little lollipops!" boomed the voice from the other side of the door.

It was opened with some enthusiasm, though this soon evaporated when the woman filling the doorway realised she was not gazing into the eyes of the children she had been expecting, but was instead staring at the crotches of two adult men.

As Hoon watched, she seemed to swell, growing larger like a pufferfish warning off a predator. Her eyes raised to meet his, and a momentary look of confusion and surprise almost immediately gave way to a scowl of disdain.

"Well, bugger me red raw," she said in a voice that had grown accustomed to not having to worry about what the neighbours thought. "Look what the cat shat out."

Hoon smiled weakly and scratched at the back of his head.

"Alright, sis?" he muttered. "Long time no see."

CHAPTER TWENTY-FOUR

HOON SAT at a scratched and scuffed oak table tucked at the far end of a sprawling old kitchen that appeared to be in the process of evolving, with three different styles of cabinets and two different wallpapers providing a visual history of its progress so far.

He nursed a mug of coffee so strong that he'd been able to stand a spoon straight upright in it. It straddled the line between liquid and solid, and even just being in this close proximity to it, Hoon reckoned, meant he'd be wide awake for days.

His sister had taken his unexpected arrival surprisingly well. After her initial outburst at him, and the, "What the suffering fuck is that thing?" that she'd hurled in the Professor's direction, she'd begrudgingly invited them inside.

Hoon had asked permission to lock the Professor up in one of the five wooden chalets that stood on the grounds around the house, and with a wave of a hand she'd told him to, "Do what the fuck you like."

The chalets had been built by the house's previous owner, who had rented them out to tourists looking to get off the beaten track. Now, they had mostly fallen into ruin, infested with damp and riddled with rot.

He'd secured his hostage in the one closest to the house— one of just two that had been at least partially maintained for the last four decades—and then returned to find the coffee-flavoured gloop waiting for him on the kitchen table.

"You're looking well, Berta," Hoon said.

It was intended as a harmless enough comment, but his sister failed to take it at face value. She wheeled around to face him, a hot teaspoon held in a way that suggested she could do some serious damage with it.

Hoon did not doubt that she could.

"Don't you even fucking think about trying to butter me up, Bobby!" she warned, squinting at him like she was channelling her inner Popeye the Sailor Man. "Or I'll bounce you out that window cradling your bollocks like they're the newborn infant Christ."

"I wasn't fucking buttering anyone up!" Hoon spat back. "I was just saying you're looking well."

Berta raised her nose to the air and sniffed. "Here. You smell that?" she asked.

"Smell what?"

"The pile of absolute fucking horseshit you're spilling! I don't look well. I'm not a kick in the arse off seventy, both hips are giving me gyp, and I've got piles hanging out of me like a bunch of dirty grapes." Berta's lips drew back over her teeth in distaste as she checked her younger brother out. "Mind you, I'm fucking Debbie McGee compared to the nick of you."

Hoon was too distracted by the obscure reference to the 1980s magician's assistant to pick up on the insult.

"Why the fuck did you choose Debbie McGee?" he wondered, then he ducked when the hot teaspoon went whizzing over his head and clattered against one of the wallpapers behind him.

"Never you bloody mind!" Berta said. She gave him another up-and-down look. "What's happened to you? You been living rough? Because you look like you have."

"What? No. Not exactly."

"And what's with the fucking T-shirt? *Mr Grumpy?* Were they all out of *Mr Useless Streak of Cat Piss* or something?"

Hoon looked down at the now filthy, bloodied garment. "I don't think that character ever made it past the publisher's desk."

He risked a sip of his coffee, almost choked on it, then set it back down. An old cuckoo clock on the wall loudly counted down the minutes to eleven o'clock. The cuckoo itself would never pop out, Hoon knew, his sister having amputated it with a pair of poultry shears after its third or fourth appearance many years prior, then taped the little swing doors shut.

"I'm in trouble, Berta," he admitted.

"Of course you're in fucking trouble," his sister shot back. "You always bloody were. You might be all haggard and dead-eyed—and fatter, you're definitely fatter—but some things never fucking change."

She pulled out the chair across from him, and he watched as she gingerly lowered herself onto it accompanied by a sound-track of creaking bones and cracking joints.

Some of Hoon's first memories were of his older sister. He would've been four or five at the time, and her almost twenty. Even then, she'd struck him as a force of nature—larger than life, impossibly strong, and the only person capable of going toe to toe with their father.

Their mother had died around about that time, and Berta had reluctantly stepped into the matriarch role. When their father had botched an attempt to follow his wife a month or two down the line, leaving him in a vegetative state for the remainder of his days, she'd become the closest thing to a parent that Hoon and his younger sister had.

Roxie had just been a baby when everything had gone to shit. She needed all of Berta's attention, and she got it, too. Hoon, on the other hand, had been forced to grow up quickly, though his efforts to do so had rarely been good enough to gain his older sister's approval.

They had moved here to *Westward* when Hoon was ten or eleven, a settlement from the hospital and a small life insurance payout providing the capital needed for them to finally get out of the house where their father had attempted to swallow a shotgun.

Hoon had hated the new place. They'd had neighbours at the old house. He'd had friends to play with. Out here, the nearest neighbours had been a mile away along the beach at low tide, or twice that distance across the hills if the water had cut off that route, and the youngest member of that family had been in their late fifties.

His childhood adventures had been largely solitary ones, involving swimming, rock pools, and epic battles with imagined foes. He'd done most of his schooling here in this room, Berta shouting at him while she gutted a trout, or plucked a pheasant, or prepared some other recent kill for the cooking pot.

Even as he'd grown, she always seemed enormous. When he reached his full height he was only an inch or two shorter than her, yet it felt like she was twice his size, and four times as strong, and she'd remind him of that with the occasional explosion of violence that came out of nowhere.

Now, though, age had chipped away at her, withering her away, shrivelling her up. She'd moved around the house in big bounding strides, always in a rush, usually carrying washing, or rubbish, or a loaded shotgun over one arm.

Her movements now were slow and steady, like she was wary of something shattering beyond repair. Everything about her seemed to have softened around the edges.

Everything but her tongue.

"The fuck are you looking at me like that for?" she demanded when she'd finally touched down onto the chair.

"Like what?"

"Like you've had your brain swapped out for a bag of fucking walnuts," Berta replied. "It's old age, Bobby. Comes to the best of us. It's got its fucking hooks deep into you already, by the looks of you. You look like a warm shite that's been pushed through a sieve."

"Cheers for that," Hoon muttered.

"Not as bad as your boyfriend, mind," Berta continued. "I mean, Jesus Christ, what's he meant to be? The Elephant Man's fucking stunt double?"

"I bit his nose off," Hoon explained.

Berta tutted and shook her head in distaste. "What you get up to in the privacy of your own bedroom is no concern of mine," she said, waving both hands like she could waft the whole conversation out through one of the open windows.

"He's no' my fucking..." Hoon sighed. "He's a prisoner. He was torturing me a few months back, and to escape I had to chew his nose off."

Berta's lips pursed. "Still sounds a bit kinky for my liking."

"Aye, well, I can fucking assure you it wasn't. I bit off his nose, then rammed a broken chair leg through his throat. Thought I'd killed the bastard, but apparently not."

His sister sniffed and reached for a bowl of sugar cubes that sat on the table between them. "Aye, well, no surprise there," she said, tossing one of the cubes into her mouth and crunching it between her blunted yellow teeth. "You always were bloody useless."

Hoon was in no mood for her withering criticisms, but didn't have the energy for the shouting match that would surely follow if he said as much. Instead, he tried to move the conversation on to more pressing matters.

"There are people after me," he said. "An organisation."

"Which one, *Fuckwits Anonymous*?" Berta asked. "You fallen behind on your membership fees again, or something?"

"I'm not kidding around, Berta," Hoon said, somehow finding the restraint to rise above the remark. "These are bad people. Serious people. They want me dead."

"Well, knowing you as I do, Bobby, I'd imagine they're not the fucking only ones," Berta said. "Aren't you still with the *po-po*?"

Hoon snorted out a laugh. "The fucking *po-po*? Where are you getting that from?"

"*Netflix*," his sister replied. "And don't fucking look at me like that, I didn't get it for me. I got it for the kiddliewinks."

Hoon looked around the kitchen like he might spot a gang of feral children lurking under the appliances, dirty faces staring back at him.

"Neighbour's two. Next house over. They come to visit most days," Berta said. "Insufferable pair of bastards. Twins, too, so always a bit creepy, but they bring a bit of life to the old place."

"Right. Fair enough," Hoon said. "And no."

"No, what?"

"I'm not still in the polis. Haven't been for a couple of years."

Berta sniffed and sat back. She nodded, like this was the first thing Hoon had said that she approved of. "Good. Never suited you." She tapped the table. "The army, that suited you. Following orders, doing as you were told. That's got you written all over it. But a *detective*?" She folded her arms across her ample bosom and shook her head. "No. I mean, they must've been fucking desperate to take you on for that. There must've been a national bloody shortage."

Hoon, once again, bit his tongue.

"Aye, well, all behind me now."

"You ever see Roxie's spawn?" Berta asked.

"Louisa, you mean?" Hoon asked. He shrugged. "Used to. No' so much now. She's got a kid of her own. Jaden."

"Oh, God!" Berta rolled her eyes so far back into her head, Hoon found himself watching for them coming all the way back up from below. "Another one. That's all the world fucking needs."

"He's a nice wee lad," Hoon said, but it was met by a disbelieving grunt from his sister. "You, eh, you been to the grave recently?"

"What, Roxie's?"

"Any of them."

"What the buggery bollocks would I do a thing like that for?" Berta scoffed. "No point clinging to the bloody past, is there? It's like I've always said—"

"Onwards and fucking upwards," Hoon said, finishing the sentence for her.

"Precisely!" Berta picked at her teeth with the corner of a trimmed fingernail. "So, these people trying to kill you. Who are they?"

"They're called the Loop," Hoon explained.

"Sounds like a bloody boogie-woogie band," Berta said.

"Make it a lot fucking easier if they were," Hoon said. "But, no. They're like a global terrorist network, or fucking criminal empire, or something."

"Sounds big."

"It is," Hoon confirmed.

Berta gave him yet another slow look up and down. "So, why on Earth would they be interested in a little scrote like you?"

"I, eh, got on their wrong side," Hoon told her. "Repeatedly."

Berta jabbed a thumb back over her shoulder. "Biting that bingo hat's nose off?"

Hoon frowned. "What the fuck's a bingo hat?"

"It's a hat you wear to the bingo," Berta explained, in a brusque, offhand manner that suggested he should've been able to figure that out for himself.

"Right. Aye. Fair enough. But, no. Not that. Or no' just that, anyway." Hoon brought his coffee up to his mouth again, but the smell of it gave him all the caffeine hit he needed, and he immediately returned it to the table. "I freed some women they were trafficking, killed a few of them, got one of their main guys locked up."

"You've been busy."

"Aye. Fought a big spooky giant, too."

"I see," said Berta. "And at what point did you sustain the head injury?"

"Which one?" Hoon asked.

Berta jabbed a finger against the tabletop and scowled at him. "The one that's made you come here talking a big old load of shite! I mean, you've either been watching too many action movies, or you've got a bleed on the fucking brain, Bobby."

"Loads of it was in the papers!" Hoon protested.

"Which ones? The *Made-Up Times* and the *Bullshit Weekly*?" Berta scoffed. "I mean, what's a 'spooky giant' when it's at home?"

"Just a big fucking spooky guy! He was one of them... what do you call them?"

"Hallucinations?"

"No! Fucking... the spooky white ones."

"Ghosts?"

"Jesus Christ. No! The fucking pale... When you've got no..." He banged his fist on the table in triumph. "Albinos! He was an albino."

Berta shook her head slowly, her features contorting in disgust. "That's a medical issue. You can't call them 'the spooky whites ones.' I thought I'd raised you better than that, Bobby."

Hoon bowed his head, genuinely chastised, as his sister folded her arms, leaned back, and sniffed.

"They are fucking weird, though," she admitted.

She eyeballed her younger brother for a few moments, her tongue rolling around inside her mouth like it was hunting for an escape route.

"Are you being serious?" she asked. "All that stuff you said. You're not on the wind-up?"

"Straight up," Hoon said. "I've pissed off a worldwide network of bastards. They've got their best men looking for me."

Berta snorted. "Their best men? For *you*? Talk about fucking overkill," she said, then she fixed him with the sort of look a long-suffering parent might give a wayward teenager. "And tell me this, what are you planning on doing about it?"

"I don't know," Hoon admitted. "I mean, from what I know, there are thousands of them. Hundreds of thousands, maybe. I can't exactly get them all."

Berta peered along her nose at him for a while. It was a long, crooked thing, that deviated a couple of times on its way down her face.

"Remember Tony Blair?"

Hoon frowned. "The Prime Minister?"

"No, the other one. Little fat fucker. Lived two doors down at the old house. Couple of years older than you. Used to leather shit out of you on the regular."

The frown deepened further. "Don't think so."

"Well, you should. You used to fucking greet your eyes out about him often enough!" Berta brought her fists to her eyes and mimed crying, *"Wah! Wah! Tony pushed me over! Or Tony kicked me in the goolies! Or Tony set my jumper on fire!"*

Hoon blinked. "Jesus."

"Awful child. Parents were no fucking better, mind you," Berta continued. "Anyway, he was much bigger than you. Not exactly difficult, given that you were built like a worm on hunger strike. But he was a big boy for his age. Ten or eleven, but could've passed for thirty."

"*Thirty?!*" Hoon spluttered.

"I'm not even exaggerating," Berta told him. "Potbelly, bags under the eyes, hair receding, beard like a pirate captain."

"Are you sure this was a fucking child?" Hoon asked. "And no' just a short man?"

"Don't be so bloody ridiculous! Of course he wasn't a..." Berta rubbed her chin, her index finger picking at a big hairy mole just below her mouth. "Actually, that would explain a lot."

"Was there a point to this story?" Hoon asked.

"What? Oh. Yes. So, he would push you around, you'd come home in tears, and I'd console you."

"You?" Hoon laughed. "*You'd* console me?"

"Well, I'd tell you to get a fucking grip, and to stop behaving like a child."

Hoon nodded. "Aye, that sounds more like it."

"And I'd tell you that bullies like that only understand one type of language," Berta continued, before hammering a hand down on the table so hard it even made Hoon jump. "A bloody good fisting!"

Hoon hesitated, just for a moment. "I don't think that word means what you think it means."

"I know exactly what it bloody means, thank you very much, and I fucking stand by it," Berta said. "And then, one day you finally listened. You remember what you did to Tony that day?"

"I dread to fucking think at this point," Hoon muttered.

"You walloped him. Square in the face. Bloodied his nose," Berta said, and for perhaps the first and only time Hoon could remember, she looked genuinely proud. "He was far bigger and stronger than you—he could've shoved your head up his arse and popped it off like the cap of a fucking beer bottle—but when you hurt him like that, none of that mattered. He ran off, tail between his legs."

"And I'm guessing he never bothered me again?"

"What? Oh, no. Leathered the absolute living shit out of you three days later. Him and a big gang of his mates. I thought they were going to fucking kill you at one point," Berta said. "But my point is..."

She raised her index finger like she was about to deliver the perfect words of wisdom to round off the story, but then just sort of froze there with her mouth open.

"Your point is what?" Hoon asked.

Berta shrugged. "Fuck knows. Can't remember where I was going with it." She pushed back her chair and, bones creaking, stood up. "Now, what the fuck are we going to do with *Shite of the Living Dead* out there in the chalet?"

"I'm going to ask him some questions," Hoon said. "You got a notepad or something?"

Berta rubbed her hands together with glee. "For paper cuts? Between the fingers is a good one."

Hoon stared blankly at her for a few moments, then shook his head. "For him to write on. Pretty sure he can't talk."

"Oh." The word came out like a sigh of disappointment. "Yes. I've probably got something somewhere."

"Good. I'll also need a pen." Hoon got to his feet. "Plus some scissors, a hammer, two blocks of wood, and any safety pins or needles you've got lying around."

Berta's grin practically split her face in two. She slapped a hand on her younger brother's shoulder.

"Now you're fucking talking."

CHAPTER TWENTY-FIVE

THE PROFESSOR WAS asleep when the Hoons entered the cabin. He let out a muffled yelp of fright when Berta kicked him on the shin, and screamed, "Wake up, you ghastly fuck!" in what turned out to be a successful attempt to rouse him.

"Alright, fucking calm down," Hoon told her. "Leave this to me, I know what I'm doing here."

"That'd be a first."

Hoon sighed. "I said you could sit in and fucking watch, as long as you didn't interfere."

"I'm not interfering."

Hoon gestured to the now wide-eyed Professor cowering on the musty armchair to which he'd been tied. "You booted him in the leg and called him a 'ghastly fuck.' How is that no' interfering?"

Berta threw her hands up and sighed. "Well, *clearly* we just have a very different understanding of what the word means," she said. "If you want me to keep out of it, you just have to say so."

"I did," Hoon reminded her. "I literally told you no' to fucking interfere."

"Fine. Fine," Berta said, acting like the injured party here. "I'll just go and sit down and keep my mouth shut. You'd like that, wouldn't you?"

"I'd very fucking much like that, aye," Hoon confirmed.

His sister stared at him in sullen silence for a few moments. Then, with the speed of an attacking cobra, she grabbed one of his nipples through his t-shirt and twisted until he hissed.

"Ow! Jesus fuck! What was that for?"

"That's what you get for trying to act the fucking big man in front of your noseless wee pal there," she told him.

And then, with great care and deliberation, like she was a new monarch taking to the throne for the first time, Berta lowered herself into the cabin's only other armchair, interlocked her fingers, and waited for the show to begin.

Hoon glanced around at the inside of the cabin, trying very hard not to breathe in.

"I like what you haven't done with the place," he remarked.

While more care had been taken with this chalet than the others, it could still best be described as a 'damp-infested shit hole.' Like the others, it had been built almost fifty years previously, to provide holiday accommodation to the growing numbers of tourists who flocked to the Highlands in the hope of escaping the rat race for a while.

Berta had no time for such people, though. She'd been on one holiday in her entire life, and that had been a day-trip to Elgin. She hadn't enjoyed it. The thought of allowing an ever-changing roster of complete strangers into her life—into her home—chilled her to the bone.

And so, the chalets had been left to rot. This one, though, had been used for storage from time to time, and Berta had carried out some basic repairs over the years to stop at least a percentage of the rain getting in. Not a high percentage, mind you, but a percentage all the same.

What it had mostly been used to store were chickens. She'd

eventually built them their own little coop with a fence to protect them from predators, and hadn't bothered to clean this place up afterwards.

So, when Hoon dragged the rickety wooden chair across the floor, its back legs cut trenches through the years-old layer of dried chicken shit.

He spun it around on one leg so the back was facing his prisoner, and then sat astride it in the wrong direction.

Something just below the seat went *crack* and the chair suddenly lurched to one side. Hoon let out a panicky, "Fuck!" then jumped off before the whole thing collapsed like a house of cards.

"That was humiliating," Berta muttered, as Hoon kicked the rotten remains of the chair away.

"Well, maybe if you'd taken fucking better care of the place!"

"Oh, like I didn't have enough to do, running after you two little shits!" Berta countered.

"You did fuck all for me!" Hoon spat back. "I cleared off to Glasgow before I was fifteen!"

"And not before bloody time," Berta snapped. She pointed to the Professor. "Now, are you going to crack on here? Your boyfriend's getting impatient."

Given his lack of nose, and all the haphazardly applied sticking plasters, it was hard to get an accurate read on the Professor's facial expression. Hoon didn't think 'impatient' was an accurate way of describing it, though. If anything, he looked like he was happy for the argument to continue for as long as possible.

Hoon fetched another chair from the corner of the cabin, checked this one to make sure it wasn't going to collapse on him, then placed it—backwards, as before—in front of the Professor. He straddled it with a little more care this time, and was pleased when it didn't give way.

He sat there, saying nothing, for a good minute or two, just eyeballing the other man like he might be able to break him with just a look.

The Professor, however, was made of sterner stuff. Although, going by how he shifted his weight around in the chair and averted his gaze, not all *that* much sterner.

"The fuck you looking at?" Hoon asked. He glowered at the prisoner, then broke into a smile. "Just messing wi' you, pal. Don't worry. Been a rough couple of fucking days, eh? Sorry about all that in the van, by the way. Didn't know you were there to start with. And then, I mean, when I did, I probably could've gone a wee bit fucking easier on you, too. My bad."

"Oh, just hurry up and cut his bollocks off!" Berta called from her seat. "That's what we're all here for, isn't it?"

Hoon rolled his eyes like he and the Professor were sharing a secret. "Don't mind her," he said, keeping his voice low. "She's demented."

"What was that?" his sister demanded. "Did I just hear you say 'demented' or 'dementia' there?"

Hoon turned and looked back over his shoulder. "I said you're demented."

Berta sniffed. "Well, that's alright, then. Carry on."

The Professor's gaze was flitting between them both, never settling on one for long, like he was worried the other might attack him when he wasn't looking.

"Don't listen to her," Hoon said, directing his attention back to the man in the armchair. "I'm not going to cut your bollocks off. Not unless I really have to, and I'm sure it won't come to that."

He shuffled his chair a little closer. Made his smile a little friendlier.

"Here's what we're going to do, in order to ensure all your bits and bobs remain attached. We're going to have ourselves a wee pub quiz. You been to a pub quiz before?"

The Professor said nothing. From across the room, Berta let out an impatient sigh and heaved herself to her feet. She produced a pair of scissors as she hurried over, and snipped at the air with them.

"Oh, for fuck's sake, let me have a crack at him."

"*Mmmph! Mmmph!*" The hostage hurriedly shook his head, eyes bulging like he was trying to telepathically implant his response in Hoon's head.

Hoon held a hand up to stop his sister, but kept his gaze locked on the Professor.

"You've never done a fucking pub quiz?"

Another shake of the head, a little less frantic this time.

"Jesus Christ. What, never?"

"What about a Karaoke?" Berta chipped in. "Ask him if he's done a Karaoke."

"What the fuck does it matter if he's done...?" Hoon sighed, pinched the bridge of his nose, then relayed the question to the man in the chair.

Yet again, the Professor shook his head.

"He's a bastarding liar!" Berta announced, then she lunged with the scissors, drawing a yelp of fright from the Professor, who was only saved by a last-second intervention from Hoon.

"Just give me them fucking things and go and sit on your arse!" Bob barked, wrenching the scissors from Berta's hand. "You nearly had his fucking eye out there. Poor bastard's already down a nose."

Berta glowered at her younger brother, and Hoon brought his hands up, ready to protect himself from an unexpected pinch, punch, flick, or other sudden outburst of violence.

It proved unnecessary, though, and she returned to her seat with only a snarl and some light muttering, then lowered herself carefully back down onto it again.

Hoon twirled the scissors around on one finger, then pointed the sharp end in the Professor's direction.

"Right, where were we? Pub quiz. OK. Well, it's a pretty fucking pointless analogy now, so let's scrap that. Think of it like... a game show. You've seen a fucking game show, aye?"

The Professor nodded this time, and Hoon gave the scissors another celebratory twirl.

"Now we're fucking getting somewhere!" he said. "So, this is like a game show. But, instead of winning money, or holidays, or caravans, or whatever, you win your own body parts. There's no gimmicks, or anything. No fifty-fifty, or phone a friend. I'd say you could ask the audience, but I don't think she's really on your side, to be honest, so I probably wouldn't bother. Totally your call, though."

Hoon stood up enough to allow him to reach into his pocket. He produced the little notebook that Berta had found in a drawer, and unclipped the stubby wee pencil from the top. He placed them both on the Professor's knee, so that he'd be able to reach them, even tied as he was.

"Right, then, question one. The woman you were with. Called herself Suranne. Who the fuck is she?" Hoon asked. He tapped the scissors on the back of the chair, and pointed to the floor. "And, just so there's no confusion, in this round, you're playing for your toes..."

———

A couple of hours, a lot of questions, and a disappointing lack of amputations later, Hoon stood down at the shore, watching the water of Loch Nevis licking across the white sand. Berta's little powerboat, *The Dirty Slapper*, bobbed up and down at the end of a short jetty.

The engine looked relatively new, but the rest of the boat appeared to be unchanged from when he'd last seen it. That could've been his imagination, of course. With the rainy summers and bitter winters around here, it would be a miracle if the wooden hull had stayed intact for that long.

He picked up a stone, turned it over in his hand until he found the flattest edge, and skimmed it out across the water. His record was eleven hops. Today, he barely managed four.

The Professor hadn't needed a lot of motivation once he'd got started. He'd scribbled down answers to all of Hoon's questions, with only the occasional reminder about the scissors needed to keep him focused.

Berta had been very disappointed at that. She'd particularly been looking forward to finding out what Hoon had planned to use the blocks of wood for, and was gutted that she never got the chance.

The only problem was, none of the answers really helped him. He knew a bit more about Suranne—her real name, he insisted, though Hoon found that hard to believe—but otherwise he hadn't really known what questions to ask.

He'd asked if the Loop would keep coming for him, and the Professor had answered with just a single word scratched onto the paper.

'Always.'

Hoon had known that would be the case, but seeing it in black and white still made his heart sink a little. Up here, miles from anywhere, it was easy to believe he had escaped. That he was free.

But that word on that paper told him he'd never be free. They'd find him, sooner or later, and there was fuck all he could do about it.

Without naming names, he'd asked if the Loop was after anyone else in connection with him. The Professor had scrawled down the name 'Miles Crabtree,' and nothing else. Hoon had prompted him to continue, but he'd underlined Miles' name and left it there.

If the bastard was telling the truth, then it meant that Gabriella wasn't a target, and neither were Greig and his family.

After that, nothing he had to ask seemed all that important.

There was only one other question he really wanted to know the answer to, but it wasn't one the Professor could help him with. It wasn't one that anyone could help him with.

"What the fuck do I do now?" he muttered, and the wind stole the words from his mouth, and carried them off across the bay.

"Bobby!"

Berta's voice snapped him out of his stupor. He turned from the Loch to find her leaning out of the kitchen window, beckoning him inside.

"Soup!"

"Aye, just coming," he told her.

Before he started back towards the house, he plucked another stone from the shore, spun around, and sent it skimming across the surface of the water with a *plip-plip-splish.*

"Bollocks," he grunted.

And with that, he headed inside.

CHAPTER TWENTY-SIX

HOON STOPPED in the kitchen doorway, unable to believe his eyes. He turned to his sister, who was ladling soup into bowls from an enormous blackened pot on the stove.

Three bowls, to be precise.

"What the fuck's he doing here?" Hoon demanded.

At the table, the Professor sat staring down at a place mat that had been set out in front of him. The ropes that had bound him to the armchair in the chalet now secured him to a dining chair, instead.

"He's got to eat," Berta said. "Can't have him starving to death, can we?"

Hoon stormed over to her. "Then he can eat out there! You do know the cunt tortured me, aye?"

Berta wheeled around and hit him on the top of the head with the ladle. It was hot, and covered in soup, and made a hollow *clonk* as it struck him.

"Ow! Christ!"

"We don't use that word in this house, Robert Hoon!" she scolded. "That word despises women."

Hoon stared at her, rubbing the top of his head, and inadvertently massaging soup into his scalp.

"Aye, well, I'm starting to know how it fucking feels," he muttered, then he backed off when Berta shooed him towards the table.

He took his seat across from the Professor, leaving the head of the table free for Berta. Only then, when he was seated, did he allow himself to fully appreciate the aroma that filled the kitchen.

If the sight of the house and his disappointing stone skiffing down on the beach had triggered a few memories, then the smell of Berta's soup brought the rest of them rushing back like an avalanche.

Suddenly, he was four again, back in the old house, waiting for his mum and new baby sibling to come home, blissfully unaware that only one of them ever would.

Suddenly, he was five, sitting on the step of the old back garden, listening to Berta and their dad shouting inside, while Roxie screamed in the bedroom upstairs.

Suddenly, he was ten, sitting here in this room, reciting his times tables while one sister prepared the dinner, and the other drew rainbows with her crayons, each one beautiful, despite being all the wrong colours. Or perhaps because of that.

And then, suddenly, he was back here, with the ravaged face of a killer regarding him with nervous curiosity.

"The fuck you looking at?" Hoon asked, and the Professor quickly averted his gaze.

Bowls were deposited in front of them with little in the way of care or ceremony. The soup slopping around inside them was the same kind as Berta always made, though no two servings were ever quite the same.

It was always vegetable soup, but made with stock from a ham hock, or the boiled up remains of a chicken. The actual vegetables in it always varied, depending on the time of year, and what she had to hand. Neeps, leeks, and onions were usually guaranteed. After that, it was anyone's guess.

Today's serving included big lumps of partially blitzed carrot, and what looked like chunks of parsnip. There was never any point asking Berta what the ingredients were, because the only response you'd get was, "Vegetables, obviously," or, if she was in a particularly foul mood, a clip round the ear.

Hoon had been shocked when he'd first ordered soup from a wee cafe in Glasgow, shortly after he'd moved there to find work. He'd even brought it back up to the counter to complain, as the stuff he'd been given had been liquid, whereas the soup he was used to erred more towards being a solid. Berta's soup was all big mushy lumps with just a wee runny drizzle at the bottom of the bowl that might as well have been a dollop of sauce.

"You not having any?" Hoon asked as Berta set about the washing up.

"Well, I'm not going to sit and eat looking at his face, am I?" she replied. "Turn my fucking stomach, that would."

Hoon picked up his spoon and set about the contents of his bowl. Years of alcohol and dodgy kebabs had dulled his taste buds, but he would've sworn that the soup tasted *exactly* like the stuff from his childhood.

Across the table, the Professor looked longingly at his bowl, his mouth opening and closing like he might be able to will it into his mouth.

"What you need is one of them big fucking insect tongues, pal," Hoon said, smooshing some soggy turnip between his back teeth. "You'd be hoovering it up by now."

Berta looked back over her shoulder, tutted, then dried her hands on a tea towel.

"Oh, for fuck's sake. Here."

She snatched the other spoon off the table, scooped up some

of the soup, then inserted it into the Professor's open mouth. He grimaced in pain as he swallowed it down.

"Oh, grow up. It's not that bloody hot!" Berta said, preparing another spoonful.

Hoon picked up a piece of bread from the table, tore a chunk off, and used it to point at the prisoner's scars.

"Think it's his throat being all fucked up that's the problem," Hoon said. He held the other man's gaze and smiled. "From when I put the chair leg through it." He dunked the bread in the soup. "Remember that? When I bit off your nose and nearly killed you?"

"No work talk at the dinner table, Bobby."

"It's hardly fucking work talk!" Hoon protested, but a warning look from his sister shut him down before he pushed it any further.

Instead, he just watched her shovel another spoon of soup into the Professor's open mouth, and shook his head in disgust.

"This'd better no' turn into some weird romantic thing," he said. "Like Beauty and the Beast, only with two Beasts and none of the fucking Beauty."

"What, me and him?" Berta yelped. "Fuck off! He looks like a fucking wasp's nest cut in half. He should be so bloody lucky!" She rested a hand on his shoulder, said, "No offence," then dropped the spoon back into the bowl.

"What are you doing?" Hoon asked when Berta went around to the back of the prisoner's chair and started messing with the ropes.

"I'm untying him so he can eat."

"You can't fucking untie him!"

The ropes fell slack. Berta shrugged. "Well, I just have, so evidently I can."

"He's fucking dangerous!"

"Yes, well, so am I, as I'm sure you'll attest. I'm sure,

between us, we can keep him in check long enough for him to eat some fucking soup. Don't you?"

Hoon *harrumphed*, but quietly, so that his sister didn't pick up on it. "Aye, well, we're fucking tying him up again afterwards," he said. "And until I figure out what we're doing with the dead-eyed sack of *Muppet* shite, he's staying locked up in that fucking cabin."

————

Once the soup had been polished off, and the Professor returned to 'that fucking cabin,' Hoon prowled through the rest of the house, memories lunging at him from every cobwebbed corner.

There was the burn mark on the carpet from when he'd dropped a candle during one of the many power cuts. There were the markings on the wall, tracking his and Roxie's changing heights.

And there was the mirror, in its gilded frame, that he and Berta had both stopped to check themselves in before heading out the door for their younger sister's funeral.

Berta had tutted and fussed as she'd fixed his tie for him. Then, as they'd stood making the final checks of their reflections, her hand had slipped into his. Not for long. Just for a few seconds. But in that moment, without uttering a single word, she said all the things she had always wanted to say, but had never been able to bring herself to.

It had been a flying visit for the funeral. He'd barely been in the house for fifteen minutes, and when he and Berta had walked out through the front door together, he was of the firm belief that'd he'd never return again.

And yet, here he was, standing beneath a bare bulb in the hallway, directly outside what it now occurred to him was his old bedroom. He didn't really need to look. He would've known where he was in the house with his eyes shut, the familiar creaks from the floorboards, and the wear pattern on the carpet would've allowed him to navigate the place with his eyes shut.

Not just the house, either. *Westward* sat on nine acres of land, and he'd explored every last inch of them a hundred times over. There were places in the world he knew well—Glasgow, Inverness, he was even starting to get a handle on London—but this place he knew better than he knew himself.

Better than anyone.

He realised he was staring at his old bedroom door now, but not really looking. Not really seeing it. Instead, his mind was racing with possibilities. With thoughts of bloodied noses.

And of last stands.

There were a handful of ways to get to the house, all of them exposed. From a decent vantage point, he'd be able to see anyone approaching.

He could think of three such positions right off the top of his head.

There were a lot of hiding places, if you knew where to look. The chalets were obvious. The stretch of woods that ran up the hillside to the back of the house was too.

But there were ditches and hidey-holes, and places no one else knew about.

Anyone wandering into that blind could quickly find themselves deep in the shit.

He'd thought about taking the fight to them in London, even though he knew that would be suicide. Here, though, he had something those bastards didn't.

Here, he had home advantage.

Hoon turned away from his old bedroom door without opening it. He found Berta in the back garden, hanging out the washing, and she watched his approach like she could see the change in him, and wasn't sure if she approved.

"What now?" she asked. "What are you up to?"

Hoon stopped on the other side of the washing line. A half-pegged sheet flapped loosely between them, like it was trying to shoo him off.

"You got any guns around the place?" he asked.

Berta snorted. "Guns? What sort of a question is that to ask your sister?" she demanded. "Of course I've got fucking guns. There's a couple of twelve-bores in the house. Why?"

"Two shotguns. Couple of pistols. That's not enough," Hoon muttered. "That's no' nearly enough."

"For what?" Berta asked. "What are you planning?"

"Give them a bloody nose. That's what you said," Hoon replied. "That's what I'd planned, down in London, but it would've got me killed. But here?" He gestured around them. "Here, I could do it. Bring those snatch-eyed shite-jugglers here, and I could fucking do it. No' just bloody their noses, but cut off their ears and feed them to them up their arses. I fucking know this place. They don't. I bring them here, fight them my way, on my fucking territory, and they've no' got a chance."

Berta drew herself up to her full height, and Hoon had to fight the urge to duck and cover.

"What are you saying, Bobby?" she scoffed. "That you want to turn this place—turn my home—into a bloody warzone?"

"Uh, aye. Aye, I suppose that is what I'm saying," Hoon admitted.

Berta finished pegging up the wayward sheet. When she stepped out from behind it, her face was fixed in a grim smile.

"I thought you'd never fucking ask."

CHAPTER TWENTY-SEVEN

THE DIRTY SLAPPER churned its way up Loch Nevis, leaving the jetty of *Westward* somewhere far back in its foaming wake. The boat wasn't a particularly speedy thing—just over twice a brisk walking pace—but it let him take the most direct route to Mallaig, and stay off the roads. The van, with its fake plates, was safely tucked away in the little car park. Take it out in public, and there was a risk of him being rumbled before he was ready.

Getting ready was the purpose of this little jaunt. The boat wasn't fast enough to get him all the way to his destination in any sort of timely manner, but it would get him to Mallaig, and from there, he could get the ferry across to Skye.

He'd already put a call in to Iris from Berta's landline. Iris hadn't answered, but then that was no surprise. Hoon knew the protocol, and had left a message on the answering machine, taking care to make sure the recipient fully grasped the urgency of the situation.

The sun was shining, which was a rare treat, though it had started to wane towards the hilltops in the west, and the wind coming in across the loch was quick to steal away any warmth it might have offered. Berta had given him an old jumper of hers to wear on the trip, partly to keep him warm, but mostly to, "Cover up that fucking awful T-shirt."

He'd initially refused, as it was far too big for him, but she'd insisted, and now he was grateful for it, as the wind continued to swirl, and the cold set about him.

Still, the scenery made up for it—the oaks and Scots pines gathered like onlookers along the shore, the rolling mountains far off on his right, and the vast, still expanse of the loch itself, where white horses galloped alongside the boat.

Chugging along there on the water, not another soul to be seen, he could almost have allowed himself to forget his troubles, to convince himself that everything that had happened in the last few months had been a bad—and at times completely fucking ludicrous—dream.

He could almost have done all of that.

Almost, but not quite.

It took him the better part of an hour to reach Mallaig, where he tied up the *Slapper* and climbed a rusted metal ladder up onto the docks. The last ferry was still loading up, and he was able to grab himself a foot passenger ticket before the cars were all aboard.

There were half a dozen other foot passengers milling around on the upper deck when he reached it. He took a moment to appraise them, making sure none of them were there to kill him. Given that most of them were women over sixty, he thought it was unlikely.

He relaxed a little, and stood breathing in the smell of diesel and salt, watching the seagulls circling overhead, their beady eyes scanning the dock below. Hoon followed their gazes and saw some unwitting bugger emerging from the chippie, already in the process of unwrapping the paper from around his food.

Poor bastard.

Hoon thought about shouting a warning, but knew it would be too late. Instead, he watched in quiet amusement as the bag was unwrapped, and a dozen gulls immediately dive-bombed it, screeching furiously, their wings beating in the terrified man's face, their beaks hungrily snapping at the steaming hot chips.

With a strangled cry of fright, the would-be chip-eater abandoned the lot to the gulls, and ran for cover. By the time he had made it ten yards, the pavement swarmed with grey and white bodies, and rang out with the *clacking* of beaks.

"Aye, they don't call it 'Seagull City' for nothing," Hoon remarked, then the ferry blasted its horn, and set off over the sea to Skye.

———

Iris, like Berta, lived off the beaten track. Hoon hitched a lift from the ferry terminal at Armadale, and got off a few miles north at the turn-off for Ord, thanking the elderly couple who had given him the lift, and taking a moment to pat their elderly terrier who had taken an immediate shine to him.

From there, Hoon set off up a narrow, single-lane road, flanked by towering Scots pines on both sides. He hiked for a couple of miles, keeping his head down and standing aside whenever a vehicle approached, then setting off again the moment it passed.

After thirty-five minutes of walking, he reached a foot-tall stack of rocks at the side of the road. The cairn had been built and rebuilt countless times over the years, Hoon knew, its proximity to such a narrow road putting it in a state of constant jeopardy.

He hung a sharp right there, and headed into the trees. Brown pine needles crunched softly underfoot as he entered the darkening forest. The texture of the sound changed around him, the branches diffusing the wind, while at the same time adding their own haunting melody of creaks and groans. It felt like stepping into another world, and something about it made him realise, all of a sudden, how tired he was.

As he trudged through the woods, he tried to remember when he'd last slept. There had been the nightmare at Welshy and Gabriella's. Was that just the night before?

No, he'd been driving the van the night before. Two nights ago, then, and even then he'd only been able to snatch a few disturbed hours. And it wasn't like he'd exactly been sleeping well in the weeks and months prior to that.

The exhaustion dragged at his feet, each step harder than the one before. The ground looked soft and welcoming, and he almost contemplated stopping for a few moments to take a seat. To lie down, maybe, just for a few minutes. Just to catch his breath. Just to get his bearings.

A burst of movement in the woods beside him snapped his heavy eyelids open. He turned, fists raised, to find he was being watched.

"Fuck off, you squirrelly wee bastard," he snapped, and the creature scampered up the tree it was clinging to, then vanished into the branches above.

The jolt of adrenaline, brief as it was, kept him awake and focused enough to find Iris's place. It was a low, grey stone bunker with moss on the walls and grass growing on the sloping roof. If you weren't looking for it, you'd walk right by it. You might even do that if you *were* looking for it, as Hoon discovered. Twice.

It was a tripwire that gave it away. He spotted the line strung between two trees, only just in time to clumsily step over it without setting it off. Hoon couldn't see what it was connected to. It might be some pots and pans, set up to rattle when a potential intruder entered the area, or some C4, primed to blow them to smithereens. You never knew with Iris.

Though, it was usually the latter.

Once Hoon knew he was in the right area, finding the actual bunker was easy. Hoon picked his way carefully to the front door—the only door, in fact—then hammered on the metal with the heel of his hand.

"Iris! It's me. Open up."

There was silence from inside for a few moments, then a nasal voice with a Scouse accent piped up, "I can't let you in. You need to do the code-knock first."

Hoon sighed. "I'm no' doing the fucking code knock. You know it's me, ya daft bastard. I know you've got fucking cameras watching me."

He turned and raised a middle finger to the surrounding trees. He couldn't see any cameras, but they'd be there somewhere. Hoon was probably being recorded from at least three different angles.

"How do I know it's you if you don't do the code knock?" Iris asked from the other side of the door.

"Because I've got my fucking face and voice," Hoon said.

Iris let out a derisory "Ha!" from inside the bunker. "I'm not falling for that. They might've cloned you," he said. A floorboard creaked. His voice became softer, but closer. "They can do that, you know? They can totally do that. I've seen them with my own two eyes."

"You haven't fucking got two eyes, ya mad bastard!" Hoon barked. "Now hurry up and open the fucking door!"

There was a lengthy silence, before Iris finally replied.

"Bit harsh."

Hoon buried his face in his hands. "What the fuck am I doing?" he muttered, then he sighed, raised a fist, and rattled off a complex series of knocks.

Nothing happened.

"Right, I fucking did it! Open the door!"

"You missed one," Iris told him.

Hoon's fists and jaw all clenched. "Just open the fucking—"

There was a weighty *clunk* from inside, then the door swung open to reveal a short, scrawny man dressed in combat fatigues. He was bald up top, but rocked a ring of wild white hair around the sides and the back of his head, giving him the mad scientist vibe that he'd always aspired to.

One eye bored into Hoon as they came face to face, the other apparently more interested in checking out his own nose.

It was a stray bit of shrapnel that had taken Iris's right eye, and the glass one he'd had ever since always seemed to have a mind of its own. Every time Hoon looked at it, it seemed to be pointing in a different direction, and never the same direction as Iris's actual eye, either.

Most people assumed the nickname had come about as a result of the injury, but Iris had been Iris long before then. The name had been given to him by one of the NCOs during basic training. None of them had quite understood it, until it was eventually explained that Iris was an acronym.

Once someone had gone on to also explain what an acronym was, Iris was informed that it stood for, 'I Require Intense Supervision.' It had not, of course, been meant as a compliment, but he'd worn it as a badge of honour ever since.

"That you, Boggle?" Iris asked.

"No, it's a government fucking space lizard wearing my skin," Hoon retorted. He sighed when he saw the look of alarm on the other man's face. "Of course it's fucking me. I phoned ahead."

"Did you use the code word?" Iris asked, then he yelped and danced back when Hoon shoved his way into the bunker.

"Out the fucking road. My feet are killing me," Hoon told him.

He flopped down onto a padded bench that ran most of the length of one wall. Three screens were fixed to the wall opposite, each showing a different angle on the bunker. Hoon watched one as the door was closed again, and a slow *sssh-kukt* told him some sort of vacuum seal was engaging.

"Sorry about that, Boggle," Iris said, turning away from the door. His movements were fast and fidgety, like a mouse sensing danger. "You know what they say, though."

"That you're a fucking headcase?" Hoon replied. "Aye, I've heard that, right enough."

Iris giggled. "Good one. Good one. But no. They say, 'You can't be too careful.' That's what they say."

"Clearly, the people who say that have never met you," Hoon told him. "Or they'd say, 'You can't be too careful, unless you live in an airtight bunker in the middle of fucking nowhere, obviously, in which case, you definitely fucking can.' I mean, you didn't really think I was a clone, did you? Surely you're no' that far fucking gone?"

Iris let out a laugh that was all in the nose. "Nah, course not, Boggle. No way their cloning tanks would be able to handle you!"

Hoon momentarily considered delving deeper into the subject, then concluded that he didn't have the energy. Instead, he spat out his reason for coming.

"I need guns, Iris," he said. "And explosives."

Iris sat on the bench and slid closer. His good eye studied Hoon. His glass one, meanwhile, looked down at the carpet.

"Oh yeah? What sort of thing?" he asked.

Hoon had been giving it some thought on the boat over, and went through his current wish list.

"Sniper rifle. L115A, ideally, but anything with a bit of range and penetration power. Thermal sight's a must."

"You want to shoot through body armour or vehicles?" Iris asked.

"Armour. They'll be on foot."

Iris double-tapped the side of his head, like he was locking in the selection. "What else?"

"Two or three SMGs. Couple of assault rifles—"

"SA8os?" Iris suggested, then both men laughed.

"No. Preferably something that fucking works when you want it to," Hoon said.

"M16, maybe?"

Hoon nodded. "I wouldn't complain."

Iris double-tapped his temple four times, with a tiny break between the second and third.

"I've got a couple of pistols, but a few more wouldn't go amiss," Hoon continued. "And then whatever explosives you can get your hands on."

Even Iris's glass eye seemed to light up at that. "Now you're talking my language!"

It was impressive that Iris had managed to retain his love of explosives, considering the shrapnel that had cost him his eye had been entirely self-inflicted.

"Anything you think I've missed?" Hoon asked.

Iris pressed his finger to the side of his head. He looked up, like he was reading the list he'd stored up there. His glass eye, for once, looked directly at Hoon.

"Depends. Are you overthrowing a small country?" he asked.

Hoon shook his head. "Just holding my own against a handful of bastards."

Iris dropped his hand to his side and did that nose-laugh of his again. "Well, then the good news is, I think that should cover you," he said.

"That implies there's some bad news," Hoon pointed out.

"Yes. There is," Iris admitted. "I don't have any of that stuff."

Hoon scowled. "For fu... Why didn't you say that at the start, then?" he demanded.

"You seemed to be in the flow. I didn't want to interrupt."

"You were interrupting every two fucking seconds!" Hoon

pointed out. He took a breath, quelling his building anger. "Fine. Fine. Just tell me what you do have."

"Nothing," Iris replied.

Hoon stared at him. He partly stared back.

"What the fuck do you mean, 'nothing'? You must have something. You've always got fucking something."

Iris shook his head. "Sorry, Boggle. I got ripped off. Totally cleaned out."

"Fuck's sake! When? Who by?"

"Serious lads, Boggle. Proper big boys, from Peterhead."

Hoon snorted. "You can't use 'proper big boys,' and, 'from Peterhead,' in the same fucking sentence. That's a fucking contradiction in terms, unless you mean their fucking waistlines."

Iris pulled an exaggerated shrug, holding his hands out, palms up, like he was trying to weigh a giant's testicles. "That's just what I heard. Think they supply some terrorist outfit somewhere. Or drug barons, or something. Either way, they're coining it in."

He slid a little closer along the bench, and both eyes checked different corners of the room, like they were worried someone might be hiding there, listening in.

"It's not just me they ripped off. From what I hear, they've got everything you asked for, and a lot more to boot. They only did me over a couple of days back. I reckon, if me and you were to go up there and put our heads together, we could take it all back. Me and you, Boggle. Like the old days."

Hoon glowered back at him. "You mean like the old days where you nearly got us killed on a regular fucking basis? Them old days?"

"Exactly!" Iris said, completely failing to pick up on the sarcasm. "Me and you, together again, cracking heads and taking names."

"The only fucking head you've ever cracked is your own, you skelly-eyed belter."

Iris slid further along the bench until he was shoulder to shoulder with his house guest. "You know what I mean, though. And you know I'm right, Boggle. You need those guns. I want my stuff back. Help me, and I'll sort you out with everything you need."

"Free of charge," Hoon said.

"At a generous discount," Iris replied.

Hoon said nothing. He didn't need to.

"OK, five free items, and credit for the rest," Iris said. "Can't do better than that, Boggle. These are difficult times we find ourselves in."

"It'd better be interest-free credit."

"A very attractive percentage," Iris countered. "Have you seen the inflation rate lately? I mean, yeah, the government—the world government, I mean, not that shower of yes-men down in Westminster—they set the rate, and money doesn't even exist, but still."

He gave a, 'What can you do?' sort of shrug, then spat on his hand and offered it out for Hoon to shake.

Hoon regarded it, but didn't yet accept the offer. "Do we know what we're walking into?"

"Ah, they're nobodies. Nothing you and me can't handle."

"You said they were serious," Hoon reminded him. "You said they were 'proper big boys.'"

"They're from Peterhead, Boggle," Iris said. "They're a joke. Me and you'd wipe the floor with them. Not that we even have to, mind you. We won't even need to see them."

"How come?" Hoon asked.

Iris pressed the side of his head. He gestured at an empty patch of air in front of them, like he was showing something written there. "Because I know where they're storing it all.

Quick job. You, me, and my van, and all your dreams come true."

He spat on his hand a second time, because apparently once wasn't lubrication enough.

"You in?"

Hoon sighed. "Christ," he muttered, then he pressed his hand into Iris's, much to the other man's obvious delight. "Aye. I'm in."

CHAPTER TWENTY-EIGHT

THE HIKE BACK out of the woods was made in near darkness, with only the glow from Iris's head torch to pick out the route. Fortunately, he knew exactly where he was going, and after just five or six minutes of traipsing through the forest, they emerged at a stretch of road Hoon had never seen before, but which he guessed was a little further along from the cairn where he'd turned off earlier.

A white *Ford Transit* van was parked in a layby, the livery for a plumbing company emblazoned across both sides, complete with an email address and phone number.

"You branching out from arms dealing?" Hoon asked as they clambered into the front of the vehicle.

"Cover story, innit?" Iris replied. "Real company, too. Not from around here, mind, but phone number and email address both work. Helps sell it if anyone starts digging around. It's a win-win. They get free advertising, I get to stay off the radar of you know who."

He pointed upwards and made some suggestive shapes with his eyebrows. Hoon elected not to pursue it any further.

"Aye, handy that," he said. He clipped on his seat belt and yawned. "How long until we get there?"

Iris's face contorted with the effort of calculation. "Well, we'll go across the bridge, through Inverness, out towards Aberdeen until... what? Huntly? Or before then? Keith, maybe?"

Hoon shut him down before he could go any further. "I wasn't asking for the fucking turn-by-turn navigation, Iris. Just an ETA'll do."

"About... four-and-a-half to five hours, thereabouts?"

"Are you telling me, or asking me?" Hoon asked. "Because it sounds like you're asking me, and I fucking asked you first."

"About that," Iris said, with a fraction more confidence.

Hoon crossed his arms and angled himself towards the door. "Right. Good. I'm going to sleep."

"Sleep?! You can't sleep, Boggle. We've got catching up to do!"

Hoon closed his eyes. "That can fucking wait. This can't," he said.

Iris started the engine. "Alright, fine. If that's what you want, Boggle."

Hoon didn't respond.

"Boggle?"

Still nothing. Iris reached over and gave him a nudge.

"Boggle?"

"For fuck's sake! What?!" Hoon barked, whipping his head around to shoot the other man a warning look.

"You alright with me driving?"

Hoon's face turned a shade of puce, like he might be about to explode. "Well, you're the one with the fucking steering wheel, so aye. I'm alright with it. I'm more than fucking alright with it, in fact. So, away we go."

"Right. Yeah. OK." Iris pointed from himself to the road ahead. "It's just, you know, depth perception's not great."

Hoon groaned. "Aw, Jesus. Aye. Fair point," He gave it but a moment's thought, then shrugged and settled down again. "Fuck it. If we die, we die," he said, then he closed his eyes as the van pulled away, and willingly surrendered to some long overdue sleep.

———

Hoon woke just twice on the journey across to the northeast, despite Iris's near-constant narration detailing every turn and rise in the road.

The first time he'd opened his eyes had been when the van was passing the roundabout at Inverness's Eastfield Retail Park. Hoon had immediately spotted the illuminated signage for the *Tesco* superstore, where he now held the record for the briefest spell of employment.

He'd stayed away just long enough to note that a lot had happened in his life since then, but not long enough to actually dwell on any of it. Still, fleeting as the job had been, it would always mark a boundary between his old life and his new one, he knew. The Bob Hoon who'd rocked up for that security guard gig had no idea about the fate of Caroline Gascoine, or the Loop, or any of that stuff.

"Lucky bastard," he'd slurred, and then his head had fallen back onto his arm, and he'd been snoring again in moments.

The second time he woke up was when the horn of an oncoming vehicle blared at them just outside Banff, and Hoon had found Iris frantically correcting the steering after nodding off at the wheel.

A burst of swearing and a quick seat change later, and they were back on the road, with a partially refreshed Hoon driving the final stretch.

Iris, despite having almost fallen asleep, seemed wide awake now that he was on the passenger side of the vehicle, and Hoon found himself wondering if the bastard had staged the whole thing.

"You're looking older, Boggle," he announced. Hoon shot him a sideways look, and saw the glass eye looking up at the roof above his head. "I was checking you out when you were sleeping."

"You creepy fuck," Hoon spat. "What do you mean you were checking me out?"

"I just meant I was looking at you. I wasn't touching you up or anything, if that's what you're thinking," Iris replied.

Hoon did a double-take. "Well, I wasn't, but I'm starting to fucking wonder now." He faced front again. The van's headlights cut trenches through the darkness ahead, revealing a long, empty road. "And you're no' exactly ageing gracefully yourself, you wrinkly old bastard. You've got more lines than a fucking *Ordnance Survey* map, and I see you and your hair have long-since parted ways."

"Good riddance!" Iris replied. He ran a hand across his shiny domed head. "It was just a load of hassle. Never behaved itself. Going left, going right, lying flat, sticking up, you couldn't predict it, Boggle. I for one am glad it's gone. And all the ladies love a bald guy, don't they?"

"Oh aye, I can imagine them all queuing up to visit you in your creepy fucking bunker in the woods."

Iris chose to ignore that remark. "All the top sexy guys are bald, aren't they? The Rock. Um... Who else is there?"

"What the fuck are you asking me for? You're the one making the point."

"Bruce whatshisname," Iris said.

"Forsyth?"

"No! Of course not Bruce Forsyth! Bruce Forsyth wasn't bald!"

It was Hoon's turn to almost crash the van, when he tore his eyes from the road to shoot the man in the passenger seat a look of disbelief. He tightened his grip on the wheel before responding. "What are you talking about? Bruce Forsyth? Of course he was fucking bald!"

"Was he bollocks! He had hair!" Iris insisted, pointing to his own head for emphasis. "He had loads of hair! He had too much hair, if anything."

"What are you...? That was a wig! You didn't really think that was his actual real hair? He'd have to have come down from fucking outer space. It's no' humanly possible to grow hair in that shape."

"Why would he wear a wig, though?" Iris asked, and he seemed genuinely bewildered by the very notion of it.

"Well, I'd imagine so that no bastard knew he was bald," Hoon guessed.

Iris ran his hand over his head again, this time drumming the fingers so they all got a turn at feeling his shiny scalp. "Why would you do that, though? All the ladies love a bald guy."

Hoon sighed and shook his head. "I feel like I'm stuck in a fucking time loop here," he muttered.

"Anyway, you're pretty much bald, Boggle."

"Am I fuck. I shave my head. That's very different." He leaned over and pointed at his scalp. "See? Shaved. No' bald. Big fucking difference."

His point made, he went back to driving.

Silence fell for a while. Hoon yawned and thumbed each of his eyes in turn, clearing away the crusts of sleep. They couldn't be far away from Peterhead now. Ten miles. Maybe less.

"Willis," Iris said.

Hoon frowned. "What?"

"Bruce Willis. That's who I was thinking of. Not Bruce Forsyth. You know? From *Die Hard* 2."

"Aye," Hoon muttered. He drove on a little while further. His fingers began to tap out a beat on the wheel. It was no use, he couldn't hold it in. "Why *Die Hard* 2?" he asked.

Iris frowned. "What?"

"Why say he was in *Die Hard* 2? Why no' just say he was in *Die Hard*?"

Iris shrugged. "Haven't seen it. Is he in that one, as well?"

Hoon exhaled slowly through his nose, shut his eyes for as long as he dared, then gave a tiny shake of his head. "Doesn't matter. But aye, of course he fucking is. But, doesn't matter. We're nearly at Peterhead. Where am I going when we get there?"

"The harbour," Iris told him.

"It's Peterhead. It's pretty much all fucking harbour. Which bit?"

Both of Iris's eyes looked in different directions. Notably, neither of those directions was the one Hoon was in.

"Don't tell me you don't fucking know!" Hoon cried. "You said you knew where they were storing the guns!"

"I do!" Iris insisted. "They're storing them at—"

Hoon removed a hand from the wheel and jabbed a finger right under the other man's nose.

"If you say 'the harbour,' I'll launch you through this fucking windscreen."

Iris swallowed. "The *docks*," he concluded, then he flinched like he thought Hoon was about to hit him.

He was correct. Hoon thumped him hard on the right thigh, and Iris clutched at it, yelping in pain.

"Aah! Dead leg! Dead leg!"

The van's tyres squealed as Hoon pulled into a layby at speed, then stamped on the brake until the vehicle skidded to a halt.

"You're lucky it's just your fucking leg!" Hoon hissed. "Are you telling me we've driven all this way for fucking nothing?"

"No!" Iris protested. "And, to be fair, I drove most of it, anyway, so—"

He buckled when another punch hit him in exactly the same spot as the last one.

"Ow! Jesus, stop doing that!" Iris cried, squashing himself right up against the passenger door, as far out of Hoon's reach as it was possible to be without leaving the van. "I can find it, don't worry. I've got a sixth sense for this sort of thing, trust me!" He clicked his fingers and pointed at the man in the driver's seat. "*Sixth Sense*. That's another one. Bruce Willis. You seen that one?"

Hoon balled all ten fingers into fists, and Iris almost merged with the metal and glass of the door in his attempt to get away.

"Alright, alright! Easy, big man!" he said. "All we've got to do is go to the harbour and drive around a bit. I'll know it when I see it."

"And what if the fucking polis sees us?"

"What if they do?" Iris asked.

"You don't think that might look just a wee bit suspicious?" Hoon spat. "Two guys in a fucking plumber's van prowling the harbour area in the middle of the night?"

"What's suspicious about that?"

"Well, hang on, let me think..." Hoon rubbed his chin for a second, before spitting out the answer. "Oh, aye, fucking everything!"

Iris shook his head. "Nah, they won't think anything of it," he insisted. "They'll probably just think we're on the hunt for a couple of prostitutes."

"Jesus Christ. That was the point I was trying to fucking..."

Not for the first time that night, Hoon buried his face in his hands. He ejected a cry that sat balanced on the knife-edge between anger and exasperation, then gripped the wheel again until his knuckles turned white.

"Right, fine. I mean, there's fuck all else we can do now, anyway," Hoon muttered. "But, see if this is a complete waste of time, Iris? You'll have no fucking eyes left by the time the night's over." He shook his head quite forcefully. "In fact, no. No. You'll have *half* an eye left. That's how fucking raging I'll be. I'll no' even take it all out in one fucking go. I'll fucking peck it away, bit by bastard bit."

Iris's shaky smile became a big, confident grin. "Relax, Boggle. No need to get yourself all wound up, mate. Uncle Iris has got it all in hand. I'm on it." He clapped his hands, rubbed them together, then pointed to the road ahead. "Fraserburgh, here we come!"

Hoon's head snapped around. "*Fraserburgh?!*"

"What?"

"You said fucking Fraserburgh!"

Iris frowned. "So?"

"We're no' going to Fraserburgh!"

The smile remained fixed, but Iris's good eye began to look a little worried. The other one, however, wasn't getting involved. He swallowed. Again.

"Peterhead, I meant," he replied. "It's definitely Peterhead." He made a weighing motion with both hands, and squashed himself even harder against the passenger side door. "What if I said I was ninety-five percent sure?"

"I'd punch you so hard in the teeth that they'd come firing out your ears like fucking popcorn," Hoon replied.

Iris nodded. "Well, in that case, I'm a hundred percent sure," he said, then he rapped his knuckles on the dashboard, and pointed to the road ahead, and in a voice like an old Etonian cried, "Onwards, Jeeves!"

CHAPTER TWENTY-NINE

HOON HAD BEEN EXAGGERATING. There was more to Peterhead than just the harbour. There were also two supermarkets, a *McDonald's*, and even a golf course, although, granted, these could all be described as being *harbour adjacent*.

There was a lot of harbour, though. Proportionally, there was probably more harbour here than anywhere else Hoon had ever been to.

And, fair play to the people who lived here, they were running with it, too. Every second business Hoon drove past had the word somewhere in its name. *Harbour Spring. The Harbour Lights. Harbour Hostel. Harbour Haulage.* The place had one defining characteristic, and by Christ, they were making the most of it.

They were passing the Buchanhaven Harbour viewpoint on Harbour Street when Iris let out a low groan like he was having an uncomfortable bowel movement. Hoon looked across to find him sitting with his eyes closed, a finger pressed to the side of his head like he was a US Secret Service agent who couldn't find his earpiece.

"The fuck's wrong with you?" Hoon asked.

"We're close. It's not far from here," Iris said. "I can smell them. The guns. Even with my eyes shut."

Hoon's instinct was to ask why having his eyes shut would make any difference to his ability to smell, but it was overruled by a deeper, more primal urge to bark, "Don't talk shite."

"Trust me, Boggle. Trust me," Iris said. His eyes were still closed, but he suddenly pointed off to the left, and declared, "There!"

"That's the fucking North Sea," Hoon informed him. There was no anger or venom behind it. At this stage, what would be the point?

Iris opened his good eye. It swivelled to look out at the water, then closed again.

"Wait, no," he said. "That way!"

This time, it was his right arm that came up, and Hoon had to lean sideways to avoid getting a finger in his ear.

"Just fucking admit you don't know where it is!" he hissed.

Both of Iris's eyes opened this time, for all the good the other one did. He sat up a little straighter, and peered out in the direction he was still pointing.

"No, it is. That's it," he said. "That warehouse down there. With the green doors. That's the one."

"How do you know?" Hoon asked. "And don't even try and say you can sense it in your bones, or some bullshit, because I'm no' in the fucking mood."

"Well, that," Iris said. "And the guy who told me about the whole thing, he described it. Big green doors. Just off Harbour Road. That's got to be it, Boggle. It's got to be! The guns are in there. I know it. I can taste them, even if I shut my eyes."

"What fucking difference would...?" Hoon began, but he cut himself off before he could finish the question. Best to let it go. It wasn't the time or place. Nowhere and *nowhen* ever would be. "The guy who told you? What do you mean?"

Iris paused, just for a nanosecond. "Just a guy. He got ripped off by them, too. He, eh, he followed them here."

Hoon considered the response, eyes narrowed, then decided he was going to take it at face value. He didn't have the energy for anything else.

He pulled onto the access road leading to the warehouse, and tucked the van in around the back, out of sight. Shutting off the engine, he cast his gaze across the building, scoping it out.

"Don't see any cameras. Do you?"

"No, he's got none of that," Iris muttered, then he quickly corrected himself. "They. They've got none of that." He gave Hoon a nudge. "Like I said, Boggle, piece of piss, this. In, out, shake it all about, and we're golden. It'll be too easy."

The look Hoon gave him was cold and callous. "I don't want it to be *too* fucking easy. Too easy means there's something gone wrong. I want it just fucking easy enough."

"Yeah, well, it'll be just easy enough, then. That's what I meant," Iris told him. "It'll be exactly as easy as you want it to be, Boggle. I'm telling you." He opened his door. "This'll be a piece of fucking cake!"

The big green roller doors were around the front of the building. Spotlights washed the area around them in a jaundiced yellow glow, so anyone out there would be clearly visible to traffic passing along the road.

After getting out of the van, Iris had gone around to the back, climbed inside, then emerged carrying a couple of balaclavas and a crowbar. He was also clipping on a large, chunky belt, with about twelve different pockets and pouches all around it.

"Jesus Christ. Did you fucking mug Batman?" Hoon asked. "What are you wearing?"

"Utility belt," Iris said. "Not Batman's though." He grinned. "Mine's better."

"What's in it?"

Iris began pointing to some of the pockets in turn. "Ball bearings. Thermite. Cyanide pills—can't be too careful. Travel sickness tablets."

"Fuck me, Iris. You just keep them two right next to each other, do you? You don't think that's maybe a bit risky?"

Iris stole a look around, then leaned in closer. "They're not real. They're just for effect."

"The cyanide pills?"

Iris shook his head. "Both." He came closer still, dropping his voice until it was barely a whisper. "I don't even get travel sick," he said, then he winked, tapped the side of his nose, and pointed to the next few pockets. "Garrotting wire. Smoke bomb. Condoms."

"Alright, alright, I'm sorry I fucking asked," Hoon said. He took the balaclava and pulled it on, hiding his face. "So, you're sure we're no' going to face any resistance in here?"

"None," Iris assured him. He climbed back into the van again, so the rest of his reply had a metallic echo to it. "Their security's shit. We'll go in, find the gear, then I'll bring the van around the front and we can load up and get out. We'll be back on the road in twenty minutes."

He jumped down from the van, now wearing a large and deadly looking slingshot that was fastened to his forearm by a series of straps and buckles. Fishing in the first pocket of his belt, he produced a couple of ball bearings, motioned at Hoon not to move, then took a few shuffled steps closer to the back of the warehouse.

On the fifth or sixth step, a security light illuminated high on the wall on Iris's right. He spun, already drawing back the elastic of the catapult, and immediately let fly with one of the ball bearings. Glass shattered, and the area was once again plunged into darkness.

From there, he turned anti-clockwise, raised the slingshot up to his left, then fired again, this time into the darkness. There was another sound of breaking glass, and Iris hummed below his breath as he set about unfastening the slingshot from his arm.

"What the fuck was that?" Hoon asked.

"Lights," Iris said.

"No, I know they were fucking lights. How did you know about them?"

Iris focused his attention quite intently on the straps and buckles for a moment. "My guy told me."

"Oh, he told you exactly where they fucking were, did he?"

"Yeah. He's good," Iris said.

He had just returned the catapult to the back of the van when Hoon caught him by the front of his camo jacket and slammed him up against one of the rear doors.

"I'm getting a bad fucking feeling about this, Iris," Hoon spat. "My arsehole sense is tingling."

Iris gently cleared his throat. "That, eh, that would make you the arsehole in this situation, Boggle."

Hoon's eyes became dark slits in the holes of the balaclava. "Eh?"

"Spider-Man, he doesn't say his bad guy sense is tingling, he says his Spidey sense is tingling. So, if your arsehole sense is tingling, that means you're saying that you yourself are the arsehole."

"Forget the fucking arsehole sense!" Hoon hissed. "The point is that I think you're full of shite, Iris. I'm starting to get gravely fucking concerned about what we're going to find in there, but unfortunately for me, I don't have a lot of other fucking options right now."

"Chill, Boggle. Deep breaths. It's all going to be OK," Iris promised. "In, out, shake it all about, remember?"

He reached back into the van and retrieved the crowbar from where he'd sat it down, then brought it between them, presenting it to Hoon.

"Now, let's go steal some guns!"

———

Iris wanted to use the thermite to burn out the lock on the door at the back of the warehouse, but Hoon had overruled him. There was no need to bother with any fancy shite, when the simple application of force would do the job.

Iris had begrudgingly agreed, before pointing out that the thermite was about twenty years old, anyway, so probably quite unreliable.

He'd kept an eye out while Hoon jammed the crowbar into the frame of the door, and had then taken it upon himself to cough loudly and repeatedly to mask the sound of the wood *cracking*. This, if anything, would only have drawn more attention, and Hoon had hissed at him to, "Shut the fuck up!" on more than one occasion.

When the door finally gave, Hoon was almost knocked over by Iris rushing inside. Hoon watched as the other man hurriedly keyed a series of digits into a pad on the wall, then a long, soft *bleep* indicated an alarm system had been deactivated.

Hoon stared at him expectantly. Iris smiled, shrugged, and whispered, "My guy told me the code."

"He knows a fucking lot, this guy of yours."

"He does," Iris confirmed.

"So, why am I here with you, then, and no' your fucking guy? You and your guy could've been doing all this."

"He's not any good at confrontation," Iris said, then he flashed an unconvincing smile before Hoon could pick up on the comment. "Not that there's going to be any confrontation. He's just... Between you and me, he's a bit paranoid."

"Fucking hell. Coming from you?" Hoon muttered, then he grimaced and turned away when Iris activated a head torch, dazzling him. "Watch where you're fucking pointing that thing."

"Sorry, Boggle."

He turned away, and the light swept across the inside of the warehouse, reaching about a third of the way into the cavernous space. It illuminated thirty or more wooden crates, most of them marked on the side with Chinese writing.

"You sure this is it?" Hoon asked.

"Aye, this is the place," Iris replied in an awestruck sort of whisper.

His feet shuffled forwards, dragging the rest of him along. He moved like he was being drawn in by the crates, like a cartoon mouse to a block of cheese.

"Why the fuck's it all in Chinese?"

Iris shot a look back over his shoulder, and Hoon barely managed to avert his eyes to avoid being dazzled again.

"You're hardly going to write 'guns' on the side, are you? That'd be a dead giveaway."

Hoon plodded along behind his one-eyed companion, the head torch illuminating more and more crates as they progressed through the warehouse.

"These can't all be guns," Hoon muttered.

"I think they are," Iris said, and there was a tremble of excitement in his voice.

"Who the fuck are they arming? The whole of the Northern Hemisphere?"

Iris stopped at a crate that looked more or less identical to all the others. He tapped it with a finger, and turned to Hoon just enough to not blind him with his head torch. "Try this one."

"Why that one?" Hoon asked.

"Just got a good feeling about it."

Hoon scowled at him, but the balaclava robbed the look of

much of its power. With a sigh, he dug the flat end of the crowbar between the lid and side of the crate, and pushed down slowly until one of the nails that fastened the box shut gave way.

Sliding the bar along to the other end, it took significantly less pressure to pop the next nail all the way out, creating enough room for Iris to shove a head and arm in and check inside.

"Well?" Hoon asked, still holding the lid open with the metal pole. "We got what we're after?"

There was some rummaging, then a little orange head with a shock of bright green hair popped up from inside the crate. Its fabric mouth flapped open and closed, and it spoke in a muffled lisp.

"Hewo Boggle! Can we be fwiends?"

"The fuck is that?" Hoon hissed.

Iris extricated himself from inside the crate. Even with his mask on, it was clear that he was grinning from ear to ear.

"He's not real, it's just a puppet."

"Course it's not fucking... I can see it's a fucking puppet!" Hoon replied, the words somehow making it out through his gritted teeth. "It's no' a fucking gun, is the point I'm making."

"Must be a different box," Iris said, turning and wandering off. He stopped at another, sniffed it, then nodded. "This one. They're in here."

Hoon hefted the crowbar from one hand to the other. There was a part of him—a worryingly large part, in fact—that wanted to swing it at the bastard's head.

He'd known, even back in the bunker, that this had been a bad idea, but he'd been much too desperate and far too exhausted to say no. Everything about the mission felt off, from Iris's weirdly erratic intel, to the fact that he was still wearing a tiny, green-haired man on his left arm.

"Will you put that fucking thing down?" Hoon said.

"What's your problem, Boggle? He's just a puppet.

Everyone loves a puppet, don't they?" He flapped the mouth open and closed again, and adopted the same accent as before. "Eveywone wuvs a puppet."

"I'll shove my arm up your arse and use *you* like a fucking puppet, if you don't get rid of it."

Iris stopped. His eyebrows dipped into view in the eyeholes of his mask, as his brow furrowed in concentration. He stood there in silence for a while, as he tried to figure out if what Hoon proposed was actually possible.

He dropped the puppet, just in case.

"Right, come on, crack it open," he instructed, tapping the box in front of him. "This is it. This is the one."

"That's a different fucking box to the one you said a minute ago," Hoon pointed out. "You do know that, aye?"

"Is it?" Iris looked down at the crate, then turned one-eighty and studied the one behind him. "No, you're right. You're right. It's this one. Definitely this one."

Hoon's fingers tightened their grip on the crowbar. He stared at the side of Iris's head for an uncomfortably long time. Then, muttering angrily, he jimmied the lid off the box with far less care and attention than the last time.

Again, he held it prised open while Iris wedged his top half in through the gap. For the first few seconds, there was no reaction from the man half-inside the box. Then, dozens of polystyrene packing peanuts were ejected from inside the crate and onto the floor at Hoon's feet.

"There's a lot of stuff to dig through," Iris announced.

More of the packing material was launched out through the gap. Hoon watched as it piled up in a mound on the floor, then gave it a kick, scattering it.

"It might just be all packing stuff, actually," Iris said. "That might be all that's in here." He stopped digging for a moment. "Why would you pack packing stuff?" he wondered, then he went back to rummaging around.

"Just fucking leave it," Hoon told him. "Obviously there's nothing—"

He was silenced by a cry of triumph from inside the box.

"Hang on, hang on!" Iris declared, then he emerged holding something with the circumference of a large dinner plate. His good eye looked delighted, while the other one stared at the thing in his hand with a note of glassy concern. "It's a landmine!"

"For fuck's sake, watch what you're doing with it!" Hoon warned.

Iris tossed the explosive device from hand to hand, then passed it around his back like he was showing off his basketball skills. "Don't worry, Boggle, it's not armed. At least, I hope not..." He studied the top of the device, then shook his. "No, it's fine. But, see? I told you, didn't I?" He tapped the top of the box. "And this is just the start. It's all here. Everything we could ever want, ours for the taking!"

Hoon glanced around at the other crates. "Aye, maybe," he conceded.

"No 'maybe,' about it!" Iris crowed. "Like I told you, big man, this is going to be a piece of piss."

As if they'd been waiting for just the right cue, the overhead lights came on, revealing a raised metal walkway that ran all the way around the top of the warehouse.

And, more importantly, revealing the ten or more armed men standing all around it, taking aim.

Hoon groaned. "Oh, aye," he said. "*Too* fucking easy."

CHAPTER THIRTY

"TAKE YOUR FUCKING MASKS OFF!"

"Put your hands up!"

"Show your fucking faces!"

The shouts came from on high. Different directions. Different voices, too, though the accents were the same. Both local, though not as densely Doric as some of the others Hoon had heard in the past.

There was a loud *clack* as Iris dropped the landmine. Both men standing in its immediate blast radius froze to the spot as it bounced once on the concrete, then landed, face-down, between them.

"You fucking idiot!" Hoon hissed.

"Sorry, Boggle. Hands sweat when I'm nervous." His eye flicked down to check out the explosive device. "Think we're OK, though."

"How can you tell?"

"Because it hasn't blown up," Iris replied.

Hoon kept his head down, but scanned the upper level of the warehouse with his eyes. The guys were mostly mid-thirties and up, he reckoned. Looked serious. Held their weapons in a way that told him they knew how to use them.

They were well spread out, too. Taking cover would do no good, because the bastards had them covered from every angle.

The shouting from the walkway came again. "Take off the fucking masks, or we'll shoot."

"No, you won't, you toad-eyed yokel fuck!" Hoon shouted back. "You've got a box of landmines here. No' to mention whatever the fuck else you've got stashed around. One stray shot and the whole fucking lot goes boom, you pricks, an' all. So, if you want to shoot, son, just you fucking go ahead. I'm game if you are."

Footsteps clanked along the metal floor of the walkway. Hoon turned to see a giant with ginger hair and a face full of freckles peering down at him, his rifle lowering to his side, and the start of a smile playing across his mouth.

"Boggle?" he asked. "Is that you?"

"No fucking way!" Hoon pulled off the balaclava. "Redneck?"

Up on the walkway, the man known as Redneck threw back his head and laughed. It was a big, joyous sound that seemed to come all the way up from his toes, and went booming off to the far walls of the warehouse.

"I knew it!" he cried. "I mean, 'Toad-eyed yokel fuck!' Who else is going to say that to a guy with a gun pointed at his head?" He nodded to the man beside Hoon, who was still wearing the balaclava. "Who's that you've got with you?"

"What, this tube? It's Iris."

Iris yelped and grabbed at his mask, but too late to stop Hoon pulling it off. Iris danced awkwardly on the spot, moving his arms around as if he had suddenly become completely naked, and was trying to hide his embarrassment.

The revelation did not seem to come as any surprise to the

man on the walkway. He laughed, though it was far more measured than the last one.

"Course it is. Aye. I should've guessed that," Redneck replied. He motioned to the other men to lower their weapons. "It's alright, lads. These two and me go way back. They're not going to give us any bother."

"They're trying to nick the gear," another of the men pointed out.

Redneck shook his head and gazed down at Hoon and Iris. "I'm sure it's just a big misunderstanding that we'll all laugh about together. I'm sure it's a funny story. Right, Boggle?"

Hoon hesitated. Redneck was a good lad, but there was an edge to his words. A thin seam of pure danger running right through the middle.

"Aye, well, I'm no' sure it's *ha-ha* funny," he replied. "But it's definitely a story."

"Now, *this*, I can't wait to hear!" Redneck clapped his hands and rubbed them together. "But first, what's say we get some coffee?"

———

Hoon and Iris were beckoned through to what they guessed was an area of the warehouse designed for meeting clients and customers. It was certainly nicer than the rest of the place, in that it had four nice couches, a coffee table with some glossy magazines on it, and the whole room had apparently been given a lick of paint in recent months.

Redneck had told the rest of his guys to go home, and while they'd all looked surprised by this, none of them had offered any complaints. It was the middle of the bloody night, after all.

Besides, there was something about the man that made you want to do what he said. He rarely raised his voice, and Hoon couldn't remember hearing him ever get angry. And yet, there was something about him that made you want to obey.

It was the way he looked at you, all big, honest eyes and trusting smile. It wasn't that you were scared of him, it was more that you just didn't want to let him down.

The nickname was an obvious one, but very fitting. With his short shock of ginger hair and ghostly white skin, it took just a couple of hours in the Basra afternoon sun to burn the back of his neck into a thick layer of crimson scar tissue. Hence, *Redneck*.

After the others had been sent away, Hoon and the big ginger lad had done some enthusiastic mutual shoulder grabbing, which was about as close as they were ever going to get to an embrace.

Iris, meanwhile, skulked around behind one of the couches, like an unruly schoolboy who knew full well that a bollocking was coming his way, but didn't know quite when to expect it.

Redneck stuck the kettle on, prolonging Iris's suffering for a few moments longer. Then, when the water was starting to roll towards the boil, the red-haired giant turned, folded his arms, and smiled.

"What the fuck are you two up to, then?" he asked. "I mean, it's good to see you, Boggle, but you could've just phoned."

"I didn't know it was your place," Hoon said. He fixed Iris with a look of contempt, but it went unnoticed. "Far as I knew, we were taking back this bellend's stuff from some guys who nicked it."

"Nicked it?!" Redneck cried, and Iris flinched back in fright. "I bought it off you, fair and square."

"No! Bought it, yeah, but not fair and square. Not even close. Below market value. Well below market value," Iris replied. "You didn't literally steal it, but you more or less did."

"We agreed on the price!" Redneck reminded him. "In fact, you named the fucking price!"

"I undervalued it!"

"How's that my problem?"

Hoon looked Iris up and down with contempt. "I knew this was a weird set-up," he said. "You were getting me to come rip Redneck off, you treacherous fucking Cyclops."

"I'm sorry, Boggle."

"Don't fucking apologise to me," Hoon said, then he shook his head. "In fact, no, *do* apologise to me, because I had to put up with you in a fucking van for hours on end, but say sorry to Redneck first."

"Sorry, Redneck," Iris mumbled.

"Tell him it won't fucking happen again."

"It won't happen again."

"He's your fucking mate," Hoon said. "You're no' supposed to rip off your mates."

"Sorry, Redneck," Iris said again, and this time he hung his head in shame.

The kettle rolled to a boil, then clicked off. Redneck considered the apology for a few moments, then waved it away. "It's fine. Forget it. Just don't do it again, eh?"

"You hear that?" Hoon asked, staring at Iris, but pointing to the other man. "That is a very fucking generous response. I'd have shot you. How would you have fucking liked that?"

"I wouldn't," Iris admitted. "I wouldn't have liked that, Boggle."

"No. I should fucking think not," Hoon said.

For a moment, it looked like he was going to continue berating the Liverpudlian, then Redneck sidled in with a couple of mugs, defusing the situation.

"Coffee? Tea?"

"I'll have a coffee, Red, cheers," Hoon said.

"Iris? What you having?"

Iris raised his head. "You're not angry with me, are you, Redneck?"

"What, for breaking into my business and trying to steal a load of stuff off me?" Redneck raised his eyebrows, then shook his head. "I'm not angry, Iris, I'm just disappointed."

Iris almost crumbled at that, and had to lean on the back of the couch to support himself.

"I'm really sorry, mate," he said, then he nodded at the mugs the other man was holding. "Don't suppose you've got nettle tea, do you?"

"No. Of course I don't," Redneck said. "I've got normal tea, or normal coffee."

"Can I just have the hot water?"

Hoon and Redneck swapped looks, one of confusion, the other of utter exasperation.

"Suit yourself," Redneck replied, then he busied himself preparing the drinks.

"What's the score with the set-up here?" Hoon asked, looking around the room. "Never had you pegged for an arms dealer."

"Hmm? Oh. I'm not," Redneck said. "I mean, I suppose technically I am, but not really."

Hoon cocked his head towards Iris. "This wedge of fudds said you were supplying some terrorist outfit."

"Ah right, aye. But then, we've established he's full of shit."

Redneck passed out the mugs, then raised his own and they all clinked them together with a, "Cheers."

"I've been getting them shipped into Yemen of all places. The civil war there's something else. Way worse than a lot of what we saw."

Hoon took a sip of his coffee. "What are you doing, supplying the rebels or something? You always were a fucking bleeding heart."

Redneck smiled. "Not exactly. It's a complex situation. Changing all the time. I've been trying to get weapons into the hands of civilians. They've been getting hammered from all sides, so I'm just trying to give them a fighting chance."

"Making a pretty penny on it, I bet," Iris chipped in.

"Eh, no, actually," Redneck confessed. "Losing money. But, you know, it's not just about that, is it? See, most people, they don't want to get involved. Governments, big business, they don't give a shit about anyone, as long as they're still making money. They'll let any atrocities happen, as long as their accountants keep smiling."

"Preach, brother!" Iris whooped.

"Eh, aye. Cheers," Redneck said, before turning back to Hoon. "But that's the difference between them and us. The good guys and the bad guys. The good guys help each other. The good guys do the right thing. So, I'm just doing my bit."

"And we're the good guys then, are we?" Hoon asked.

"We'd better be. Otherwise, all that stuff we did... what was it for?"

Hoon chuckled. "Good to see you haven't fucking changed, big man."

"Ha. Aye. Well, some of us never do, eh, Boggle?" Redneck took a swig of his coffee, then pointed at both men with the mug. "Mind you, I wouldn't have you down for getting mixed up in this sort of thing. Breaking and entering. Were you not with the police?"

Iris's eyes became so wide that the glass one fell out and landed on the floor, staring upwards. "What?! You never told me you were a copper!" He gasped. "You were in me house! I told you me secret knock!"

"Right, one, pick your fucking eye up," Hoon instructed. "Two, it's no' a house, it's a metal shed. And I'm not in the polis, no. I used to be, but I'm no' anymore."

"Right. Phew. Good for you, Boggle!" Iris said, stooping to pick up his eye. He blew on it to clear off the dust, then popped it back into the socket. "You tell the man where to stick his fucking job?"

"No. They fired me for being a corrupt bastard," Hoon said. "Fair play to them, too, they had me bang to fucking rights."

"Oh. Right," Redneck said, and he looked so disappointed that Hoon had to stop himself from apologising. "Well, I'm sure you had your reasons."

"Aye. So I tell myself."

The big redhead took a seat on one of the couches, and gestured for the others to do the same. He waited until they were both sitting down, before continuing with his questioning.

"It's a big jump from getting fired from the police to nicking a load of guns from a warehouse, though," he said. "I'm guessing that's where the story you mentioned earlier slots in?"

"Good guess," Hoon said. He sat back, sighed, and checked his watch. "It's a fucking epic, though. How long have you got?"

"Long as it takes," Redneck told him. "I'm not going anywhere."

"OK, fine. Buckle the fuck up, then," Hoon told him. "Because this is going to get wild."

And with that, he started to explain. He told them about the job at *Tesco*, and his almost immediate firing. He told them about Bamber turning up, about his daughter, everything that happened to her, and everything he'd done in his quest to bring her home.

He told them about the men he'd killed—those he could remember, anyway—and about the twisted wee fuck who'd started it all in the first place.

"Chuck?" Redneck said, sitting forward on the couch. "Chuck did that?"

Hoon just nodded in reply.

"So, where is he now?" Redneck pressed. Then, when Hoon's next reply came in the form of a long, meaningful look, he said, "Oh. Wow. Right," and sat back again.

The coffees and hot water were finished by the time Hoon was nearing the end of the tale. Both other men had looked a bit sceptical when he started talking about fighting a giant mute albino, but they hadn't questioned him on it, or otherwise called bullshit.

Redneck had read about Chief Superintendent Bagshaw's death in the paper the day before. This was news to Hoon, who hadn't realised it had been announced. The death had been put down as suicide. This was not news to him, of course.

They had all shared a moment of silence when Hoon told them about Welshy. He left out the details. Didn't tell them what he'd done to hasten their old mate's journey towards its end. Although, to be fair to them, he doubted either of them would have judged him for it.

They made appropriately sad sounds. Nodded. Sighed. Sucked air in through their teeth. Considering the amount of death that all three of them had not just witnessed, but dished out over the years, none of them were very good at talking about it.

"So, that's how I got roped in with Captain fucking *ChuckleVision* over there," Hoon concluded, once he'd brought them both fully up to speed. "If these bastards are going to come for me—and they are—then I at least want to make them seriously reconsider their fucking career choices."

"And what's the plan, exactly?" Redneck asked. "Bob Hoon, one-man-army, is it? Going out in a blaze of glory?"

"Something like that, aye," Hoon confirmed. "I got myself into this mess, I'll get myself out of it."

"Lone wolf. Like me," Iris said. "You can't cage a lone wolf, can you, Boggle? Or a tiger."

"What the fuck are you talking about?" Hoon asked.

"I'm just saying..." Iris shifted his weight around on the couch. "You can't cage a tiger."

"Course you can cage a fucking... They cage tigers all the

fucking time," Hoon spat. He swallowed back a deep breath, then exhaled slowly, bringing his temper under control. "Here, listen, Iris. You know what you should start contributing to the conversation?"

"No. What?"

"Nothing. Not a fucking word. Just an eerie, unsettling silence," Hoon told him. "Like a fucking haunted doll with a child's soul trapped inside. You just sit there creeping us both out by saying absolutely nothing. You think you can manage that?"

"Yeah, but—"

Hoon made a pinching motion towards him, and hissed out a sharp, *psssht!*

"We've started," he explained. "Not a fucking cheep now. Come on. You can do this, I've got fucking faith in you here, don't let me down."

He waited to make sure that Iris had got the message. When he turned back, Redneck was sitting all the way forward, his elbows resting on his knees, his gaze boring into Hoon as if it might allow him to read his mind.

"I know that fucking face," Hoon told him. "What are you thinking? What are you going to say?"

"You really think you can take these guys solo, Boggle?"

Hoon shrugged. "I've managed alright on my own so far."

"Aye, but you weren't on your own, were you?" Redneck pointed out.

"What the fuck's that supposed to mean?"

"Jesus, Boggle. Did you even listen to anything you told me? You've had help. Every step of the way. From your detective fella in Inverness to your MI5 guy. That police chief woman in London. Welshy's missus. Your sister..." He indicated Iris with the briefest of nods. "Even this idiot. And me."

Hoon frowned over the rim of his mug. "You?"

Redneck looked almost offended. "Obviously, I'm going to

give you the guns. Anything you need, mate. What's mine is yours." He smiled. "Like I said, we're the good guys. That's what we do. We help each other out."

"Can I have some guns, too?" Iris asked.

"No, you fucking cannot," Redneck replied, not even looking at him. "I mean it, Boggle. This thing you have to do, this path you're on, I get it. I do. But, you can't walk it alone. You might think you have been so far, but you haven't. Not even remotely." He sat back. "And, I mean, come on. You were never some fucking... *lone warrior*. We might like to think so, all of us, but we're not. We never have been. You were a leader. That's who you were then, that's who you are now. I think you've just forgotten that."

"So... what you saying, Red?" Hoon asked. "You volunteering to come kill a gaggle of fucks with me?"

Redneck smiled. "I mean, I'd love to for old time's sake, if nothing else, but we're walking different paths, brother. I've got my own mission going on. Got a lot of people depending on me to help keep them alive. But, I can give you whatever you need. On the house."

"Cheers," Hoon said. "Shame, though. You're the best fucking sniper I know."

"Nah." Redneck shook his head. "Second best."

Hoon's eyebrows journeyed downwards on his forehead, before rising almost all the way to the top.

"Shite. Aye," he said, then he shook his head. "No. Can't get him involved."

"From what you've told us, I'd say he'd jump at the bloody chance. I know I would in his..." He smirked. "I was going to say shoes..."

"Oof. Brutal!" Hoon winced. "And you've the cheek to call yourself one of the fucking good guys?"

"That was a bit below the belt, wasn't it?" Red admitted. He knocked back the last of his coffee, then stood up. "Right, then," he announced. "Let's go get you tooled up!"

"Nice one," Hoon said, getting to his feet. "But, eh, you mind if I use your phone to make a quick call first...?"

Redneck checked his watch. "You're aware it's the middle of the night?"

"Aye," Hoon replied, the corners of his mouth tugging upwards. "That's what makes it funny."

———

The sun was rising over Peterhead Harbour by the time the van doors were all closed. Hoon sat in the driving seat, awake enough now to not even contemplate the possibility of letting Iris take the wheel.

He had just started the engine when Redneck appeared at the window, motioning for Hoon to slide it down.

"Good luck, mate," Red said, once the window was opened.

"Cheers, big man. I appreciate this," Hoon replied. He gestured down at himself, now kitted out in far more appropriate attire for a man about to go to war. "And thanks for the clobber, too."

"No bother. And mind what I said, eh?" Red pointed past Hoon to where Iris was fiddling with his seat belt. "Don't be like this arse, all withdrawn from society and paranoid. You've got friends. People who care about you. You might not like it, but you do. Make the most of that."

Hoon grunted. "Aye," he said, firing up the engine. "We'll see."

Redneck smiled. "Well, can't say I didn't try," he said, then he fired off a salute.

It took Hoon a moment or two, but then he returned it.

"Cheers, pal," he said, then he wound up the window, and the van thundered off up the hill towards Harbour Road.

"He's a nice guy, isn't he?" Iris volunteered, as they drove away. "He could've completely lost his shit with us there, but he was pretty cool about it."

"Iris?"

"Yeah, Boggle?"

"Shut the fuck up."

Iris nodded. "Right, Boggle. Sorry, Boggle."

And with that, they set off on the long journey west.

CHAPTER THIRTY-ONE

THE DIRTY SLAPPER sat much lower in the water on the return trip to *Westward*. Hoon had needed to take the van across on the ferry to avoid any questions about the big wooden box he was carrying, then Iris had helped him manhandle it down the ladder and into Berta's boat.

It hadn't been easy, there had been a lot of swearing involved, and on two occasions it looked like they were going to drop the whole thing into the water, but eventually they got it aboard, leaving just enough room for Hoon to squeeze in beside the crate.

After that, they had said some stilted farewells, and Iris climbed back up the ladder, only to reappear at the top a moment later.

"Good luck, Boggle," he said, then he vanished again, and Hoon heard the sound of the van door closing, and the engine starting up.

Hoon had sat there alone for a few minutes, weighing up all the potential consequences of the next action he planned to take. Do it, and there was no going back. He'd be bringing the war to him.

Could he really do this? To Berta? To everyone?

"Ah, fuck it," he'd said out loud, then he'd taken out the phone that Miles had given him, slipped the battery back in, and made what he fully expected to be the most difficult call of his life.

It turned out to be a lot easier than he'd been bracing himself for.

After that, he'd untied the boat and set off, the additional weight making the waves lap ominously against the sides, and occasionally splash over the top so it sloshed around at his feet.

He wasn't as lucky with the weather this time. A fine mist of drizzle seeped into him from Mallaig all the way back to the dock at his sister's house. It reduced visibility down to just a few metres, and he was forced to take his time for fear of smashing into some bugger coming the other way.

When he was a bit further down the loch, and into a wider stretch, he opened the *Yamaha* engine up a bit, making up for lost time. Even then, it was approaching lunchtime by the time the dock at *Westward* reared up at him through the mist.

He brought the *Slapper* in alongside it, tied it up, then hauled the box out onto the little wooden jetty. He could just about carry it on his own, but it wasn't going to do his back any favours. Instead, he dragged it onto solid ground, then left it there while he went to fetch Berta to give him a hand.

The further he got from the water, the thinner the mist became. As he drew closer to the house, he was able to make out a shape. A figure, an axe raised above its head.

He heard his sister cry out, "No!" and instinct launched him into a run.

With every step, the fog fell away. He saw the Professor, his scarred face slick with sweat, hoisting the hatchet with both hands, readying to bring it down.

Roaring, Hoon launched himself at the bastard, slamming into him with a flying tackle that took him clean off his feet.

They hit the ground as a tangle of arms and legs, Hoon grabbing for the axe, wrenching it from the Professor's grip.

"What the suffering fuck do you think you're doing?" demanded a voice from somewhere above and behind them.

Hoon secured the weapon, pinning it to the ground, then looked back over his shoulder to find his older sister standing there, hands on hips, a look of fury etched across her features.

"Well?" she demanded.

"He had a fucking axe!" Hoon yelped.

"I know he had a fucking axe. I gave him said fucking axe," Berta replied. "He's been chopping wood for the fire. Badly, I might add. He's almost as clueless as you are, and fuck me, that is saying something, is it not?"

"But... he's dangerous. He shouldn't be untied."

"I don't get to sit around on my arse all day, so why should he? Why have a dog and bark your-fucking-self?" Berta boomed. She stood back and made a beckoning motion. "Now, get off Paul before you break him. Even more than you already have, I mean."

Hoon looked from Berta to the man pinned below him, then back again. "Paul?"

Berta sniffed. "Well, I can't call him 'the Professor,' can I? We're not inhabiting a fucking cartoon. It's the real world. People have names."

Hoon released his grip, but took the axe with him as he stood up. The Professor lay motionless where he'd fallen, only his eyes shifting to warily follow Hoon's movements.

"So you called him Paul?"

"Yes, well, I had to call him something, didn't I? And he wasn't exactly forthcoming, so Paul it is. If he doesn't like it, then tough titty, he shouldn't have played silly buggers. Besides, he looks like a Paul, doesn't he?"

Hoon glowered at her like she'd lost her mind. "What are you...? Of course he fucking doesn't! Look at him! He looks like a fucking Halloween mask made of raw chicken. Or, like someone's ordered a paper mache Albert Einstein off of *Wish*. He's about as far removed from looking like a Paul as it's possible to get without a fucking spaceship and a sense of adventure."

Berta rolled her eyes at her brother's response, then clicked her fingers and pointed at the man sprawled on the ground. "Right, up you get. That wood's not going to chop itself, is it?"

The Professor raised himself gingerly onto his elbows. Then, still watching Hoon, he clambered slowly to his feet.

"Give him the bloody axe, then!" Berta urged.

Hoon looked down at the hatchet. "No chance am I giving that bastard something fucking sharp to play with. He's a killer. You're lucky he didn't take your fucking head off."

Berta tutted. "Come on, Bobby, what do you take me for?" she asked, then she directed his attention to the shotgun that lay across the deckchair she must've recently vacated.

"I'm still no' giving him the axe," Hoon insisted.

"Fine. Suit yourself," Berta said, shrugging her big, broad shoulders. "Wood still needs chopping, though, so you'll have to do it."

Hoon considered the big pile of logs that stood against the side of the house.

"Fuck it, then," he said. "I'll take my chances."

He presented the hatchet to the Professor, who stared at it in mute disbelief for a moment, then reached out and gripped the handle.

Hoon didn't let go. Not yet.

"But I'm fucking warning you, pal, try any funny stuff, and I'll insert this into every fucking orifice in your body, one by one, starting with those ugly fucking nose holes o' yours. Got that?"

The Professor croaked out a sound, and accompanied it with a nod.

"Good boy," Hoon said, releasing his grip. "Now, get your finger out your arse, and get to fucking work."

The Professor turned the axe over in his hand, his beady eyes fixed on Hoon, sizing him up, assessing his chances.

Hoon planted his feet. Stared back. Made the other man's chances very fucking clear.

"Aye," he muttered, when the Professor scurried over to the woodpile. "That's what I thought." He turned his attention to his sister, and set off back towards the boat. "Right, here you. Come and give me a hand carrying this box."

Berta scowled. "What did your last fucking slave die of?"

"Underwork," Hoon retorted. "Now, shift."

She started to hobble towards the jetty, wincing and drawing in a hissed breath as if every step was playing havoc on her hips. Hoon wasn't buying it, though. Instead, he let her get a few metres along the dock, before pointing back to the firearm sitting abandoned on the chair.

"You might no' want to leave that with him," he pointed out.

"What?" Berta looked back. "Oh, doesn't matter. Wasn't loaded. I wasn't exactly going to shoot the bastard, was I?"

Hoon's eyebrows raised in surprise. "Weren't you?"

"Of course I bloody wasn't!" Berta replied. She set off again, and this time didn't bother with the limp. "I'd have bludgeoned the fucker to death with the heavy end."

———

Twenty minutes later, both Hoons stood staring into the open wooden crate on the kitchen floor.

"That's a lot of guns," said one.

"Aye," agreed the other.

"And is that...?"

"Plastic explosives. Aye."

"Where did you get all this?"

"Peterhead."

"Where's that?"

The younger of the Hoons turned to his sister. "What do you mean? You don't know where Peterhead is?"

"Why the fuck would I need to?" Berta asked.

Hoon conceded this point with a nod, then closed the lid of the crate again.

"It's nowhere important," he told her.

Outside, through the window, he could see the Professor half-arsing his wood chopping. For a man who was so adept with small sharp blades, he appeared to be pretty hopeless with a large one.

"You eaten?" Berta asked. "There's soup."

Hoon smiled, although mostly on the inside. Of course there was soup. There was always soup.

"Aye, wouldn't say no," he replied, then they both froze at the sound of someone knocking on the front door.

"Who the buggery bollocks is that?" Berta hissed.

"What about them kids who come visit?" Hoon asked. "Could be them?"

"Only if they've started themselves on anabolic fucking steroids," Berta shot back. "Didn't you hear that knock? Nearly put the fucking door in!"

"Where's my bag?" Hoon asked.

"At your arse, where you left it," Berta said, pointing to the kitchen table. There, below it, was the bag Hoon had first brought to the house with him. Reaching in, he took out the Glock, then motioned for Berta to stay where she was.

He slipped out into the hall, the gun held in two hands, half-raised in front of him, ready to bring up all the way.

The *thudding* on the door came again. A silhouette moved beyond the dimpled glass. Someone big. Almost monstrously so, though that could've just been the blurring effect of the shadow hitting the glass.

Tucking the gun behind his back, Hoon approached the door, unfastened the lock, and threw it wide open.

It hadn't been his shadow on the glass. The man standing on the front step really was that large.

Large, and judging by both the expression and the perspiration on his face, not very happy.

"Right, then, you inconsiderate bastard," grunted a somewhat breathless Detective Chief Inspector Jack Logan. "Whatever it is you called me here for, it had better be bloody good."

CHAPTER THIRTY-TWO

LOGAN SAT at one end of the kitchen table, with Berta directly across from him, and Hoon sat slap bang between them. The DCI blinked slowly, trying to process the information he'd just been given.

"So... Roberta?" he said. "Roberta and Robert Hoon?"

"Named after the old man," Hoon said. "Aye, he was Robert, I mean, no' Roberta."

"Well, I guessed that, aye," Logan replied.

He looked from brother to sister and back again. There was a definite family similarity. Looking at Berta was like looking at Hoon in elaborate stage makeup. If Hoon had ever appeared in Panto as the dame, Logan reckoned he wouldn't look a million miles away from the woman at the opposite end of the table.

The woman, he noticed, who was currently staring at him with a look on her face that could best be described as 'curious contempt.'

"He's got piggy wee eyes, hasn't he?" Berta remarked. "Your friend here."

"He's no' my friend," Hoon said. It was an auto-pilot

response, and he almost felt guilty for letting the words out. Not guilty enough to retract them, though.

"An unnecessarily broad face, too," Berta continued. "You know what he looks like? One of them... What do you call them? The ones with the tusks?"

"Elephant?" Hoon guessed.

Berta tutted. "Well, of course not a fucking elephant!" she cried. "He hasn't got a fucking trunk for starters, has he?"

Logan side-eyed his former boss. "She's got you there, right enough."

"Walrus!" Berta said. "That's what he looks like. A walrus."

Hoon leaned closer to his sister's end of the table and looked along it to where Logan sat in stony-faced silence.

"I'm no' seeing it," Hoon told her. "He's nothing like a fucking walrus."

"Cheers," Logan said.

"If you'd said sea lion, maybe, I'd have given you that one."

Logan placed both hands on the table, sighed, and got to his feet. "Right, tell you what, I'll just bugger off home, will I?"

"Alright, alright!" Hoon said, gesturing for him to wait. "Don't get your fucking knickers in a knot. Come on, sit on your arse."

It wasn't so much Hoon asking, as the thought of the hike back to where he'd parked his car, that made Logan return to his seat.

"Ooh. Sensitive fucker, isn't he?" Berta muttered.

"Not really," Logan said, jumping in before Hoon could answer. "But I'm a very busy man, and I'll be honest, I don't much appreciate getting mystery phone calls in the middle of the night directing me out to the arse end of nowhere, only to be told I've got piggy wee eyes and look like a sea lion."

He clicked his fingers, then pointed to Berta. When he did, her mouth became a single thin red line of disapproval.

"You, get the kettle on. And do I smell soup? If so, yes, please."

He turned his attention to the younger of the two Hoons.

"You, start explaining. And fast. But first..." Logan pointed to the window. "Do you know your man out there is in the process of running away?"

Hoon jumped to his feet and looked outside. The Professor was halfway along the dock, looking back over his shoulder, as he raced towards the boat.

"Fuck!" Hoon cried, then he barged out through the back door, and set off in hot pursuit.

Logan and Berta stood watching in silence as Hoon quickly caught up with the older man, and floored him with a running tackle. They listened to an outburst of swearing so loud and forceful that, halfway across the loch, a couple of geese were startled into the air.

"Thank you for coming," Berta said, not looking away from the scene outside. Her voice was soft, with none of the scorn or venom that had coloured it previously. "He'll never admit it, of course, but he appreciates it. And he needs you. He needs someone, anyway. And you're the one who turned up. That means a lot. To both of us. Though, if you repeat any of this fucking conversation to anyone, I'll have you over my bloody knee."

"Aye. Well, your secret's safe with me," Logan said, desperately trying to distance himself from that mental image. He shrugged off his coat and draped it over the back of his chair. "Now, how about that soup?"

———

Logan made a point of not looking when Hoon dragged the protesting older man back along the dock and escorted him past the house in the direction of one of the cabins the DCI had passed on the way in. It was a safe bet that the guy was being held against his will, so until Logan knew more, he thought it best to know nothing.

Hoon returned a few minutes later, by which point Logan was already scraping the last dregs of his soup up with the side of his spoon.

It was tasty enough, but more than that, it was *hearty*. It was the kind of soup that stuck to the ribs and put flesh on your bones. And, as a bonus, he reckoned he'd ticked off his recommended five daily portions of vegetables in just that one sitting, with enough banked up to see him through the weekend.

He pushed the empty bowl away and patted his stomach, just as Hoon took his seat.

"That was delicious, thanks," Logan said.

Berta, who was chopping up yet more vegetables to start on another batch, shot a look back over her shoulder at the bowl in the centre of the table.

"Aye, well, you know where the fucking sink is."

"Oh. Right. Aye, sorry," Logan said.

He reached for the bowl, but Hoon got there first, snatching it up before Logan's fingers could get to it.

"It's fine, I've got it," Hoon said, taking the bowl over to the sink.

Logan watched him in a sort of startled confusion all the way to the sink and back.

"What?" Hoon asked. "The fuck are you looking at me like that for?"

"Just..." Logan nodded to the sink. "You took my bowl for me."

"And?"

"I think that's the first thing you've ever done for me."

"Bollocks, I—"

"The first thing you weren't contractually obliged by the polis to do, I mean," Logan added.

This took the wind from Hoon's sails a bit. He kept his

mouth open and a finger raised like he still had a point to make. For the life of him, though, he couldn't find the words to support the gesture, so he just shrugged and let his hand fall back onto the table.

"Aye, well, as a mate of mine made me realise last night, things change. People change." Hoon frowned and shook his head. "Or maybe they stay the same. Fuck knows what the point was he was trying to make. One of the two, anyway."

"Sounds like an enlightening conversation," Logan replied.

"It fucking was, actually, aye," Hoon said, a little defensively. "You're probably wondering why I called you out here."

"What do you mean, 'probably'? You called me up in the middle of the bloody night. No 'probably' about it."

"Alright! Fuck's sake. You get out of the wrong side of fucking bed this morning?"

"It wasn't the direction that was the problem, Bob, it was the bloody time," Logan fired back. "You got me out here without any explanation, you've clearly kidnapped a man—and I'm really hoping there's a good explanation for that one—and you look like you've spent the last six months being bounced around inside a bloody pinball machine."

"That's no' actually far off the truth," Hoon muttered.

"What I'd really like—what I'd really appreciate—is for you to tell me just exactly what the fuck is going on."

Hoon sat back in his chair and crossed his arms. For a moment, it looked like he might launch into a rant, but then he sighed, rubbed his eyes with thumb and forefinger, and leaned in closer again with his hands clasped on the table in front of him.

"Right, well, first of all, I wouldn't say I'd *kidnapped* him, exactly."

"That's a relief," Logan said.

"He just happened to be in the back of a van I stole," Hoon concluded.

"OK. Relief fading fast..."

"And, in the interests of full fucking transparency, I bit his nose off and tried to murder him with a chair leg."

It was Logan's turn to sit forward. He glanced out of the window to where he'd seen the prisoner trying to flee.

"When was this?"

"Oh, ages back. Months," Hoon said. He gave a dismissive wave, like the passing of time had made the offences irrelevant. "Your mate, Deirdrie, she knew all about it." Hoon glanced down at his hands, then met Logan's eye again. "You, eh, you heard what—"

"Aye," Logan confirmed. "Suicide, they say."

"You believe that?"

Logan hesitated, and from the look on his face, it was clear that he did not. "I suppose you're going to tell me otherwise?" he said, then a thought troubled him. "You're not going to say it was you, are you?"

"What?! Fuck off!" Hoon ejected. "No. She was... I mean, she wasn't a friend, but she knew the score. She was on the right fucking side."

"Well, aye, she was in the polis."

Hoon laughed. "Aye, but no' everyone in the polis is on the right fucking side, Jack. Let's not fucking kid ourselves on that front."

Logan said nothing. Bringing up Hoon's dismissal would've been a cheap shot, and while he wasn't above the occasional one of those, now wasn't the time.

"But she was fighting back against that," Hoon continued. "I didn't fucking appreciate it—didn't fucking appreciate her—until the wee speech my mate gave last night."

He shuffled his chair in a little closer, and dropped his voice to a whisper, like he was sharing some private insight.

"See, most people, they don't give a flying fuck."

"About what?" asked Logan, trying to follow along.

Hoon shrugged. "About anything. Anything except themselves. They see a jakey dying on the street, they step over him. They see kids with fuck all to eat, and they turn a fucking blind eye. And it's no' because they're bad people. I mean, they are, obviously, but so's every other bastard out there. It's because most folk don't want to rock the fucking boat. They build a life for themselves—no' perfect, maybe, but decent enough—and they want to protect that. And helping others, getting involved, that puts everything at risk, doesn't it? That might throw plans into fucking disarray."

"Is there a point here somewhere, Bob?" Logan asked.

"Aye, there's a fucking point, I'm just getting to it," Hoon retorted. "Deirdrie wasn't like that. Deirdrie could've been chilling in a mansion in fucking Marbella if she'd just done that. Turned a blind eye. Looked the other way. No' gotten involved. But that wasn't her. She fucking stood up to be counted."

"Stood up against what?" Logan asked. "Against who?"

Hoon blew out his cheeks and ran a hand down his face. Logan was a cynical bastard at the best of times. Getting him to believe in international criminal cabals with members seeded through everything from royalty downwards was going to be a big ask.

Still, he had to try. For all he knew, the bastards were on their way here now.

"There's an organisation, I suppose you could call them," he began. "Calls itself the Loop. Shite name, I know. Sounds like a fucking ITV game show. But, these fuckers—"

"I know," Logan said, cutting his old boss short. "I've heard of them."

Hoon stared back, unblinking, a jumble of thoughts tumbling around inside his head like dice in a cup. When he finally did settle on something to say, it wasn't particularly inspired.

"What?"

"The Loop. Owen Petrie—Mister Whisper—in one of his interviews, the first one after the brain damage, I think, he mentioned them. It's in the case file. Big network of bad bastards, he said. Claimed he was a member of it. Convinced they were going to come and get him out. Obviously, they never turned up. We wrote it off as a delusion."

"Aye, well, it wasn't," Hoon said. "I've met the fuckers. And that skeletal muff-trumpet who tried to make a break for it there, he's one of them."

Logan's chair creaked as he sat forward. "They're real? You've met them?"

"No' just met them, killed a bunch of them, too," Hoon said. "That was off the record, by the way. And it was all in self-defence, anyway. Well, about eighty percent." He thought for a moment. "Let's say seventy."

"You know I'm still in the polis, aye?" Logan reminded him.

"Aye." Hoon swallowed, then grimaced, like he was mentally preparing himself for something deeply unpleasant. "But, you're also one of the only fuckers I can actually trust. Even after all the shite I've put you through, no matter how I've fucking treated you over the years, you've been there."

Logan grunted. "Aye. Well."

Hoon's eyes narrowed. "I mean, when I put it like that, it makes you sound pretty fucking pathetic, actually." He caught the look on Logan's face, then shook his head, dismissing the realisation. "Anyway, doesn't matter. The point is... These fuckers, these Loop bastards, they're coming for me, Jack. They're coming for me. Here."

"What? What do you mean?"

"There's a team of them. Like a fucking, I don't know, assassin squad. They're after me."

"Jesus Christ, Bob!" Logan yelped. "You leave town for a couple of months and you've got a worldwide fucking crime ring sending hitmen to kill you?!"

Hoon nodded. "That's pretty much the size of it, aye."

Logan turned and looked around the room, like there might be a big sign somewhere that revealed all this was just an elaborate joke. To his disappointment, he didn't find one. He leaned his head on a hand, and eyeballed Hoon through a gap in his fingers.

"So, what are you saying? You're hiding out here?"

"No' hiding, exactly," Hoon replied. "See, I thought, if they were going to come for me, it might as well be on home turf. You know? Like, give me a bit of a chance. So, I came here. And then I told them where I was."

Logan's elbow slipped off the table, jerking his hand from his head. "You did what?!"

"Well, no' exactly. That'd be too fucking obvious," Hoon said. "But I reckon they're tracking my phone. So, I made a call today. Gave them a nudge in the right direction. If they've got any fucking savvy about them, they'll know where I am."

Logan got to his feet and crossed to the window. From the kitchen, he could see all the way along the dock, to where *The Dirty Slapper* bobbed around on the surface of the loch.

"They're no' going to be here yet," Hoon assured him. "They'll probably come tonight. Try and catch me off-guard." He snorted. "Fannies that they are."

"What the fuck were you thinking?!" Logan demanded. He reached into his pocket and pulled out his mobile. "I need to call this in."

Hoon got to his feet. "Don't be fucking daft, Jack. You can't call it in."

"What are you...? You've got hitmen coming to kill you. I mean, presumably to kill all of us now—thanks for that, by the way. Of course I need to call it in!"

"And do what? Arrest them?"

"Well, that's my job, aye, unless you've forgotten?" Logan said.

He tutted when he saw that he had no network signal. Hardly a surprise, of course, but a pain in the arse all the same. He set off in search of a landline phone, but Hoon blocked his path.

"I didn't get you here to do your fucking job, Jack," he said.

"Then why the hell did you bring me here, Bob?" Logan demanded. "Hm? What was the fucking point in dragging me all the way out here?"

"To say goodbye."

Over at the kitchen worktop, the sound of Berta's knife on the chopping board fell silent. Logan didn't say anything. Not at first. Not for a while.

"You're not dying here, Bob," he eventually replied.

Hoon nodded. "Aye, I am," he said. "And that's fine. I'm A-O-fucking-K with that. I've lived a lot fucking longer than I've any right to have lived, Jack. Guys like me are meant to go out in a blaze of fucking glory in our twenties, no' drag on into old age. This is good, Jack. This is how my fucking story was always meant to end."

"Just let me make a few phone calls. I can get ARU on standby. I'll get my team working on it from their end. Ben, Hamza, Tyler."

Hoon snorted. "Boyband? The fuck's he going to do? Provide backing harmonies? Get up off his stool on the key change?"

"Will you quit fucking kidding around, Bob?" Logan barked. "This is serious. Assuming you're not having some sort of bloody psychotic episode here, there are people coming to kill you!"

"All the more fucking reason not to drag people into it and put them in danger."

"What about me?" Logan cried. "You were quick enough to drag me into danger!"

Hoon tutted. "You don't fucking count!" he said. "And that's no' a fucking insult by the way. That's a compliment."

"I'm touched, Bob. Really," Logan said, scowling.

Hoon took a deep breath, and tried to arrange his mouth into something that might pass for a smile. He achieved this with limited success, at best.

"Jack. It's fine," he said. "If they kill me, they kill me. I've made my peace with that. I just wanted to say thanks, that's all. And, you know, goodbye. Or, fuck off, or whatever."

Logan stared down at him, eyes slowly narrowing. Hoon's face remained a picture of innocence—or as close to it as he was ever likely to get.

Which, truth be told, wasn't all that close at all.

"You're lying," the DCI said.

"What? No, I'm not. What do you mean?"

"Bollocks you wanted to say goodbye. No chance. You've not got a sentimental bone in your body, you crotchety bastard. That's not why you brought me here, is it?"

Hoon nodded. "Aye," he said, but there was a flash of something on his face that said otherwise.

"No. That's definitely not it," Logan insisted. "You had an idea last night. That's why you phoned me then, because you knew you'd change your mind. You knew if you didn't do it then, you wouldn't do it at all."

"Wrong. It was just a rare moment of fucking sentimentality, Jack," Hoon insisted. "A lumpy wee dribble of the milk of human kindness."

"Kindness? You thought you were doing me a favour dragging me all the way out here?" Logan pointed past him towards the front door. "I had to walk fucking miles to get here, Bob. You weren't doing this for my benefit."

He took a step closer, so he was almost looking straight down at Hoon's upturned face. Hoon, for his part, didn't budge an inch.

"No," Logan said, shaking his head. "You called me last night because you needed me for something. You had a plan."

"I do have a plan, aye. I'm going to take out as many of these Loop bastards as I can, then go out with a bang."

"That might be your plan now, but that wasn't it then," Logan continued to insist. "You had another one, didn't you? And, since it involved me, I'm going to go out on a limb and assume it's better than getting yourself killed. Because, let's be honest, as plans go, that one's shite."

There was a *clunk* and a *boing* as Berta embedded her big kitchen knife in the wooden worktop. "Oh, for fuck's sake, Bobby. Whatever it is, spit it out, before I come over there and thrash it out of you." She raised a finger and jabbed it towards him, eyes narrowing into slits. "And don't you fucking think for a moment that just because your friend's here I won't do it, because we both know I will."

Hoon glanced over at his sister, and the knife wobbling in the worktop. He took a step back, so it didn't look like he and Logan were about to start swinging punches.

"Well," he muttered. "I did have one idea..."

CHAPTER THIRTY-THREE

THE LIVING ROOM of *Westward* was a place that very rarely got visitors. The kitchen had always been where the action was, and the living room was sort of an add-on space that they hardly ever set foot in.

Berta didn't believe in replacing or renewing something that wasn't literally falling apart, and as such, the mostly untouched living room was even more outdated than the rest of the house. It smelled of mothballs and mould, though neither were anywhere to be seen.

The old furniture, from the fold-up writing desk, to the burgundy leather couch, was all clean and dust-free. Berta might not come into the room very often, but when she did, she was always sure to bring some polish and a damp cloth.

Logan and Hoon sat on armchairs on either side of the open fireplace, both sitting forward, facing each other across a small oak table as old as them both combined.

Of the two of them, Hoon had sounded the most sceptical about the plan he was proposing, and he'd abandoned the telling of it three or four times, with an increasingly exasperated Logan urging him to continue each time.

And now—now that it was all explained, and the cards were on the table—Logan sat there in silence, processing everything Hoon had proposed.

"It's risky," he said, after some more thought.

"Aye. Like I kept trying to tell you, complete waste of fucking time," Hoon agreed.

"I'm not saying that," Logan replied. "I'm saying it's risky. But it's got potential."

Hoon gave a nod, like these were the words he'd been secretly hoping to hear. "You think?"

"We'd need help, obviously," Logan said. "I'd want to call in the armed unit."

Hoon's response was immediate and emphatic. "No. These Loop fuckers are everywhere. If we're calling anyone in, it's people we trust. No one else."

"You don't trust anyone, Bob," Logan pointed out.

"I trust you," Hoon said, though it visibly pained him to do so. "And if you say someone's solid, I'll take your word on it."

Logan raised an eyebrow. "Even Tyler?"

"Come on, Jack, be fucking reasonable," Hoon retorted.

Logan allowed himself a chuckle at that, then got back down to business. "It's a big leap of faith you're making," he said. "For this to work, I mean. What you're proposing."

Hoon shook his head. "No' a leap of faith, a leap of deduction. I used to be polis, too, remember? I still know a fucking thing or two about detective work. And it makes sense. I'm sure of it."

"Aye, well, I hope you're right," Logan said. "But if you're going to do this, you need to be up close. You need to be face to face. What makes you think they're going to let that happen?"

"I'm no' going to give the bastards a choice," Hoon replied.

"If what you say is right, they're going to outnumber you. You're going to be outgunned."

Hoon shook his head. "Outnumbered, maybe. But I won't

be outgunned. I've got the best fucking shot in the business coming."

Right then, as if the person outside had been waiting in the wings, there came a knock on the front door. Hoon bounced to his feet, his eyes alive with excitement.

"Speak of the fucking devil!" he said, hurrying out into the hall.

"Bob, wait!" Logan called after him. "You don't know who's out there."

Hoon didn't notice the lack of outline on the glass of the front door. It didn't occur to him that he hadn't heard a boat approaching. It was only when he pulled open the door that he realised the person knocking was not the one he'd been expecting.

Instead, Hoon found himself staring down into the upturned faces of two identical-looking five-year-old girls.

"Who the fuck," he spat, "are you?"

One of the girls leaned in closer to the other, cupped a hand, and whispered in her ear. Both of them giggled at whatever was said.

They were both short, even for their age, and a little pudgy with it. They looked like a badly resized photograph, where someone had forgotten to lock the dimensions correctly, making the subjects appear strangely squished and out of proportion.

Hoon had never really been a fan of children, and though he'd only just met them, he'd already concluded he disliked this pair more than most.

"Away you go," he said, making a big *shooing* motion with one hand. "Fuck off, the both of you."

"Bobby!" Berta barked. She came thundering along the hall from the kitchen, shouldering Logan aside. "You watch your language in front of the little ones!"

Hoon stepped aside to avoid being steamrollered by his sister. "What, you know these two wee bastards?" he asked.

An elbow caught him a glancing blow to the ribs and knocked him into the coat stand beside the door.

"Ignore him, my little poppets," Berta said. "He's just being silly."

The twin who had been on the receiving end of the earlier whispered comment pointed to her sister. "Mandy says he's got a face like a bum," she said, barely able to get the words out through squeaks of laughter.

"He does, doesn't he?" Berta cried. "He's got a face like a big fat bum!"

"Do I fuck!" Hoon objected, then a violent poke to the stomach forced him to stumble back along the hall to safety.

Berta bent down, her hands on her thighs, and smiled at each of the children in turn. "Now, then, girls. Hands up who'd like some scones."

Both hands shot up. Berta laughed, then stepped aside, making room for the twins to go clattering along the hallway towards the kitchen. They split up when they reached Hoon and Logan, weaving around them, then reunited on the other side.

Hoon watched them until they had disappeared into the kitchen, then turned back to his sister.

"Here," he said, visibly outraged. "You never told me there were fucking scones!"

———

Hoon had Logan help him carry the crate out to the front of the house. He didn't tell him what was in it, and Logan didn't ask. Not that he needed to, of course. Still, it was good to keep *plausible deniability* as an option in the back pocket for as long as possible.

"You get through alright on the phone?" Hoon asked.

"Once I remembered how to use the old dial system, aye," Logan replied, miming turning the numbers with a finger.

Hoon nodded for quite a long time, like he didn't want to know the answer to the question he was about to ask.

"And?"

Logan blew out his cheeks. "And they have some concerns," he said. "But they'll go along with it."

"Good. Right. Aye," Hoon said.

He checked his watch. It had been turned around so it was on the inside of his wrist. An old habit. Worn on the outside, there was always the danger of light reflecting off the glass and giving away your position.

Still, he couldn't remember moving it.

"You'd better get a shifty on," Hoon told him. "And don't go dragging your fucking heels. You were doing all that jogging before when you were trying to fire it up that pathologist bird. Time to put that to fucking use."

"I wasn't trying to..." Logan began, then he shook his head. "You know we're living together now, aye?"

"Ah. Right. Got you," Hoon said. "Is that why you've started to let yourself go?"

Logan stood a little taller, sucking in his stomach. "I haven't let myself go! Cheeky bastard."

"Well, it's been fun fucking chatting, but come on," Hoon urged, tapping his watch. "Chop chop. I'm no' having this all go to hell because you can't stop talking shite."

"Right, fine. Fine," Logan said. He took a few steps, stopped, sighed heavily, then turned around. "Be careful, Bob."

"Don't you fucking burst into tears on me now, Jack," Hoon warned. "Or I'll never let you fucking live it down."

Logan smiled. "No," he said. "No, I don't suppose you would."

He was about to set off again, but something out beyond the house caught his eye. An old fishing boat was approaching around the bay, chugging through the water towards the *Westward* jetty.

"You've got company," Logan said, pointing.

Hoon followed his finger until he spotted the boat, then jabbed a thumb back in the direction of the path. "Right, go. Fuck off," he urged. "I'll deal with whatever this is."

"Sure you don't need me to stick around?"

Hoon snorted. "The day I need help from a bulbous fucking calamity like you is..."

The sentence fell away into an awkward silence. Hoon cleared his throat and pulled a grimace that might, under scrutiny, pass for a smile of apology.

"Sorry, force of habit," he admitted. "But I'm fine. Get going."

Logan watched the boat come closer. He couldn't see much through the dirty glass, but he thought a woman stood behind the wheel. She seemed to be singing to herself, and Logan wasn't getting 'contract killer' vibes off her at all.

"Right, then," he said. "Try and not get yourself killed until I get back."

"No promises," Hoon said, then he set off at a jog to intercept the boat as it coughed to a stop at the end of the jetty.

A rope was thrown out for him to catch, all grease and algae and stinking of fish. He caught it, fumbled with it, then looped it around the same mooring point to which he'd tied *The Slapper*.

The woman who emerged from the wheelhouse was closer to Berta's age than his. She was dressed in a dark green waterproof Mackintosh that covered her all the way down to her Wellies, which contrasted with the jacket in a shade of blindingly bright pink.

She looked down at him from the boat, her hands on her hips, a light misting of rain and saltwater fluttering around her head.

"Hang on. You're not Bobby, are you?" she cried, her eyes

widening and her face lighting up, like she was delivering the punchline to a particularly racy joke. She put a hand at waist height. "Wee Bobby Hoon?"

"Eh, aye," Hoon confirmed.

"You don't remember me, do you? Course you don't. Kirsty. Kirsty Ward. From Mallaig. Used to take you back and forth here all the time."

"Oh. Aye. I remember," Hoon said.

The woman on the boat snorted. "My arse you do, but I appreciate you saying it," she said. "Anyway, I'm guessing it's you I've got a delivery for."

She slapped the flat of her hand on the side of the rusted metal cabin that stood on the boat's equally weathered deck. A door swung open, and—with a fair amount of grunting and effort—a man in a wheelchair dislodged himself from inside.

"You alright there, Bamber?" Hoon called.

Bamber fired the boat's captain a scathing look. "No. Not really. I nearly threw up twice. I'm sure she had us pulling fucking wheelies on the way here."

Kirsty laughed. "Just keeping it lively for the two of you!"

Hoon frowned, his gaze darting between captain and passenger. "Two?" he asked, eyeing the open door at Bamber's back. "Who else is there? Don't tell me you've brought the fucking wife. It's no' a holiday, Bam."

"Course I haven't brought the wife!" Bamber replied. "But I met this weirdo at the harbour in Mallaig."

Behind him, a scrawny man emerged from inside the cabin, one eye fixed on Hoon, the other pointing straight up like it was searching for satellites. He had a large rucksack on his back, bulging with Christ knew what.

"Alright, Boggle?" Iris asked. He shoved his hands deep in his pockets, and shrugged his slender shoulders. "I know, like, in the van earlier, you repeatedly told me to fuck off, but I thought... that stuff Redneck said. I think... I think I want to be one of the good guys again. So, I thought maybe I could make myself useful. If, like, that's alright with you?"

Hoon looked at both men in turn, Iris missing an eye, Bamber legless from halfway down each thigh. This was it, then, was it? This was his army?

He smiled. Those other bastards didn't stand a chance.

"Aye, Iris," he said, reaching out a hand. "That's alright with me."

———

Hoon and Iris stood at either end of the crate of weaponry, while Bamber leaned forward in his wheelchair, peering at the contents assembled inside.

"Jesus," he said, then he followed it up with a low whistle through the gap in his front teeth. "You're expecting them to come in hard, then? That's some arsenal, if not."

"I don't know what I expect," Hoon told him. "So better safe than sorry, I say. I'd rather have..." He counted below his breath. "Thirteen, fourteen, fifteen. *Fifteen* guns too many, than not have enough."

Bamber pointed into the box, just like Berta had done. "And is that...?"

"C-4. Aye."

Iris rubbed his hands together, his face a picture of glee. "I can deal with that, Boggle. You know me and explosives. Leave that in my hands."

Hoon found his attention drawn to Iris's glass eye, but he ignored the flickering doubt and just patted him on the shoulder. "Cheers, Iris. I reckon they'll come in from here, here, and over there," he said, indicating the most likely entry points to the bay. "Anyone else think otherwise?"

Bamber and Iris both shook their heads. "Makes sense," Bamber said. "Anywhere else leaves them too open."

"Right, well, crack on then, Iris," Hoon said, patting the other man on the back. "You know what to do."

Iris suddenly looked unsure. "What? You're just going to let me go and do it? On my own?"

"Aye," Hoon said. "You know what you're fucking doing, don't you?"

"Eh, yeah. Yeah, I do," Iris said. "It's just... you know." He flinched with embarrassment as he unpacked the acronym of his nickname. "*I require intense supervision.*"

Hoon shook his head. "Once upon a time, maybe. But now? I don't think you do. You've got this, pal. Go do your thing."

Iris *boinged* up to his full height, like a button had been pressed on his back. He saluted more crisply and cleanly than he'd ever done in his life, then he reached into the box and started pulling out armfuls of plastic explosives and detonators.

"Maybe be a bit less fucking gung-ho with it, though," Hoon suggested. Beside him, Bamber's wheelchair gave a *creak* as it rolled back a few inches.

"No problem, Boggle. You got it, Boggle!" Iris replied. Then, arms fully laden, he spun three times on the spot, so he was facing a different direction each time, and set off at a scurry once he'd settled on the last one.

"That wise?" asked Bamber, once Iris was out of earshot.

"Probably not, no," Hoon admitted. "But then I don't know if any of this is."

Bamber laughed. It was a sharp and sudden thing. Had it been anyone else, Hoon would've said it sounded like the laugh came all the way from his toes, but Christ knew where those had ended up all those years ago.

"What?" Hoon asked. The laughter was proving infectious, and he chuckled as he asked again. "What is it? What are you fucking laughing at?"

"I don't know!" Bamber wheezed. "It's not even funny. I

just... I mean, Jesus Christ. Look at us. The three of us. All the way out here, about to do God knows what!"

He was still laughing, but it was on the wane now, and Hoon could watch the doubt creeping across the other man's face.

"You don't have to do this, Bam," he said. "I shouldn't have asked you. You don't have to be here."

"How fucking *dare* you," Bamber said, and all the humour had left his voice now. He adjusted himself in his chair, and set his jaw as he stared deep into Hoon's eyes. "After what you did? For me? For Caroline? You think I'd be *anywhere* else right now? Anywhere at all?"

His voice cracked. He banged a fist on the arm of his wheel-chair, forcing back the tears that were now threatening to over-whelm him.

"You found my girl. You found her, and you brought her home to us, Bob." A tear rolled down his cheek. He moved quickly to wipe it away, but he didn't bother with the next few that followed. "I don't care if it's the armies of Hell that come over that ridge. I stand here. With you. Until the end."

Hoon sniffed. Dabbed at his nose with the back of his hand. Cleared his throat.

"I'm no' sure your word choice was entirely appropriate at the end there, Bam," he said. "But I appreciate the fucking sentiment."

Bamber frowned, took a few moments to retrace the last part of his speech, then laughed again. "OK, maybe I don't *stand* with you, but aye, you get the point."

"I get the point," Hoon confirmed. He put a hand on his old friend's shoulder. "But you owe me nothing."

Bamber rested his hand on top of Hoon's. "Guess we'll have to agree to disagree on that one."

Hoon was about to say more when a flying plastic hoop

whanged him on the side of the head, followed by the sound of girly giggling from over by the house.

The twins stood in the doorway, hands over their mouths, faces lit up in a panicky excitement, like they weren't sure whether to cheer or run for their lives.

"What the fuck is this?" Hoon demanded, stooping to pick up the hoop. "Did you fucking throw this?"

"Can we get it back?" one of the twins asked, holding out a hand.

"No. Can you fuck," Hoon said.

He twisted so he was facing away from the house, and threw the hoop with all his might. All four of them watched as it climbed up, up, up at a forty-five-degree angle...

...then came down, down, down on an almost exact reverse path.

"Jesus!"

Hoon ducked to avoid being brained by the thing for a second time. Before he could do anything to stop them, the twins had grabbed the hoop and gone running back inside the house with it.

"Berta! Is it no' time you sent your wee pals home?"

"Don't you worry about the girls!" came the reply from inside. "They're heading back when their parents get home at eight."

"Eight?! Fuck's sake, it'll be nearly dark by then!"

Berta appeared in the doorway, filling the frame in all directions. "What part of, 'Don't you worry about the girls,' didn't you get?" she asked. "You concern yourself with your friends, Bobby, and I'll concern myself with mine."

She retreated inside, and slammed the door with enough force to rattle the windows all the way up in the attic.

Bamber shrugged. "Kids, eh?"

"Aye, you can say that again," Hoon muttered. He bit his lip, and chewed off a little strip of skin. It was the perfect opportunity to ask, he knew. The perfect time to ask the question he'd been wanting to ask for months. "Speaking of which... How is she? How's Caroline?"

Bamber's face tightened. Thinned out. "She's, eh... She's got a long road ahead of her," he said. "I'm not going to lie. But she's talking now. She's... I don't know. I can see her in there now. I feel like she's there somewhere, buried under it all. A few weeks ago, I wouldn't even have said that."

Hoon stared out over the water. He looked to the ground, then to the sky, then to the mountains rising in the distance.

He saw none of it. Not really.

"So, you're up for killing some of these pricks, then?" he asked.

"I'm counting down the minutes, mate," Bamber told him.

"Well, then," Hoon announced, finally turning back to the man in the wheelchair. "Let's get to work."

CHAPTER THIRTY-FOUR

HOON STOOD by the kitchen table, watching and listening as Iris walked him through everything he'd done so far. The one-eyed man had sketched out a map of the area to make things easier to follow. At least, that was the theory.

"And what are these?" Hoon asked, pointing to some oblong blobs scattered around the map.

Iris hesitated. "I told you. That's the cabin things."

"Why are they fucking round?" Hoon asked.

"OK, it's not *exactly* accurate," Iris admitted.

"It's no' remotely accurate. They're not that shape, and they're not in that fucking position."

"Right, OK, it doesn't matter, just pay attention. Listen," Iris continued. "I've primed some so I can trigger them remotely, and others to go off based on proximity. Pressure plates and door handles. So stay away from them ones."

"How do we know which is which?" Hoon asked.

"Easy. Odd numbers are on a remote switch, even numbers are automatic."

Hoon regarded the page spread out on the table again. "They don't have numbers."

"Yeah, they do. Up here," Iris said, tapping the side of his head.

"And how the fuck does that help me?" Hoon asked.

Iris's smile faded a little. "Oh. Yeah." He started to point to the blobs in turn. "One, two, three, four, six, five, seven, eight."

Hoon shot him a sideways look. "Why'd you do it like that?"

"Like what?"

"Like, 'six, five, seven'?"

"What?"

"Fuck's sake." Hoon pointed to the blobs again. "You said, 'one, two, three, four, six, five, seven, eight.'"

Iris's head made a series of little jerks while he retraced the movement of Hoon's finger. This made his glass eye shift around in its socket like a jumping bean.

"And?"

"And that's no' the fucking order!"

"What, of the cabins?"

"Of fucking numbers!" Hoon cried. "It goes one, two, three, four, five, six, seven!"

Iris stared at him for what felt like quite a lengthy period of time. "And what did I say?"

"For fu— Are you fucking...? You went six, five, seven, no' five, six, seven!"

"I don't think I did."

Hoon snatched up the map and the pen Iris had used to draw it with, then shoved him out through the back door of the kitchen. "Go! Fucking get out there and mark up what's what! And don't come back until you've learned to fucking count!"

He forcibly ejected the other man from the kitchen, slammed the door, then turned around and jumped when he saw two identical children standing just a few feet away.

"Jesus fuck, ye pair of creepy bastards!" he yelped. "What do you want?"

"Auntie Berta says you've to get us juice," they both said in unison.

"Does she now?" Hoon pointed to the fridge. "It's probably in there, so you go for your life," he said, then he reconsidered and sidestepped in front of them to block their route. "In fact, no. It's nearly eight. Time you girls were getting home."

"But Auntie Berta said—"

"Berta!" Hoon bellowed.

There was some groaning and muttering from through in the living room, as Berta struggled to heave herself up off the couch. Hoon continued to block entry to the fridge while he listened to her mumping and moaning her way along the hall.

"What's the problem?" she demanded.

Hoon tapped his watch. "I think it's about time the cast of the fucking *Shining* here went home, don't you?"

He shot a meaningful look out of the window. The sun was on a downward trajectory towards the horizon, and the still surface of the loch reflected a sky of pinks and purples and oranges so bright they looked almost radioactive.

"Yes. Yes, I suppose so," Berta admitted.

The girls both started to complain, but she shushed them with a smile and a flap of her hands.

"We can carry on next time," she promised, then she dunted her brother aside with a single swipe of a hip, and opened the fridge. "And you can take this with you."

She removed a metal tray that had been lined with baking parchment. A solid light brown block filled all the available space, scored along the top to segment it into rough squares.

"Here, is that tablet?" Hoon asked. "You didn't tell me there was fucking tablet!"

"Because it's not for you," Berta said, then she smacked away his hand when he tried to reach out and break himself a piece off from the block.

The twins giggled at this slapstick display of violence, then followed hot on Berta's heels as she carried the tray over to the worktop and fetched an old ice cream tub down from a shelf.

"You're no' giving them all of it?!" Hoon cried, watching helplessly while Berta broke the big slab of tablet down into manageable bite-sized chunks. "You might as well just inject them straight in the face with fucking Type 2 Diabetes."

"No, because the girls are more sensible than you, Bobby. *They* won't eat it until they're sick, like you used to. They'll take their time, and share it with Mum and Dad." She closed the lid of the tub, then held it up, just beyond their reach. "Won't you, girls?"

"Yes, Auntie Berta!" the twins said together.

"Do you two fucking rehearse this, or something? Speaking at the same time?"

"Language, Bobby!" Berta snapped. "That's enough!" She glowered at him until his face registered his submission, then gave him a curt, authoritative nod. "Now, is it safe for the girls to head home?"

"Far as I know, aye," Hoon said.

"That's not good enough," Berta said. She stabbed a finger out along the hall in the direction of the front door. "Check."

Muttering under his breath, Hoon marched out of the kitchen, through the house's hallway, and stormed outside. Iris had brought some of his own equipment from his bunker, including a set of five walkie-talkies that he insisted were all tuned to a secret channel of his own making.

Hoon hadn't bothered to argue. They worked, and that was the main thing.

He unclipped the radio from his belt, and looked over at the roof of the chalet that lay furthest from the main house. It stood a little apart from the others, and wasn't on any likely approach that the incoming hit squad was likely to take.

It hadn't been easy to get Bamber up there—especially given how firmly rot and decay had taken root in the wood—but he was now installed on the roof, lying flat, covered up, and scouting the area with a variable range scope.

"Bam. Anything?" Hoon asked.

A few seconds passed before Bamber's voice came crackling out of the radio. "Clean as a whistle."

Hoon turned back towards the open front door and made a beckoning motion.

"Right. We're fine," he said. "You send those two packing. I'm going to go get Frankenstein's Munter out of the cabin, so he's locked up in the house."

He waited a moment to check that Berta had heard him, and when he saw her fetching the girls' jackets down from a hook in the kitchen, he set off towards the closest chalet. Iris was standing near it, struggling to keep his hand-drawn map straight in the wind long enough to mark it up.

"This one's no' going to blow me to bits, is it?" Hoon asked, striding past him.

"No, Boggle, that one's fine," Iris said, consulting his map.

Hoon was almost at the front door when a voice cried out in panic behind him.

"Wait, wait!"

He froze, just a few feet from the chalet, craned his neck to look behind him, and saw Iris hurriedly turning his map upside-down.

"No, it's OK, you're safe," Iris said, after a few tense moments.

Hoon sighed, shook his head, then cautiously entered the cabin, half-expecting the whole thing to erupt in a fireball as soon as he opened the door.

Mercifully, it did not.

The Professor, bound and gagged on the floor, lay motionless as Hoon untied the ropes that had been used to restrain him. He didn't remove them all—just enough so that the bastard could get up and walk with him back to the house. He was the only bargaining chip they had, if it came to that, and there was no way Hoon was leaving him out here on his own.

The twins were coming out of the house just as Hoon and the Professor were returning to it, and the girls both squealed in horror at the sight of the old man's ravaged face.

Hoon wished he could say the timing had been accidental.

"Oh, don't you worry about Paul," Berta told them. Her voice was light and carefree, but the look she fired in her brother's direction was laced with pure venom. "He might look a bit... bedraggled, but he's nothing to be afraid of."

"Aye, don't let him scare you, girls," Hoon said. "Don't imagine him standing at the bottom of your bed tonight when you go to sleep, or anything. Or creeping across the ceiling like a big spider."

One of Berta's sensible brogues hoofed him on the shin, and he let out a sharp cry of pain.

"Ow! What was that for?" he hissed.

"You know full well what that was for, Bobby Hoon!" Berta said. She put herself between the children and the Professor, and finished fastening their coats. "Now, straight home, you two. No dilly-dallying. And get Mum and Dad to phone me when you're in, OK?"

"OK, Auntie Berta," they both said, in pitch-perfect harmony.

"That is just fucking unsettling," Hoon mumbled, and then the radio in his hand crackled out a sharp blast of static.

"Boggle," said Bamber, his voice low. "I've got movement on your six."

Hoon didn't turn. Turning would be a giveaway. Instead, he looked directly at his sister, and he saw the dread there in her eyes.

"Berta. Take the girls inside," he urged. He gave the Professor a light shove that sent him stumbling towards the older

Hoon. "Him, too. Get your gun. Get up to the loft, and pull up the ladder."

"Jesus, Bobby," Berta whispered, but she didn't argue any further than that. Instead, she plastered on a big, broad smile, and put a protective arm around the twins. "Come on, girls. Change of plan! Let's go get stuck into that tablet, will we?"

The twins cheered and went scampering back into the house. Berta grabbed the Professor by the arm, and then looked back at her brother again.

"Don't you fuck this up," she warned.

"Here's hoping," Hoon told her.

They shared a smile—just a brief one—then Berta bundled the Professor into the house and closed the front door behind her.

Hoon strolled as casually as he could around to the other side of the house before bringing his radio to his mouth. "Bam. Talk to me."

"I'm not seeing much," Bamber admitted. "Movement in the trees to the east a minute ago. Could be nothing, an animal maybe, but might not be. Definitely saw someone back on the hill path, though. Backed up quickly, but they were there."

"Right. Eyes peeled," Hoon told him. "Iris, where are you?"

There was a rapping on glass, and Hoon turned to find Iris standing in the kitchen, knocking on the window.

"I'm in here," he said, the voice coming over the radio and through the glass with just a split second delay.

"You all set?"

Iris held up a cobbled-together control panel. It looked like the sort of thing that might be used to control a very complicated radio-controlled plane. Or, more likely, to control several very complicated radio-controlled planes all at the same time.

"I'm all primed and ready, Boggle!" he announced.

Hoon spoke into the radio again. "Bam, can he get to you?"

"If he comes along the shore and around the back, aye. Nobody's going to see him."

It was Iris who replied. "On my way. Cover me, big boy!"

The kitchen door opened, and Iris came running out, clutching his control pad to his chest like it was the love of his life. His face was a picture of pure excitement when he ran past Hoon, calling out a, "See you on the other side, Boggle!" as he ran towards the shore.

It wasn't clear which 'other side' he was referring to. It could've been the battle, but it could've been something far bigger and more permanent.

Either way, despite Iris's many, *many* shortcomings, Hoon looked forward to their reunion.

He headed inside, closed the door, then locked it behind him. The crate of weaponry had been brought back inside while the twins were watching TV with Berta, and had been stashed under the kitchen table. It scraped the tiled floor when Hoon dragged it out again.

He removed the lid and discarded it with the care of someone who never intended to use it again. There were fewer guns there now, Iris and Bamber having both been suitably equipped already.

Still, in the right hands, there were enough firearms here to win any war on Earth. It was just a case of picking the right targets, and getting close enough to get off a clean shot.

There was one gun in particular he planned to take with him, no matter what. It wasn't the most sensible choice, not by a long shot, but he was taking it, all the same.

It had been buried on the verge alongside the boat down in London. He'd dug it up, and carried it with him, kept it close, ready to give it one last outing.

It sat there in the crate, still wrapped in the tape that had protected it from the elements. He fetched a knife from a drawer, and hacked away enough to let him get a firm hold. The tape left a sticky film as it peeled away from the handgun, dulling the shiny gold plating and the ridiculously bejewelled grip.

Welshy's Desert Eagle was a souvenir from a private-sector gig involving a Colombian drug cartel. The gun had belonged to the head of the organisation, but he'd had no further use for it by the time Welshy was finished with him.

Hoon passed it from hand to hand, remembering the weight of it. It was a ridiculous gun. It was obscene.

It was perfect.

"Right, then," he said, reaching back into the crate. "Here we fucking go."

———

No part of *Westward* could ever be classed as minimalist, but the only one that came even remotely close was the attic.

It had been floored when the Hoons had moved in, and had been sold to Berta as the perfect place to house any unwanted old junk. Berta had never been the type to hoard, though. If a thing had a purpose, it should be used for that purpose. If it had outlived its usefulness, or had no role to play, then why on Earth would she hang onto it?

As a result, the loft space was mostly empty. Alongside the house's water tank, it held a couple of ancient leather suitcases, three sturdy cardboard boxes, and a Christmas tree wrapped in black bin bags, which hadn't seen the light of day in years.

The windows were small squares cut into the wood and slate. Neither one of them was designed to open, and the only view they offered was of the darkening sky overhead.

Access was difficult, particularly for someone of Berta's age and size. It involved climbing up a steep wooden ladder that unfolded as the hatch was pulled down.

If it was difficult for her, though, it was impossible for the

Professor, whose hands were still tied behind his back. Berta had made him get down on his knees while she undid his bonds, then had hurriedly fastened them together again at his front, so he could at least support himself on the ladder as he climbed.

Once they were all up—the children sitting on the wooden lid of the water tank, and Professor down on the floor with his back against a sloping roof beam—Berta had reeled in the ladder, and set about securing the hatch from the inside.

The twins both watched the Professor with a sort of morbid fascination. He considered them both in turn, the tip of his tongue flitting, snake-like, between his teeth, as the corners of his dry, cracked lips curved upwards into a mockery of a smile.

He waved, his fingertips dancing like a magician casting a spell.

And his hands squirmed between the ropes.

CHAPTER THIRTY-FIVE

IT WAS dark by the time Hoon heard the *swishing* of oars through water. He thumbed the volume button all the way down on his radio, and quickly tapped out a Morse Code message to warn the others.

From his vantage point, tucked low behind the ruins of an old hen house, Hoon watched a dinghy approaching around the headland. He counted three occupants, all dressed head to toe in black. They clutched weapons to their chests, though they were still too far away for him to make out what they were. SMGs, he thought, judging by the size.

So, they were anticipating a close-up battle, then. They probably thought he was in the house, oblivious to their presence.

He felt himself start to grin, then wiped it away. It wouldn't do to get cocky.

Not yet, anyway.

He held his breath. Waited, as the boat glided to a stop at the end of the jetty. He watched carefully, his face blackened by soot from the house's fireplace, his eyes narrowed to slits.

Their next move would tell him a lot. The next few seconds

would determine if there was even a chance of surviving the night.

He had to swallow back a little *cheep* of relief when all three men clambered out of the boat and onto the wooden jetty. He'd have stuck to the water. Waded in, spreading out to make three targets instead of one.

The fact that they hadn't, told him everything he needed to know.

They were halfway to the shore when the first plank gave way beneath them. Hoon heard the *clunk* of a skull hitting wood as one of the men dropped out of sight into the icy cold water below. He tapped out a series of dots and dashes on the walkie-talkie, and something flashed below the murky surface of the loch, directly below where the other two men stood.

The whole structure collapsed in a chorus of cracks and crunches and panicky screams. Flailing limbs became tangled in the weighted fishing nets strung below, dragging them down, forcing them to relinquish their weapons to the deep as they fought to keep their heads above the surface.

Somewhere, out front, another explosion rang out. This one was bigger, and didn't have the benefit of being muted by the water. The dark sky was briefly painted in a palette of oranges and reds, and a round of panicky machine gun fire followed hot on the heels of the *boom*.

Hoon turned the volume of his radio up a couple of notches in time to hear Iris hissing excitedly over the airwaves.

"Now that," the one-eyed man declared, "was *epic*!"

———

Berta sat on the water tank, one girl tucked under each of her arms, pulled in close. They had their hands over their ears, and their eyes screwed shut, as the sound of gunfire echoed across the *Westward* grounds, and another explosion turned night into day.

It faded quickly, leaving the attic in near darkness again, save for a candle that flickered on top of one of the cardboard boxes.

"Shh, now, don't you worry about a thing," Berta said. "This is all going to be over soon. We could sing a song. Will we sing a song? What songs do we know?"

There was shouting, muffled by the roof. A *crack* of a sniper rifle. A series of frantic cries.

Berta put her hands on their heads, and pulled them in closer still, rocking back and forth as a song she hadn't spared a thought for in decades tumbled freely from her lips.

"Dreams to sell, fine dreams to sell, Angus is here with dreams to sell. Hush now wee bairnies and sleep without fear, for Angus will bring you a dream, my dear."

There was another sniper *crack*, then the *rat-tat-tat* of returned gunfire. A window shattered elsewhere in the house, and both girls jumped and squealed at the same time.

Berta raised her voice and continued to sing.

"Can ye no hush your weepin'? All the wee lambs are sleepin'. Birdies are nestlin', nestlin' taegether. Dream Angus is hurtlin' through the heather.

"Sweet the lavrock sings at morn, heraldin' in a bright new dawn. Wee lambs, they coorie doon taegether, alang with their ewies in the..."

Her voice fell away into silence. In the chill of the roof space, her breath rolled out as a mist.

On her right, a floorboard creaked. A rope fell away.

And two girls screamed as a monster came lunging from the shadows.

CHAPTER THIRTY-SIX

"HOW MANY?" Hoon barked into his radio. He was taking cover behind one of the chalets, listening to the crackling of flames from the three burning cabins, the short-barrelled assault rifle he'd grabbed from the crate—an Ultra-Compact Individual Weapon, or UCIW—clutched in both hands.

"I make twelve," Bamber said.

There was another *crack*. Even with the suppressor on the sniper rifle, Hoon saw the flash from up on the furthest cabin roof.

"Make that eleven."

Hoon checked his watch.

"Any sign of the cavalry?"

"Not unless they've come dressed like these other pricks," Bamber replied.

"That'd be an unfortunate fucking fashion faux pas, right enough," Hoon replied, then he checked his watch for a second time and winced.

Where the fuck were they? If this was going to work, they had to be here soon.

There was always Plan B, of course. It might actually be his preferred option—kill all these fuckers and burn their bodies in a big bonfire—but Plan A was better. With Plan B, he'd always be looking over his shoulder. If things worked out properly, though, then there was a chance he could be free of these fuckers for good.

Of course, that relied on backup arriving on time, and they were cutting it fucking fine.

"Fire in the hole!" Iris announced.

Hoon ducked and jammed his fingers in his ears, then grimaced as another explosion shook the ground. This one was closer than the others. He heard glass shattering and wood splintering in the chalet he was hiding behind. A chunk of fiery debris punched a hole in the wall just a few feet on his left.

"Watch what you're fucking doing!" he hissed into the walkie-talkie, but Iris was laughing too hard to hear him.

"You should've seen them!" the one-eyed man spluttered. "One of them did a triple backflip!"

"You nearly fucking took me out, too!" Hoon spat back.

"What? Aw, sorry, Boggle. Wasn't my fault. One of your men there stood on a plate."

"Then how the fuck did you have time to say, 'Fire in the hole,' first?"

There was a pause. "Oh. Aye," Iris replied. "Maybe I did press it, then."

Before Hoon could say anything more, he sensed movement on his left. A figure dressed all in black crept around the side of the chalet, crouching low, his SMG clutched in both hands.

When he saw Hoon, the whites of his eyes doubled in size. He brought his weapon up, but too late. The UCIW kicked in Hoon's grip. At that range, the other man's body armour was little more than an inconvenience. He was launched backwards, body convulsing, his finger tensing on the trigger so his bullets ripped holes in the sky.

"Fuck!" Hoon groaned.

So much for hiding.

Bamber's voice came over the airwaves. Raw. Urgent.

"Boggle," he spat. "*Run!*"

She woke to the smell of smoke. Not the odours that had been finding their way in through the gaps in the roof from outside, but closer. Stronger.

Berta peeled open a bloodied eyelid and saw two boxes and the skeletal remains of an artificial Christmas tree blazing away in the corner of the loft.

A rope lay on the floor. The hatch stood open.

The girls, and the Professor, were gone.

Her head spun as she dragged out the arm that had been pinned beneath her, and struggled into a sitting position on the floor. The smoke—thick, and black, and pungent—was gathering right up at the apex of the roof, carried by the breeze coming up through the hatch from below.

She looked for the shotgun. Gone, of course. Then, she shuffled herself over to the opening, and peered down at the upstairs landing.

The ladder had been unhooked, and now lay discarded on the floor below her. It was a drop of nine feet, maybe more.

"Fucking high ceilings," she muttered, contemplating the drop.

It would have been no bother to her once-upon-a-time, but that time had long passed. Now, it was a sprain or a breakage waiting to happen.

She looked over at the flames now licking their way up the inside of the roof. The water tank was just a few feet away, but she had nothing to transport the water in. And, even if she had, the attic was too far gone for her to save it now.

Somewhere, in the house below, two girls screamed in terror.

"Right then, you skeleton-faced cockhole. You asked for it."

And with that, she dangled her legs over the edge of the drop, and jumped.

———

Hoon ran, firing blindly into the blazing darkness. Bullets tore up the ground at his feet, spiralling clods of muck and grass into the air.

There was another cabin thirty feet ahead. He could take cover behind it, catch his breath, reload.

Twenty feet.

Fifteen.

"No, Boggle!"

The shout didn't come from over the radio, but from the chalet where Iris and Bamber were hiding. The panic in Iris's voice told him just how big a mistake he'd made.

Something beneath the soil went *clunk*. Hoon twisted, throwing himself clear just as the front of the chalet became fire and thunder and flaming splinters. The force of the blast clipped him, spinning him in the air, stealing the breath from his lungs, and making the world ring like an old school bell.

He felt weightless. Motionless. Like he was hanging there in empty space, as the world whirled around him.

And then, impact. Hard. Jarring. Dragging at him, flipping him over, gradually robbing him of all his momentum until he was just a mound of flesh and bone, wheezing and gasping on the cold, hard ground.

Over the ringing in his ears, he heard shouting. More gunfire. Racing feet.

From where he'd landed, he could see the old house. Flames

leaped from the roof, a column of black smoke rising steadily towards the distant stars.

Hands grabbed at him. Turned him. He jammed the UCIW into an unfortunately positioned crotch, and squeezed the trigger. There was blood. Squealing. The man who'd been turning him went down like a broken toy, but before Hoon could take advantage, something heavy hit him on the back of the head.

He fell, face-first, into the muck.

And, behind him, *Westward* continued to burn.

CHAPTER THIRTY-SEVEN

BERTA HEAVED herself along the upstairs landing, then recoiled when she reached the top of the stairs. The ground floor was ablaze, even more so than the attic above. Whatever had smashed through the window must've been on fire at the time, and the flames had been quick to take hold.

"Fuckity-bollocks," she whispered.

Was there another way out? She couldn't think. Her bedroom was on the ground floor. A perfectly serviceable bathroom, too. She couldn't even remember when she'd last been upstairs. She'd had very little need to.

The smoke was becoming thicker and more pungent. It dried out the back of her throat and burned away at the lining of her lungs.

The flames were licking up the staircase now, consuming the bannister, blistering the paint on the walls. If the girls were down there, then she had no hope of reaching them.

If they weren't—if they were still up here somewhere—then it was only a matter of time before they burned.

But she'd be damned if they were burning with that goblin-faced fuck.

There were five doors running off from the upstairs landing. Wasting time wasn't an option. If they were here, they were behind one of those doors.

She picked one, turned the handle, then let her weight and her momentum do the rest and stumbled into a long-abandoned guest bedroom. White sheets, made grubby by the passing of time, covered most of the furniture. The casual observer would be forgiven for thinking they'd entered a domain of ghosts, albeit quite a low budget one.

Berta stood in silence, eyeing the shapes beneath the sheets. The fabric shifted, just a few millimetres here and there, buffeted by the warm air rising from below.

She listened, breath held, her heart pounding up her throat and into her mouth, until her whole head shook with it.

And then, from somewhere along the landing, came a loud *thunk* of something heavy hitting glass.

And the sound of two little girls crying out in fear.

———

He could only have been out for a few seconds. When he came to, he was being dragged across the ground by his feet, his head bumping over rocks and mounds of tightly packed dirt.

He played dead, getting his breath back, getting his bearings, getting the lay of the land. There was, he noted, a distinct lack of gunfire. Flames still crackled and spat in the darkness, but no more explosions rang out.

The sounds of the battlefield had fallen silent.

He opened an eye and saw fire continued to consume *Westward*. There was nothing he could do. No way he could get to those inside without being instantly shot dead. All he could do was hope that Berta had got herself and the kids out safely.

Though hope had never been his strong point.

From somewhere on his right, he heard Iris cry out in

protest. "Watch what you're doing with him! He's got no legs, or hadn't you noticed!"

"I'm fine, wee man." That was Bamber's voice, hoarse and shaken. "Don't you worry about me."

Shite.

That was it, then. Barring a miracle last-minute rescue, it was over.

The grip on his legs was released. His feet fell, heels smashing against the ground.

There was a creaking of leather. Boots approached and stopped beside him.

"You're not fooling anyone, you know?"

His ears were still ringing from the blast, but Hoon recognised the voice. Suranne, or whatever the fuck her real name was.

Hoon continued to play dead. His head was still spinning, his breath still short. He just needed some time to recover. To think. To find a Plan C.

"Shoot the cripple," Suranne ordered.

"Wait!"

Hoon's eyes flicked open. He brought up a hand, palm towards her, fingers splayed wide. "Wait, don't. Fuck sake. I'm awake. I'm awake!"

Suranne smirked down at him. She wore the same black SWAT-style gear as the seven or eight men standing in a circle around them, but had rolled her balaclava up to reveal her face. There were black circles around her eyes. It was for camouflage purposes, of course, but it made her look like she was embracing her inner Goth.

"Thought that might get through to you," she said, then she stepped back and made a beckoning motion with her finger. "Up. On your knees."

"Alright, alright, give me a minute." Hoon grimaced. "You're lucky I can even find my fucking knees."

He groaned and complained as he righted himself and assumed a kneeling position. Bamber lay on the ground a few feet away, face upwards, his hands behind his head. Iris was down on all fours beside him, blood oozing from a wound on his cheek, his glass eye missing, presumed lost.

Hoon raised his head so he was looking directly up at Suranne. There was a smile playing across her lips, like she was finding this whole thing amusing.

"Bad news, sweetheart," he told her. "I've done my best, exhausted every avenue, chased down every fucking lead I could, but I can now officially report that I've no' got a fucking clue where your ostrich is."

She hit him. It wasn't hard. It wasn't meant to hurt, just to humiliate. Just to show him that she could do it, and there was nothing he could do to prevent it.

"Aye, just you go ahead and let out all that repressed sexual tension, doll," he told her. "Don't mind me. Slap me about as much as you fucking like. I can take it."

Suranne's smile only grew at that. It became a laugh, jarringly light and carefree, given the circumstances. "I have no doubt you can," she said.

She pointed to Iris. A gloved hand grabbed him by the hair from behind, wrenching him upright with enough force to make him cry out in shock. He faced Hoon and Suranne, his one eye darting between them, his features contorted in pain.

"But I wonder," Suranne began, "can *he*?"

———

Berta entered the room just as the Professor slammed the butt of the shotgun against the window again, with another disappointing *donk*.

In hindsight, she should've crept in, but the sound of the twins in distress had brought her storming into the room, and she barely made it a few feet before the Professor spun to face her, and both barrels of the shotgun snapped in her direction.

It was another bedroom. Christ, how many of them did she have? Not that there would be any left soon, of course, judging by the way the smoke was rolling across the ceiling.

The girls were over by the window, hugging each other, tears cutting clean lines down their soot-blackened cheeks. They were close to him, well within grabbing range.

Well within firing range, too.

He watched Berta, hawk-like, as she took another slow step into the room, her hands raised to indicate her surrender.

Out on the landing, flames were now leaping up the last few steps, and the second fire crackled above them, eating its way through the ancient roof timbers.

They had just minutes to get out. Moments, maybe.

Berta locked eyes with the man with the gun. "Will you get them out?" she asked him.

He nodded, just once, to confirm that he would.

Berta tore her eyes from him just long enough to steal a look at the children. They were staring back at her, their bodies rigid with terror, their faces collapsing under the weight of their snot, and their tears.

"When you get them out. When you get them down from here. You're not... You won't hurt them, will you?"

He didn't respond. Not directly. There was no nod of confirmation, or head shake of denial.

But his eyes told her everything. There was a hunger in them. A longing.

This was not a rescue. He wasn't helping the girls.

He was taking them.

Roberta Gwendoline Hoon drew herself up to her full height. The heartbeat that had been thrumming around inside her head returned to her chest and settled there.

"In that case, let me ask you something, *Paul*," she said, spitting out the name like it was poison in her mouth. "When he was chewing your nose off, did my brother bite off your fucking ears, too?"

She took another step. The barrels of the gun moved to follow.

"Because clearly, you weren't fucking listening earlier when I pointed out that the gun wasn't bloody loaded!"

The Professor looked down at the weapon clutched in his shaking hands.

And, ignoring the pain in her legs, and the lightness in her head, Berta launched herself towards the bastard, fists swinging like the arms of a windmill.

CHAPTER THIRTY-EIGHT

"WHOA, WHOA, WHOA," Hoon urged. "Let's back the fuck up and calm the fuck down. That wee runt's done nothing to nobody."

Iris grinned, showing his bloodied teeth. "Bollocks, Boggle." Laughter sniggered through his crooked nose. "I blew half of them to fucking Kingdom Come! It was brilliant!"

An SMG was jammed against the back of Iris's head. His shoulders heaved, but Hoon couldn't tell if he was still laughing or crying, or maybe stranded in some tortuous No Man's Land between the two.

"Wait, wait, steady!" Hoon cried. "Let's no' be too fucking hasty here. Shoot him—shoot either of them—and you'll never find out where your taco-faced effigy of a pal is."

Suranne's smile lost some of its shine, and Hoon knew then that he had her. She wanted the Professor back. And that meant he had something to bargain with.

"Here's what's going to happen," he said. "You let these two go. Give them five minutes to get out of here on your boat, then I'll tell you where he is."

"We don't need his help," grunted one of the men, and

Hoon heard the guttural drawl of an Irish accent. "We can look for him ourselves."

"You can look, aye, for all the fucking good it'll do you," Hoon said. "He's hidden somewhere you'll never fucking find him. Not in a million fucking—"

There was a *boom* of shotgun fire from an upstairs bedroom of the burning house. It was followed, almost immediately, by the sound of shattering glass. This, in turn, gave way to what sounded like a large sack of animal parts hitting the ground with a *splat*.

"Oh, look, you ghoul-eyed fucker!" Berta cried. "Looks like it was loaded, after all!"

Hoon smiled weakly up at the now furious-looking Suranne.

"Maybe she meant a different ghoul-eyed fucker?" he ventured. He sighed, then shrugged. "Still, if it's any consolation, he sold you out in a fucking heartbeat. Told us everything he knew. About you, about the Loop. I didn't even have to raise a fucking finger, which was disappointing. But, what was interesting, was that he didn't actually know much. Funny that, eh? Him being fucking balls deep in the organisation, he seemed a bit fucking clueless about it all. *Out of the loop*, you might say, were you the type of unfunny prick to make puns."

Suranne sighed and raised her handgun, pointing the muzzle directly at the centre of his forehead. Hoon acted fast to avoid being shot in the face.

"I know you," he said. He spat the words out quickly, partly to keep her on the back foot, but also because he was now all-too-aware that Berta and the kids hadn't yet got out of the house. "All of you. Everyone here. I know who you all are."

"You really don't," Suranne told him.

"Aye, I do," Hoon insisted. "I know you fucking intimately, sweetheart. You're me."

There was some slight dippage of the woman's eyebrows.

"What are you talking about?"

"You're him, too. And him," Hoon said, indicating Iris and Bamber. "We're the fucking same. All of us. You know why?"

"I'm sure you're going to enlighten me."

"Because we're foot soldiers." Hoon shook his head. "We're less than that, even. We're fucking cannon fodder. We're the guys who take the risks, so some big rich fucker sitting in an office somewhere can reap the rewards."

He looked around the circle of armed men, nodding at them, like he was urging them to agree. Nobody did.

"Aye, well, suit your fucking self," Hoon muttered. Keeping his hands raised, he lowered a finger so it was pointing at Suranne. "But you've got something I don't," he told her. "You've got ambition. You don't want to be down here in the fucking mud, shit, and blood with the rest of us. You want to be up there somewhere, penthouse floor, corner fucking office, *ding-ding*, thank you very much. You want to be one of them fuckers in the fancy suits, sending the likes of us to do their dirty work, while they all stand around shitting gold bars and fucking applauding each other."

Hoon blew out his cheeks and shook his head. "I never had that. I never saw the fucking appeal. That shite? That's no' the fucking real world. Down here? Down in the filth? That's where life fucking came from, and that's where it stayed. But you, sweetheart? You've got big ideas, don't you?"

Suranne looked pleased by the assessment. "Nothing wrong with setting your sights high, is there?"

Hoon looked around them. Bodies lay scattered around the grounds of *Westward*. The burning cabins had been completely consumed by fire now, and the flames had reduced to a low smouldering glow.

The same couldn't be said for the house. It was far enough away that he couldn't feel the heat on his back, but he could see the light from it dancing across Suranne's face, making her eyes sparkle and shine.

"That depends," Hoon said.

"On what?"

"On how many of us poor foot soldiers have to die to make all your fucking dreams come true."

He let that sink in, not so much with her, but with the men around them.

"See, here's what I think, *Suranne*," he said, managing to make the name sound like something offensive. "I think you're a fucking nobody. If you were as connected as you say you are, you wouldn't have turned up at my place on your own. You wouldn't have dragged in a family of what I assume were fucking Irish travellers to rough me up. Big international crime syndicates don't use fucking *Rent-a-Mick* to do their dirty work."

He gestured around to the surrounding men.

"And as for this lot, they're no' special forces. They're no' even special fucking needs," he scoffed. "They're a bunch of amoeba cocks. And by that, I don't mean they've got cocks the size of amoebas, I mean their cocks are the size of amoebas' cocks. And no' well-endowed amoebas, either. Saddo wee shrivelled-dick amoebas, who need to drive wee fucking amoeba sports cars to compensate for their all-too-fucking-evident inadequacies."

Boots creaked behind him, as some of the men shifted their weight. He braced himself for a battering, but it didn't come.

Thank Christ for that.

"So, when I realised that—when I realised that you're not the big fucking *I Am* that you're under the delusion that you are, I started thinking things through a bit," Hoon continued. "I've had quite a few cracks to the fucking head over the past few months, so it takes a bit longer to get the old brain warmed up, but I get there eventually. And what I realised was that you murdering that nappy-wearing fuck... The Eel?" He clicked his fingers and frowned. "What's his name?"

"Godfrey West," she replied, and there was a hint of smugness to the way she said it. Pride in her accomplishment.

"That's him. Aye. I don't think the Loop killed Godfrey West. I think you killed him, all on your own. I think that was a fucking power play on your part," Hoon said. "I think you're so desperate to move up in the Arsehole Premier League that you had him killed, and the poor fucking driver, too, to try and win favour with the big boys upstairs."

"And? Like I said, nothing wrong with ambition."

Hoon nodded along, not disagreeing. "Same with Deirdrie Bagshaw. That was fucking bold, by the way. Killing her in her own house. Making it look like suicide. I was almost fucking impressed."

Suranne dipped her head, as if taking a bow. "Thanks. That means a lot."

"You'd literally fucking murder your way to the top if you could, wouldn't you?" Hoon said. "Anyone above you is fair fucking game if it means you get to keep moving up the board."

"Again, nothing wrong with ambition," Suranne replied.

"And that's why you came after me, isn't it? Nobody sent you to do that, either," Hoon said. "Why would they? Because, really, I know fuck all. The Loop—if it even exists in the form you fucking power fantasist boot-licking bawbags think it does—it doesn't give a shite about the likes of me. I can't hurt something that size. No one can.

"That's why nobody's ever gone after Greig. That's why Welshy and Gabriella were never in fucking danger. They're fleas. We all are. Less than that, we're fucking microbes on the arses of fleas, and they're giants, no' even noticing that we fucking exist, much less expending any energy dealing with us. Because if they did, they'd be exposing themselves. Why take that fucking chance? Why draw attention to yourself?"

Suranne adjusted her grip on the gun. Behind Hoon, the

flames continued to crackle and crack, as his childhood home was devoured by the flames.

"A mate of mine said recently that nobody wants to get involved these days. Nobody wants to disrupt the organised chaos of their own fucking lives. And he's right. They'll go out of their way no' to go out of their fucking way. And they'll create whole fucking narratives in their head so they can still feel good about themselves afterwards. He reckons only the good guys stand up. Only the good guys put themselves out when they don't have to." He shrugged. "I'm no' even sure about that, but I do know that the bad guys certainly fucking don't."

"Is there a point coming soon?" Suranne asked.

"Aye. Here it comes," Hoon said. "The only person I'm a fucking danger to is you. Because I saw your face. I know what you've done. I could cause you problems. And because you're so far down the chain of command, none of your wannabe supervillain pals would bat so much as a fucking eyelid if anything happened to you. I said the Loop doesn't give a fuck about me. But, I don't think it cares about you, either. So, you have to take me out, right? You have to find me, and you have to kill me."

Suranne stared down at him in silence for a moment, then nodded. "Thanks for reminding me," she said, and she pressed the gun against his forehead.

Iris and Bamber both tried to move, to intervene, but hands held them. Boots pressed them down.

Hoon laughed. It was a sharp and sudden thing that seemed to take even him by surprise.

"Thank fuck," he said.

"Yeah. I suppose I am doing you a favour, aren't I?" Suranne said.

"What? Oh. No. It's no' that," Hoon said. He shifted his gaze to the masked man standing on Suranne's left, and winked. "What do you think of her tits?"

There was a moment of confused silence, during which the eyes of all the men were instinctively drawn to Suranne's chest.

And to the single red dot that was projected there, right over her heart.

"What the fuck?" an Irish accent hissed. The men spun, searching the darkness, finding more red points picking them out from all sides.

"You know how else I knew this lot weren't fucking pros?" Hoon asked, eyes locking onto Suranne.

He brought his left hand across, knocking the gun from his head, and grabbing her wrist. He stood, and as he did, a shiny gold monstrosity of a handgun was pulled from below his waistband.

"Clueless fannies didn't think to search me."

He gave the arm a twist, and she squealed as something went *snap*. Her gun fell to the ground, where Bamber snatched it up and took aim at the man still holding Iris.

"Let him fucking go," Bamber spat.

Iris fell forwards immediately as the masked man raised his hands in surrender, watching red dots float like fireflies across the heads and chests of his comrades.

"Down on the ground," Hoon urged, putting a hand on Suranne's shoulder.

Her face had turned almost pure white, giving her the appearance of a particularly distraught looking panda. She knelt, though it was more like a giving way of her legs beneath her, than a conscious decision to do so.

"I'd put your guns down, lads," Hoon urged. "Unless you're looking to start a new career as a slice of fucking Swiss cheese."

They didn't need telling twice. Weapons were quickly discarded. Iris snatched a couple up, and took great pleasure in forcing the man who'd been holding him to lie face down on the ground.

Suranne hissed as the beam from a high-powered torch hit

her in the face, blinding her. Hoon kept the gun on her until the shadows came alive behind him, and an imposing figure in a big coat came shuffling over to join them.

"Cutting it a bit fucking fine there, Jack," Hoon said.

Logan inhaled deeply, filling his barrel-like chest. He held up a finger. "Gimme a minute," he wheezed.

"Fuck's sake," Hoon muttered. "This was meant to be my big fucking moment here. Tell me you at least got her fucking confession?"

"Got it," came another voice from the darkness.

An Asian man appeared around the beam of the torch, holding up a portable recording device.

"You remember DS Hamza Khaled. Right, Bob?"

"What do you mean? Course I fucking do!" Hoon cheered. "Guy's a fucking legend! Well done, Detective Sergeant. You'll be replacing this fat prick in no time."

Hamza smiled awkwardly and shot Logan a cautious sideways look.

"Eh, cheers," he said.

Hoon made a beckoning motion, and he started to hand over the recorder.

"No' that. The other thing," Hoon urged.

"Oh. Aye."

Hamza handed over a small silver cylinder. Hoon peered down one end, pressed a button, then hissed when he almost blinded himself.

"Fuck, that's bright."

"Lasers generally are, aye," Logan confirmed.

Hoon grinned as he shone the laser pointer down at the woman on the ground, drawing pictures on her face with it.

"Hook, line, and fucking sinker," he said.

She sneered up at him through gritted teeth. "What now? You going to kill us?"

"No. They won't fucking let me, unfortunately," Hoon said.

"They're going to arrest you. All of you, but mostly you. They're going to put you in the fucking jail, and nobody's going to come for you. Nobody's going to game the fucking system. Nobody's going to pull any fucking strings. Because the only time those fuckers care about us little guys is when they're sending us to die. After that? We're on our own."

He stepped aside, lowered the gun, and nodded to DCI Logan.

"Jack, will you do the honours?"

"Don't mind if I do, Bob," Logan said, but before he could read anyone their rights, a voice piped up from the other end of the torch's beam.

"Eh, boss?" said DC Tyler Neish. The torch angle changed, so it was shining upwards, casting a young, wide-eyed man with a stupid fucking haircut into spooky shadow.

"Who the fuck's he?" Hoon asked.

Tyler ignored the comment, and instead pointed back over his shoulder. "We, eh, did all notice that house is on fire, aye?"

"Fuck!" Hoon yelped, breaking into a run. He pointed back to Iris and Bamber. "Keep them fucking covered. If anyone moves, you have my full permission to shoot them!"

"Don't listen to that. He can't actually give that permission," Logan pointed out, lumbering after him. He slowed and looked back. "Maybe a leg, but only if you have to."

Hoon passed DS Khaled and DC Neish, moving so fast that his voice trailed behind. "Don't just stand there, you pair of fucking arsemuppets, *move!*"

They were halfway to the house when one half of the roof gave way with a sound like Armageddon itself. Hoon missed a step, stumbled, then ran faster, ignoring the pain that jolted and jangled through his body every time his feet touched the ground.

The shifting of weight as the roof collapsed proved too much for the rear of the house. He saw the wall of the kitchen buckling and becoming rubble, flames rushing to fill the space the old stone had occupied.

From upstairs, beyond the broken window the Professor had been so unceremoniously ejected through, Hoon heard a sob. Or possibly two sobs, both made at exactly the same time.

"Creepy wee bastards," he muttered, then he skidded to a stop beside the Professor's bleeding, broken body and cupped his hands around his mouth. "Berta! *Berta*, can you hear me?"

There was no movement but the smoke and the flames. No sound but the hissing of old wood becoming embers.

The three detectives clattered to a stop behind him, but Hoon was already climbing, teeth gritted as he found handholds in the hot stone wall.

A pair of big hands grabbed his foot. Logan grunted as he straightened, hoisting Hoon higher up the wall until he could grab the ravaged frame of the shattered window.

Muscles burning, hands tearing on the glass, he hauled himself up and into the house. The detectives stood below, anxiously shifting their weight from foot to foot, watching and waiting.

"Should we call the fire brigade, boss?" Tyler asked.

"Bit fucking late for that, son," Logan told him.

"There he is!" Hamza cried, pointing up to the window.

Hoon leaned out, a wriggling child in his arms, all coughing and black.

"Catch!" he shouted, then he let the girl go.

"Jesus Christ!" Logan yelped, lunging, arms out, and grabbing the child before she could hit the ground.

"Don't worry, there's a spare one," Hoon called down from above.

Logan quickly passed the first girl to Hamza, then made another dive to save the other one when Hoon tossed her through the air.

"Right, you're going to want to fucking brace yourself for

the next one," Hoon called, then he vanished back into the house, leaving the detectives to handle the trembling, terrified twins.

———

The flames were everywhere. The smoke clogged the air like an oil spill in the ocean.

Hoon found Berta doubled over on the floor, not coughing exactly, but not exactly breathing, either. He knelt beside her, draped an arm across her broad shoulders, then spoke softly but urgently into her ear.

"Alright, sis? We need to get you out of here fucking pronto."

Berta raised a shaking hand and waved it, shooing him away. "The girls," she croaked.

"They're fine. We've got them. They're OK," Hoon said. "Your turn now, Berta. Come on. Up you get."

She shook her head and tried to push him away, but there was no strength to her now. For the first time in his life, Hoon reckoned he might stand a chance against her in a straight fight.

"Fuck off," she wheezed. "Leave me be."

Hoon looked back over his shoulder. There was no door now. No doorway, either. Just a wall of flame, and a black hole where the rest of the hallway used to be.

"Cut your shite. You're fucking coming," Hoon told her. "But I can't lift you, sis. I can't. So, I need you to shift your fat arse for me, OK? Can you do that for me?"

She raised her head, just enough so that their eyes met. She laid a hand on his cheek. Her skin felt weathered. Shrunken. So very, very old.

"You're a good boy, Bobby," she whispered. "You've always been a good boy."

"Have I fuck. Come on," Hoon said. "Shift."

"I don't think... I ever told you that I loved you." A tear ran down her cheek. Quite possibly the only one she'd ever shed. "Did I?"

Hoon looked back at the fire again. Closer still. He could feel the heat from it blistering the back of his neck. "No," he whispered. "No, you didn't."

Berta smiled. It was a sad, thin thing, yet mischievous, too.

"Aye, well, maybe one fucking day, eh?" she whispered, and Hoon broke into laughter.

"Aye. Maybe one day," he said, then he slumped down onto the floor beside her.

"Go," she told him. "What are you doing? Fuck off."

Hoon shook his head. "Nah."

"What?"

"Don't think I'll bother," he said. "I mean, might as well both go, eh? Seems fitting. This place, us, all fucking burning up at the same time."

She shoved him. Once. Twice. He felt it the second time. "Get to fuck!" she urged, then she grimaced and clutched at her chest, a spasm of pain turning her next words into a sob. "Please. Just go."

"If you're staying, I'm staying," Hoon said. "I'm no' having you saying I left you here to burn up. I'll never hear the fucking end of it."

A floorboard creaked. Hoon looked up at the ceiling above, before realising it had come from right behind him. He watched, genuinely awestruck for perhaps the first time in his life, as his sister rose to her feet.

"For fuck's sake," she said, coughing the words out one by one. "One day, you'll start doing as you're fucking told!"

"Aye, maybe," Hoon said, standing beside her. "But no' today."

———

"Right, you lot ready?" Hoon shouted from the window.

Logan, Hamza, and Tyler all looked up to find him helping Berta out through the broken window.

"Oh, for fuck's sake," Logan yelped.

He called over the others, whipped off his coat, and they all held a corner of it, stretching it between them to form a landing zone.

"Right, here she comes. Ready?"

Tyler shot a look at Logan. "I don't think I'm ready, boss," he admitted.

"Here she comes!" Hamza cried.

The detectives all looked up as Berta fell from the window. And it was a fall. Not a leap. Not a calculated, well-aimed jump. It was like her legs gave way, and her arms lost their ability to grip. She fell, limply, hit the coat, and the crashing down of her weight brought everyone but Logan to their knees.

It wasn't the most dignified of landings, but it was significantly better than a direct hit on the ground. She finished up sprawled across Tyler and Hamza, pinning them to the grass so they were able to wrestle their way out from below her bulk.

They rolled her onto her back just as Hoon slid down the wall beside them.

"Out the fucking road," he instructed, pushing between them and dropping to his knees beside her.

Another jolt of agony arched her back. A hand went to her chest, her fingers digging in like she could tear out the pain and be done with it.

Her eyes were glassy. Unfocused. She spoke, but it was a babbling whisper, barely audible above the roaring flames.

"B-Bobby. Where's Bobby?"

"I'm here, Berta. I'm right here," Hoon replied.

He took her hand. There was no resistance in it. She had been the strongest person he'd ever known, for better or worse, and now all that strength was leaving her before his eyes.

She looked up, not at him, but past him, like she could see something up there in the heavens above.

"You were meant to get the house," she whispered. "So fucking much for that."

"Forget the house. I don't want the house," he assured her.

She shifted her gaze so she was looking at him. "Why? What the fuck are you saying about my house?" she demanded, then she let out a sharp cry and hammered desperately at her heart, like she was trying to beat it into submission.

Hoon pointed to Tyler. "You. Boyband. Get the boat ready. We need to get her to the fucking hospital."

Tyler stood there, staring back. "Um, I don't know about boats," he confessed.

Down on the ground, Berta chuckled. "Course he fucking doesn't. Look at him. He looks like someone enchanted a fucking mannequin."

"Somebody get the bastarding boat ready!" Hoon cried.

Berta's hand tightened in his grip. He looked down at it, and a blackened tear fell between their fingers.

"It's OK, Bobby. It's fine," she told him. She brought his hand to her mouth, kissed it, and let it rest against her cheek. "You were the best wee brother I ever had."

"I was the only fucking brother you ever had," Hoon reminded her, each word almost choking him on the way out.

Berta managed a smile. A wink. "Aye," she said. "I know."

And with that, her head tilted back towards the heavens.

And the flames of *Westward* stretched high towards the sky.

CHAPTER THIRTY-NINE

THE FUNERAL WAS A SMALL, quiet affair, attended only by close friends and family. Bamber came. Iris, too. Even Redneck took a break from saving the world—or at least arming it—to pay his last respects.

The service had been, in Hoon's opinion, the usual pish. A lot of generic words used to say not a lot about a life the minister had known next to nothing about.

He'd sat through it with his head down, standing when told to, and pretending to pray when prompted.

He'd even joined in on the singing part. He was sure the old bugger would get a right laugh at that.

Now, with the service over, and the coffin in the ground, he stood back from the hole, watching the gravediggers filling it in.

"Doesn't really feel real, does it?" asked Bamber.

He'd broken a wrist when they'd hauled him off the roof of the chalet, and Redneck was pushing his chair across the grass. Iris followed, but he hung back a safe distance, like he was still waiting for some sort of punishment for the attempted robbery.

They all stopped next to Hoon, and watched the mound of soil being returned to the Earth.

"Keep expecting him to come bursting out," Redneck said. "That big grin on his face."

Hoon chuckled. "Aye. That'd be just like the bastard, right enough."

A dented old hip flask was presented to him by Iris. The one-eyed man had got a replacement glass eye. It was a completely different colour to the original, though just as prone to roll around in the socket.

Hoon took the flask, unscrewed the lid, then raised it towards the grave in a toast. "To Welshy," he said.

"Welshy," chimed the others.

Hoon took a swig from the flask, then coughed it all back up again, wheezing like he'd just taken a haymaker to the chest.

"The fuck is that?!" he ejected.

"Homemade peach schnapps," Iris explained. "But, I don't like peaches, so it's mostly just schnapps."

"What the fuck do you...?" Hoon began, then he sighed, shook his head, and passed the flask to the next man. "Doesn't matter. Cheers, Iris. It's the thought that fucking counts."

Across the graveyard, he saw her, and his feet turned to stone.

Gabriella stood at the gate, shaking hands with those who'd turned out, acknowledging their sympathies with a nod and a smile.

He hadn't spoken to her. Not today, and not on any of the days since he'd seen her last.

He'd made sure Miles knew what had happened. He'd given assurances that they were all safe. And, as far as he knew, they were. Suranne and her cronies were now guests of the Scottish legal system, and the world, it seemed, was continuing just fine without them.

Hoon, too, was going to have a lot of questions to answer. Logan had made that very clear. But questions he could handle, now that he knew Gabriella and the others were safe.

He understood it now, the Loop. He understood it better than most people in it, he reckoned.

It wasn't coming for him.

Of course, that didn't mean he wasn't coming for it.

"You going to go say hello?" Bamber asked.

Hoon tore his gaze from the woman at the gate. The gravediggers were almost done now. The funeral was over.

Hoon had done what he'd come to do.

"No," he replied. "I think everything we needed to say has already been said."

Hands were shaken. Hugs were half-given.

And, with his best funeral jacket swishing around his knees, Hoon turned towards the back gate of the graveyard, and set off on his way.

He took the sleeper train back up north. Having learned his lesson on his first trip down, he'd splashed out for an upgrade, so he had a full cabin to himself, rather than a seat.

The room was tiny, and he'd had to sidestep along the corridor just to reach it. But, having spent so many years in the military, fighting for every available cubic inch of sleeping space, the cell-like berth felt positively palatial.

She was awake when he arrived back at Raigmore Hospital. Awake and, by the sounds of her, absolutely raging.

"Where the fuck is he? Silly little fucker that he is!" Berta bellowed. A nurse tried her best to settle her, but was quickly shouted into submission. "Don't you fucking tell me to calm down, young lady! I've got every right to be making a fucking fuss!"

Hoon knocked on the open door, and popped his head inside, bracing himself for what was to come.

"Ah, speak of the fuckwit and he shall appear!" Berta

snapped. She gestured around her at all the wires and tubes. "What the fuck is all this?"

"You're in hospital," Hoon told her. He gave a nod to the grateful looking nurse, who quickly scarpered past him out of the room.

"Well, *clearly* I'm in the fucking hospital, Bobby!" she spat. "I know a fucking hospital when I see one. The question is, *why* am I in a fucking hospital? The last thing I remember, I was slipping away into a well-earned death, and then suddenly here I fucking am, with people poking and prodding at me like I'm a specimen in a fucking zoo!"

She shook her head, grabbed a couple of pipes and some wires, and gave them a firm yank.

"Well, no, I'm not fucking having it!" She pointed to one of the machines just beyond her reach. "Switch me off. Come on. Unplug me. Get it fucking over with."

Hoon pulled out a chair and sat beside her. "Too late," he told her. "They reckon you're going to be fine. I managed to keep your heart going until the helicopter arrived."

"*You?!*" Berta cried, the betrayal scrawled all over her face. "I might have fucking known you'd have had a hand in it."

"Aye. You're welcome," Hoon said. "There's no point pulling any of that stuff off, by the way, they'll only come and stick it back on. And you're out of danger now, anyway. They say you've got the heart of a fucking racehorse. You've got decades left in you yet, they reckon."

"Oh, well, that's just fucking marvellous!" Berta ejected. She let her head sink back into the pillow, shut her eyes for a moment, then snapped them open again. "The girls! The twins!"

"Both fine. They're at home," Hoon said. He winced. "No' sure their parents will be that keen on you babysitting again, mind you."

"Probably for the best," Berta said. "They were trying to get me to watch something called *Avatar*."

"What, the thing with the blue people?"

Berta frowned. "What the fuck are you...? No. A little bald lad. He's magic, or got special needs, or something. I wasn't paying much attention. You heard of it?"

Hoon shook his head. "Can't say I have."

"Awful shite. Absolutely fucking tedious. Stay away, is my advice."

"I'll keep that in mind," Hoon told her.

She sniffed and ran her tongue across her yellowed teeth, building up to the next question.

"I assume the house is fucked?"

"No' all of it," Hoon said. "I think your big soup pot's still intact."

"Yes, well, it was built to last," Berta said. "Buy cheap, and you buy twice, that's what I always say."

"I assume you've got home insurance?" Hoon asked.

Berta waved a hand. "Yes, yes. I remember paying something once."

"Once?" Hoon asked.

"Aye. Ages back."

"You're supposed to pay every year."

Berta shot him a doubting look. "Well, I don't think that can be right."

"What do you mean? Of course it's right!" Hoon insisted. "You pay it every year. Don't tell me you haven't been paying it."

"Every bloody year?!" Berta spluttered. "What, even if nothing happens? What sort of fucking racket is that? That needs shutting down, that does. Absolute fucking scam."

Hoon massaged his temples. Two minutes back in his sister's company and he could already feel the headache starting.

"So, you've got no house, and you've got no money?"

"Aye, well, if *someone* had just done the decent fucking thing and left me dead, neither of those would be a problem, would they?" She crossed her arms, tutted, then sighed. "I'll just have to stay with you, I suppose."

Hoon sat bolt upright in his chair. "Me?!"

"Yes, you! This is all your fucking fault, after all! I could've been cheerfully rotting in the fucking ground by now, but oh no, you wanted to keep me around. Well, actions have fucking consequences, young man! You wanted me around? Fine. You'll be sick of the fucking sight of me by the time I'm finished!"

"I'm already sick of the fucking sight of you," Hoon told her.

Her hand grabbed him by the front of his shirt and almost yanked him out of his chair. She had her strength back, then. Great.

"Oh, well just you get fucking used to it, Bobby," she told him. "Because you're going to be stuck with me for a long time to come."

She released her grip. Hoon smoothed himself down, then leaned over and flicked the power switch of the machinery she was connected to. He watched her lying there in the bed, scowling back at him, then shrugged and sighed.

"Worth a try," he said. He got to his feet. "I wonder if Redneck needs anyone else to go out to Yemen with him?"

"Why the fuck would you go to Yemen?" Berta demanded.

Hoon smirked. "I wasn't thinking of me."

Then, with the sound of his sister's voice booming in his ears, he left the room, stalked through the fluorescent-lit corridors of Raigmore Hospital, and out into the world beyond.

Out there, he took a breath. He was standing right by the car park and bus stop, so a lot of what entered his lungs was petrol fumes.

But it wasn't London petrol fumes. These were *Highland* petrol fumes, better in every way.

He walked across the hospital grounds, and stopped at the top of the road. Traffic flowed past in both directions, headed towards Inverness city centre on the right, and out towards Culloden on his left, past the big *Tesco*, and the polis HQ.

He looked both ways. He clapped his hands, and rubbed them together.

"Right then," he muttered, directing it out to the world at large. "What the fuck am I going to do now?"

The world didn't answer. But it didn't matter. For the first time in months—for the first time in years, maybe—he felt like he had time. And he felt like he had options.

And one option, in particular, was more immediately appealing than the others.

"Pub, then," he decided.

With the scent of fresh Highland petrol fumes filling his lungs, and a light spray of rain starting to fall, Robert Hoon shoved his hands in his pockets, hunched his shoulders, and strode off towards futures unknown.

THE END

NEXT IN SERIES

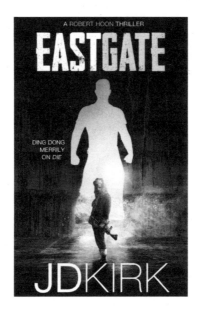

Hoon returns in EASTGATE, his fourth novel.

JOIN THE JD KIRK VIP CLUB

Want access to an exclusive image gallery showing locations from the books? Join the free JD Kirk VIP Club today, and as well as the photo gallery you'll get regular emails containing free short stories, members-only video content, and all the latest news about the world of DCI Jack Logan.

JDKirk.com/VIP

(Did we mention that it's free...?)